By the author of NOW, HEAR THIS!
CLEAR THE DECKS and
STAND BY-Y-Y TO START ENGINES

Daniel V. Gallery

U-505

"Brimming with thrills." — *Philadelphia News*

"An engrossing tale. . . . Pungent, entertaining, informative." — *Navy Times*

"A humdinger of a sea story . . . a highly readable book, trimmed from stem to stern with the writer's irrepressible sense of humor."
— *Chicago Sunday Times*

"Excellent in several ways: it provides a fine quick survey of the whole Atlantic war, it describes the operation of the German U-boat service, and, most dramatically, it tells how an American task force under Admiral Gallery achieved the unique feat of capturing a German submarine."
— *Publishers' Weekly*

ALSO BY ADMIRAL GALLERY

Cap'n Fatso
Stand By-y-y to Start Engines
Clear The Decks
The Brink

Published by
WARNER BOOKS

U-505

(original title: *Twenty-Million Tons Under The Sea*)

DANIEL V. GALLERY
Rear Admiral, USN (Ret.)

WARNER BOOKS

A Warner Communications Company

TO
MY WIFE VEE
who kept the home fires burning
during the Battle of the Atlantic

WARNER BOOKS EDITION

Warner Books, Inc., 75 Rockefeller Plaza, New York, N.Y. 10019

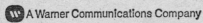 A Warner Communications Company

Printed in the United States of America

First Printing: November, 1967

10 9 8 7

CONTENTS

Chapter

1

PROLOGUE

EACH WEEK at the Museum of Science and Industry in Chicago, thousands of wide-eyed school kids explore an eerie, improbable exhibit. It is the ex-German submarine U-505, once one of Hitler's best U-boats. Boarded and captured by our Navy in 1944 off the West Coast of Africa during the Second Battle of the Atlantic, since 1954 it has rested high and dry among the trees in Jackson Park alongside the Museum near the shore of Lake Michigan.

In Chicago it is now a must for young Davy Crocketts, Supermen, and Captain Videos, to take time out from Indian fighting and space travel, and become Captain Nemos probing the secret vitals of this former enemy ship and brushing elbows with the mysteries of the ocean's depths. The unique exhibit is dedicated as a memorial to the 55,000 Americans who lost their lives defending our country at sea.

This is a strange end for one of the U-boats that made a shambles of our ocean shipping lanes in 1942-43. . . . A deadly instrument of war, built to help Hitler conquer the world, becomes a trophy at a museum, a permanent memorial to the American seamen who helped shatter *der Führer's* dream of world conquest! A killer that once prowled under the seas jammed with high explosive projectiles for sinking ships is now crowded daily with eager laughing children!

The story of how this came about is one of the epics of World War II. It takes us back a century and a half in naval history to the lusty days when full rigged sailing ships with smooth bore guns slugged it out yardarm to yardarm, and when the cry, "Away all boarding parties," sent gangs of swashbuckling, salty characters scrambling over the rail with cutlass and marlin spike to board and capture the enemy vessel.

Since the War of 1812, such things have happened only in story books. That kind of naval warfare went out of style with sails and muzzle loading guns. Now naval battles are fought at long range, and when modern weapons hammer an enemy ship into submission, she blows up and sinks.

But on June 4, 1944, a jeep carrier task group of the Atlantic Fleet took a page from the story books by boarding and capturing the U-505, 150 miles off Cape Blanco, French West Africa. It was my great good fortune and high honor to command the task group that did this job. This was the first capture of a foreign man-of-war in battle on the high seas by our Navy since June, 1815, when the American sloop-of-war "Peacock" boarded and seized the British brigantine HMS "Nautilus" in the Straits of Sunda near Singapore.

This statement requires explanation to meet the objections which readers familiar with naval history are sure to raise. I say "foreign enemy man-of-war," which eliminates captures by either side in our Civil War—and there were very few. I also say "on the high seas," which eliminates the Spanish ships that we raised from the bottom of Manila Bay or salvaged off the beach near Santiago. I also exclude the many German ships that were turned over to the Allies after the Germans surrendered in World Wars I and II. They were not captured in battle. So far as I have been able to find out from much research, the U-505 is indeed the first foreign enemy man-of-war captured in battle on the high seas by the U. S. Navy since 1815.

The Museum of Science and Industry has gone to great lengths restoring this submarine to its original condition. Everything in the Museum belongs to the modern era and is in working order. This submarine is no exception. The German firms that built the U-505 have cooperated with the Museum in restoring the sub, on the theory that if one of their U-boats is to be on display, they want it to be in such condition that it will at least be a credit to German technology.

The submarine is now practically in operating condition, except for the holes the Museum has cut through the pressure hull so a constant stream of visitors can file through it and see all its complex machinery. There are also a few shell holes in the thin outer plates, put there by my boys in 1944, which the Museum is leaving untouched, perhaps to give evidence that this otherwise healthy looking craft wasn't built where it now stands. But otherwise the boat is in the same condition as when she was sinking our ships off Panama in 1942.

Everything that you find inside an operating submarine is there: torpedoes, diesel engines, periscopes, pumps, gyro compass, underwater listening devices, radio and radar gear, plus a bewildering array of hand wheels, gages, indicators and switches. It all works, and periodically the Museum kicks the main diesels over for a few revolutions under their own power.

The crew's spaces, officers' quarters and captain's cabin, have the bunks all made up ready for the off duty watch to turn in. The galley range is ready to cook the next meal and pots, pans and crockery are all in their proper places. An official U-boat chart and pencils supplied from Germany are laid out on the Navigator's table under the ship's clock which still runs. If her former crew could walk aboard today, they would feel completely at home, and might even get her underway again if they could break her loose from the concrete cradles among the trees!

When I look at the U-505 alongside the Museum now, I can't help thinking that it was her destiny to wind up at her present moorings from the moment her keel was laid. That submarine and I simply had a rendezvous to keep and neither one of us really had much control over it.

I could easily make out quite a case showing how shrewdly I anticipated every move she made during the last week before we captured her, and took proper action to counter it. In fact, all I'd have to do is to simply lay her track alongside mine on a chart without comment and let the reader draw his own conclusions from the way they converge to a point at 11:20 A.M., June 4, 1944.

But I don't intend to do this. The German skipper and I both had what we thought were sound reasons for every move we made that last week. Looking back now, our reasons were wrong in almost every case. It was a snafu of errors on both sides in which his mistakes counteracted mine, and produced a fantastically improbable result.

It was much too improbable to just happen that way as

9

a result of pure chance. All of us who did this job know very well that Some One more powerful and wise than any of us was guiding our footsteps that morning. I don't mean to imply that God took time out from His regular duties to personally intervene in a puny sea battle off the coast of Africa. But it so happened that in World War II we were on God's side (as Joe Louis put it), and the U-505 was not.

People sometimes say to me, "You were very lucky that day." I agree with them—up to a point. Apparently our plan of operations for that day agreed with God's. How much luckier can you be?

There are two ways of "explaining" such things as this, although in my book they both boil down to the same thing. One is to say that life on this earth is controlled purely by chance and that man has no control over his destiny—it depends on the roll of the dice. If you want to defend this proposition, I can give you a list of about twenty incidents in the Battle of the Atlantic which might seem to support it—incidents in which apparently pure chance produced effects beyond any reasonable expectation of their importance.

However, I don't subscribe to this doctrine. I think this universe was created by an All-Wise Being, for a purpose, and that whatever happens in it, on this puny planet or in the Dark Nebula, over a squillion miles away, happens in accordance with this purpose. In other words, I believe in God.

When you get right down to brass tacks, the people who say it is all luck, believe in Him too. They just call Him by a different name than I do. Nobody with common sense can believe that this wonderfully regulated universe in which we spend our brief lifetime is run by pure chance and nothing else. It is too well organized, consistent, and logical except for the things that men do. There must be a Controlling Intelligence. I call Him God; agnostics call Him "chance," "probability," or "fate." But call Him what you will, there is an Intelligence greater than man's that created this universe, is therefore greater than the thing He created, and laid down laws that govern its destiny. When men go crazy and try to destroy themselves, He may nudge the dice that His creatures are rolling and make them come up the way they should. Seafaring men are close enough to God's handiwork every day to recognize His help when they get it.

The story of the U-505's capture, told to successive generations of youngsters as they troop through her, will be an inspiration to young Americans for a long time. The ship itself, now peacefully resting among the trees, should be a stern reminder to their elders of the debt this country owes to its seamen, who in two World Wars fought grim mid-ocean battles against prowling killers like the U-505, bent on destroying the sea power which keeps this country of ours alive.

Few Americans realize how close we came to losing both those battles, and what the disastrous result of losing them would have been. In April 1917, the Allies nearly lost World War I at sea. Churchill, in his *World Crisis* says of this period: "The U-boat was rapidly undermining not only the life of the British Islands, but the foundation of the Allied strength, and the danger of their collapse in 1918 began to loom black and imminent."

Twenty-five years later, in April 1942, a similar desperate crisis was at hand. In April, May and June, we lost over two million tons of ships. Had that rate of loss continued a few more months, Hitler might have won the war.

Writing of this period in the Second World War, Churchill says, in *Their Finest Hour*, "The only thing that really frightened me during the war was the U-boat peril. . . ."

The two Battles of the Atlantic will never take their proper place in the public mind as crucial campaigns in world history. They lacked glamor and headline appeal. They were relentless, drawn out, monotonous struggles that covered a whole ocean and lasted four to five years. The tempo was slow, and the action repetitious.

Only forty years ago a great naval battle was the most spectacular event of history, jammed with violent, fast moving and dramatic action. In a few hours a naval battle fought within visual range of all ships involved, could settle the fate of nations for years to come. The battle reports of every ship in the action could be expanded into an exciting book. There's a whole shelf full of such books about Jutland, fought in 1916.

11

But the battle reports in the Atlantic struggles were tables of cold dreary statistics, balancing the tonnage of merchant ships sunk against that of new ships launched and of new submarines joining the pack against wolves killed since the last table was compiled. These statistics were jealously guarded secrets until the war was over and then nobody cared about them any more. There were occasional moments of high drama, like the Night of the Long Knives, Murmansk Convoy PQ17, and other great convoy battles, the sinking of "Bismarck," "Graf Spee" and "Hipper," and the Channel break of the "Scharnhorst," "Gneisenau" and "Prinz Eugen." But these were mere incidents in the overall campaign. The real story is in tables of statistics which read as dramatically as the telephone book to all except a few naval men. For this reason the Battles of the Atlantic will never be enshrined in our national memory alongside those of John Paul Jones, or the Battles of Manila Bay, Guadalcanal, and San Bernardino Strait, although the Battles of the Atlantic were much more decisive than any of these in shaping the future of our civilization.

The British understood this much better than we do. Prolonged periods on a hunger diet have impressed it on two generations of Englishmen as it has never been impressed on us whose country is self-sufficient in food production and has not yet been blitzed.

Until we broke the back of the U-boat fleet early in 1943, the control of the seas so vital to the existence of the free world hung in a precarious balance. Had we lost this control, the United States' great industrial machine, that supplied the sinews of war to our Allies, would have come to a grinding halt deprived of the strategic overseas imports of raw materials that keep it going. Our vast armies would have been bottled up within our own shore lines, unable to exert any influence on the course of the war in Europe. England faced an even grimmer prospect—slow starvation.

This country of ours has survived two world wars primarily because its industrial capacity has made us invincible—*up to now*. But our capacity to produce the stuff of war depends absolutely on importing several million tons per year of strategic raw materials which we can only get from overseas. Cut off these imports and you throw our whole industrial machine out of gear because certain essential parts for airplanes, tanks, ships and guns simply cannot be made out of raw materials found in the United States.

This stuff must come in by sea because the number of ton miles involved just cannot be handled by air lift. The great Berlin airlift that bailed us out of trouble in 1948 was a wonderful thing. But the monthly ton mileage involved in this all-out air effort, which taxed the Air Force to its utmost capacity, can easily be moved at sea by two medium-sized cargo ships. Even if it were possible to wave a magic wand and create the colossal fleet of cargo aircraft necessary to haul all our strategic imports by air, this fleet would be a Frankenstein. It would soon burn up the world's reserve of petroleum and would thus shove us back to the era of sailing ships!

Both Battles of the Atlantic belong on any list of the decisive battles of world history. But between World Wars I and II, in a mere twenty-five years, we forgot the bitter lessons of 1917 and had to learn them all over again in 1942. Let's hope we don't forget again, because even in the Atomic Age, to survive we must control the seas.

For two years the U-505 was one of the great fleet of U-boats that challenged our control of the seas and almost wrested it away from us. In her first six months at sea she sank eight Allied ships, totalling 46,200 tons. She is typical of the commerce raiders that prowled the Atlantic and made a shambles of our eastern seaboard early in '42.

As time goes on, this submarine in Jackson Park should keep reminding our people, who forget so easily, that sea power is vital to the security of any great nation.

This book tells the story of the U-505, from her keel laying in Germany to her final "docking" in Jackson Park, Chicago. The story is put together from interviews with her crew, and study of her official papers, complete War Diary and logs. The tale of this U-boat, told against the background of the Battle of the Atlantic in which it played an important part, should help drive home the moral of sea power which so few of our people understand, and maybe some other lessons too.

It may show that there was not so much difference between the individual men who met far out on the eternal sea to fight this battle. They were similar human beings

13

with similar motives and emotions, directed by fallible superiors who could make equally bad mistakes. I like to think that our men were fighting for a better cause than the others and that's why we won.

(NOTE: In telling this story I sometimes quote conversations between crew members of the U-505. Obviously I have no way of knowing whether or not these exact words were said.

(But all the main facts of the story are historically correct and are documented by official records, War Diaries and ship's logs. The minor incidents are based on interrogation of prisoners, and on letters I have had from the U-505's crew, who are now back in Germany.)

Chapter

2

THE PHONY WAR

THE FIRST six months of the war on land were known as the phony war, but there was no phony war at sea. On the very first day one of Hitler's U-boat skippers committed a blunder that had far reaching repercussions. Within hours after the outbreak of hostilities the U-30 torpedoed and sank the British passenger liner "Athenia" without warning. One hundred twenty-eight civilians, twenty-eight of them Americans lost their lives in this ominous sample of things to come.

This sinking shocked the whole civilized world. In the twenty-one years intervening since 1918, nearly all nations had solemnly signed high sounding and supposedly binding agreements that never again would they wage unrestricted submarine warfare as the Germans had in World War I. Many restrictions had been placed on sinking merchant ships and passenger ships were not to be sunk under any circumstances. Despite all this, the Second Battle of the Atlantic began exactly where the first one had left off—a passenger ship was sunk without warning.

This drove home some hard facts of life to the naive

people who had assumed that solemn peacetime promises between nations mean anything when a global war breaks out. The Nazis' callous disregard of solemn commitments put them in bad odor right off the bat. The immediate sequel to it proved even worse for Germany.

Hitler had deployed his U-boats around England before invading Poland despite his assurances to his Admirals that England wouldn't fight. But he had issued strict orders to them, that in the unlikely event England did fight, they were to operate in accordance with Prize Warfare Rules, and under no circumstances would they sink unarmed passenger ships.

The young skipper of the U-30 in his first command, mistakenly identified the "Athenia" as an auxiliary cruiser and let her have it. After discovering his mistake he kept radio silence and didn't report what had happened till he got back to Germany some weeks later. Meantime, the German Admirals couldn't believe they had a skipper so egg-headed he would disobey their ironclad orders and advised Hitler to this effect.

Hitler and his propaganda chief Goebbels, promptly issued a hysterical statement accusing Churchill of having had a time bomb placed aboard the "Athenia" in order to blame her sinking on the Germans.

Nothing could have aroused England more than this obviously false and stupid statement from the Nazi government. All hope of appeasement went down the drain with it. By the time the U-30 got back to port and her skipper made his contrite report to Doenitz, Hitler was too far out on a limb to recant. The skunk had busted up the lawn party for keeps.

Actually, the skipper of the U-30 was just a few months ahead of his times in what he had done. The Rules of Prize Warfare were as obsolete in 1939 as the sailing ships for which they had originally been framed. All naval men knew this and had subscribed to the Prize Rules with tongue in cheek because politicians had required them to. The Rules forbid sinking passenger ships and require that before any legitimate targets, except war ships, are sunk their crews must be placed in safety. They specify that unless close to land the ship's boats are not considered a place of safety.

Obviously these rules, drawn up in the days of sailing ships, cannot be applied to steam vessels equipped with radio. If submarines observed these rules they would be useless except against warships. But all great nations, including the United States, had ratified this pious hypocrisy knowing full well it would go down the drain as soon as a major war broke out. It was like agreeing that from now on when we drop atom bombs on cities we will kill only combatant males. Such rules of warfare make no more sense than a set of rules for rape.

Even so, the Germans went through the motions of observing the Rules of Prize Warfare for a while. But mistakes by U-boat commanders, retaliations by the British and counter-reprisals by the Germans soon made the whole silly business another scrap of paper. The Germans were trying to establish a hunger blockade around England and sinking warships does no good in that kind of operation. Within a few months Hitler lifted all restrictions on attacking British ships, and two years later in the Pacific, U.S. subs were sinking all enemy ships on the same basis as the U-boats.

That's the only way a submarine fleet can operate. A sub on the surface is out of its element, hopelessly vulnerable to air or gun attack. A submarine's only advantage over her prey is invisibility. She must operate by stealth, strike without warning, and slink away unseen. She can't pick up survivors because there is barely room enough on board for her own crew.

Submarine warfare, whoever wages it, will always be a ruthless, cold-blooded business following no rules except expediency. But all civilized nations justify bombing cities without any difficulty, and the women and children killed by U-boats in World War II were a drop in the bucket compared to those killed in the bombing of cities. Nobody gets very indignant about the civilians buried in the rubble of industrial cities, now that we think atomically.

Those who are inclined to get excited about the flagrant violations of Prize Warfare by the Nazis may be interested to know that the United States is still officially committed to the Prize Warfare hokum. We are also building atomic submarines designed to remain submerged for months at a time. I wonder if any readers are naive enough to think that an atomic submarine which is nearly impregnable as long as it remains submerged will convert itself into a surfaced sitting duck just to comply with Prize Warfare rules. All past experience answers "no."

Survivors of World War I who were still going to sea in 1939 might well have said, "This is where we came in." For the first few months U-boats operated in the World War I hunting grounds close to the British coasts and there had been very little change in submarine or anti-submarine tactics between wars. The U-boat was essentially unchanged and its main weapon was still the straight running, steam driven torpedo, with a contact firing device. Destroyers still used depth charges against subs and the only new development was an underwater echo ranging device called Asdic by the British and Sonar by us, which was highly overrated at first. Aircraft had made great strides between wars, but the RAF had paid no attention to anti-submarine warfare. Its pilots were not trained for it and they had not developed proper weapons for planes to use against submarines. In the early months of the war, RAF aircraft were little more than scarecrows to the U-boats. So, with the sinking of the "Athenia" the Second Battle of the Atlantic began just about where the first had left off twenty-one years before.

The broad strategy of Germany was exactly the same this time as it had been before, to set up a starvation blockade around England. Island empires like Japan and England cannot survive long if you cut their imports of food below a certain definite minimum. No matter how firmly their people are convinced that their cause is just, no matter how determined they are to fight to the bitter end, nor what powerful military forces may be based on the island, when starvation sets in, surrender becomes as inevitable as death and taxes. Twice within two generations, England has stared this gaunt prospect in the face. Japan was on the threshold of starvation with no possibility of escape when we gave them a face saving reason for surrender by opening the Pandora's Box of the atom bomb, and letting them off the hook.

In 1939, England's hour of trial was still three years away. The plans of the German Navy for war against England called for 400 U-boats, and in 1939 they had

17

only 57. Hitler plunged into war over the alarmed protests of all his Admirals, who knew they were not yet ready to fight England. Hitler was certain that England wouldn't fight. When she did fight his Admirals were filled with gnawing fears despite *der Führer's* spectacular successes throughout the first year. They understood, as ex-corporals like Hitler and Napoleon never did, that you can overrun continental Europe and still lose a war if you don't control the seas around Europe.

The Germany Navy immediately launched a tremendous U-boat building program which by the end of the war produced a total of 1102 new boats. Production rose from two boats per month in 1939, to over thirty a month in the middle of the war. Fitting such a production program into the overstrained wartime economy of Germany was a great feat of organization, planning, and political intrigue. Admirals Raeder and Doenitz had to fight Air Marshal Goering and the Army for every ton of steel and every man hour of labor they needed. The unpredictable *führer* sometimes solved hassles about priorities by giving overriding number one priorities to four or five competing projects at once so that U-boats, jet fighters, V weapons and tanks might all have priority over each other. Allied bombing of U-boat building yards played havoc with production schedules, but the U-boat fleet grew from 57 in 1939 to 450 in 1943. Training the crews for these boats was just as big a job as building them. The staff work, planning, and logistic effort that went into the building and training of this fleet was as thorough and efficient as the operational handling of it, which wrought such havoc at sea.

The balance sheet for U-boats during the whole war can be summarized as follows:

On hand at start	57	Sunk	781	
		Captured	1	(U-505)
		Scuttled	215	
Built	1102	Surrendered	162	(Incl. U-570)
Total	1159	Total	1159	

The personnel losses in the U-boat flotillas were staggering. Out of 40,000 U-boat sailors only 12,000 survived the war. The rest went to the bottom with their boats.

On the other side of the ledger, 5,700 Allied ships totalling 23,000,000 tons were sunk and 48,000 merchant seamen went down with them.

The men who directed the production and operation of the great U-boat fleet were a strange group. At the top of the heap was Adolph Hitler himself, an ex-corporal from World War I who couldn't even make sergeant in four years of front-line service, but twenty years later nearly became the greatest conqueror in military history. He was fascinated by ships and made a hobby of memorizing technical details of warships. He could tell you the speed, armament and displacement of his own and all the principal enemy ships. He had flashes of genius and often plunged into desperate ventures against the advice of all his military experts. Many of his harebrained schemes succeeded simply because they were so daring they caught a complacent enemy flat footed. He did this in the naval field when he rammed the Channel break of the "Scharnhorst," "Gneisenau" and "Prinz Eugen" down the throats of his protesting Admirals. But every other time he butted in and issued tactical orders to ships at sea he loused things up and brought on disaster as in the cases of "Tirpitz," "Hipper" and "Scharnhorst." He didn't understand the sea and didn't like it, but he was an egomaniac who often interfered in fields about which he knew nothing and parlayed his hunches to phenomenal success, but didn't know when to quit. In fact, he got himself into a position where he *couldn't* quit until he conquered the world. It was the sea that finally stopped him from doing that.

Two of Hitler's principal military advisers were Raeder, Commander-in-Chief of the Navy, and Goering, Chief of the Luftwaffe. These two cordially hated each other and spent much of their time trying to poison Hitler's mind against each other. Goering sneered at navies and claimed his Luftwaffe would win the war single-handed. He insisted that every German airplane should come under his command, prevented the Navy from ever getting its own air force which it needed so badly in the Battle of the Atlantic, and would have no part of sending *his* airplanes out to help submarines at sea. When his Luftwaffe bombers could sink ships themselves, he was all for it, but he didn't propose to have them act as scouts just to help Doenitz's U-boats roll up a score.

Doenitz, as Commander-in-Chief of U-boats, was Raeder's principal subordinate. Even these two didn't get along together. Raeder envied the phenomenal growth of the U-boat flotillas while his surface fleet was being knocked out of the picture. Occasionally he ordered sweeping changes in the U-boat organization without even consulting Doenitz, and then had to back water on them when Doenitz was able to show the changes were ill advised.

Goering eventually succeeded in knifing Raeder in the back and getting him sacked as C. in C. Doenitz moved up and succeeded him in January, 1943. This finally backfired on the fat Air Marshal who himself lost favor with *der Führer* when his bombastic claims for his air force proved phony. Hitler's last official act before committing suicide was to appoint Doenitz his successor and order him to liquidate the fat man for treason. Considering all the bickering and intrigue that went on at the top level and the number of vitally important decisions that were based on nothing more that Hitler's brain flashes, it's a wonder the Nazis didn't lose the war in the first year instead of overrunning Europe as they did.

Looking back on it now, the war was suicidal right from the start for Germany. Hitler simply bit off more than he could chew. He pitted 83 million Germans against the rest of the western world, dragging half a dozen conquered countries along with him by their bootstraps and carrying Mussolini's Italy on his back. Once he got the wild bull by the tail he couldn't let go. He wound up fighting 380 million people, the unlimited cannon fodder of Russia, the combined sea power of England and the U.S., and the tremendous production capacity of the U.S. It seems incredible now that the result could ever have been in doubt.

Sea and air power played the decisive role in Hitler's eventual defeat. They barred the advance of his seemingly invincible armies at the English Channel. They enabled the United States to import raw materials from all over the world, manufacture them into arms and transport them to England and Russia. They bought time for the United

States to train vast armies and transport them overseas. Finally, they enabled us to land armies in Africa, Italy, and France, and to keep them supplied while we drove the Germans back across the Rhine. The integrated sea-air power developed by the U.S. Navy in the preceding twenty years proved invaluable in this battle for control of the seas. But had Doenitz's U-boat fleet numbered 400 when the war began, as the German Admirals planned, none of these things would have been possible.

Although there were many colorful and dramatic incidents in the great battle for control of the sea, the real strategic story on which the outcome of the war depended was told by columns of figures in the Admiralty and in Doenitz's headquarters. The reports of battles at sea were gripping reading, but the really vital reports were cold tables of statistics; tonnage sunk, new tonnage built, and tons of stuff to be shipped versus U-boats sunk, new boats built, and operational boats reporting to Doenitz for duty from the training command. Heroic deeds and lives lost were incidental in the columns of figures which accumulated relentlessly week by week.

In any large operation involving the interplay of many opposing factors, the people who run the show, whether it's a peacetime business or a Battle of the Atlantic, always find some one combination of figures more significant than any other in telling them how they are doing. In the Battle of the Atlantic, both sides soon arrived at the same criterion. It was known on our side as the "exchange rate." This was simply the number of merchant ships sunk in a given time, divided by the number of U-boats sunk in the same period. If in a given period fifty merchant ships were sunk and two U-boats went to the bottom, the exchange rate was twenty-five to one. Davy Jones' accountants at the bottom of the sea would check off twenty-five merchant ships settling into the primeval ooze on the ocean's floor before they spotted one U-boat coming to rest there. This exchange rate varied from twenty to one during the first few months, to eighty-nine to one in 1942, and dwindled down to less than one to one near the end of the war. This one simple figure eliminated all the incidental heroics, sifted out many other interesting but relatively unimportant statistics, and told both sides the

21

answer to the really vital question, "How are we doing?" If it was ten to one the battle was just about even. If it was higher than that the Allies were in trouble. When it was less, Doenitz's staff burned the mid-night oil to bring it up again.

A month after the war started and while the Battle of the Atlantic was still taking shape, one U-boat scored the most spectacular victory of the whole war at sea. On October 14, 1939 Kapitän Leutnant Prien took the U-47 through the British defenses and into the Royal Navy's main fleet base at Scapa Flow where he torpedoed and sank the battleship "Royal Oak" with a loss of 850 lives. Scapa Flow at this time was supposed to be an impregnable stronghold. It was unthinkable that anything except aircraft could get anywhere near the ships in Scapa Flow and aircraft bombing was so innacurate at this time that it presented no serious threat.

There are several channels through which a ship as small as a submarine can get in to Scapa Flow. The main entrance channel was protected by nets and was, of course, so heavily patrolled that not even a fish could get in undetected. The smaller channels, all narrow, rocky, and difficult to navigate even in daytime because of swift tides, were obstructed by sinking block ships in the narrowest part. All ships in Scapa Flow felt as safe as if they were in dry dock in their home yards.

But near midnight on October 14, Prien squeezed the U-47 past a block ship that was sunk only a few yards out of its proper position in a rocky, swift running inlet and got into the holy of holies at Scapa Flow. He spent three hours in there, made two attacks on the "Royal Oak" a half hour apart, sank her, and got out again.

While Prien was threading the needle past the block ship on the way in, at the narrowest part of the inlet, a motor car parked on one bank focussed its headlights on the U-47, the driver got out and watched the intruder for a moment and then drove off. The history books don't say what the driver did when he got to his destination. But even if he had recognized the U-47 for what she was, I doubt if it would have made any difference. If any rural resident had rung up British Naval Headquarters at one o'clock in the morning to report he had just seen a U-boat coming into their impregnable stronghold, they would have sent the nearest constable to heave him into the local looney bin. At this time the Royal Navy was still rather complacent about its control of the seas and regarded Hitler's Navy with contemptuous amusement. When Prien's first torpedo hit the "Royal Oak," her skipper and the Admiral on board wouldn't believe it and suspected an internal explosion. This belief persisted for half an hour while Prien circled, reloaded his tubes, and then blew them clear out of the water.

Churchill says of this episode, "It must be regarded as a feat of arms." I agree. In my opinion, it was the greatest individual feat of arms performed at sea for many years. It shook the Royal Navy to the core and served notice on them that despite the phony war ashore, they had a real fight on their hands at sea. The staggering shock which this dealt the British is clearly shown by the fact that from then on week-end leaves for Admiralty personnel began on Saturday night instead of Friday forenoon!

Prien's victory had important results in Germany too. It highlighted the possibilities of submarines and helped Doenitz get number one priority for his U-boat building program. It made Prien a hero of the Fatherland, and Hitler himself presented the Rittercross to him.

Prien was the first of the three great U-boat aces. In little over a year the names of Prien, Kretschmer and Schepke were household words throughout Germany. I will say more of them later.

Only two months after Prien's great feat, a dramatic incident of the surface war occurred in the South Atlantic. The pocket battleship "Admiral Graf Spee" had been on the loose since the war began, prowling back and forth between Africa and South America and sinking 50,000 tons of ships. She incidentally had been following the Rules of Prize Warfare meticulously, stopping and searching ships before sinking them and rescuing all hands in their crews.

Merchant seamen faced many hazards in World War II: U-boats, aircraft, surface raiders and mines. If given their choice as to how their ship would be sunk, they would always have chosen the surface raider—at least you see it coming and have perhaps a half hour's warning of your fate. Besides, there is a peculiar brand of international brotherhood among sailors, and surface raiders always picked up survivors.

On December 13, 1939, the "Graf Spee" was confronted by three British cruisers under Commodore Harwood off the coast of South Africa. The "Graf Spee" displaced 10,000 tons, had six eleven-inch guns, and was well armored. The biggest British cruiser displaced 7500 tons, the total weight of metal thrown by a broadside from all three cruisers was less than that of one from the "Graf Spee," and all were lightly armored. This was very much like a grizzly bear facing three angry terriers. But in this case the terriers were skillful and daring as well as angry. After an all day running fight, which cruiser captains will regard as a classic from now on, the "Graf Spee" sought refuge in Montevideo to lick her more or less superficial wounds, leaving the British cruisers waiting for her outside. By the end of three days when the Uruguayan government required the "Graf Spee" to depart, clever British propaganda had created hobgoblins in the German skipper's mind, and convinced him that a great armada including a battle cruiser, was assembled outside waiting. Actually, one of the British cruisers had been so grievously hurt she had limped off to the nearest dockyard and only the other two, badly battered themselves, were outside. The German skipper, rather than face what he thought was certain destruction, blew his ship up and sank her in the Platte River. Two days later he committed suicide.

I relate this incident in detail because suicide plays an important part in the story of the U-505, just as it did in the collapse of the Nazi regime. Germany's greatest general, Rommel, committed suicide when charged with treason toward the end of the war. Hitler brought the whole business to a Götterdämmerung finish with his suicide when the ruins of the Reichschancellory were crashing down around him. Goering furnished a grim anti-climax after the Nuremberg Trials by beating the hangman to the drop with poison. As will be seen later, two of the principal characters in the U-505 story also took the easy way out. In a godless, totalitarian regime where nothing matters except success on this earth, failure leaves no choice except suicide. The whole war was a suicidal business for Germany . . . and perhaps for all of us when we released the Frankenstein of atomic fission after we had Japan hopelessly defeated.

After the sinking of the "Graf Spee," the Battle of the Atlantic settled down to the cruel relentless struggle to enforce a starvation blockade that was to drag out for five years. In that first year prior to the laying of the U-505's keel, three names stand out among the U-boat skippers—Prien, Kretschmer and Schepke. Between the outbreak of war and April 1941, these three took a grim toll of Atlantic shipping. Prien and Schepke both exceeded 200,000 tons. Kretschmer scored the phenomenal total of 325,000. The highest total attained by any U.S. sub skipper in the Pacific was less than 100,000. Between the three of them, the German aces sank over 150 ships. All three got the highest military awards that Germany can give—the Rittercross with oak leaves and diamonds.

While these three aces were rolling up their scores and blazing trails for their comrades to follow, the Royal Navy and RAF were learning the elementary facts of life about anti-submarine warfare. By the time the phony war on land was over, they had learned enough to make it tough for U-boats patrolling in close around the shores of England. The U-boats had to move out further into the Atlantic and stay beyond the range of RAF planes which had now learned how to navigate at sea and were carrying depth charges instead of the comparatively harmless aircraft bombs. This move out into the Atlantic increased the distance of the hunting ground from the German bases and made the U-boats spend more time enroute to and from the payoff area. Even so, they continued to take a heavy toll of Allied shipping. By the time the U-505's keel was being laid in June 1940, the box score was:

Allied ships sunk (all causes)	249	(1,016,000 tons)
Submarines sunk	23	
Exchange rate	11 to 1	

The war at sea had settled down to the grim pattern of the starvation blockade, it was progressing reasonably well from the German viewpoint and the U-boats were beginning to set taut on the noose around England's neck.

In another year or so they might strangle her—if the war lasted that long.

But the war on land had suddenly become a rout and as the U-505's keel was laid, the Germans were at the gates of Paris. Maybe the war would be over before this U-boat could be finished!

Chapter

3

THE U-505 COMMISSIONED

THE U-505's story begins in the Deutsche Werft Shipyard at Hamburg, Germany, where the sub's keel was laid on June 12, 1940. As they drove the first rivets in this new sea wolf's keel Hitler's panzer divisions were roaring across France sweeping all before them, apparently invincible. They had overrun Poland, conquered Norway, driven the British into the sea at Dunkirk, and within two days they would make their triumphant entry into Paris. There was just one barrier left to halt Hitler's conquest of Europe— the sea.

In fact, it was just a small arm of the sea, the English Channel, only eighteen miles across, that barred his victorious armies from England. The big question mark was, could this historic barrier still hold back the crushing power which the Luftwaffe and panzer divisions had just demonstrated to a stunned world? On many building ways in Germany marauders similar to the U-505, designed to break this barrier, were taking shape.

On the very day that the keel of the U-505 was laid, French resistance collapsed. So, with world shaking events occurring, no Nazi bigwigs were on hand for such a routine and unimportant event as the keel laying of another submarine in Hamburg. The Luftwaffe and the panzers seemed irresistible, few of the Nazi General Staff doubted that the end of the war was close at hand. What difference did it make whether an extra U-boat keel was laid or not? History was in the making, and according to Hitler the peace that would soon be signed, "would last for 1,000 years."

Two days after the keel laying, the conquering German armies entered Paris, Hitler danced his little jig in the Compiègne Forest, and there were many who thought that this U-boat and her sister ships, then being rushed to completion, would never see action in this war.

How wrong they were. History followed its time honored habit of repeating itself—and the panzer divisions remained poised on the French side of the English Channel for the next three years. The Luftwaffe crossed the Channel almost at will and rained death and destruction on London, Coventry, Plymouth and many other English cities. But control of the seas, precarious though it was, saved England from invasion just as it had over a hundred years before, when Napoleon, another conquering ex-corporal who didn't understand sea power, had seen his legions halted opposite the Cliffs of Dover. Thanks to sea power, the British bled and sweated it out . . . and conquered Hitler.

So, although Denmark, Holland, Belgium and France were crashing to defeat when her keel was laid, construction of the U-505 proceeded apace during the eventful year which followed.

During that year, the Luftwaffe fought and lost the Air Battle of Britain. They inflicted grievous punishment on the civil population of England by aerial bombing, but they paid a heavy price to the fighter defenses, and it became obvious they could not win by aerial bombing alone. Hitler reluctantly abandoned his plans for invading England when his Air Marshals and Admirals could not guarantee safe passage across the Channel for his invading force. Eighteen miles of salt water which could be crossed in a couple of hours but which were dominated by the Royal Navy and the RAF, stopped the Wehrmacht which had blitzed Poland and the low countries, and had made the "impregnable" Maginot Line a laughing stock.

Meantime, the fall of France enabled Doenitz to move his U-boat bases from Germany to the Biscay coast of France. This was a welcome break for Doenitz because things were getting too hot for him close to the shores of England. The RAF had learned a lot since the war began, and it was necessary for him to shift his zone of operations further out into the Atlantic beyond the range of shore based aircraft. This increased the distance to the hunting ground by about 1,000 miles per round trip, but the shift to Biscay bases evened it up again.

So far, the war at sea had been indecisive, a mere preview of what was to come. The Allies had lost 374 ships totalling 1.5 million tons, but this was hardly enough to even cause food rationing in England. The German sea-borne traffic, except with Sweden and Norway, had been completely cut off. But Hitler had conquered so much new territory and acquired so many new resources, that he didn't feel the pinch of the Royal Navy's blockade too badly . . . yet. The war had reached a temporary stalemate. England had braced herself for a last-ditch fight on the beaches, the hills, and in the streets, if Hitler's conquering panzers ever got across the Straits of Dover.

During the first ten months of war the size of the U-boat fleet had remained static. Twenty-three new boats joined the fleet, but twenty-three had been sunk. However, the number of U-boats available for operations decreased because half of the fleet had to be assigned to training new crews for the great building program then getting into high gear. When the U-505's keel was laid, Allied shipyards were still in low gear but U-boat production was building up to thirty per month. For the next year, the U-boat fleet was growing rapidly and our total merchant fleet decreased by nearly 3 million tons.

When Doenitz moved his zone of operations out into the broad Atlantic, new tactics became necessary. While close to England, where the shipping lanes converged, his U-boats had operated as lone wolves, simply waiting near the bottle necks for the shipping to come to them. But out in the open sea where the convoy routes could be shifted around, lone wolf operations didn't pay off because too much depended on the luck of the hunt. One boat might intercept a convoy and make a killing while a sister boat patrolling only fifty miles away might see nothing and bring all her torpedoes back to port.

Doenitz had an ace up his sleeve, the *rudeltaktik* or wolf pack, which he had worked out in prewar exercises. This was a revolutionary concept which recognized that to get the most out of submarines they had to be operated as surface vessels most of the time, and which took a well calculated risk in discarding radio silence.

Doenitz's headquarters took over operational control of the boats at sea and spread them out in a long line on the surface across the convoy lanes. When one of the boats sighted a convoy he no longer drove in submerged and expended all his topedoes. He stayed on the surface and shadowed the convoy, keeping the masts in sight just over the horizon, reporting by radio to Doenitz. Doenitz rebroadcast the convoy's position, course and speed to other boats on the line and they converged on their prey at high speed on the surface. Often they were guided in by homing signals from the shadower, who being out of range of shore based aircraft, could get away with this. When five or six boats had assembled on each flank of the convoy, Doenitz would turn them loose to charge into the convoy at night overwhelming the escorts by sheer weight of numbers.

This seems very simple and logical as I describe it now. But when Doenitz did it, it was a complete break with previous submarine practice in all navies. Submarines were traditionally lone wolves, and radio silence was a sacred cow. This daring shift in tactics caught the Allies unprepared and Doenitz's new idea met with immediate spectacular success. For the next two years the wolf packs took a terrible toll from our convoys in the North Atlantic.

German histories of the war refer to the nights of October 18 and 19, 1940, as the "Night of the Long Knives." On these two nights a pack of twelve U-boats, led by the three great aces Prien, Schepke and Kretschmer, ripped into two convoys like a pack of hungry wolves turned loose in a flock of sheep. A nautical version of Dante's *Inferno* was enacted out in the cold Atlantic several hundred miles from the English coast.

After lurking on the surface all day just beyond the horizon, the packs struck with unprecedented fury after dark. Surfaced U-boats charged back and forth through the convoy like the Horsemen of the Apocalypse, firing torpedoes right and left. Star shells lit up the sky, guns of all calibres blasted away, and the muffled thunder of torpedo explosions and depth charges reverberated all night. For hours there were scenes of wildest confusion. Tankers blew up with flash mushroom explosions that were previews of the atom bomb, and subsided into flaming beacons on the surface of the sea that burned for hours giving a garish light for the continuing nightmare. Ships, maneuvering wildly to avoid torpedoes, rammed and sank each other. Gun crews firing at U-boats racing between columns of the convoy shot into ships in the adjacent column. Escort vessels pursuing the U-boats were mistaken for subs and shot up by ships in the convoy they were trying to protect. The escorts were utterly futile that night and didn't damage a single U-boat. The merchant ships which escaped slaughter did so simply because there weren't enough attackers to sink them all.

Seamen whose ships were shot out from under them did not suffer long in the bitter cold sea that night. After five minutes or so in near freezing water, the body becomes numb and death comes fairly comfortably in about fifteen minutes. Tanker crews had their bodies freeze while their heads, faces and hands were being burned to a crisp by the flaming oil that covered the surface of the sea. There were few survivors from torpedoed ships and most of them had both arms and legs frostbitten beyond repair. The doctors clipped them off neatly, close to their bodies.

For the merchant sailors, these were nights of panic with unseen terror striking out of the blackness time and time again from all sides. Survival was a matter of blind luck as torpedoes fired from the center of the convoy often missed their intended targets but hit ships in the next column. Blazing tankers illuminated friend and foe alike, but the black submarines with decks awash were much harder to see than the great cargo ships, and a conning tower is a tiny target for a gun crew on a rolling ship.

For Schepke, Prien and Kretschmer, these nights were wild orgies of power and victory. When the gray dawn of October 19 ended the slaughter, 32 ships out of 83 in the two convoys had been sunk. A total of 150,000 tons went to the bottom in the most overwhelming success of the Battle of the Atlantic for Doenitz and his three great aces.

To the Germans, the "Night of the Long Knives" is one of the high spots in their naval history. But to Davy Jones' cold blooded accountants, it is merely an incident in the great table of statistics compiled at the bottom of the sea, recorded in their barnacle covered ledger simply as "October 18 and 19, 1940, Convoys SC7 and HX79—32 ships, 150,000 tons." Numerous similar incidents would be recorded in the next few years, but none equal to the "Night of the Long Knives."

Six months later, in March of '41, the British exacted poetic vengeance for this night of terror. Up to that time they had sunk a total of thirty-one U-boats in nineteen months, but for the past three and one-half months had not sunk a single one. Between 8 and 17 March, they sank three. These three sinkings were consecutively recorded on the Admiralty's master list as follows:

Date	U-Boat	Cause of Sinking	Position
8 March	U-47	HMS Wolverine	60°-47′ N 19°-13′ W
17 March	U-99	HMS Walker	61° N 12° W
17 March	U-100	HMS Walker— Vanoc	61° N 12° W

U-47 was Prien, U-99 Kretschmer, and U-100 Schepke. The three great aces were swept off the board in 9 days! This was the heaviest blow of the war so far to Doenitz and to the morale of his whole U-boat fleet. Prien and Schepke went down with their boats. Kretschmer was captured and spent the rest of the war in prison camp. He is now a Kapitän zur See in the new German Navy.

Kretschmer's capture is of interest in this story of the U-505. He was cornered at night while stalking a convoy by two British destroyers, one of which had just killed Schepke half an hour before. Badly damaged by depth charges while submerged at 300 feet, he lost control of his boat and she started toward the bottom in thousands of fathoms of water. He had the choice of sacrificing himself and his crew by simply riding her down to crushing depth or of blowing his tanks, bringing her to the surface, and giving his crew a chance to be rescued. He chose the latter and broke surface very close to the two destroyers. When he came up he was helpless and intended simply to surrender and scuttle. But there was no way the destroyers could know this, especially at night. Ordinarily, a cornered submarine is treated the same way as a cornered tiger. Surrender is impossible for either of them. The

British opened fire on U-99 and for ten or fifteen minutes Kretschmer and his crew huddled on deck behind the bridge while the destroyers blasted away. When the British finally realized the U-boat was out of action and ceased fire, Kretschmer sent his crew below to put on warm clothing before going overboard. For another fifteen minutes or so the U-boat and the two destroyers wallowed in the darkness, eyeing each other suspiciously. Finally, one destroyer drifted down very close to U-99 and seemed to be lowering a boat. Kretschmer sent his Engineering Officer below to open the vents and scuttle. The Engineer did his duty well and went down with the boat. Kretschmer and the rest of his men were fished out of the water and taken to England.

The question arises, what would have happened if the destroyers had lowered whale boats and sent armed boarding parties over as soon as U-99 surfaced? Your guess on this is as good as mine. There is at least a possibility that U-99 might have been boarded and captured. I bring this up because some people in Germany are critical now of the U-505's crew for "allowing" their boat to be captured. But Kretschmer, the greatest ace of all, lay helpless on the surface for half an hour with destroyers within hailing distance before scuttling his boat. The crew of the U-505 behaved just about the same as Kretschmer's crew. The difference in the final outcome of these two engagements resulted not from what the German crews did or didn't do, but from what their enemy did.

In May of 1941, another one of the epic incidents of the battle at sea occurred when the giant battleship "Bismarck" almost got loose in the Atlantic. The "panic button" in the Admiralty was held down for a week while this great ship was making her break north and west of Iceland for the convoy lanes.

The "Bismarck" was the most powerful surface ship ever built up to this time. She displaced at least 50,000 tons, had eight fifteen-inch guns, could make thirty knots and was so heavily armored and so well subdivided that she was almost unsinkable. Had she gotten loose along the convoy lanes, she would have been like a bull in a china shop. She could have paralyzed our transoceanic commerce as long as she remained at large.

She was intercepted and brought to action in the Denmark Strait between Iceland and Greenland by HMS "Hood" and "Prince of Wales." The "Hood" had been the pride of the British Navy and symbol of England's sea power for twenty-five years. She was the most impressive looking warship in the world, had the same main battery as the "Bismarck," was about the same size and could make thirty knots. But she was a glass jawed heavyweight with light armor and had no business within gun range of a tough customer like the "Bismarck." The British Admiralty should have known this.

The "Bismarck's" second salvo blew up her magazines. The "Hood" disentegrated in a huge ball of fire and only three out of her crew of 1500 survived.

The "Bismarck" shifted her sights to the "Prince of Wales," a brand new battleship, heavily armored, and with gun power equal to her own. Within minutes she staggered this second heavyweight with hits that knocked out half her battery and make a shambles of her bridge. The "Prince of Wales" put her helm over and reeled out of action. At this point, the German Admiral threw away one of the greatest opportunities ever given to a German naval officer. Had he pursued the "Prince of Wales," he would probably have sunk her too. But he was a literal minded man of no vision. His orders were to break out into the Atlantic and when the "Prince of Wales" limped off and left his path clear, he bugged out and headed for the wide-open sea.

He didn't make it. After a three day game of hide and seek involving every ship and airplane the British could muster, the "Bismarck" was cornered while trying to get in to Brest and was hammered to pieces by an overwhelming armada. The savage punishment which she absorbed was unbelievable. The British literally held target practice on her at point blank range with their heaviest naval guns, but couldn't sink her. They finally put her on the bottom by pumping torpedo after torpedo into her helpless, wallowing hulk.

Looking back on this affair now, it was a grim comedy of errors on both sides. The German Admiral should have sunk the "Prince of Wales" and then have gone back to Germany to become a hero of the Fatherland greater even than Prien. Instead, after proceeding too far into the Atlantic to turn back to Germany, he decided that superficial damage to the "Bismarck" required him to head for the dockyard at Brest. Although he had actually given the British the slip by this time, he thought British cruisers were still trailing him. Convinced that his location was known, he opened up on his radio to send a lot of dramatic messages to Hitler, thus revealing his position to the alert direction finder system of the Admiralty. Soon the British, still seeing red from their humiliation in Denmark Strait, lowered the boom savagely on the garrulous German Admiral.

There were many flagrant bloopers on the British side too. The explosion of the "Hood" duplicated the explosions of the three similar British battlecruisers twenty-five years before at Jutland. The mills of the Admiralty grind slow, but you might think that in twenty-five years they would get around to reading the action reports of World War I. In addition, the British were within hours of having to call off the chase for lack of fuel when the "Bismarck" was finally cornered. Refueling at sea was commonplace in the U.S. and German navies at this time, but the successors of Nelson are slow to adopt ideas that other navies think of first and the British had not yet taken up this newfangled business.

On the day before the "Bismarck" was finally sunk, a squadron of torpedo planes from a British aircraft carrier mistook one of their own heavy cruisers for the "Bismarck" and fired a salvo of a dozen torpedoes at her. They all missed! Finally, when the "Bismarck" was reduced to a helpless battered hulk that refused to sink, no one even thought of trying to put a tow line aboard and drag this priceless token of victory back to England.*

* Lest my British friends accuse me of being smug I hasten to say that the three most important new developments in aircraft carriers since World War II have come from the Royal Navy. We in the U.S. Navy have always figured that we were the experts on aircraft carriers and have been rather patronizing toward British effort in this field. So who invents the canted deck, the steam catapult, and the mirror landing system? Answer—the Royal Navy!

There is one other improbable incident of this battle which is worth telling in a book about submarines. The U-556 was known throughout the submarine flotillas as the "Bismarck's" little brother. One day in the Baltic, the U-556 had met the "Bismarck" on her shakedown cruise and sent a rather flippant message from "Captain to Captain." When a brusque reply came back demanding the U-boat skipper's name, he replied, "I'll bet you can't do this," and submerged until the "Bismarck" was well out of sight. Some time later the bumptious sub skipper paid a formal call on the Captain of the "Bismarck" and presented him with a certificate saying the U-556 would look after and protect the "Bismarck" wherever she went. The young sub skipper's bravado broke the crust of the "Bismarck's" captain and a firm friendship was thus established between the giant battleship and the U-boat.

On the day before the "Bismarck" was cornered and sunk, U-556 was returning from a war patrol in the Caribbean, running submerged, when the "Reknown" and "Ark Royal," racing to intercept the "Bismarck," steamed smack across her course five hundred yards ahead of her. The setup was a U-boat skipper's dream—an unescorted battleship and aircraft carrier at point blank torpedo range, unaware of the U-boat's presence. But the U-556 had expended all her torpedoes! To cap the climax, it was a torpedo hit a few hours later by a plane from the "Ark Royal" that finally sealed the "Bismarck's" fate, jamming the battleship's rudder when she had almost made good her escape. The "Bismarck's" little brother had promised a little more than he was able to deliver! Just a month later, when starting off for her next cruise, U-556 joined the "Bismarck" in the mud at the bottom of the sea not far from the spot where her big brother had sunk the "Hood."

On May 25, 1941, the day that the U-556 failed her big brother, and the day before the "Bismarck" was sunk, a new U-boat slid down the ways in Hamburg—the U-505. It was just two weeks short of a year since her keel had been laid.

Incidents such as the "Night of the Long Knives," the end of the three aces, and the killing of the "Bismarck," added color and drama to the war at sea, but the real battle dragged on methodically and relentlessly day after day with the fate of the western nations at stake. These things, and others that happened on the surface, the great convoys plodding back and forth, wolf packs prowling, hideous night battles, narrow escapes, and drifting wreckage and lifeboats, were all just incidents. The final score was kept down at the bottom of the sea. When the U-505 was ready to go in commission on August 20, 1941, the box score of Davy Jones' accountants since the beginning of the war was as follows:

Allied merchant vessels sunk 1653
Tonnage lost 8,000,000
New construction 3,000,000
Net loss 5,000,000

New U-boats commissioned 153
U-boats sunk 40
Net gain 113 (plus 57 original boats = 170 total in fleet)

The U-boats were getting the upper hand, food was now strictly rationed in England, and another year or so of blockade by a steadily growing U-boat fleet might force her to the wall. But Hitler couldn't wait. A maniacal urge drove him on and when he was stopped in one direction, he had to lash out in another. He couldn't get across the Channel to finish England quickly, blockade is a slow process, so he launched his attack on Russia. The frantic pleas of his military advisers against the Russian campaign had little effect any more. They had advised against every major move he had made so far, and every move had hit the jackpot. Who could blame him for thinking he had a magic touch and was infallible?

On August 26, 1941, more than a year after France surrendered, the U-505 was commissioned at Hamburg, Kapitän Leutnant zur See Axel Loewe, Commanding. By this time the war with Russia was in full swing, but the slogan inscribed on the first page of the U-505's guest book, now in a glass case at the Museum of Science and Industry, reads, "Wir fahren gegen England," ("We are sailing against England"). Actually, they were going

4,000 miles further than England—but not even in their zaniest nightmares could any of the U-505's crew foresee that she would end up among the trees next to a museum in Chicago.

What they did think about is indicated by the following jingle translated from the early pages of the U-505 guest book. It was written the day she was commissioned, each of the various guests at the ceremony and visiting officers from sister ships composing and signing one verse:

10 proud British merchant men cruising in a line,
Along came U-505 and then there were nine.
Amfert—Oberleut. zur See

9 proud British merchant men with lookouts not awake,
The U-505 caught one and then there were eight.
Engemann, Oblt. Ing.

8 proud British steamers at a quarter past eleven,
When we squeeze the firing switch, then there are seven.
Habberg, Lt. zur See

7 British cargo ships loaded to their sticks,
But after our torpedo hits, there were only six.
Schneewind, Ober Lt. zur See
[Note—son of Raeder's Chief of Staff?]

6 proud British freighters running for their lives,
One lagged behind and then there were five.
Wuch, Lt. zur See—U-656

5 big British steamers almost at the shore,
The 505 released an eel and then there were four.
Rolph Faustborn, Lt. zur See

4 proud British steamers were sighted by our crew,
We dive and fire a double shot, and then there are two.
Boerner, Lt. zur See

2 British freighters a big one and a small,
Loewe shot the big one down so then only one.
                    Hans Schult, Lt. zur See

One little freighter arrived at Portsmouth—then,
The BBC and Reuters announced there were ten.

The moral of this story is "Don't believe what you
read in the British newspapers."

The next entry in the guest book turns time back
twenty-five years for any naval man, no matter what his
country:

"May the boat live up to the motto of the Seydlitz,
"Always in the lead."
                    Sig. Putra—Formerly Gunner
                    SMS Seydlitz, 26 August 1941"

The "Seydlitz" was one of the Kaiser's five battle
cruisers at the Battle of Jutland in the first world war.
Even today if you mention Jutland to a British naval officer his blood pressure goes up, he clears his throat and
emphatically claims that this battle was a "strategic victory" for the British. But the German High Seas Fleet,
outnumbered two to one, escaped behind its mine fields
after inflicting losses on the Grand Fleet over twice as
heavy as it sustained. Churchill, dutifully but half-heart-
edly defending the British Commander-in-Chief in this
action says, "He was the only man who could have lost
the war in an afternoon. . . ." (by getting his whole fleet
sunk!). But he could also have shortened it two years if
he had been willing to get in there and fight.
The thing that saved the day for the Germans in this
great battle, perhaps the last fleet action that will ever be
fought, was the so-called "Death Ride of the Battle
Cruisers." These battle cruisers, including the "Seydlitz,"
were in the lead at Jutland and bore the brunt of the attack by the British Grand Fleet. The "Derfflinger,"
"Moltke," "Seydlitz," "Von der Tann" and "Lützow"
threw themselves into the path of the oncoming Grand
Fleet, and held it off for a few minutes while the High

Seas Fleet extricated itself from an impossible situation. Even the British acknowledged this as an epic incident in naval warfare.

Twenty-five years later, in the guest book of the U-505, an unreconstructed survivor of the Death Ride wishes the next generation of German sailors luck, and reminds them that they have great traditions to live up to.

By the time the above was written it seemed that the U-505 might have to hurry if she was to carry out these sentiments. The panzer armies had proven invincible and it looked as if they would soon overwhelm Russia. The war at sea had settled down to the grim, relentless and long-drawn-out business of a starvation blockade.

As soon as Russia was conquered, Hitler would turn on England again and then it would be up to the German Navy to get the panzer armies across that narrow stretch of salt water in the Straits of Dover, which the British army crossed when they evacuated Dunkirk. During the invasion of England, many Knights Crosses and Oak Leaves would be won and all hands in the U-505's crew wanted to take part in this operation and share in the glory.

By August of '41, the United States was waging an undeclared war against U-boats in the North Atlantic. Lend Lease was supplying the British with arms, we had swapped them fifty destroyers for bases in the western hemisphere, and our own destroyers were escorting British convoys, hunting out, and depth charging U-boats. But Hitler didn't want to fight us at this time and refused to let his Admirals retaliate against us. They were now waging unrestricted U-boat warfare against all non-Axis ships in the North Atlantic, but he forbade attacks on U.S. ships in our home waters. His master plan when the U-505 was commissioned was to defeat Russia, then dispose of England, and to deal with the United States after that.

I was in England as an observer before we got into the war in October, 1941. I remember well the grave faces in the Admiralty the morning the aerial photographs of submarine building yards were evaluated, showing that U-boat production would soon reach thirty per month. England had plenty of battleships and cruisers to insure control of the surface of the sea, but these were useless for protecting convoys against submarines. They were worse than useless because whenever one of them put to sea she had to have a heavy destroyer screen to protect her against submarines, thus reducing the number of escorts available to escort vital convoys.

The steadily growing U-boat fleet now numbered 200, and the Admiralty was badly scared. Everybody at the meeting that morning did some simple mental arithmetic and their faces got longer when they did. By this time it was apparent that the gallant British people could grit their teeth and take whatever punishment the Luftwaffe could deal out to them. But even the bravest people cannot hold out indefinitely against starvation and the noose of the U-boat blockade was getting tighter each week. From a long range point of view, this expanding U-boat fleet, to which the U-505 was the latest addition, was a much more deadly threat to England than the Luftwaffe or the panzer divisions.

Chapter

4

INSIDE A SUBMARINE

THE U-505, Hull 295 of the Deutsche Werft Shipyards, Hamburg, was a type IX-C boat, 252 feet long, displaced 1100 tons when fully loaded, and carried a crew of four officers and 56 men. She could make nineteen knots on the surface running on her diesel engines, and could stay at sea for ninety days cruising at economical speed. She was of the pre-schnorkel type which could not run on diesel engines when submerged, but had to use her electric motors driven by a battery. This battery had to be recharged at least every twenty-four hours, and this could only be done by surfacing and running the diesel engines.

She carried twenty-one torpedoes, each capable of sinking any ordinary merchant ship, and had four tubes forward and two aft. When commissioned, she had a 4.1

inch gun just forward of the conning tower, but this was later removed and replaced by anti-aircraft guns.

Before we go to the Baltic with the U-505 to watch her crew shaking down, let's take a look inside this strange denizen of the deep. Some scientists tell us man's ancestors were creatures that originated in the ocean's depths. If so, we have long since lost our ancestor's feeling of security under water. Even sailors who spend their lives on the surface of the ocean are regarded as a queer lot and submarine sailors are a breed apart. Man is now a dry land creature and to most people a submarine is an eerie, mysterious vessel.

Usually we think of a submarine as a craft designed to spend most of its time submerged, but the World War II submarine was actually a surface craft which could, when necessary, operate submerged for short periods of time. In an emergency, to escape an attack, it could go down to five or six hundred feet, but it couldn't stay there long and it couldn't move very far while it was down there. It was a lightly armored surface warship endowed with a special cloak of invisibility which she could wrap herself in and disappear when the going got too tough on the surface. Like any ship, it had to provide space and facilities for the crew to live, eat and sleep. It also had to be able to propel itself through the water and to perform some useful function in this world, such as blowing up and sinking merchant ships. It takes a lot of complex equipment to do this and a modern submarine crams more men, machinery and equipment into less space than any other vehicle designed by man.

The "pressure hull" of a submarine contains all the living spaces, machinery and essential equipment. It is a tough steel cylinder, about ten times as long as it is in diameter, divided internally into six water tight compartments by athwartship bulkheads, with a long narrow fore and aft passageway running from bow to stern. Circular doors three feet in diameter permit passage through the bulkheads. Amidships it has a stubby conning tower sticking up which is also a part of the pressure hull.

Inside this hull the air pressure is always just about atmospheric. Outside is the sea pressure corresponding to the depth at which the boat is operating. At five hundred feet it is sixteen tons per square foot of surface. The pressure hull must be a rugged structure to withstand such tremendous compression and if it ever cracks and admits sea water, the sub will be on the bottom of the ocean permanently in a very few minutes.

A submarine has two powerful diesel engines, a pair of heavy electric motors, a huge storage battery and many pumps. It has torpedo tubes, complex fire control gear, and intricate radio, radar and listening equipment. When you jam all this stuff inside the pressure hull, plus spare parts, labyrinths of pipes, wires, valves, switches, gauges and meters, plus sixty men and their belongings, plus food and fuel for three months, and then add the streamlining structure necessary to let it make some speed through the water and put a few guns and other useful pieces of machinery on this structure, the cylinder is just barely buoyant enough to float. Only the bridge would stick out of water and her decks would be awash.

Attached to the outside of the pressure hull are large tanks which the submariners call ballast tanks. This term is confusing to the layman because they are really "buoyancy" tanks, which, when empty, supply the flotation necessary to keep the heavy pressure hull afloat with her weather decks dry. These tanks have sea valves in the bottom and air valves on the top. When you open both the valves and the vents, sea water comes in, forcing the air out through the vents, the tanks lose buoyancy and the submarine sinks. Theoretically, if you let in just exactly the right amount of water, she will sink until only a half-inch of the periscope sticks out of water, but in practice you can't do this. It isn't possible to gage the weight of the boat and the amount of water admitted that closely. If you admit just a gallon or so too much water, and do nothing about it, the sub will start sinking slowly, but with a gradually increasing rate until the pressure hull collapses, which in the U-505 type sub would happen around 1,000 feet. The reason is that sea water is not compressible but steel is. As the sub sinks deeper and the pressure on the hull increases, the steel cylinder compresses slightly. This small compression decreases the buoyancy, which is already negative, and so she sinks faster.

The sinking can be stopped either by admitting compressed air to the ballast tanks and blowing water out, by pumping it out mechanically, or by driving the boat through the water and using the bow and stern planes to produce dynamic lift and hold the boat up as the wings of an airplane do, which is how it is almost always done in practice. When a sub dives, she admits not quite enough water in the ballast tanks to sink her and then pulls herself down by use of her diving planes. Then if something goes wrong and she loses power, she will float back up to the surface.

Sometimes it *is* possible for a sub to remain at rest completely submerged without using the diving planes and without juggling ballast. The density of sea water usually is nearly constant, but the sea is moody and doesn't always behave according to its own rules. Occasionally you can find a submerged layer of cold extra heavy water, and if you settle onto it gently enough with just a few pounds of negative buoyancy for the warmer water, the heavier cold water will hold you there suspended motionless. The only other way you can remain motionless submerged is to sit on the bottom in water shallower than your crushing depth.

The ballast tanks are not nearly as sturdily built as the pressure hull because they always have sea pressure both inside and outside, so they have no tendency to crush with increased depth. The same is true of the external fuel tanks which are open to the sea at the bottom. Oil being lighter than water it floats on top of the sea water, and as you use up oil the sea water rises higher in the tanks. Pressure inside and outside of these tanks is equal, as it is in the ballast tanks.

The whole structure of the pressure hull and its ballast and fuel tanks is enclosed in a light steel envelope of "gingerbread" which also never has to resist any unequal pressures. Its main purpose is to streamline the boat, furnish support for the outside weather deck and the guns, and stowage space for things carried externally, such as the anchor windlass, extra torpedoes, life rafts, etc.

A pre-schnorkel submarine of the U-505's type runs on its diesel engines when surfaced. But she must stop the diesels before she submerges. A diesel engine uses a lot of air, and the instant the conning tower hatch is closed for submerging, air in a submarine becomes a precious thing in short supply. If you slam the conning tower hatch and air inductions closed and submerge with the diesels running full speed, you would suck all the air out of the boat in a few seconds.

Toward the end of the war the "Schnorkel" made it possible for submarines to run their diesels when submerged just below the surface. A schnorkel is simply a long steel pipe that sticks up about as high as a periscope and allows the diesels to suck air down from the surface into the boat. But this great improvement came too late for the U-505.

When she submerged she had to switch to her electric motors which drew their power from a huge storage battery. This battery, weighing over one hundred tons, could drive her for about twenty-four hours at slow speed or a much lesser period at high speed. At her most economical speed there was enough juice in the battery to take her about sixty miles submerged. The only way pre-schnorkel subs could recharge their batteries was by running their diesel engines which turned over the electric motors acting as generators and put energy back into the battery. When the battery got low, a pre-schnorkel sub had to surface for two to three hours to recharge the battery. As will be explained later, this was one of the major facts of life about that type of submarine.

A submarine torpedo is a miniature version of the boat itself. Similar in all respects to the parent vessel except that, no crew space being necessary, the whole interior is jammed with machinery, explosives, and mechanical brains.

The standard torpedo at the beginning of the war was driven by compressed air, had a range of four to five miles, and could make thirty knots. This torpedo left a telltale white wake of air bubbles behind it and thereby often gave its target warning of its approach. Later, the Germans developed an electric torpedo driven by a storage battery, which left no wake.

The early torpedoes were straight running missiles which had to be carefully aimed, allowing for the course and speed of the target vessel. If the target zigged or zagged after this torpedo was fired, the torpedo would miss. Later the acoustic torpedo, equipped with mechanical ears which picked up the sound from the target vessel's screws, could maneuver to make the sound equal in both ears, and thus "home" on the source of the noise. It was only necessary to aim it in the general direction of the target and turn it loose. No careful analysis of target course and speed was necessary and a zigzagging target didn't bother it a bit. This was a deadly thing until we learned how to counter it.

The electric acoustic torpedo was worse than a rattle-snake for a while, giving no warning and never missing. It was the first guided missile developed by man. It was the embryo from which whole families of airborne guided missiles are now developing. These modern missiles in one form or another are simply aerial torpedoes. But instead of sinking one ship and its crew, these missiles with atomic warheads can blast a whole city of a million human beings into eternity without warning. . . . Civilization progresses rapidly these days!

The counter to this first guided missile, the acoustic torpedo, was ridiculously simple, when we finally thought of it! We just towed raucous noise makers on a long cable astern of our ships. The torpedoes homed obediently on the loudest noise they heard and blew their own brains out harmlessly far astern of their intended targets! Let us hope similar booby traps can be devised to lure airborne missiles away from our big cities. Maybe we can hang "noise" makers on man launched satellites or the moon!

Another type of torpedo, for use against convoys where many ships were crowded together in a small space, ran straight till it got to the middle of a convoy and then darted around like a ferret in a chicken yard making erratic figure eights until it plunked one of the many ships trying frantically to maneuver out of its way and at the same time to avoid colliding with each other.

Torpedo exploders also went through various stages of development. At the beginning of the war they were per-cussion affairs and the torpedo had to physically hit the side of the target to make them work. If the torpedo depth control mechanism was inaccurate and the eel ran too deep, it could pass smack under the target ship and go on harmlessly beyond. Early in the war, the Germans had trouble with their depth mechanisms the same as we did, and many a U-boat skipper saw fat targets get away from him after a perfect approach and well-aimed shot because the torpedo ran deeper than the setting he had put on it. These skippers returned to port spouting curses at the torpedo designers—just as ours did. No matter what his nationality, if you give a submarine skipper a defective torpedo, he'll damn your eyes to his dying day.

To counteract erratic depth performance, the Germans developed a new type of exploder which didn't have to hit a ship but merely had to come close. Like the magnetic mine, it was fired by passing through the magnetic field that surrounds a ship. If it passed ten or fifteen feet under a ship it would explode the war head and break the ship in two. This worked for a while but then it and the magnetic mine were countered by demagnetizing all our ships. We wrapped electric cables clear around the ship fore and aft, and kept a heavy current flowing through them, setting up a man-made magnetic field exactly opposite to that induced in the ship by the magnetic field of the earth, thus sterilizing the ships so they would not fire the magnetic exploders. For a while the demagnetized ships caused the U-boat skippers to damn their own designers again, when they should have been cursing the Allied countermeasure boys.

Designers of new weapons and designers of the countermeasures for them, are never more than half a jump ahead of each other. It is a deadly, continuous battle of wits that absorbs the best scientific brains on both sides. We bring out a new weapon, catch the enemy flat-footed with it, and for a while it takes a heavy toll. Then the enemy's countermeasure people figure out how to confound it, and the weapon is useless—except that our own countermeasure people are busy too, and they knew the Achilles heel of this new weapon when they brought it out, foresaw the countermeasure to it, and are ready with a counter to the countermeasure. It's a scientific chess game involving a lot of mind reading and calculated risks, with thousands of lives at stake, which has been in progress ever since man has been inventing weapons. Up to now, almost every revolutionary new weapon since Hannibal's elephants—gun powder, the machine gun and the airplane, to name only a few—have been hailed as the ultimate weapon which would make war so terrible it would be banished from the earth. We seem to have such a weapon now in the H bomb. But the lesson of all previous history is that we will develop other things that will enable us to live—and to die—with the H bombs.

Strange to say, this new magnetic torpedo firing device of the Germans was not new at all. The U.S. Navy had developed it long before World War II. But in an attempt to gain complete surprise when and if we ever used it, and to be sure the enemy wouldn't have a countermeasure ready for it, we clamped a super-duper top secret label on it. In general, the fewer who know a secret, the better chance you have of keeping it. In this case, to confine the knowledge closely, tests of the new firing mechanism were run by a small group under laboratory conditions which nearly, but not quite, duplicated wartime conditions at sea. Our submariners knew nothing about this device until war broke out and the ordnance experts smugly handed it to them and said, "Here you are, boys—you don't even have to hit with this—just come close."

But the first few patrols by our subs in the Pacific proved there was a bug in the mechanism. Our skippers came ashore tearing their hair out by the handful, telling of daring attacks they had made, perfect approaches on fat targets, torpedoes running "hot and straight smack under the target, but no BOOM!" The scientists blamed it on faulty adjustments by the submariners so the boys went out and risked their lives again getting the same result. A rhubarb of some proportions developed, and for a time our submariners regarded our own Bureau of Ordnance as hostile forces.

Meantime, the Germans, with no knowledge at all of our great secret, developed the same thing themselves—except that theirs worked! And so it goes in this battle of brains. Smart people sometimes outsmart themselves, and Lady Luck is always hovering over their deliberations, ready to upset their applecarts with some outrageously improbable cast of the dice.

Another little gadget you find in a torpedo is the arming device. You can't afford to cruise around in a submarine with twenty torpedoes fully armed and ready to explode from any slight jar or some magnetic fluke that could be caused by the aurora borealis. So the detonating cap which originates the explosion of the warhead is kept a few inches away from the hammer which will strike and fire it eventually. Even if the cap fired itself in this position it wouldn't detonate the warhead.

On the nose of the torpedo warhead there is a small propellor-like water vane, which turns when the torpedo drives itself through the water. The shaft of this vane has a screw thread connected to the detonating cap and as it turns it moves the detonator into line with the firing device, completing the alignment after the fish has traveled a safe distance from the firing sub.

This device may have saved the U-505 from a premature end. One day in 1942, while attacking a ship in the Caribbean, one of her own torpedoes ran eratically, and some of her crew think it turned back and hit her square amidships. But the U-505 had a rendezvous to keep with Destiny and her number hadn't yet come up, so the screw thread hadn't quite finished unwinding and all the sub got out of it was a dent in one of her ballast tanks.

Some people think the oceans depths are sepulchral, noiseless voids where eternal silence reigns. How wrong they are. If you lower a sensitive microphone into the ocean you can hear many sounds. Maybe you even hear the heart beat of this planet, if the scientists are right when they say all life originated in the sea.

Water is an excellent conductor of sound—the submarines and their hunters both made constant use of this fact. The noises made by the screws of a ship can be heard many miles in an underwater microphone. The noises of the machinery and people inside her, transmitted into the water by the ship's hull, can also be heard at great distances. Breaking waves make noises and so do many kinds of fish. Schools of shrimp make rhythmic throbbing sounds that are very similar to the screws of a ship. The ocean has temperature, density and salinity layers that sometimes trap sound and channel it for phenomenal distances.

The ability to hear is of vital importance to a submarine, and all submarines are equipped with a sensitive array of listening devices. Very often they can hear an approaching ship much further than they can see her even when fully surfaced. When a sub goes deep to evade an attack the *only* way she can tell what goes on up on the surface is by sound.

The principal means used by surface vessels for finding submarines submerged is the sonar gear. The guts of this apparatus is housed in a dome which sticks out a few feet below the keel of the surface ship. A gadget inside the dome makes a "ping" which spreads out in all directions through the water. The sonar operator, in a compartment just above the keel, surrounded by banks of delicate instruments, watches his outgoing ping spread out on a video scope like the ripple from a pebble on a pond. If there is nothing out there but sea water of uniform temperature, density, salinity and emptiness, he gets no echo and pings again. But occasionally, after hours of endless pinging, he gets an answering echo "pong." All this "pong" tells him is that there is something out there besides emptiness, but whether it is a ship, a school of fish, or a temperature gradient, is up to him to figure out. The direction from which the echo returns tells him the bearing of the "something," and the time interval from ping to pong, multiplied mechanically on a computer, by the speed of sound in water and divided by two, tells him its range. An expert sonarman can often tell from the quality of his echo whether he has got a school of fish, a thermocline, or a submarine.

By listening, without pinging, you can often find out a lot more of interest. You can hear the sound generated by a propellor driving a ship through the water, and count the revolutions per minute it is making. The sound expert on submarines can tell the skipper, from the screw noises he hears, how many screws the ship has, and whether it is a plodding harmless merchant vessel which he can safely attack, or a prowling high speed destroyer which he had better avoid. When the sonar operator on a destroyer gets a solid "pong" echo, he listens for screw noises. If he hears them he knows he has got a submarine—unless it turns out to be a school of "talking" shrimp.

A friend of mine who had a destroyer squadron out around Guadalcanal in the early days of the war, tells a story about the strange sounds you can hear from the ocean's depths. He says that one day it was the good fortune of his group of "cans" to witness the most colossal bit of romancing (at least so far as physical bulk is concerned) that ever takes place on this earth—the mating of two whales. This creates quite a commotion in the water because the whales go at it enthusiastically. While all the watch standers on the bridges of the destroyers were eagerly training spyglasses and binoculars on this rare sight, the sonar operators down below, conducting their routine probe of the ocean's depth, bounced a ping off the two great fish and reported "unidentified echo," on the precise bearing and distance of the amatory leviathans. Then, in accordance with regular procedure, they quit pinging and listened. My friend swears that his experts on underwater sound reported "screw noises."

The behavior of sound in water is a field of science which absorbed the effort of our best scientific brains in Vannevar Bush's OSRD. In water of uniform temperature, pressure and density, sound travels at constant speed in straight lines. But the ocean seldom duplicates standard laboratory conditions. Usually the temperature of the water decreases as you go down and this will cause a sound beam projected just under the surface, to curve down and go deep till it either dissipates itself or hits bottom. Sometimes you get inversions, and the temperature increases as you go down. Then your sonar beam curves up, hugs the surface and you may get echoes from unusually long ranges. A surface vessel with its sonar and "ears" at a fixed depth has to do the best it can with water conditions as it finds them. A submarine can sample the water all the way from the surface down to about three or four hundred feet and cruise at the depth where it finds the best listening conditions on a particular day.

The submariners in the new atomic submarines we are building now claim they will hardly ever surface, except maybe to leave and enter their home base. They say they will stay down several hundred feet all the time where listening conditions are best, will find and stalk their targets by the screw noises and will sink them by firing acoustic homing torpedoes without ever actually seeing the target. I tell them this may be possible theoretically, but that it won't work in the U.S. Navy. They will have to surface after each shot because the boys in the Pentagon won't believe their claims on sinkings unless the submariners can produce photographs for the Public Info boys to put in the newspapers!

Underwater explosions can sometimes be heard for phenomenally long distances—under proper conditions for several thousand miles. A sinking ship makes characteristic noises as her boilers explode and parts of the hull are crushed in by the terrific pressure as she goes down. So when a global war is in progress, with hundreds of ships being sunk and depth charges being scattered all over the ocean, it's no wonder that the ocean reverberates with strange noises. The fishes must wonder what Man is up to.

You can tell that sound is of great importance to a submariner from reading any book about submarines. It is full of words designed to suggest the noises heard under the sea. Kachung, kachung, kachung is the day-long beat of the diesels. Thum, thum, thum is the noise made by high speed propellors approaching for an attack. Ping is the ominous warning from a destroyer's sonar gear. Kerblam . . . crump . . . whang is a salvo of depth charges close aboard. To a great extent, sound takes the place of sight as the main link with the outside world to the men who live inside a pressure hull.

Radio is another link that connects a submarine to the outside world. Submarines can receive certain types of long distance radio transmissions when they are shallowly submerged, and while receiving them they put out no indication of their location. But to transmit an answering message, they must surface, or at least stick a whip antenna above the surface. When they do, their neck is out as soon as they hit the key of their transmitter because they are then linked to friend and foe alike.

If you have direction finders all around the edge of the Atlantic Ocean, constantly on the alert for any message on the known submarine frequencies, it takes only a few seconds for three or four of them to swing their loops and get a good bearing on the source of the message. These far flung stations flash their readings to a central plotting room where experts on a twenty-four alert, can soon lay a small polygon down on your chart of the Atlantic which probably contains a submarine. Many a sub went to the bottom a few hours after sending a routine message in mid-ocean because of information furnished by our direction finder networks.

Laymen may ask, "Why didn't the Germans set up a similar system to tell their submarines where our killer groups were?" They just didn't control enough of the world's geography to do it. We occupied the whole rim of the Atlantic and could get simultaneous bearings from all around a German sub. The Germans in France could only get one bearing on our sub killers, and it takes two or more intersecting bearings to give you a "fix."

A layman listening in on a radio circuit hears a jumble of dots and dashes as monotonous and humdrum as rain on a roof. But to a radio operator there is a rhythm and beat to every incoming message that is just as peculiar to the man who is sending it as the sender's voice. Radiomen call this characteristic beat the sender's "fist" and it identifies him to his contemporaries as surely as his fingerprints. Our direction finder operators got to know the fists of many U-boat radiomen, so in addition to locating a U-boat that surfaced to transmit a message, they could often tell you which U-boat it was.

Even a U-boat's radio transmitter also has its own individuality. You can seldom detect this by ear, but if you make a tape recording of a transmission and blow it up many times on an oscilloscope, the experts can put their finger on any other transmissions from that particular radio set.

The moral of all this is, that whenever you touch a radio transmitting key in wartime, you are announcing not only your location, but also your name, rank and serial number if the enemy is as alert as he should be. This is why all Navies make a fetish of radio silence. Hitler's inability to understand this caused an upheaval in the German High Command that resulted in his sacking Raeder as the naval Commander-in-Chief.

When the cruiser "Hipper," and the pocket battleship, "Lutzow," intercepted one of our Murmansk convoys, they were driven off by much inferior British forces and the BBC immediately broadcast this stirring naval victory to the world. Hitler, who was pretty well fed up with the impotence of his surface Navy by this time, heard this broadcast and demanded that Raeder get an immediate report from the flagship "Hipper" giving their version of the battle. The "Hipper" was keeping radio silence while returning to port; and Raeder refused to order her to break it until she reached safe waters. Meantime, *der Führer* fumed and waited, his fury against the surface Navy mounting under skillful needling by Goering.

When the "Hipper" finally got to port, Hitler and all his top brass gathered around the teletype machine in his headquarters to get the long awaited news. Just as it started coming in, the teletype circuit to Norway went dead for several hours.

Adolph blew his top, threw a tantrum that was memorable even for him and heaved Grand Admiral Raeder out of his job.

There is another side to the radio silence business. As related above, you could sometimes hurt yourself by too deep a silence. In the jeep carrier task groups we used our radios almost promiscuously. You can't operate an aircraft carrier, and accomplish anything worth while, unless you do. You've got to talk to your planes in the air to give them landing instructions. You've got to let them test their radio sets right after launching and make sure they are working. Otherwise, when one of them finally spots a submarine a hundred miles from the ship after several weeks of hunting, you experience the utterly frustrating experience of having him fly back to the ship and send you a blinker message saying, "There was a submarine out that-a-way an hour ago—but she's gone now."

This business of uninhibited radio traffic with our planes is what we military "experts" call a calculated risk. We knew there was some chance the enemy might hear our transmissions, but we weighed this chance against the known fact that there was little use flying airplanes if you couldn't talk to them, and decided to use radio. As things turned out, we were right, so this was a calculated risk. The U-boats used their radios too much so this was not a calculated risk. The definition of a calculated risk is a gamble which military men take when they can't figure out what else to do and which turns out to be right. When it turns out wrong, it wasn't a calculated risk at all. It was a piece of utter stupidity.

The German scientists were slow getting wise to the facts

of life about radar. For a long time they wouldn't believe that British destroyers were equipped with it. German technology was way behind the British in this field, and all the radars their scientists knew anything about were too big to put aboard small ships.

Even after sad experiences convinced the unscientific U-boat sailors that the British had seagoing radar because destroyers were charging straight at them out of the arctic mists, the "experts" in Berlin gravely assured Admiral Doenitz that airborne radar was impossible. But it didn't take many attacks on his U-boats by aircraft on pitch black nights to convince Doenitz that the experts were wrong again. At his urgent insistence the scientists developed radar detectors which were eventually installed in all U-boats.

To install active radar sets (rather than detectors) would have been suicidal. Planes and surface vessels would home on the magnetic pulses sent out by such sets. Radar works on the same principle as sonar, except in a different element. A radar set emits an electromagnetic "ping" into the atmosphere, and waits for an answering magnetic "pong" from some reflecting surface. Any time you make a radar "ping" you risk giving away your location the same as you do when you put your fist on a radio transmitting key.

But a radar detector is a passive device which puts out no indication that it is operating. It's like the listening gear of a submarine as opposed to the active sonar of a surface ship. An active radar puts out a pulse of energy, gets an echo and measures the number of microseconds between the pulse and echo. A radar detector simply picks up the original pulse and indicates that a transmitting set is somewhere in the vicinity. It can't tell you how far away the transmitter is because it has no way of knowing just how many microseconds ago that pulse was triggered.

To compensate partly for this, the detector picks up a pulse about twice as far away as the triggering set can detect a usable echo. The detector works on the original outgoing pulse, whereas the active set must detect and measure a weak echo with only a fraction of the energy in the outgoing pulse.

These radar detectors sometimes did more harm to the

Germans than they did good. Their warnings saved some U-boats from surprise attacks at night. But they also caused many a U-boat to crash dive for an aircraft many miles away, and to stay submerged for hours when there was no real danger at all.

All a radar receiver tells you when it shows a blip is that there's a radar transmitter somewhere within about fifty miles of you. From about the middle of 1943 on, Allied aircraft were so thick over the Atlantic shipping lanes that it was a fairly good bet there would be an aircraft within forty or fifty miles of any U-boat that surfaced near the shipping lanes, and all the U-boat skippers knew this. But when they surfaced and got a blip on their radar receivers, their heart beat increased and they submerged forthwith. It's one thing to know before you blow your tanks and come up that there will *probably* be an enemy aircraft within fifty miles of you. It's a much more urgent thing, when you break surface, to see a little dancing blip on a scope confirming the fact that you were right, but leaving you in doubt as to whether he is half a mile or fifty miles away. You will probably assume he is half a mile and get below again as fast as you can.

Doenitz and his "experts" finally got so panicky about radar that they conjured up hobgoblins that didn't exist. When the Allies shifted the frequency of their radar transmitters beyond the range of the German's detectors, the Nazis wrongly suspected their own passive receivers of putting out signals which the Allies could detect. Several of their U-boats were surprised on dark nights by aircraft equipped with new high frequency radars which had produced no blip on their detectors. The Nazi scientists jumped to the conclusion that their receivers were somehow enabling Allied aircraft to home on their subs. They junked one type of receiver and developed another called Naxos—of which more later. Actually, we never detected any usable signals from the German radar receivers, despite the suspicions of the Nazi long-hairs.

So much for the mechanical insides of the U-505 when she started her training in the Baltic. The essential facts about the U-505 type sub were:

(a) She was primarily a surface vessel.

(b) She was compelled to surface for several hours in

every twenty-four to recharge her batteries.

(c) She had no schnorkel.

(d) She could go down to about 600 feet.

(e) She had excellent listening gear and only primitive radar detectors.

(f) Her primary armament was twenty-one torpedoes, but at first she also carried a four-inch gun.

Chapter

5

SHAKEDOWN CRUISE

ON THE FIRST of September, 1941, the newly commissioned U-505 went through the Kiel Canal to the Baltic to spend the next four and one-half months "shaking down." In this shaking down process a new ship works the bugs out of her machinery and digests and assimilates the men who have moved into her vitals. During this process she is somewhat like a young puppy developing its muscles, eyes, and ears, and learning to run, feed and take care of itself.

There are three major ingredients in the complex reaction that occurs on the shakedown cruise of a new ship, changing her from a floating machine shop into a weapon of war. They are the skipper, the crew, and the machinery. Their relative importance is in the order stated.

The machinery of the U-505 was the best that German scientific and technical brains could produce. The diesels, batteries, torpedoes, listening gear, periscopes and other equipment were the equal of any in the world. If skillfully operated, this mass of machinery would be a deadly instrument of destruction able to smash with one blow great merchant ships twenty times her tonnage and value. With a well trained crew, and fighting on her own terms, she could sink the biggest battleships in the world.

But a U-boat, like any other ship, is just so much cold metal until her crew comes aboard. Then each man in the crew loans her a little piece of his soul to keep as long as he serves in her—and often longer if she's a good ship. These little pieces all added together make up the soul of the ship, bring her to life, give her personality, and make her a member of the seagoing community of ships.

So long as a ship has a crew in her, whether she be the "Queen Mary" or a seagoing tug, the "Forrestal" or a submarine, she is a living, breathing thing, equal in a sense to any other ship, at least to the same extent that all men are supposed to be equal. Sometimes a little spit-kit of a tug is a better ship than a huge ocean liner, just as a carpenter can be a better man than a king.

To a seafaring man the ship he lives in is his home regardless of her tonnage, or of the size, shape and purpose of her hull. Some ships exist to transport man or his goods to the far corners of the earth and to bring back raw materials to the homeland. Others exist to protect these kind of ships, or to drive them off the seas. But the sort of a home that a ship is depends not on how she justifies her existence or even on the amount of elbow room a sailor has in his bunk. It depends on the men who live together in her.

The U-505's crew was a typical cross section of German youth. At this stage of the war they were a carefully skimmed cream of the crop, fired with zeal for the Fatherland and hate for England. Like most of the German Navy, they were not Nazi party members, but were convinced Germany's cause was just simply because it was the cause of their Fatherland, and were eager to get their U-boat to sea to join their sister ships striking back at England.

The average age of the crew when she went into commission was twenty years. They were born soon after World War I, most of them sired by soldiers and sailors who fought for the Kaiser. By 1928, when they started to school, Hitler had staged his abortive beer hall putsch, had served his term in prison for it, and had written *Mein Kampf*. He and his Nazi party were on the way up.

In 1933, Hitler took over as Chancellor of the Reich when these war babies were eleven years old. During their most impressionable years, Hitler was practically a god in Germany. Their parents regarded him as a messiah. Is it any wonder these kids believed in him and swallowed his stuff about the master race?

Many of them spent their teens in the Hitler youth movement but were too young to be full-fledged Nazi party members. Besides, the Navy discouraged party membership. The career officers who ran the Navy were willing to go along with Hitler and rebuild their service under him, but they avoided joining the party when possible. I fished men from three submarine crews out of the Atlantic and all of them said, "I am a German soldier—but not a Nazi."

Some were on the arrogant side, after they dried out a bit, but that is understandable. In their brief, unhappy lifetime, they had seen Hitler change their Fatherland from a conquered, helpless country, to the most feared nation on earth. When the U-505 went in commission in 1941, these youths had every reason to believe that Germany was invincible and they were on the winning side. None of those kids had much control over their destiny on this earth. Like our own youngsters, they were the product of their environment, and the mistakes of their elders.

But, I'll say this for them—they were worthy opponents and fought bravely for an evil cause. They risked their lives to torpedo ships and then steamed off and left the survivors to make the best of their way ashore or to the bottom, as the case might be. They did not machine gun life boats as our propaganda claimed they did. When we sank one of their subs and paused to fish them out of the water they were grateful—and surprised. Their propaganda had told them to expect machine-gun bullets instead of rescue!*

The U-505 was one of the standard type commerce destroyers which bore the brunt of the Battle of the Atlantic. There were perhaps eight hundred such type U-boats built, and in outward appearance you couldn't tell them

---

* When we tried to hang Admirals Raeder and Doenitz at the Nuremberg war criminals trial one of the charges was that they had ordered U-boat skippers to machine-gun the survivors of torpedoed ships. This was disproved. In the whole war there was only one authenticated case of machine gunning survivors at sea. This was done by a U-boat skipper named EMS. The British shot him after the war.

apart. But identical sister ships, as alike physically as two swab handles, can have totally different personalities. One will be happy and successful, another surly, unlucky, and no good. The skipper makes the difference. This is true of any ship. But on a submarine, even more than on a surface craft, the skipper is literally the heart, soul and brain of the ship. When the chips are down he is at the periscope and often he is the only man aboard who really knows what the score is. His snap judgment on when to take her down, when to blow main ballast and surface, when to attack and when to retire, will mean life or death to all on board. If he is timid, his sub will behave timidly in battle, no matter how tough his crew. If he is daring, his boat can perform great exploits with a crew of weak sisters.

The skipper depends on his crew, of course, and one dumbkopf who fumbles his own small job can ruin a daring attack for the skipper. But with the right kind of skipper, the dumbkopf is less apt to fumble. A tough, expert crew can sometimes stiffen the backbone of a mousy skipper, but usually whatever influence is exerted comes the other way. The skipper's personality profoundly affects every man in the crew, and each man in the crew, individually, exerts a much smaller effect on the skipper. You will see as this story unfolds how the whole character of a U-boat can be changed overnight just by putting a new skipper aboard, because he alone makes the decisions which determine whether the boat will be a lion or a mouse. The U-505's first skipper's name, Loewe, means lion in German. He painted a lion rampant on his conning tower and as long as he was aboard, she behaved like one.

All navies, except perhaps the Japanese, recognized the skipper's importance, and rewarded their top submarine skippers handsomely. Prien, Schepke, and Kretschmer were the top aces of the U-boat fleet, acknowledged as such even by the Allies. No one submarine skipper in any Navy has ever rolled up a score to equal Kretschmer's 325,000 tons. Prien, Schepke and Kretschmer had far reaching effect on the war at sea by convincing Hitler that the U-boat was the answer to England's supremacy at sea and persuading him to go all out on production of U-boats.

The Germans had a fixed scale of awards for successful raiding operations. Ace U-boat commanders who sank over 100,000 tons of Allied ships, got the Knight's Cross of the Iron Cross from Hitler and were great heroes in Germany. Their crews shared in these awards and were also marked men in the Fatherland. We had submarine aces in our own Navy. Fluckey, O'Kane, Street, Ramage, Gilmore, Cromwell and Dealey, all got the Congressional Medal of Honor—the last three named being posthumous. All these men, whether American or German, were modest chaps who would tell you that their crews deserved all the credit for their success, and in a sense this is true. But ask their crews about this and they will all tell you that if you replaced any of these lions with a mouse, their now famous submarines would have behaved in a mousy manner.

The U-505's pressure hull was never breached by enemy action, but her second skipper cracked under pressure when she was being severely punished by a depth charge attack. I can think of no more devastating experience for a U-boat's crew than to have the brain and heart of their ship fail them when the chips are down as this one did. I doubt that her crew ever recovered from the shock, and I believe this had something to do with her eventual capture. (This will be told in detail later.)

But her first skipper, Axel Loewe, Kapitän Leutnant zur See, Reichskriegsmarine, was a good one. You would expect him to be good because the U-boats were the elite branch of the service in the German Navy and got the pick of the officer personnel. This U-boat was one of the early ones of the program that finally produced 1100. The first skippers of these early U-boats were professional career officers and competition for these commands was keen.

Loewe came from a substantial family in eastern Germany and was thirty-one years old when he commissioned the U-505. His father had been an officer in the Kaiser's Navy who fought in the "Seydlitz" at the Battle of Jutland. The son followed in his father's footsteps, entered the Naval Academy at the age of nineteen and served in surface ships until war broke out. Then he volunteered for submarines, spent six months in the sub school and made one "makey-learn" war cruise under an experienced skipper before taking command of the U-505. So far as submarines were concerned, his inexperience was comparable

60

to that of his crew. But he had twelve years of regular Navy service behind him; he was a professional, and a good one.

He knew, as all pros do, that the best way to advance your own personal interests is to shove them into the background and make the welfare of your men your first concern. As soon as any crew knows they have this kind of skipper, that ship is on its way to becoming an efficient and successful one. As Loewe expressed it to me in a letter written ten years after the war, "I tried to follow the principle of the British Admiral Nelson and make my ship a happy band of brothers."

Judging from other things in this letter, Loewe is quite a man and a worth-while citizen. Although he lost all his worldly goods in the war and his naval career was abruptly ended, he has reestablished himself since. He now holds a responsible job in West Germany, and says he considers that his life on earth so far has been lucky and happy because, "I have my health, my wonderful wife has stayed with me, and we are raising three fine children." I think that sentence explains why the man who brought the brand new U-505 into the Baltic in late 1941, soon made her into a good ship.*

Loewe spent the next four months in the Baltic, beyond reach of the RAF and Royal Navy, whipping his boat and crew into shape for the grim work ahead.

Only three of the fifty-six enlisted men in the U-505's crew had ever served in a submarine before. I thought the U.S. Navy did a marvelous job of making sailors out of farm boys in World War II, and toward the end, 80 per cent of our sailors were lads who had never been at sea before the war started. Training submariners is much more difficult than training surface sailors. But when a submarine fleet expands in war time from 57 boats to over 600, keeping as many boats on the hunting grounds as possible and losing trained crews regularly due to enemy action, the level of previous experience in the new boats is bound to be spread mighty thin.

* A recent letter from Loewe says he has rejoined the newly formed German Navy and is now a Fregatte Kapitän.

With only three old submarine hands on board Loewe had to start with the ABC's of the business. The crew were very willing and specially selected, but they had to be taught everything—Loewe practically had to begin by explaining which end was the bow. Under such conditions the shakedown period is very important indeed.

On a submarine, more than on any other type of ship, each of the men who will live together for a year or so has a very high stake in the welfare and efficiency of this boat —his own life. Every man in a submarine knows that whatever future he has in life is bound to the fate of that submarine. If the boat dies, the odds are three to one he dies with her. He therefore not only does his own job to the very best of his ability, he checks to see that every other man does likewise. There is no such thing as an unimportant job and everybody knows that a single mistake by any one of them can be the end for the whole lot of them. Everybody resents any carelessness or inefficiency because the guilty party gambles with all their lives when he does anything that risks his own. A crew can be reconciled to a daring skipper who takes long chances and wins great glory for them to share, but they can't tolerate a stupid shipmate who doesn't pull his weight in the boat.

After a submarine crew have made a couple of war cruises together, there is a bond between them that lasts for life. It bridges whatever gaps there may be in their background, education, and station in life, and makes them permanent members of an exclusive club who have shared certain experiences together that no other group in the world have shared. They may not all like each other, but for a certain period they pooled their lives together in a dangerous business and brought each other through it safely. They can therefore make allowances (ashore) for the failings of these shipmates which they wouldn't make for anyone else.

When the U-505 joined the U-boat kindergarten class in the Baltic, the first thing they had to learn was how to handle the boat. It's easy enough in a book of this kind to "explain" how a submarine submerges by opening the flooding valves and vents to fill up the ballast tanks, pulls herself under with her diving planes, and then adjusts trim and buoyancy by taking just enough water into the internal tanks of her pressure hull. Anyone can understand that if you close the vents and shoot compressed air in at the top of the ballast tanks, forcing the water out through the flood valves at the bottom, the sub will become buoyant again and come up to the surface.

But before a sub can do either one of these maneuvers, every man in her crew must become thoroughly familiar with his own little part of the sub's intricate anatomy. This little part may contain dozens of valves, switches, and levers, all of which must be operated not only correctly and in proper sequence, but also in correct relation to what dozens of other men are doing at the same time. It's hard to make a "small" mistake when everything is so closely integrated that one flip of the wrist in the wrong direction can dangerously snafu a thousand correct operations performed precisely right. Doing even a routine maneuver is a complex operation requiring perfect teamwork of all hands.

When the diving alarm sounds, all hands who are on deck tumble down the conning tower hatch and someone who *knows* how many were topside must check them off as they come down. The last man down slams the conning tower hatch closed provided he is sure the diesels are stopped, as they should be by that time. Then a lot of valves and vents must be opened in exactly the right order, the motors must be started, and the men on the diving planes must keep the bubbles in their inclinometers exactly where they should be. The diving officer must know exactly how much water he needs in every ballast tank and must close the valves and vents at exactly the right point. Otherwise he could scuttle the boat instead of just giving it slight negative buoyancy.

He must keep track not only of the total weight of the boat but also of the fore and aft distribtuion of this weight. Both of these vary continuously. The total weight changes as the crew eats up the food and discharges the waste products over board. Water is heavier than oil, so as you burn oil and sea water replaces it in the external tanks, the boat tends to gain weight. Three men moving from the after torpedo room to the forward one make an important change in the trim of the boat in half a minute. Since the external ballast tanks usually are full when submerged, there are a few internal tanks inside the pressure hull which are used for final adjustments to trim and buoyancy.

A boat can be in good trim on the surface where it has tons of positive buoyancy, but badly out of trim submerged when the buoyancy is near zero. An exaggerated example of what can happen when you get badly out of trim submerged, is the famous picture of the U.S. submarine "Pickerel" skyrocketing out of the water at a 45-degree angle, which appeared in *Life* a few years ago. That was done deliberately "for public relations" purposes. But it could happen accidentally if the diving officer doesn't know what he is doing, and would generate very bad public relations for him with the Captain. It did happen once to the U-505.

On the lighter side, a standard gag on almost every submarine in any Navy involves the toilet and the latest recruit to report aboard. When a sub is running submerged, flushing the toilet (which is, of course, inside the pressure hull) involves a rather complicated sequence of opening and closing water and air valves. All submariners will gravely tell you that to take care of your routine bodily functions you need a college degree in hydraulics.

Some rather Rabelaisian pranks can be played on a newcomer to the submarine service by giving him only slightly inaccurate instructions as to how to operate the valves the first time he has need to do so when the boat is submerged. Of course, to be sure the newcomer doesn't drown himself and swamp the boat you had better be standing by outside the door of the "head" after you give him these instructions.

There are two kinds of dives for submarines—a "normal" dive and a "crash" dive. On a normal dive, there is no hurry, everything can be checked and double checked, and you take her down gradually, keeping her on an even keel. A crash dive is an emergency maneuver when you've got to get down fast to save your hide. When an airplane screams down out of the clouds, seconds can mean the difference between life and death. Then a crash dive is a slam bang maneuver, in which the big idea is to get under as soon as possible, adjusting trim and buoyancy later, before you plunge so deep that your pressure hull cracks. Even on a crash dive you must be sure the conning tower hatch is closed and the diesels are stopped. When time permits, you will get all the crew below before slamming the conning tower hatch. As will appear later, I encountered one U-boat skipper in the Atlantic who couldn't wait for three of his men to get below when we surprised him. One of those three is the only survivor from that U-boat now.

After the crew of the U-505 had mastered the ABC's of their business, they held full power trials and tested their guns, torpedoes, and all other equipment. Then, graduating to a higher class and working with friendly ships and planes, they got into the business of learning to fight their ship. Their radio operators learned how to get quick accurate bearings on any transmissions they picked up in order to track down unwary merchant vessels who broke radio silence at sea. Their sound crews learned to follow an unseen ship by the noise of her screws while she was still beyond the horizon, and to determine from sound alone whether she was a merchant ship for them to torpedo, or a destroyer for them to avoid. Her "dirty trick" department learned to shoot *pillenwerfers* out of small tubes to create chemical bubbles in the water astern which sent back false echoes and baffled the probing sonar beams of destroyers trying to hound them down. They practiced ejecting oil and wreckage to convince a gullible destroyer skipper or aviator that his first attack had made a kill. Loewe perfected his technique for making a submerged approach and attack on a zigzagging target. They made crash dives to deep water as they would have to do when attacked by aircraft. They practiced lying doggo on the bottom in shallow water with all hands practically holding their breath and not making the slightest sound as they would have to do to fool tormenting destroyers. They drilled at creeping away quietly, submerged, their screws barely turning over, while destroyers dropped depth charges on the phony *Pillenwerfer* bubbles astern. When trying to sneak away in this fashion, a U-boat crew walks around on tip toes, because the sensitive listening gear on a destroyer can sometimes pick up the footsteps of a heavy lummox clumping along on the steel floor plates. They ran slam bang submerged at full speed, making erratic maneuvers to be used only in extremis when noise wouldn't matter, because the hellish din of depth charges close aboard was drowning out all other noises, including the destroyer's sonar gear. They simulated all sorts of casualties, pretending that many important pieces of machinery had been smashed by depth charge attacks, and that they were limping home in badly battered condition.

During this shakedown period, a change was occurring inside the U-505 like the change that goes on in an egg during incubation. Sixty strangers were adjusting themselves to each other, getting to know and have confidence in their skipper and each other, giving up pieces of their individuality, and changing from an amorphous mass of strangers into an integrated, purposeful, intelligent whole, much greater than the sum of its original parts. Each of these sixty became a limb, organ, or nerve of the complex body that took shape inside the submarine's tough shell. Each felt that he was an important part of the new organism and that his destiny and its destiny were one and the same. Loewe was its brain, and about half its soul. As we shall see, so long as he was on board it was a lion that had hatched in the shell of this U-boat.

Finally, the U-505 had to pass a rigid operational test and prove to the Admiral in charge of training that they had learned their lessons and were ready to graduate. Late in November they had their final operational readiness inspection. The Admiral's team of seasoned U-boat experts gave the new ship a merciless grilling, running her through every maneuver a U-boat can ever be called upon to perform. They sprung unexpected casualties to the engines, torpedoes, and attack director on the green crew and skipper. They pulled critical switches at the wrong time, secretly opened valves that should be closed, and tried every way they knew to snafu operations. Inspecting officers pretended to get angry at boot seamen and ranted at them to see how they would behave under pressure.

Loewe had done his job well. On 24 November, U-505 passed her exams and went back to the yard at Hamburg for her post-trial overhaul and loading of live torpedoes. On 19 January 1942, they were pronounced ready for the final test of battle, and the U-505 shoved off from Kiel to join the Second U-boat Flotilla based at Lorient.

This first operational voyage took them through the Kattegat and Skagerak into the North Sea. In World War

I, when both sides of the English Channel were in Allied hands, a mine field clear across the Channel near Dover blocked that passage to the Kaiser's U-boats. In World War II, with the Germans holding the French side of the Channel, it was impossible for the British to lay such a mine field. But swarms of RAF aircraft and Royal Navy motor torpedo boats made it too dangerous for Nazi subs to use the Channel regularly. Toward the end of World War I, the great North Sea mine barrage, extended all the way from Scotland to Norway, had practically bottled up U-boats in the North Sea. But in World War II, the Germans held Norway and no such barrage was possible. The U-505 avoided the English Channel and took the longer passage north around Scotland, between the Faeroes and Iceland, and into the Bay of Biscay to Lorient on the Gironde River in France.

Although this took them directly across the converging convoy lanes to England, the voyage was apparently uneventful. The leather covered book, now on display in the Museum of Science and Industry, simply records the dates of her departure from Kiel and arrival in Lorient. But the war diary shows that Loewe kept his crew busy constantly for these 15 days with more drills of every kind, crash dives, and simulated casualties. In addition, all their regular watches were now being stood "for keeps" in enemy waters, and all hands were under a tension they had never felt in the Baltic. In this part of the ocean there was no such thing as a friendly ship or aircraft. Submarines were treated as rattlesnakes by anyone who sighted them.

U-boat sailors didn't trust the Luftwaffe any more than our own submariners trusted American flyers. There were recognition signals, of course, for use between planes and submarines. But all submariners used to say, "There's only one recognition signal we really trust—if it flaps its wings, its friendly!"

On that first cruise to Lorient the crew of the U-505 began learning how to live with the idea that sudden death lurked constantly just beyond the horizon and they could never be sure of living another fifteen minutes. But nothing much happened to impress it on them that time.

As the U-505 reported for duty in Lorient early in '42, and prepared for her first foray against Allied shipping, the Battle of the Atlantic was entering its grimmest year. In 1942, the Germans terrorized the shipping lanes and almost knocked England out of the war by sinking 1570 Allied ships, totalling 7,700,000 tons.

During this "Happy Time," as the U-boat skippers still call the year of 1942, no outstanding aces succeeded in filling the shoes of Prien, Schepke and Kretschmer. But there were a dozen or more who exceeded 100,000 tons and the greatly increased number of U-boats at sea more than made up for the lack of phenomenal individual performers like those of the three aces. The U-505 was joining the U-boat fleet just in time to take part in the good hunting that would prevail for the next year and a half.

On her trip to Lorient, the U-505 passed about 200 miles south of Iceland where I had just taken over Command of the U.S. Navy Fleet Air Base at Reykjavik. I was to remain there for the next year and a half, operating a squadron of Catalinas on anti-sub patrol, helping the RAF to escort the hard-pressed convoys through the toughest stretch of the North Atlantic. During this time the U-505 would make three far ranging cruises and sink nine ships. Two and a half years later she and I had a strange rendezvous to keep off Cape Blanco, French West Africa. But many things were still to happen before this meeting occurred—and in February, 1942, she sailed past me two hundred miles away south bound, unmolested by my PBY's.

Chapter

6

ICELAND

WHILE nothing much is happening to the U-505 as she makes her way to Lorient, I digress from her story now to relate an Icelandic saga in the Battle of the Atlantic.

Iceland is strategically located to dominate the North Atlantic convoy lanes. It was an ideal base for long range patrol planes helping to fill in the mid-Atlantic gap which our planes based in England and Newfoundland couldn't reach in 1941.*

The Icelanders had sat out all the wars of the world for a thousand years as neutrals, and didn't want any part of this one either. But in a global war the big nations don't pay much attention to International "Law" or the protests of weak neutrals. We muscled in on the Icelanders as gently as possible in July, 1941, during the undeclared war, brought our friends the British in with us, and stayed there the rest of the war. (If you're interested, any international lawyer can spout legal gobble-de-gook for hours "justifying" this invasion.)

I arrived in Iceland on 31 December 1941, for duty in command of the U.S. Navy Fleet Air Base at Reykjavik. I was a Commander then. The undeclared war which we had waged for five months around Iceland was over. Still numb from the shock of Pearl Harbor, we now plunged up to our necks into the Battle of the Atlantic to sink or swim with the British. The Battle of the Atlantic was just entering the black year of 1942, in which things went steadily from bad to worse throughout the year.

My main job in Iceland was to tie in the operations of our PBY airplanes up there with the efforts of the RAF and the Royal Navy to escort convoys through the "gap" where the U-boat wolf packs prowled. For the next year and a half, the Battle of the Atlantic raged relentlessly from 300 to 500 miles south of us and my planes helped the RAF beat the wolf packs off many a beleaguered convoy.

We lived primitively in Nissen huts on the edge of Reykjavik air drome, and a big part of my job was doping

---

*When I say "our" I mean Allied forces not simply the U.S. Navy. Lest readers of this book in which the U.S. Navy plays the leading role should get an exaggerated idea of the part the USN played in the Battle of the Atlantic, important though it was, let me hasten to state that the final box score on submarines sunk was

British and other Allied Forces	600
US Forces	181
Total	781

out ways and means to keep the boys from going nuts during the long arctic nights in a cold, strange land.

The command set-up under which I had to work was one of the typical snafus of the early war days. Almost every Allied officer in Iceland senior to me had some sort of authority to issue orders to me. For a while, whenever one of them happened to think of it, he did.

I had five official bosses who could tell me what to do —two U.S. Admirals, one British Admiral, one U.S. General, and an RAF Air Commodore. It says in the Gospel, "No man can serve two masters," and I agree that serving two is a very difficult job indeed. But I soon found that serving five is easy. All you have to do is to exercise a little judicious stupidity and get your bosses debating among themselves about their respective prerogatives and about who does what to whom. The situation becomes confused and to avoid any high-level rhubarb about it, they finally let you write your own ticket. You wind up becoming a small scale Commander-in-Chief, hobnobbing with all five bosses on an equal basis and running your own show to suit yourself.

As soon as I acquired this status, I found the RAF Air Commodore was the boss I had to work with to pull our weight in the U-boat battle. For all practical purposes, I joined the RAF, and the Air Commodore's planes and mine worked together over the convoy routes as if we were one outfit.

This didn't happen quite as quickly as you can tell it in one short paragraph. The Air Commodore was inclined to be a bit skeptical of me at first. He took one look at my face, which my friends tell me resembles a relief map of Ireland, and decided that anyone whose ancestry was so obviously Gaelic would probably make things as difficult as possible for His Majesty's representatives. This coolness eventually melted and we became fast friends, seeing eye to eye on every operational question that came up during our year and a half of close association.

After we had warmed up to each other, the Air Commodore said to me one day, "Y'know, Dan old boy, I was dubious about you at first, thinking that your Irish background might make dealing with you a bit difficult."

I replied, "I bear no ill will whatever toward the British

70

for what they did to my ancestors. In fact, Commodore, I am eternally grateful to your ancestors for persecuting mine and driving them out of Ireland, so that I was born in the U.S.A."

As we got to know each other better and could recognize a twinkle in each other's eyes, further high-level ribbing resulted. Working closely with the Royal Navy and the RAF, I often had to exchange official memoranda with the Air Commodore and the British Admiral.

Whenever you address a note to a high ranking British officer, you must stick a whole flock of initials behind his name on the envelope—DFC, DSO, KCB, etc.—indicating the orders and decorations which he holds. The only thing I could put behind my name when I signed these memos was "junior," and this made no impression whatever on our gallant fighting Allies.

After a while, when I got to know them well enough, I began putting "DDLM" after my signature on notes to the Admiral and the Air Commodore, figuring that sooner or later one of them would ask me about it.

Sure enough, one morning the Air Commodore did. I met him in RAF headquarters and after the customary exchange of courtesies, he remarked, "I say, Dan old man—what does DDLM mean that you put after your name?"

"Oh-h-h," I said vaguely, "That's the American equivalent of your KCB."

Knight Commander of the Bath is one of the biggest and best things to which a British military officer can aspire. The Air Commodore was properly impressed. There followed a pause during which I could practically hear the gears grinding inside the Air Commodore's head as he tried to figure out the meaning of the cryptic initials. Finally he gave up and said, "But . . . just what do the initials stand for?"

I said, "They stand for 'Dan Dan the Lavatory Man!' "

This kind of high-level monkey business was not just for fun. Word of it flashed through the camp rapidly and helped to keep the boys on an even keel during the long arctic nights.

Another incident helped us to break the ice and make friends with the British. One day when a blustery wind

71

was blowing, the first shipment of recreational gear for our camp arrived from the United States. Opening up the boxes of this consignment like a bunch of kids on Christmas morning, we found, among other things, a push ball which we promptly blew up to its full five foot diameter. Exploring the crates for more loot, we left the push ball sitting outside the storeroom unattended.

You should never leave anything as big and light as a push ball unattended in Iceland, because the wind comes along and blows it away. This happened to our push ball. I emerged from the storeroom just in time to see it go skipping down the road, bounce over the bluff into the water, and start sailing across a small inlet on which our camp was located. It soon grounded on the opposite shore where a British anti-aircraft battery had its camp.

I wanted that push ball back, so I picked up my field telephone to call the CO of the AA battery and ask him to hold my push ball till we got over there and reclaimed it.

Our field telephone system consisted of a labyrinth of wires laid out over marshy ground. Short circuits and grounds were frequent, and strange things happened on this command circuit. Connections often got crossed—as they did this time.

Just as I picked up my phone, I heard my friend across the way calling Royal Navy Headquarters and reporting, "The biggest bloody mine you've ever seen in your life has just washed ashore at our camp, and will you please send a mine disposal squad over to deal with it?" I hung up without saying a word.

After a few minutes I called the Royal Navy Headquarters and reported that I too had seen this huge mine wash ashore, that I had a qualified bomb disposal party at my place, and that if the RN wished me to do so, I would be happy to deal with this situation.

There was nothing in the world that the Royal Navy wanted more at that time than to have someone else take this nasty job off their hands. The Watch Officer promptly replied that this would be "quite satisfactory."

I burst into our Officers' Club, rounded up about a dozen helpers, explained the pitch to them, and we organized a bomb disposal squad on the spot. We had all read enough about bomb disposal to know what sort of equipment we needed and how to go through the proper motions. We scrambled around the camp grabbing a half dozen rifles and commandeering a stethoscope, a voltmeter, a field telephone set, and a couple of tool boxes. Dumping this equipment into jeeps, we roared over to the British camp where we found a crowd of our gallant Allies standing back at a respectful distance, casting nervous glances at the "mine."

The arrival of the American "experts" obviously relieved the tension. We immediately stationed our sentries and shoved the crowd back to a safer distance.

Leading out our field telephones we placed one at the mine and another about a hundred yards back, so our mine disposal boys could phone back every move they made to be recorded in a note book, in case they made the wrong move and blew themselves up.

Then, after a few minutes of hocus pocus with the stethoscope and voltmeter, much telephoning back and forth and scribbling in the note book, we finally gave the signal that the big moment was at hand.

While the crowd watched in awed silence, we unscrewed the valve, let the air out, and then got the hell out of that camp at four bells and a jingle.

I was always getting into "situations" with the British. One icy day in January, I accompanied Admiral Dalrympyle Hamilton to a conference with Commander-in-Chief, Home Fleet, on board his flagship anchored near Reykjavik in Havlfjordur.

When we departed from the great battleship, the guard, band, and six side boys were drawn up on the quarterdeck to shove us off with appropriate ceremony in accordance with time honored naval custom. In deference to the foul weather, two sailors were also stationed at the foot of the gangway to help the visiting brass into the boats.

As our boat was shoving off one of the sailors slipped on the icy gangway and plunked into the near freezing water. His buddy promptly hauled him back on the gangway platform and then, though both were drenched in icy brine, they snapped to attention and stood at salute till the boatswain's mate finished piping the barge away.

I complimented Admiral Dalrympyle-Hamilton on this

"good show . . . traditions of Nelson, and all that sort of thing."

"Nothing at all old boy," the Admiral replied modestly, "I'm sure any of your sailors would have done the same thing."

"I suppose so," I said, but then all my Irish ancestors rose up in their graves and compelled me to add, "Except, of course, that none of my sailors would have fallen overboard in the first place."

Don't think from all this monkey business that life was just fun and games in Iceland. In January '42 The Battle of the Atlantic was mounting to a smashing climax, and we were smack in the middle of it and brand new at the business. This was the heyday of the wolf packs and the outcome of World War II hung in the balance a few hundred miles to the south of us. Our planes flew fourteen-hour patrols every day taking the weather as it came —and it came in stinking doses of fog, wind, and freezing rain. Our pilots, flying lumbering PBY's, often spent ten hours going and coming from a convoy, but during their four-hour patrol around the convoy they kept the wolf packs down, forcing them to use up their precious batteries and to lose distance on the convoys.

The logistics of an operation of this kind are worth looking at, since military men are so frequently accused of padding their requirements outrageously. To keep one PBY over a convoy 500 miles away twenty-four hours a day, you have a perfect right to demand a twenty-six plane squadron. This probably sounds like a typical Pentagon overestimate, but I can really justify that one. Your planes spend ten hours on each sortie going and coming to put in four hours on the convoy so it takes six planes to do the twenty-four hours of flying time over the convoy. You've always got to have at least one spare plane sitting on the line with its crew briefed and ready all day long, so that makes seven. The six planes that flew fourteen-hour hops yesterday are in check today being readied for tomorrow's operations, so that makes thirteen. In the flying business you hope there will never be an accident, but you know there will, so you add a certain percent for "attrition." Let's say you are really conservative and only demand one extra plane for this factor. That makes fourteen. After a plane has flown let's say 1,000 hours, it has to be laid up for a major overhaul, which takes a month as opposed to a routine check of one day. This means you will always have about two planes in the shop, so now we are up to sixteen. Just as Doenitz always had 50 per cent of his U-boats in training, you have to back up your operational force with plane crews in training. Being acutely cost concious and frugal with the taxpayers' money instead of demanding an equal number of planes "on the line" and in training as Doenitz always did for his U-boat fleet, I'll settle for only half as many, which brings our total up to twenty-four. Any sensible military man always adds a certain percentage to the best honest guess he can make as to what he needs, and, again being a thrifty soul, I'll add only ten per cent. So we wind up with a requirement of twenty-six planes to keep one over the convoys in the mid-Atlantic gap.

Some critics have accused the military of being profligate wastrels because we didn't win World War II by killing the last Jap with the last bullet we had in our ammo locker. I would much rather defend myself against such charges than try to explain to my three kids why we lost our liberties because military planners didn't want the war to end with a lot of surplus junk on our hands.

So if you ever have to fight wolf packs, operating from a base in Iceland, don't settle for a squadron of less than twenty-six planes. (I had to get along with sixteen.)

Many of our pilots in Iceland flew hundreds of hours around the convoy before sighting their first sub. Sometimes it seemed to them that it was utterly futile and useless to stick their necks out flying through foul weather only to bore holes in the air around a convoy with no submarines anywhere in sight. But the subs were there, submerged, and by keeping them submerged we were doing a lot to help defeat the wolf packs. My boys needed their first kill to boost their morale and enable them to rub elbows with their blooded compatriots in the RAF without any inferiority complex.

Early in 1942, we sighted three U-boats and fumbled the opportunities for this first kill due to buck fever, bad luck, and inattention to seemingly minor details. I blew my top, called all the pilots together and read the Riot

75

Act to them. At the end of my tirade, I announced that our recently opened Officers' Club was hereby closed and would remain so until we got our first kill. This was cruel and unusual punishment, but I had decided I would rather be a son-of-a-bitch and help win the war, than to help lose it and be thought a "swell guy."

Soon thereafter, one of our pilots, Lieutenant Hopgood, en route to meet a convoy out of England caught the U-464 surfaced about 50 miles from the convoy. His attack crippled her so she couldn't submerge but could still limp along on the surface.

Hopgood had dropped all his depth charges on the first attack and his single thirty-caliber machine gun was useless against the thick hide of the U-boat. He radioed to the convoy and a British destroyer broke off at full speed in answer to Hoppy's plea for help. Meantime, the crippled sub went alongside an Icelandic fishing vessel and as Hoppy circled, the Germans abandoned and scuttled the sub, took over the trawler and headed for Germany. Hoppy duly reported all this by radio and spent the next couple of hours shuttling back and forth between the trawler and the onrushing destroyer coaching her how to steer.

This was an exciting three hours for all of us back in Iceland. Hoppy's electrifying message that he had a cripple on his hands but couldn't finish it off brought everybody piling in to the RAF operations room where we sat with our ears glued to the radio following the dramatic developments at sea.

Hoppy's radio reports right up to the end were terse and official giving a clear and complete picture of what was happening out in the Atlantic mists. His next to last one was, "Destroyer is alongside trawler and has taken off 52 prisoners." We were still cheering and slapping each other on the back when he came through with his final one in plain English—a paraphrase of the well known and wholly inaccurate, "Sighted Sub, Sank Same," message of dubious fame. It read, "Personal for Commander Gallery. Sank sub, open club."

We opened the club all right. We almost blew the roof off the joint that night, and while this celebration was at its height, we conceived a happy idea of getting a suitable trophy of this victory to grace the lounge of the club. Obviously the most suitable trophy would be the U-boat skipper's pants.

Next morning I addressed an official letter to the First Lord of the Admiralty in London, outlining the previous day's action, explaining the American expression, "Caught with your pants down," and its obvious application to what had happened, and requesting that when the British destroyer arrived in England with the prisoners, the skipper's pants be forwarded to the Fleet Air Base for framing. To make this deal legal and to prevent leaving the German skipper in an embarrassing position, I sent a pair of my own pants along with this letter and forwarded the correspondence via the British Admiral in Iceland.

At first the Admiral was horrified at the idea of addressing the First Lord with such an irregular proposal. But the Air Commodore persuaded him to "bung it on in to London." By return mail I received a very pleasant letter from the First Lord congratulating us on our first kill and saying he had instructed the Admiralty "to deal with" my request.

A month or so later a very stuffy communication arrived from the Director of Naval Intelligence, quoting several sections of the Geneva Convention about humiliating prisoners, etc., etc., and regretting that my request could not be granted.

I took a very dim view of the matter. I didn't mind the malarkey about the Geneva Convention so much, but I did resent the outrageous injustice of not even getting my own pants back!

In any story of Iceland the ordeal of the Murmansk convoys clamors for a hearing. The merchant sailors who survived that murderous run from Reykjavik to Murmansk and back (back only if you were lucky) were the unsung heroes of the war. In wintertime the Arctic Ice Cap extended down nearly to Bear Island and forced the convoys to cruise well within bomber range of the Norwegian coast. In summertime the midnight sun gave both subs and planes twenty-four hours of daylight to find their targets and do their deadly work. Our planes escorted these convoys as far as they could and often the Luftwaffe planes practically relieved us "on station" at the limit of our range. Thus the convoys had air escort all the way to Murmansk and back, but most of the way it was hostile. The Russians made sweeping promises about heavy fighter escort for each successive convoy as soon as it came within their range, but they made no attempt to meet their commitments. Our ships were bombed by the Germans even when they were unloading at the docks in Murmansk.

If the Luftwaffe and the German Navy had been able to cooperate harmoniously, nothing would have gotten through on that run. On the few occasions when they did work together such as on convoy PQ17, they decimated our convoys. Luckily for us Goering and Raeder hated each other, and the U-boats seldom got the help they needed from the air.

The ordeal of PQ17 was one of the saddest chapters of the Battle of the Atlantic. Several Murmansk convoys had been roughly handled and as PQ17 assembled at Reykjavik in June 1942, there was unrest among the merchant sailors, some of whom refused to sail with their ships. To quiet the unrest, word was passed that we were going "all out" on PQ17. It would have a close escort of six destroyers in addition to the usual dozen corvettes. It would also have a covering force of four heavy cruisers escorted by three destroyers to beat off surface raiders. To top all this off, a task group of the newest British and American battleships, "Duke of York" and "Washington," plus four heavy cruisers, plus a dozen destroyers would follow close behind them to trap and destroy the "Tirpitz" in case she was rash enough to venture from her hideout in Norway. This is probably the most formidable escort any convoy was ever given—or more accurately, was ever promised.

On June 27, 1942, thirty-four merchant ships sailed from Reykjavik for Archangel, their crews lulled with a sense of security that the combined naval might of Britain and the U.S. would see them through. The ships were loaded to the gunwales with tanks, planes and ammunition —all badly needed in Russia.

What followed is a shameful page in naval history, and I must say that so far as the U.S. Navy ships in this operation were concerned, all they could do was obey the preemptory orders of the British Admiralty in London, under whose control our ships were operating.

One of the many things that the merchant sailors didn't find out until after they sailed was that when the Admiralty said the battleship force would be "close" behind the convoy, they meant 150 miles—at least five hours steaming at full speed. They also meant only until the convoy reached Bear Island at which time the big ships would bug out for home.

On July 1st, when the convoy was just passing Jan Mayen Island and was still six hundred miles from Bear Island, the Germans located it by air, and shadowed it from then on. On July the 4th, when the convoy was passing between Bear Island and Spitzbergen, the attacks began and four ships got sunk.

I'll never forget that 4th of July in Reykjavik if I live to be a hundred. The Air Commodore and I knew that this convoy had the heaviest surface escort ever assembled and that the mission of this armada was to lure the "Tirpitz" out and destroy it. But we didn't know the details of what was in the Admiralty's mind. any better than the merchant sailors did.

We met in the RAF operations room early that morning and spent most of the day watching the drama unfold hundreds of miles to the northeast. Early in the forenoon we got a flash from London saying, " 'Tirpitz' is proceeding to sea." So far as we knew, our two great battleships were still following "close" behind the convoy. The "Tirpitz" was heading into a booby trap.

The Air Commodore turned to me and said, "It looks like this is going to be the best 4th of July since you blokes declared your independence." I agreed. All afternoon we smacked our lips in anticipation of the coming triumph. As we found out later, by this time our battleships were on their way back to the safe haven of Scapa Flow.

Late that unforgettable day we intercepted the message from London, "All warships retire to the west at high speed. Merchant ships scatter and make best of way to Archangel." Too stunned and ashamed to say a word we just drifted out of Headquarters, went back to our huts and wept or cursed.

When the U.S.S. "Washington" came into Reykjavik some weeks later her people wouldn't come ashore. They didn't want to face their friends although God knows all they did was carry out orders from London which left them no discretion.

Fortunately, the merchant sailors in the convoy never saw our battleships, so it was a long time before they found out how the battleships deserted them. But they did see four heavy cruisers turn and run, taking the six destroyers assigned to escort the convoy along with them and leaving the convoy to its fate. The merchant ships scattered in accordance with the Admiralty's orders and did the best they could in lone battles against the Luftwaffe and the U-boat fleet. Only 11 out of the 34 ships which sailed from Iceland ever got to Russia. Some of them limped in months later, having hidden themselves in the ice pack to repair their damages. Out of 200,000 tons of vital cargo in this convoy, only 70,000 got to Russia.

Churchill in his book, *Closing The Ring,* says of PQ17, "The consequences for us were painful." This is a classic understatement by one of the masters of the art. He spends seven pages in this book trying to "explain" the snafu of PQ17. But anyone familiar with the Churchill style when he means what he is saying, as in his "blood, sweat and tears" oration, can see that his heart isn't in it when he tries to justify what happened to PQ17. He is just going through the motions of defending knotheaded subordinates for whom he was responsible. He sent Stalin a 1500 word telegram trying to justify his inept helpers in the Admiralty —clearing it first with F.D.R. Churchill never needed more than about 150 words to explain his position when he was sure he was right, nor did he clear it with anybody. In this case, he got a rude reply from Stalin, and it was deserved.

Much as I deplore the conduct of our naval forces in this action, I must, in justice, state the Admiralty's side of the case. Singapore, where the "Prince of Wales" and "Repulse" got sunk, and Pearl Harbor were still fresh in their minds. Many of our finest surface ships had been sunk in the previous seven months and British dock yards were jammed with badly damaged battleships. The whole future of surface navies seemed to be at stake and the heirs of Nelson in the Admiralty were taking no chances on having two more new battleships caught out on a limb where the Luftwaffe might nail them.

Maybe this explains why the two battleships were told to stay 150 miles behind the convoy. But I'll never understand why the four cruisers and a dozen destroyers were ordered to scram for home as soon as the "Tirpitz" was rumored to be coming out. (Actually, the "Tirpitz" turned back soon because Wilhelmstrasse could make just as big blunders as the master minds in London could.)

Churchill solemnly says that this cruiser force would not have had a chance against the "Tirpitz." Perhaps in theory he is right. But on December 13, 1939, three small cruisers wrote a glorious page in British naval history when they defeated the German pocket battleship "Admiral Graf Spee" in an all-day running fight and drove the big ship fleeing into neutral waters at Montevideo. Theoretically, these three frail British cruisers were foolhardy to venture within gun range of the "Graf Spee."

Churchill also knows, perhaps better than anyone alive, that to win great victories you sometimes have to take long chances. Even after the Admiralty pulled the battleships out of PQ17's escort, the four cruisers and nine destroyers still with the convoy might have written another page for the history books if the Lords of the Admiralty had had as much guts as their compatriots at sea. But shore-based bureaucrats never take chances which would make them look bad in case of failure. When you put a good seafaring and fighting man ashore at the Headquarters of the government, his mind doesn't work as it does at sea. It gets stultified by contact with bureaucrats and politicians, and he sometimes does things that shame his brethen at sea.

Soon after the PQ17 fiasco, we quit running the Arctic convoys until the long winter nights set in again. When we started again, Berlin soon proved that the Nazi bureaucrats could foul up their sea going forces just as badly as the Admiralty could. While attempting a raid on a Murmansk convoy the great cruiser "Hipper" and the battleship "Lutzow" turned tail and ran for shelter when a few destroyers peeled off from the convoy and made what they expected to be a suicide attack on their huge opponents.

81

The odds against these destroyers were at least as great as those against the escorts which abandoned PQ17. But despite the odds these bantamweights went in slugging and routed the heavyweights.

The German ships ran because of ironclad orders from Hitler issued after the loss of the "Bismarck," that German surface ships were not to fight a battle in which they had to take any risks! There is no such thing as a battle in which you don't take risks—unless you call shelling and sinking a hospital ship a "battle." But Raeder, who was a competent seafaring man aboard ship, held still for this absurd order from *der Führer* and passed it on to his people at sea. The "Hipper" and "Lutzow" went out on that next to last raid of the Germany surface navy with orders to "Hang their clothes on a hickory limb—but don't go near the water." We know now that the "Tirpitz" had similar orders when she made her shortlived feint against PQ17, causing the convoy to scatter and our warships to abandon the merchantmen and flee for safety. PQ17 might have been an entirely different story if the officers on duty in the Admiralty had exercised the intestinal fortitude that the British Navy always displays at sea.

To sum up the Arctic convoys, in 1941 and '42, 219 ships sailed in these convoys for Archangel and Murmansk—155 got through and delivered 24,000 vehicles, 3200 tanks, 2600 airplanes and 700,000 tons of ammunition and oil. Despite Stalin's angry reply to Churchill's telegram about PQ17, we supplied Russia with the stuff that kept her in the war and did so at great cost to ourselves. But if the German Navy and Luftwaffe had fought together against us as Goeing and Raeder fought against each other, they could have stopped the Arctic convoys cold, and might have knocked Russia out of the war.

One incident that occurred in Iceland before we got up there has a place in this story of the U-505. It is the strange business of the U-570. This submarine, although of a later number than the U-505, was at sea on her first cruise when the U-505 was being commissioned in August, 1941.

One morning, three hundred miles south of Iceland, she surfaced simply to air out the boat for a few minutes. It was her bad luck to pop up half a mile in front of an RAF plane returning to Iceland after a fruitless antisub patrol with all her depth charges still in the bomb racks. Within seconds the plane plastered the U-570 with a full salvo of depth charges which shook her up severely and, although doing no fatal damage, crippled her so she couldn't submerge. Then to the amazement of the circling pilot, as the sub limped along on the surface, the whole crew came scrambling up on deck holding their hands aloft and waving a sheet in token of surrender!

The plane had no more depth charges left and there is no way in which the pilot of a land plane can negotiate surrender terms with the skipper of a crippled submarine. The pilot sprayed machine-gun bullets in the water to let the U-boat crew know that he was in charge here and could take disciplinary action if necessary and then sent them a blinker message to steer for Iceland. The U-570 meekly obeyed! For the next twenty-four hours the RAF kept planes circling the U-570 as she plodded through the stormy weather toward Iceland, and the Royal Navy rushed a tug out from Reykjavik to meet her.

I can see why a skipper who was not yet willing to die for the Fatherland might be reluctant to scuttle his U-boat in the North Atlantic hundreds of miles from land with nothing in sight but an airplane. There was a gale blowing, even in August the water is cold, and the circling airplane could do little for 50 men in the water. But when the British tug appeared a new situation was presented. The British were well aware of this and had prepared for it.

As the tug neared the submarine the Royal Navy skipper hailed the Germans and expressed grave doubts that he could rescue any of them in the prevailing heavy seas if the U-boat happened to sink. He urged them to keep her afloat at all costs. I'm sure he stayed within the limits of the Geneva Convention, but he must have been a very persuasive man, because the German crew accepted a towline from him and continued their voyage toward Iceland.

Just off the south coast of Iceland the towline broke in the heavy weather and the U-570 with her crew still on board was washed ashore on a sandy beach. By this time her crew had thrown her codes and secret papers overboard and had smashed most of her secret equipment. When the storm abated, the British salvaged the U-570, towed her to England and eventually repaired her and commissioned her in the Royal Navy as HMS "Graph" (see Churchill's *Grand Alliance,* page 519, for an account of this episode).

I have related this story in detail because some British naval officers will dispute the claim that the U-505 is the only German submarine ever boarded and captured at sea. There is no doubt whatever about what happened to the U-505. She didn't surrender, we took her by force. I don't know how to classify what happened to the U-570, but it was a different sort of thing entirely.

This strange tale does have a bearing, even though remotely, on the story of the U-505. The arctic nights are long, the social whirl in Iceland was slow, and we often gathered around the fireplace in the Officers' Club after dinner to swap lies about our flying experiences and to discuss global strategy. The strange story of the U-570 was hashed over many a time. One night after Hopgood's exploit with the U-464 and the Icelandic trawler, and while a marvelous aurora borealis display outside made all things seem possible, a fantastic plan was hatched. Somebody tossed the question out on the hearth—"Why can't we board and capture a sub with one of our PBY's?"

If you analyze this idea now it seems crazy—in fact, next morning when we got up in the dim arctic light, it seemed a little bit farfetched. But when you are gathered around a fireplace in Iceland with a dozen active young imaginations at work on an idea, and especially when the bar stays open late, small difficulties are solved immediately and big ones are soon whittled down to small ones.

We started from the known facts that a depth charge attack which doesn't sink a sub may cripple her so she can't submerge, and that submarine crews had a strong desire to stay alive. We all knew that you can land a PBY in a pretty rough sea and get away with it—much rougher water than you can take off from afterwards.

We visualized another situation like Hopgood's with a cripple limping along on the surface. We decided we would circle close aboard for a few minutes peppering the hull with machine gun bullets to convince the crew they had better stay below. Meantime, we would crack off a previously agreed code word to the base which meant,

"We are about to board and capture this guy—send a destroyer out to accept the prize from us." *Borealis* was to be the magic word.

Then our PBY would land in the water just short of the U-boat's stern, taxi rapidly up and hook her wing over the sub's deck just abaft the conning tower. All this time the bow gunner would be beating a tattoo on the conning tower with his machine gun. The plane would, of course, be equipped with boat hooks, tommy guns, and about a fathom of steel chain.

While the pilot gunned his outboard engine to hold the plane alongside the moving sub, the rest of the plane crew would pile out of the side gun blister onto the deck of the sub and after lashing the PBY securely to the U-boat, rush up to the conning tower. The man with the chain secures one end on deck and heaves the other down the conning tower hatch, making it impossible to close the hatch and submerge in case the Nazis are able to effect repairs. His pals pump a few slugs down the hatch from their tommy guns to convince the boys below that it isn't safe to try and come up on deck. Then the only thing left is to pound out another message to base on our portable transmitter asking, "What the hell is the delay in getting that destroyer out here?" About this time the bar closed and we all went to bed.

Call this plan fantastic if you will. I suppose it was. But it is the germ from which an equally fantastic plan sprouted two years later—a plan that put the U-505 on the end of a towline astern of a jeep carrier and eventually, alongside the Museum of Science and Industry in Chicago.

Chapter

7

LOEWE'S FIRST MISSION

On February 11, 1942, the U-505 and the veteran U-68 sailed from Lorient, the U-505 on her first war mission and the U-68 on her fifth. Escorted by a minesweeper to the hundred-fathom curve, they parted there to proceed independently as lone wolves to their assigned hunting ground off Freetown, just above the Equator in the big bulge on the west coast of Africa.

The shipping lanes for traffic going round the Cape of Good Hope pass close to Freetown and there was lots of traffic going that way now. The battle for Egypt was raging along the northern rim of the Sahara Desert, with Rommel and the British chasing each other back and forth from Bengasi to El Alamein. The Mediterranean was practically closed to Allied shipping and all supplies for the British Army had to go clear around Africa. Doenitz, keeping a shrewd eye on shipping and on the deployment of Allied naval and air forces, had found a spot off Freetown with heavy traffic and weak defenses. The hunting would be good there.

As Kapitän Leutnant Axel Loewe took the U-505 to sea for her first raiding mission, he had every reason to look forward eagerly to the future. He had a splendid new U-boat, and a crew which he had trained himself. His orders to operate as a lone wolf gave him an independent command and made him the master of his own destiny as much as it is possible to be such on this earth. He had reached the top spot to which any young German could aspire at this point in world history and had a better opportunity to win fame than any of his contemporaries in the Army or even in the Luftwaffe. Within a few months he might be a hero of the Fatherland like Prien, the giant-killer who sank the "Royal Oak." Prien was now a corpse on the bottom of the sea, put there by the little "Wolverine," a mere spitkit compared to the "Royal Oak." But Loewe didn't let his mind dwell on things like that. All aviators expect to die in bed and so do U-boat skippers starting off on their first cruise.

Loewe had nineteen torpedoes on board and it only took 50,000 tons of enemy ships sunk to win an Iron Cross. If he was lucky, if most of his torpedoes hit, and if his targets were average sized ships, he might make it on this cruise. Hessler in the U-107 had sunk 90,000 tons on one cruise. The U-68, now also enroute to Freetown, was already well on her way to 100,000 tons and a Knight's Cross for her skipper. The luck of the chase would, of course, play a big part in the score that Loewe would make on this cruise. But he had drawn a good hunting ground so his own guts, skill and intuition would play a big part too. Every U-boat skipper who ventured out of Biscay was crossing the doorstep of destiny and Loewe must have had a few dreams of glory as he stood his night watches on the bridge working his way south.

The crew were just as anxious as the skipper to get into action. Up to now Germany was certainly winning the war and none of them doubted final victory. They were anxious to play a part in it which they could brag about in later years. Members of famous U-boat crews were great heroes in Germany now. During their eight-day stay in Lorient, the unproven crew of the U-505 had been tolerantly patronized by the combat veterans of the U-68, U-124, U-515, and some of the other famous boats. With a little luck they would be able to do some patronizing themselves next time they were in Lorient.

For the first two days out of Lorient, Loewe crept along at low speed submerged all day and ran at high speed on the surface all night. Then, with about four hundred miles between him and the RAF bases in England, he ran surfaced all the time except for about an hour a day of proof dives and drills. At this time the proposition that Britannia ruled the waves, and the air over them, was merely a patriotic idea in the minds of some old-fashioned Englishmen. A bold eager beaver like Loewe, who had confidence in his lookouts, could cruise on the surface any time he felt so inclined. As we shall see, when the U-505 headed for Freetown the next time—two years later—it would be quite a different story.

The one thing that the new U-boat, its Captain, and the crew needed to finally fuse them into an effective combat unit was a successful brush with the enemy. No matter how well a new ship does at drills, these are make-believe affairs. Until the chips are down and you play for keeps you can never be sure that there isn't a weak sister aboard who will get butter-fingered when his life is at stake. The U-505's first chance to prove herself came within two weeks when she was passing west of the Cape Verde Islands.

At 4:30 in the afternoon on February 24, Loewe sighted

a smoke cloud over twenty miles to the east. When he tried to close it he soon found it came from a fast south-bound convoy making fifteen knots. Such a convoy would have been hard to catch in any event because running on the surface the U-505 could make little over eighteen knots. When you are trying to close twenty miles on a convoy, holding a position abeam of it, as you must to make a successful attack, three knots margin in speed is just barely enough. But in this case, the convoy had air escort and Loewe was driven under several times when the planes made routine sweeps out in his direction. Apparently the planes never saw him, but their approach forced him to submerge. His submerged speed being only three or four knots at best, he lost distance on the convoy rapidly whenever he was driven down. Loewe hung on till one o'clock the next morning, by which time he still was twenty miles from the convoy but had dropped astern of them. Then he lost the convoy in the darkness, and he surmises in his war diary that the convoy made a sudden change of course to the east which he failed to detect. He also records for the information of his superiors, "My fault that we lost contact." This sheds a lot of light on the man's character because all his superiors could ever know about this episode was what Loewe told them, and he could easily have told them a better story to explain his first failure if he had been built that way.

Of course, the crew knew pretty well what was going on during this ten-and-half hour chase, and knew it really wasn't the skipper's fault that this convoy had escaped. They knew you can't always attack every target you sight. A lot depends on the speed of the target and your position relative to its course when you first pick it up. If there are airplanes buzzing around the convoy you'll only get in a shot if your first sighting happens to be in a lucky position. So the crew of the U-505 didn't blame their skipper for the convoy's escape. But they still needed their first kill, and Loewe knew very well that you don't build morale on good abilis for missed opportunities.

But sometimes you can build it on strange things. Next morning a lookout sighted a Sunderland bomber near the horizon about five miles away. "Alarm! Flugzeug!" he cried, and the four lookouts plopped down the hatch into the conning tower. The watch officer pulled the diving alarm and the whole boat galvanized into action.

Both diesels coughed to a stop as the maschinistenmaten spun their throttle valves and slammed the main air inductions shut. Electricians threw in the switches on the big board in the motor room and the whine of electric motors replaced the throbbing of diesels as the shafts kicked over again.

"Ready to dive," bawled the watch officer as he dropped from the bridge into the conning tower, pulling the hatch down over his head. On the level below in the control room men stood tensely at the flooding and vent manifolds, their hands on the valves ready to go into the routine that would take her down.

"Achtung!" barked the diving officer, and made a signal with his right hand. The men began spinning valve wheels in a carefully predetermined sequence.

The boat had been "riding on the vents," which means the sea valves in the bottom of all ballast tanks were open but the air vent valves in the top were closed. Sea water, had therefore enterd all tanks through the open sea valves compressing the air trapped in the top of the tanks until the air pressure equalled the sea pressure and the water stopped coming in. All ballast tanks were about half full of water and the boat was, in effect, being kept on the surface by the cushions of air trapped in the top of each ballast tank.

To take her down, all they had to do was to pop the vents open. The air would whoosh out, the water would surge in through the bottom and down they would go. You get under a little quicker if you nose the boat down about ten degrees in the process, so it was standard procedure on U-505 to pop the forward vents open first, letting water in forward to trim the bow down, and then pop the after vents. Meantime, the men on the diving planes watched the bubbles in their inclinometers and wrestled with the big wheels on the forward and after diving flippers to keep the boat at the desired angle.

A dozen operations must be performed at exactly the right instant to make a good crash dive retaining full control of the boat. When they are, your boat is completely submerged in about thirty-five seconds, she has levelled

89

off at about forty meters, the bubbles are centered, the trim tanks adjusted, and you settle down for a normal submerged run.

This time on the U-505, there was a slight hitch. Willi Bunger, an eighteen-year-old farm boy on the after ballast tank vents, missed a signal and didn't pop his vents open when he should have. Willi knew that if necessary he should open his vents at a certain point without further signal after the diving officer gave the order, "Take her down." But always in the past the diving officer had motioned with his left hand when he wanted the after vents. He did this time too, but Willi didn't see it and the diving officer failed to check. Willi waited about ten seconds too long before popping the vents on his own initiative. As a result, for fifteen or twenty seconds, water was pouring into the tanks up forward but none was coming in aft. This made the boat very nose heavy.

As Loewe climbed into the conning tower the boat had just reached its normal ten-degree nose-down trim. "Sunderland aircraft, 5 miles bearing 270, Kapitän," reported the watch officer.

"Very well," said Loewe. "Hold her at this angle."

The angle increased to fifteen degrees. "Bow planes full up . . . Stern planes full down," barked the watch officer. The angle increased to twenty degrees, the diving officer checked quickly to see that the after vents were open—and by this time they were. "Close forward vents," he yelled.

Normally this would have straighted things out fast. The inrush of water up forward would stop, water would continue to pour in aft and proper balance would soon be restored. But Willi Bunger had waited so long before popping his vents that by the time he did it the stern was clear out of water and the after flood valves were a foot above the water. Instead of more water coming into the after tanks, the water already in them was gurgling out. When he opened the vents, it just made things worse by letting the water pour out faster.

Down, down, down, went the bow. At thirty degrees Loewe shot a glance at the depth indicator, saw that it still read zero and realized immediately what was happen-

90

ing. The boat was pivoting around the conning tower with the bow going under and the stern coming out of water.

"Ausblasen," he yelled, taking over from the diving officer. "Blow all tanks." As the shafts began to race he added, "Stop motors."

High pressure air to expel water from all tanks began hissing through the boat, but she kept right on tilting till she was forty degrees nosed down. Before she reached that angle the men and all loose gear started sliding along the floor plates and piled up against the forward bulkhead in each compartment making the boat more bow heavy. Water was still pouring out of the after tanks, faster than it was being forced out of the forward ones.

For two minutes, in order to stand erect, Loewe had to brace one foot on the forward vertical bulkhead and one on the deck of the conning tower. A few more degrees increase in trim would have forced him to shift both feet to the bulkhead. Any instant he expected to feel the smashing impact of bombs from the Sunderland.

Finally the increasing trim stopped . . . the boat hovered at a crazy angle for half a minute, and then began settling back again. When she was within ten degrees of being level again, Loewe barked, "Cut off the air, open all vents and valves, start motors." The U-505 settled back in the ocean, water rushed in equally forward and aft, and the boat disappeared under the sea.

To all hands in the crew it seemed that their heartbeats had stopped and they hadn't breathed for five minutes as they were waiting for the blows from the air which hadn't come. Now, at forty meters on an even keel, everyone let out a sigh, looked at each other silently and relaxed.

In Loewe's war diary the following entry appears, "Eine schauderhafte Situation. Gottsei-dank hat das Flugzeug nichts gesehen." A liberal translation is—"A hell of a fix. Thank God the plane didn't see us."

Ten minutes after getting squared away again, Loewe and the diving officer had reconstructed the whole sequence of events and figured out why it had happened.

"Tell Bunger I want to see him," said Loewe.

Willi Bunger was in his bunk, his face buried in the mattress and his whole body quaking when they shook him and said, "The Captain wants to see you."

Willi sat up slowly, holding his head in his hands trying to conceal the tears, but he couldn't do it. "I can't help it," he sobbed looking at his shipmates miserably, "It was all my fault."

"Ja," said his friends . . . "but no harm done . . . the Captain . . ."

Willi pulled himself together, dried the tears on his skivvy shirt and made his way forward to the conning tower.

"Seaman Bunger, Sir," he said, snapping to attention.

Loewe looked narrowly at the bloodshot eyes and tear stained face. "Well?" he said.

"It was all my fault, Sir," blurted Willi. "I missed a signal and . . ." Willi choked up and began crying again.

After a pause Loewe asked, "Did you do it on purpose?"

"No, Kapitän," said Willi.

"Will you ever do it again?"

"No, Herr Kapitän," said Willi emphatically.

"Gut," said Loewe. . . . "We must have looked very funny with our head in the water and our ass up in the air, like an ostrich." Even Willi couldn't stop an embarrassed grin at this absurd picture. "Go below and get some coffee, Wilhelm," said Loewe.

Although only the Captain and Willi had been present in the conning tower during this interview, every word spoken was known to every man in the boat within a very few minutes. Each one of them said within himself, "I must be careful not to fail this Captain."

From that day forward Willi Bunger responded cheerfully to the nickname "Ostrich" and never made another mistake on the vents.

On March 2nd, the U-505 arrived in her assigned area off Freetown, and three days later, at 6:30 in the evening on the 5th, the lookouts sighted a 6,000 ton cargo ship, 120 miles off shore bound for Freetown. This time Loewe was lucky. The ship had no escort, it was just before sunset when he sighted her, and he could remain on the surface and make his attack under cover of darkness. For four hours he stalked her deliberately and just before 11:00 P.M. he fired his first torpedoes at a live target, a double shot from the bow tubes at point blank range of

600 yards. They both missed! But a third shot didn't. It hit the unsuspecting steamer smack amidships, and she coasted to a stop sending out a frantic SOS saying, "S.S. 'Ben Mohr' torpedoed," and giving her position. The U-505 had finally tasted blood. In the light of a nearly full moon, Loewe waited while the "Ben Mohr" got her boats in the water and then plunked her with another torpedo that broke her back and sank her. He then made off on the surface at high speed leaving the life boats to make the best of their way ashore. The ship had gotten off an SOS and on such a fine moonlight night there might be planes out there any minute, so it was advisable to get away from the scene of the sinking. In fact, three hours after the sinking they had to crash dive to avoid a Sunderland obviously sent out in response to the "Ben Mohr's" SOS. The SOS had given Loewe all the information he needed for his sinking report and that night he entered in his war diary, "5.3.42—Englische Frachter Ben Mohr 6000 BRT." From the point of view of a U-boat skipper and his crew, the above terse entry contains all the information of any importance in connection with an incident such as this one.

It is not quite as simple as that for the survivors in the life boats. But if they are only 120 miles from Freetown in good weather, the outlook isn't too grim. If they are in the middle of the Atlantic, that's something else, and they have an ordeal to go through before they can be sure they are survivors.

As the U-505 steamed off to the southwest from the scene of her first kill, she was a different U-boat and every man in the crew a new man. Up till now they had been on trial but hadn't proved themselves. Despite that diploma from the Admiral in the Baltic, they were still virgins at the trade of sinking ships. Now they had come up with a clean kill and wouldn't have to be bashful any more in the presence of the older crews of the Second Flotilla around the bars in Lorient. It was a jubilant group of novices that had tasted their first blood that night. They found it a heady drink.

Their next swig of it came sooner than they had any right to expect. At 9:30 the next morning, only about forty-five miles from the spot where they had sunk "Ben Mohr," they sighted a heavily laden tanker also inbound for Freetown. She was zigzagging radically, evidently having been warned about the sinking of the "Ben Mohr" in this same area a few hours before. But it didn't take Loewe and his navigator long to analyze the zigzag and determine that she was headed for Freetown and that they were right on her base course. Loewe submerged and waited for her devious path to bring her in front of his tubes, and two hours later she lined herself up with his periscope cross hairs. He fired a double shot at her as she disappeared in a rain squall and heard two explosions at the time when his torpedoes should have hit. Ten minutes later, when the squall lifted, there was nothing but a huge cloud of smoke where the tanker had been. Loewe surfaced and approached the cloud noting that the water was covered with oil and wreckage, and finally spotting two rafts and a life boat. He came close enough to the rafts to determine that the survivors were all soaked with oil and that some were burned and needed medical supplies. But as he prepared to go alongside and give them morphine, salve and bandages, the lookouts sighted an airplane. He had to submerge and get out of that area.

The entry in the log for that day's work was, "6.3.42 Engl. Tanker, Name Unknown, 8000 BRT." The sinking of 14,000 tons in two days started dreams of glory dancing in every head on the U-505. They had 13 torpedoes left and if they kept on at this rate the torpedoes would soon be gone and they would be on their way home to get Iron Crosses at the end of their first cruise! They told themselves they were no longer mere novices with only one kill. They could now strut through the bars and bistros of Lorient using the plural when they spoke of their kills. They had twisted the tail of the British Lion 4,000 miles from home out in the ocean that Britannia was supposed to rule. They regarded themselves now as seasoned U-boat veterans.

But Loewe, although pleased at these first two successes, knew that he and his crew hadn't really been tested yet. They were all still apprentices and would be until they got shaken up. There is nothing heroic about sinking a couple of unescorted merchant ships any more than there is in shooting ducks. It requires a certain amount of technical know-how in operating the boat, alertness by the lookouts to spot the game, and skill in adjusting and aiming the torpedoes. But it is no real test of the crew's ability to perform under pressure. That would come later when exploding depth charges slugged the hull with stunning blows, when each man had to grit his teeth, brace himself and find the right valves in the dark with the whole ocean quaking around him.

Actually, it was Loewe's duty to postpone this testing as long as possible. His job was to make his attacks so that the enemy had the least possible chance of doing any harm to him. The more one sided and certain he made this business of sinking unescorted merchant ships, the better he was doing his job. In submarine operations, as in all fields of military endeavor, the ideally planned and executed operation is an ambush where you kill the enemy from a position of complete safety yourself. A commander who takes any unnecessary risk is a fool.

Submarine warfare is a business in which the advantages are all on either one side or the other and the odds can change quite suddenly from one extreme to the other. The very nature of a submarine requires it to operate by stealth and so long as it remains undetected until its torpedo blows the bottom out of an unsuspecting victim, the odds are all in the sub's favor. Even Prien's great and daring feat of sinking the "Royal Oak" depended on stealth and surprise. But the moment a destroyer or an aircraft spots a sub the odds swing the other way. A sub's only real defense is to submerge and make itself invisible. That first convoy the U-505 had sighted, just after leaving Biscay got away simply because an aircraft circling around it forced the sub to submerge and hide.

Submarines seldom get into a fight, properly speaking, except when cornered. A fight is a two way battle in which the opponents stand up to each other and slug. Submarines are supposed to roll with the enemy's punch, dodge and squirm, and to get away rather than counterpunch. Even the wolf packs which charged into convoys on the surface at night did so under cover of darkness, depending on surprise and confusion to enable them to hit and run.

I don't mean to imply that the U-boat crews were not brave men. They were. But they had a different kind of courage from the kind we usually associate with military exploits. Their courage was tested not by the sinking of helpless merchant ships, for which they got their medals, but by the uneventful weeks of prowling in enemy waters between sinkings when nothing was happening. Then they had to learn how to live with the constant knowledge that sudden and gruesome death might be lurking just beyond the horizon. Even if they went for months without encountering enemy opposition, this was no guarantee that in the next ten minutes they might not be fighting for their lives, struggling to bring their boat to the surface and get overboard before her battered hull went to the bottom. Loewe knew that it took a few depth charges close aboard to sort out the men from the boys in his crew and finally make the U-505 a tested veteran.

After sinking the tanker, Loewe patrolled back and forth across the shipping lane from Freetown to Cape of Good Hope eager for the next victim. But for the next ten days he had the whole ocean to himself, and his jubilant crew had to settle down again to the tedious monotony of routine life at sea in a submarine.

Landlubbers who spend their lives ashore where they have plenty of elbow room, and can have all the privacy they want any time they feel grumpy, find it hard to believe that sixty men can live together for three months inside a pressure hull no bigger than a subway car.

It's a cramped, confined life, in which all hands get to know each other much too well . . . but so is life in a monastery or a prison. Men can get used to it, and, counting all navies of the world, perhaps 100,000 men did it in World War II.

When you are on patrol and the hunting is bad, one day is almost exactly the same as the others. In fact, you could simplify the calendar by boiling the week down to three days—Yesterday, Today, and Tomorrow.

The sixty men who go to sea together in a sub have got to make more personality adjustments than most psychiatrists have ever heard of. Before the cruise is over, every man on board will know every joke that every other man on board has ever heard. He will listen to plenty of bragging by his shipmates about their amatory exploits and probably do some himself. To three or four intimates he

96

may let down his hair and tell them what he really thinks. But although plenty of serious thinking is done on a long cruise, little of it comes out in words. A garrulous deep thinker would be a menace to the morale of a group who know they are never sure of half an hour to live. Raconteurs are what you need on a U-boat—not philosophers. A screwball character who isn't screened out of the crew soon enough, can make life hell for all on board, including himself—for one cruise. A claustrophobe would, of course, be unthinkable—a sub would be a literal mad house for him and all his shipmates. The longest walk you can take is two hundred feet in a narrow passageway from the forward to the after torpedo room.

With sixty men living practically in each other's laps, little things assume great importance, and an irritating personal quirk that might be overlooked ashore can quickly antagonize all your shipmates. Snoring is frowned on by the men in adjacent bunks. By adjacent, I mean just high enough above and below each other so that the man in the middle bunk barely has room enough to roll over. If you slurp your soup too loudly at the chow table, the guy who sits next to you for ninety days may want to strangle you at the end of the first month. You can make life-long enemies by occupying the gents' can for more than your fair share of time. This, incidentally, is the only place on a U-boat where anyone is ever alone, all by himself—except for the skipper, who can pull a curtain across the door of his cubbyhole cabin and pretend he is getting some privacy.

Everybody has got to allow for some weaknesses in each of the others, and to keep his own weaknesses, which the others must allow for, to a minimum. I don't mean to say that a sub crew get along together like nuns in a convent. But every man on board has got to get along fairly well with every other. There just isn't room enough in a sub for any real personality clash and if one occurs the skipper will probably transfer both offenders at the end of that cruise. As long as your shipmates feel that you are willing to give as much as you take, you will be accepted. If they ever feel otherwise about it, you are in bad trouble and soon learn the meaning of "massive retaliation." When your shipmates turn against you, you can be just as lonely on a crowded submarine as if you were marooned on a desert island.

A thief on a submarine is simply unthinkable, and so is a sex pervert—because there is no place to hide. I've heard of a man on a U.S. sub during the war who didn't think it was safe to leave his money behind on the paymaster's books in Pearl Harbor when he went off on a war patrol to Japan. He drew $1,200 in cash the last day in port and kept it in his clothes locker on the sub! Everybody lives in a goldfish bowl and any unusual event in the after torpedo room, such as Schmidt losing his watch, is known immediately in the forward torpedo room.

An unusually funny quip or noteworthy comment of any kind gets through the boat almost as fast as if it had been said on the public announcing system. For this reason, you had better not go off half cocked in any comment you make if it can affect the peace and harmony of the boat, because what you say will eventually get to the skipper if you are out of line.

Under some circumstances, the crew can tell the skipper gently but firmly something which he ought to know. A new skipper on one of our veteran subs in the Pacific muffed his first attack because he stuck the attack periscope up too far out of water, and his prospective victim spotted it and got away. For the next day or so, he overheard snatches of conversations mentioning a nickname which he didn't recognize as belonging to anyone in the boat. Finally, he asked one of the Chiefs, "Who is this guy I hear the boys calling Old Totem Pole?" The Chief had to tell him, and he never stuck his periscope up too far again.

Bathing facilities are primitive on a U-boat. There is no such thing as a bath tub, although you can take a salt water shower in the cooling water for the diesel engines, after it has done its cooling and is maybe too damn hot to interest you. A sub must make her own fresh water by distilling sea water, which uses up her precious fuel supply or battery. Fresh water is carefully rationed and each man in the crew gets half a bucketful per day. After a while, you learn to brush your teeth, shave, scrub your clothes, and take a sort of a bath every now and then, in half a bucket of water. You don't have to be too particular about bathing, because when everybody smells a little bit gamey, nobody gets too much of a fish eye unless he is really ripe. Our submariners say, "If you think you smell someone standing behind you but find nobody there, then you better take a bath."

Space is at such a premium on a U-boat that they can't provide a bunk for each man. As soon as one man gets out of a bunk, another one crawls in. This is known as the "hot bunk" system. At the start of a cruise with all torpedoes on board, the upper bunks have torpedoes stowed in them. Some bunks are shared by three men, being occupied around the clock. Officers double up in a stateroom with upper and lower bunks.

In accordance with the long standing custom of the sea, the Captain lives in solitary grandeur in a private cabin. He has a desk, wash bowl, locker and bunk all jammed into a space six feet square. But at least he has it all to himself, and is therefore the only man on board who can have some privacy when he wants it. Of course, he is always alone with his indivisible responsibility, and probably often wishes he could share that with somebody.

The galley on the U-505 was little bigger than a telephone booth. It had a three-burner stove on which all the cooking was done for sixty men. The food was good— the very best that Germany could produce was given to the U-boats.

What to do with spare time is quite a problem on a submarine. You can't just sit around thinking during off-duty hours, and there is certainly no use in writing letters home. Whenever possible, a skipper will run close enough to the surface to stick up a whip antenna and get the radio news broadcasts. It helps relieve the hemmed-in feeling of isolation to hear what is happening elsewhere on this planet. Most U-boats carried a record player which they could hook into the loud-speaker circuits. By the end of one cruise the discs would be worn out and the melodies etched into the brains of the crew for the rest of their lives. Books and magazines were read over and over until they became dog-eared. Decks of cards continued in use long after they were worn out, and checkers and chess were popular pastimes.

Any military man from a spit and polish outfit would be

shocked by a brief glimpse inside a submarine after it settles down on a war patrol. When he recovered enough to talk, he would certainly announce that this was a rag-time, undisciplined outfit. He would be wrong on the dis-cipline part—no U-boat lives long unless its crew is thoroughly trained to instant and precise obedience.

But life is a bit on the informal side in submarines, military protocol is sketchy, and, when on patrol, U-boat sailors looked more like pirates than members of the Third Reich's Kriegsmarine. All who could, grew beards. Their mops of uncut hair could stuff a couple of mattresses. You could make a pretty fair guess as to how long a U-boat had been away from base when you fished its survivors out of the water, from the length of the crew's hair.

The "uniform of the day" for a sub in the tropics was sneakers and a pair of drawers. When sixty men live as close together as a U-boat crew does, you don't need any insignia of rank to tell the others who you are. And when all you wear is a pair of skivvy pants, it cuts down the laundry problem. So conventional uniforms went into the lockers when they left Lorient and didn't come out again until they came alongside the dock to be received by the Admiral on return. On U.S. submarines, even the officers went around in skivvies.

After ten days of the Yesterday, Today, and Tomorrow routine, Loewe finally spotted another steamer early one morning. It was unescorted but zigzagging radically. Loewe stalked it for seven hours, maneuvering on the sur-face just beyond the steamer's horizon to get into a posi-tion ahead for a good shot. At mid-afternoon he sub-merged, closed in for the kill and fired a double shot. Both shots missed because the ship took an unexpected zig di-rectly away from him just as he fired. The water was glassy and the steamer may have spotted his periscope just in time. At any rate, he had to back off beyond the horizon, surface and maneuver for firing position again. Had this happened at night he could have regained posi-tion quickly on the surface. Several hours later, when he had worked around ahead of the steamer again, an air-plane appeared forcing him to submerge prematurely and the steamer got away.

This futile day's work highlights the fact that U-boat

operations depended completely on stealth. Whenever a prospective victim saw the U-boat more than a minute or so before a torpedo hit, she simply had to turn away to frustrate the attack. The sub would then have a long haul getting into position for another attack. (Note: The acoustic homing torpedo later changed this.) The escape of the steamer after the aircraft arrived on the scene also points up the fact that boats like the U-505 were essentially surface vessels. Whenever they had to stay submerged any length of time their victims got away.

For the next twelve days the only events to break the monotony were several crash dives in the daytime to escape planes which the U-boat's alert lookout sighted before the planes saw them. Theoretically, a plane can see a submarine much farther away than the sub's lookouts can see the plane and in peacetime maneuvers they usually do. But it often happens the other way in war time because a sub's lookouts have a much greater incentive for alertness than the plane's lookouts. When the plane sees the U-boat first and sinks it, everybody in the plane gets a medal—but everybody in the U-boat usually gets killed.

Loewe's lookouts also sighted a corvette on the horizon, but since she was all alone and proceeding at high speed, Loewe maneuvered to avoid her. His major mission was to sink merchant ships and he could not afford to waste fuel getting in position to pick a fight with a small but deadly warship.

March 28 began like any other routine Today, but turned out to be an unusual one. Shortly after midnight on that day the British made a daring naval raid on Saint Nazaire aimed at destroying the only dry dock in France that could take the great battleship "Tirpitz." They broke into the inner harbor with the ex-U.S. destroyer "Campbelltown" and rammed her into the dock gate where she remained with her bow wedged fast until the next afternoon, Then, while many German engineering experts were aboard trying to figure out how to get her out of there, pre-set time fuses solved the problem for them by blowing her to smithereens and scattering pieces of highly trained experts all over the outskirts of Saint Nazaire—putting the dock out of commission for the rest of the war.

This was very embarrassing to the Germans, and especially to Doenitz and his staff. Hitler had promoted Doenitz to four star rank only a few days before and Doenitz had sent a nice message to all his U-boat commanders saying that this was in recognition of their efforts. The daring British attack caught him with his new four star pants down.

It has long been a superstition in the U.S. military forces that the General Staff system, employed by all the German armed forces, including the Navy, renders it impossible for a Commander to make small mistakes. If subordinates stick to the system and clear everything through channels, the only bloopers they can ever make will be colossal ones such as those which lost World Wars I and II. But the U-505's war diary for March 28 reveals that even the famed General Staff system can slip a cog when somebody pushes the panic button.

Right after the "Campbelltown" barged into the dock gate, a jittery staff officer in Doenitz' headquarters jumped to the conclusion that the British were making a major landing and released an urgent radio saying, "All U-boats east of twenty-nine degrees West proceed toward Lorient at high speed."

On the U-505, 3,000 miles away off Cape Palmas in Africa, they woke Loewe up at 3:00 A.M. and handed him this dispatch. His longitude was twenty degrees West, so this was a peremptory order from Doenitz, telling him to head for Lorient. It was obviously meant only for boats in the Bay of Biscay, but this was Loewe's first command and he didn't feel justified in reading between the lines. He felt it necessary to send a radio to U-boat headquarters referring to the panic message and saying, in effect, "Who me?"

By the time this query got to headquarters, order had been restored and he got a prompt reply telling him to remain on station. Kapitän Leutnant Merten in the nearby U-68, being a veteran skipper, had merely dismissed the panic message with a contemptuous comment on chairborne strategists ashore and gone on about his business.

When things quieted down in Saint Nazaire, Doenitz, whose communiqués were usually pretty factual, sent out a message to his U-boats, recorded in U-505's war diary, saying, "British attack driven off."

This is quite comparable to the communiqués of all governments after an air raid had blasted one of their cities off the map, and when the enemy bombers were finally going home, "The enemy aircraft were driven away!"

I relate this incident because some U.S. military officers have been trying for years to persuade Congress that if we will adopt the General Staff system in this country, we will all live happily ever after.

Later on that day Loewe got sucked into a succession of incidents that nearly lost him a few tail feathers. Twice after sunset on the 28th, he had to crash dive to avoid aircraft. Just before midnight he sighted another aircraft and a corvette. Sniffing around the area to find out why there was so much activity he finally spotted a large merchant ship headed for Freetown.

Maneuvering on the surface in the moonlight he was just getting into position to shoot when the steamer suddenly headed right at him as if to ram. He had to crash dive and let her pass over him, thus putting him astern of her where it was useless to fire torpedoes. Apparently this was a chance maneuver by the steamer and she hadn't actually seen him. He surfaced and trailed her for four hours waiting for the moon to set. But again an aircraft drove him down and must have seen him and called the corvette back from its position ahead of the ship. Soon Loewe's sound man reported, "High speed screws approaching," and a little later, "Sonar pulses, growing louder."

This was it. Now he was the quarry instead of the hunter and would soon find out what his crew were made of. His only defense was evasion. He couldn't use his torpedoes without exposing himself to almost certain destruction.

Loewe took her down to six hundred feet, slowed to creeping speed, and an expectant hush came over the boat. At a time like this the men in that steel cigar one hundred fathoms below the surface are on the threshold of eternity with their lives in the hands of one man, the skipper. There must be many thoughts racing through their minds, but there is only one in the skipper's mind—escape.

All hands in the sub can hear the increasing noise of the

enemy's propellers as he approaches the firing point and the decreasing beat as he passes it. There follows an interval of perhaps half a minute while the depth charges are sinking, when everyone braces himself, and almost everyone, no matter what his background, prays and promises God he will do better from now on IF . . .

Then suddenly, massive sledge hammer blows slug the hull. That is the Old Man with the scythe on his shoulder knocking on their hideaway and demanding admittance. He pounds like a lusty young giant. The steel hull transmits each shock to the very marrow of every man's bones. But unless the explosions are very close indeed, all they do is smash the lights, jar large flakes of paint off the bulkheads and loosen the fillings in your teeth. If the skipper is a tough man, he knows within a few seconds whether his boat is really hurt or not. If it isn't, most sailors consider themselves released from the promises they recently made to their God—under duress.

The skipper of a cornered sub faces a grim dilemma in deciding how he will try to escape. If he stays near the surface, his sub is easier for the sonar operators to find and easier to hit with depth charges. But he is under less water pressure than if he goes deep and if his pressure hull is cracked, he may have time to blow all tanks, surface and give his crew a chance to escape before she sinks.

If he goes deep he will be much harder to find and more difficult to hit. But he loads his hull with tremendous water pressure. A mere tap from a depth charge too far away to hurt him at a depth of ten fathoms may crack his pressure hull at 100 fathoms. Then, even if he pulls the plug and blows all tanks, the water may gush into the pressure hull faster than the air can expel it from the ballast tanks. In that case they all go down, down, down until the sea pressure crushes them flat, and the end is like a beer can full of flies that gets run over by a truck.

When the increasing screw noises and sonar pings told Loewe that the corvette was almost at the firing point, he ordered full speed on both motors and put his rudder hard over, hoping to run out from under the depth charges while they were sinking to their set depth. Half a minute later hell broke loose all around them. The ocean trembled, great blows smashed against the hull, and the men were thrown against the sides of their steel cigar like dice rattling around in a box. For a few seconds discipline and panic scuffled with each other inside every man but soon panic was overpowered and shoved back into the depth of his subconscious. A few seconds after the battering subsided the reports were coming into the control room, "No serious damage forward." "Engine room's OK. . . ."

Loewe kept on at full speed for ten minutes and then reduced to creeping speed again. For about fifteen minutes after depth charges rip the ocean apart, reverberations, eddies and gas bubbles, disturb the water so that a corvette's listening gear is useless. Her sonar man straining his ears for telltale noises cannot pick up the sound of a U-boat's propellers over the rumbling and re-echoing that goes on in the depths. During his ten-minute speed run Loewe had moved about a mile from the scene of the attack and was still down at six hundred feet. As the ocean began to quiet down the sub's sound man was straining his ears too, and soon he reported, "Propeller noises medium distance." A minute later he said, "Propeller noises decreasing," and all hands took a deep breath and grinned at each other. At last they were indeed members of the inner circle of combat seasoned U-boat veterans.

That night Loewe wrote in his log, "Baptism of fire. Crew behaved excellently." But he didn't seek any more trouble with that particular steamer and her escorts. He remained submerged for two hours after the screw noises died away, then surfaced and moved off to the south.

Next day Loewe made a nice little gesture to his crew by dipping down across the equator for half an hour. No sailor is considered a real shellback until he has crossed the line and they all like to brag of having done so. In his war diary, Loewe records, "Appropriate ceremonies were observed modified to meet existing conditions." Even in the midst of an all-out war, seafaring tradition required that proper deference be paid to Neptune who is supposed to board every ship that crosses the equator in search of unfortunate landlubbers who have not previously made their number with him.

After another uneventful week, Loewe hit the jackpot again two days in a row. On the first day, he entered in

105

his war diary: "4-3 2132 Stmr West Irmo (Amerikaner) 5775 BRT." This ship was escorted by two corvettes and Loewe had to stalk her for twenty-nine hours before he got her. He missed her once with two torpedoes and neither she nor the escorts even knew it. But when he hit her, he had to slink away and elude the escorts so he actually didn't see her sink. He claimed her only as a "probable" because he heard the torpedoes hit and ten minutes later heard the unmistakable noises produced when a sinking ship is being crushed by the pressure in the depths of the sea.

Next day he got a Hollander, the "SS Alphacca, 5759 BRT." This one was a sitting duck, unescorted. He plunked her with one torpedo early in the evening in a surface attack, and then stuck around for a while to gossip with her crew in the life boats. He notes in his war diary, "Boats well equipped and provisioned. Crew spoke German. Upon parting we wish each other 'good sailing.' . . . Irony of war, we fight against men who speak our own language."

Twelve days later the U-505 started back for Lorient and had a comparatively uneventful passage. One day she had a brush with an aircraft that dropped twelve bombs around her in the course of a couple of hours but they did no harm, although the first one must have been close to her just as she was submerging. They later found a fragment of its case on the conning tower.

Four hundred miles out of Lorient they were again attacked by aircraft, but crash dived in time to get nothing but a shaking up from the bombs. Two hours later Loewe received a radio from Doenitz telling him an inbound sub had just been attacked in his exact position. Evidently the Germans were reading the coded reports from RAF aircraft over Biscay at this time. Loewe comments on this dispatch, "Fast intelligence work."

On May 7, the U-505 tied up in Lorient. On her maiden cruise she had sunk 26,000 tons of Allied shipping, a pretty fair record even in the banner year of 1942. Actually, it was close to the general average of all U-boats at sea during the ninety-two days that she was out. Some did better but, for a new sub on her first cruise, to equal the average was a very creditable performance.

She fired fourteen torpedoes of which eight hit. She sighted seven possible victims and got four. She crash dived to avoid aircraft twenty-four times and was only bombed twice. She had felt depth charges exploding close enough aboard to expose any weak sisters in her crew and none had been shaken out.

One very significant statistic of this cruise, showing how well the war at sea was going for Germany at this time, is the summary of miles steamed, "12,937 surfaced, and 316 submerged." This means that the U-505 travelled forty times as far as a surface vessel as she did submerged. Since subs were primarily surface craft, it indicated that at this stage of the war, they were able to operate in accordance with their nature and limitations, and explains why Germany sank over seven million tons of Allied shipping in 1942. The comment of Admiral Doenitz's staff on the U-505's war diary for this cruise was:

"First mission of Captain with new boat, well and thoughtfully carried out. Despite long time in operations area, lack of traffic did not permit greater success."

Chapter

8

CARIBBEAN CRUISE

THE exultant U-505 returned to Lorient on May 7, 1942, to overhaul her engines, get a new load of torpedoes, oil, and stores, and to let her crew blow off steam. For the next month, life was fast and easy—plenty of fresh air and sunshine, no more constant tension, and thousands of new faces besides the sixty that had grown so monotonously familiar. Many of these faces were pretty, female, and willing.

As the U-505's crew met friends from other boats ashore, their first duty was to brag about the fine bag their own boat had made on its maiden voyage. Sailors' stories of their adventures grow in stature each time they are told, but even allowing for this, the friends of the

U-505 along the waterfront were duly impressed and revised their rating of the U-505 accordingly.

After you get through lying about your own exploits in a waterfront cafe, your next duty is to listen respectfully to the tales of your friends. At this stage of the war, U-boats were making a shambles along the U.S. coasts and everybody in Lorient had plenty to brag about. When your friends have listened to your stories, have told theirs, and have finally run out of steam, there will be a sombre pause before the next inevitable series of questions begins.

". . . I don't see U-252 in her pen. Isn't she due back soon?"

"Overdue. Ten days."

"Too bad. Old Hans Schmidt was a good pal of mine. . . . We went to gymnasium together in Essen . . . lived across the street from each other. . . . How about U-577?"

"She's gone. Hasn't been heard from in two months."

"Well . . . that's the end of the two hundred marks that Muth owed me. Remember him? . . . the stocky little red-headed radioman that sang all those funny songs?"

"Ja, I remember him—he beat my time with that gal in Hamburg, but I liked the guy just the same."

"U-587. . . . How about her?"

"Sunk near Iceland six weeks ago by four goddam British destroyers. . . . But she had time to come up, get off a report and scuttle. . . . They think some of the crew may have been saved by the British, if they got pulled out of that freezing water soon enough."

This sort of grave conversation goes on till every new gap in the flotilla has been accounted for. This is a morbid topic but it was an integral part of life in the Second Flotilla. Flotilla Headquarters never posted any lists of losses, but the word got around among the crews in port just as fast as if Berlin had announced each new loss on the radio news broadcasts.

Most U-boat sailors took this sort of news with impersonal detachment—feeling sorry about their friends' bad luck, but not worrying too much about what their own luck might be. At this stage of the war they were only losing about three boats per month and a good submariner always takes it for granted that he will get back safely from the next cruise. Applying this reasoning to each successive cruise can carry him through a couple of years of bitter war.

The repairs needed by the U-505 were minor. She was soon reloaded, and, on June 7, she sallied forth again, this time bound for American waters. Reports in Flotilla Headquarters had told an amazing tale of the slaughter the U-boats were making along the U.S. coast, and Loewe was eager to join the fun and run up his score.

The United States' entry into the war brought a major shift in Doenitz' strategy and tactics. There was nothing static or hidebound about the Gross-admiral. He was a shrewd man who knew his business, and when new situations came up he reacted to them quickly. He was constantly probing for weak spots where he could make an easy haul. When he found one, he shifted his area of operations and concentrated on it until the sinkings mounted so alarmingly that the Allies had to rush reinforcements there. Then he would shift to another weak spot.

When Pearl Harbor plunged the U.S. into the shooting war, we were babes in the woods, so far as anti-submarine warfare was concerned. True, we had been fighting an undeclared war for five months with Doenitz, but on a very limited scale, and far away from our own shores. In general, we were totally unprepared at home in organization, training and equipment to protect shipping close to our own coasts.

The lights of our coastal cities still blazed at night, silhouetting coastwise ships for pot shots by subs. Our ships jabbered promiscuously on radio. There were no convoys in U.S. waters, we didn't have enough planes or destroyers to do a proper escort job, and our people simply wouldn't believe that this war that had raged for two years in far-off Europe could reach to our shores. Actually, the only reason why it hadn't gotten there long before was that Hitler hoped to keep the United States out of the shooting war until he finished conquering Europe. Despite our undeclared war, he had forbidden Doenitz to go beyond the mid-Atlantic.

Pearl Harbor surprised the Germans almost as much as it did us. But Doenitz reacted rapidly. Within a month he had recalled his wolf packs from the mid-ocean gap, revised his whole strategy, and was redeploying the packs as lone wolves against the U.S. coastal shipping. In January, his battle-seasoned U-boats ripped into our Atlantic seaboard shipping like hungry wolves turned loose among a flock of sheep.

Ships were sunk within sight of our boardwalks. On some nights the flames of burning tankers were even brighter than the city lights. Our beaches, from Sandy Hook to Key West, turned black from oil scum as the slaughter mounted. After several months of this, we finally dimmed the shore lights, organized coastal convoys and went to war. Then Doenitz simply shifted further south and had happy hunting there for many more months than I care to tell about.

Just before the U-505 sailed on her second cruise, Doenitz, keeping a sharp eye on his graphs of tonnage sunk vs. U-boats lost, had detected a levelling off in the exchange rate along the U.S. coast as we began to learn our business, and had just shifted to a virgin territory where the opposition would be feeble—the previously untouched Caribbean. This was Loewe's assigned area.

The U-505 made another easy transit out of Biscay and as soon as he got out into the mid-ocean gap, Loewe bent on knots and ran surfaced as much as possible. He didn't want the happy hunting in the Caribbean to be over before he got there.

There was a marked difference between the attitude of his crew on this trip and on the one before. The eager beaver, slightly nervous air of the trip down to Freetown, was gone, replaced by the quiet confidence of tested veterans who knew that they were good. The plank owners, who had commissioned the boat, now patronized the four new men who came aboard in Lorient to replace men transferred to new boats shaking down in the Baltic.

This run across the Atlantic was a picnic excursion. The jeep carriers had not yet appeared in the Battle of the Atlantic. You never saw an enemy aircraft out there except for high flying, harmless transport planes, heading for the Azores. The U-505 ran surfaced nearly all the way and Loewe let his crew bask topside in the balmy sunshine all day long. Everybody could have a salt water bath on deck every day, and as a gesture of contempt, they even set up a mess table and served lunch on deck. They could always depend on sighting a surface vessel first, so with no airplanes to worry about, this was indeed a garden of Eden, and they had never had it so good.

Just three weeks after they sailed from Lorient and while still several hundred miles from the Caribbean, they found their next victim. One forenoon the sunbathers were brought to their feet by the port lookout's cry, "Masts on horizon bearing twenty degrees on port bow."

"All hands below except the bridge watch," barked the officer of the deck.

The crew tumbled down the escape hatches to the forward and after torpedo rooms and the deck was cleared by the time Loewe scrambled up on the bridge and trained his glasses on what the lookout saw. It was a spar no bigger than a broomstick, poking up over the horizon at the limit of visibility.

"Good work, Muller," said Loewe to the port lookout. Then, to the watch officer, "I'm going to close a few miles on him first before submerging."

Loewe headed directly for the spar and noted that it grew in height with gratifying rapidity. With his powerful glasses he saw a crow's nest emerge over the horizon, but there was no lookout in it, so he remained surfaced. Doenitz was right that the enemy would be careless in this new territory. After half an hour the top of the pilot house peeked over the horizon. Soon Loewe would be able to see the bridge and, by the same token, those on the bridge would be able to see him.

"Take her down," he ordered and dropped down the hatch into the conning tower, followed within six seconds by all four lookouts. The last one slammed and locked the hatch, and in another forty seconds they were submerged with nothing but the periscope sticking out.

The eye piece of the periscope was now ten feet lower than Loewe's eyes had been on the bridge. The steamer had dropped below the horizon and only the masts were visible again. But Loewe had her course figured out to half a degree by this time. She wasn't even zigzagging, and all he had to do was wait for her to climb over the horizon and steam smack in front of his loaded torpedo tubes. This would be shooting fish in a barrel.

That's exactly what it turned out to be!

Date	Type	Name	Tonnage
28.6.42	Am. Frachter	Robin Hood class	6900 BRT

This time Loewe fired a double shot and both hit. He remained submerged after his first fish hit giving the crew about an hour to lower boats and get clear. Then he finished her off with a third shot, surfaced after she sank, and continued on his way to his assigned area.

So, on the first day near his new area, Loewe hit the jack pot again. The U-505's lucky star was still rising. On the second day the jack pot repeated.

Date	Type	Name	Tonnage
29.6.42	Am. Frachter	Thomas McKean	7400 BRT

This time he surfaced, after crippling the ship with his first double shot, let the crew lower boats and then finished the job with his four-inch gun. After setting her afire he photographed the sinking ship and one of the life boats, and gave the boat medical supplies and directions to the nearest land 360 miles away.

As the U-505 wishes the survivors luck, and disappears over the horizon in search of new victims, let us now look at another side of the picture in this war against shipping.

Statements obtained from all survivors of ships sunk during this period are on file in Washington with the Maritime Administration of the Department of Commerce. I reproduce below a few of these statements from the "McKean," without editing. They are given verbatim because they tell the story as only seamen can tell it. A seaman goes back to the very start of the voyage in telling a tale and, although many details may seem irrelevant and unimportant, the statements wouldn't ring true without them. To a seaman, such things are very important.

THOMAS McCARTHY,
Chief Engineer

Made the following statement:

I live at No. 20 Hendricks, New Brighton, Staten Island, New York. I have been going to sea for thirty years. I hold a chief engineer's certificate, which I have held for about fifteen years.

The "Thomas McKean" was built at the Bethlehem-Fairfield Yard, Baltimore, as a liberty ship, and I was on her when she was taken out of the yard. As a matter of fact, I was on her for about a week previous to that time, during the trial trips. She was turned over to the Calmar Line for operation and I formally joined her as Chief Engineer about May 27, 1942, at Baltimore. I was hired by the Calmar Line in New York and sent to Baltimore. The "McKean" was in command of Captain Respess when she left Baltimore. She left Baltimore on May 29th and she proceeded down to Wolf Trap for DeGaussing. At Wolf Trap, it was discovered that the vessel was too highly magnetized and the Navy Department then ordered us to Norfolk for DePermbing. After this work was finished at Norfolk, the "McKean" proceeded to the Standard Oil Dock at Norfolk for bunkers. The "McKean" then proceeded from Norfolk Light up the Chesapeake Bay, through the C.&D. Canal to Philadelphia.

At Philadelphia cargo was taken aboard, practically a full cargo with the exception of about 1000 tons. After remaining at Philadelphia for about a week the vessel then proceeded to Brooklyn to take on further cargo and from Brooklyn we went over to Edgewater, New Jersey, to finish complete loading.

On Saturday morning, June 20th, the vessel then dropped down and went to anchor off of the Statue of Liberty, and the next morning, June 21st, we left New York in convoy bound for the Delaware Breakwater. We arrived at the Delaware Breakwater about half-past eight or nine o'clock in the evening of June 21st, where we

113

anchored for the night. At 4:20 the next morning, June 22nd, we left in convoy bound for Lynnhaven Roads, where we arrived that evening about 11:12 P.M. and where we remained until the following morning.

The following morning at 4 o'clock, June 23rd, we left Lynnhaven Roads and proceeded to sea on our destination, which was Trinidad, where we were to take on bunkers. We proceeded alone and not in convoy. Everything went well until the morning of June 29 when, at 7:20, a violent explosion occurred between No. 5 hatch and the steering engine room, starboard side. At that time, I had just gotten into the bathroom and was preparing to take a shave. My room is forward, on the port side on the boat deck. The first assistant, Mr. William McClintock, was on watch in the engine room. Oiler Shepard and Watertender Hendeley were also on watch, both being in the engine room.

On this ship there was no bulkhead between the engine room and the fireroom. It is all one compartment. There was no fireman on watch as such, but the water tender is a combination water tender and fireman. In other words, just those three men were in the engine room. The engine room is amidships and the explosion did not affect the engine room—that is, it did not occur in the engine room.

When that torpedo hit I knew darned well what it was because I had just got torpedoed about six weeks previous, and I had my face all lathered up, and I was just getting the old razor out and "Wham!" I put on my sneakers and I immediately went down in the engine room, and when I got there the first assistant, the oiler and the water tender had evacuated. After she hit they took and got out of there.

In other words, when I was going down they were coming out, so I took and turned around myself, and to take and make sure that I knew they were all out I made a round of the quarters to check up to see all the men were out of there, because the fire alarm, or the emergency alarm was ringing continuously. Somebody had thrown that in from the wheelhouse and everybody was going to their boat stations, or the various stations at which they belonged, so I went back up and the engine was still running at this time. I did not stop her because I went up to the skipper and he said, "How hard are we hit?" and I said, "It looks to me like the whole stern is gone," and he said, "Take and climb over and see what you can see." And we had these cargo nettings alongside of each lifeboat so you could crawl down instead of going down the ladder, and fifteen or twenty men could crawl down into the boats at once, so I crawled down abeam of starboard boat No. 1 and I saw the ship was completely shot.

The skipper at that time was on the boat deck and hollered out, "What does it look like?" and I said, "It looks like she is finished." And he said, "Where are your men?" And I said, "Nobody is in quarters and they are evidently by the boats." So I said, "All right, I will shut off the engine," because the engine was still going like the devil, but she was not making any progress. So I went down and shut the engine off and came back up. The water tender, Short, who was on the 8 to 12 watch, shut down the service pump, that is the pump that supplies the fuel from the tanks to the burners in the boilers.

From the place where the torpedo hit, the torpedo evidently was very low. I would say offhand the torpedo hit her about 15 feet below the surface from the way she acted. She hit very low and she just took and broke the stern right off. She opened her right up in a perfect V, because I could see it very plainly when I was in the netting talking to the skipper, because I was standing in there and looking along the shell of the ship, and I could see the whole stern had dropped down. It was perfectly visible from the deck, but what we wanted to look at was how bad it was and saw she was finished.

I went back up and I took and secured the engine there and shut off the throttle valve, and that is accessible from the main deck in a small compartment there. After I shut her off I went down in the engine room to see what damage was down there. Then I went back up to the skipper and he said, "How is it lined up now, Chief?" I said, "Well, we are a dead pigeon." And so he took and said, "I will heave the papers over and you grab a case of cigarettes," and he passed them to me to throw in the lifeboat.

As soon as the torpedo struck Sparks got a message off right away, a wireless message, because I asked the captain about and he said, "Yes, the message has gone out that we got hit," and Sparks got a verification on it from the various Naval Bases who picked it up and who were listening in. So after we got the cigarettes and threw them in the boat, the Skipper said, "Is everybody accounted for?" I said, "Yes, and he said, "Pull away and we can check up on those other boats." I didn't get a chance to get anything. I went in Boat No. 1, as all of the other boats had pulled away. After we got off of the ship about fifty feet or a couple of boatlengths away Sparks came running out on deck, but there was no use to turn around because she was starting to sink back aft all of the time, and he crawled back aft, and by the time the painter on our boat got afoul of the rudder and we told Sparks to jump, and the skipper cut the painter loose and Sparks jumped then, but he didn't want to jump, and we pulled him in the boat and we squared the boat away, and hauled back aft in case anybody was back aft, and if they were they should have been in the water, but there was nobody there.

After we got about six or eight boatlengths off of the starboard quarter we came right around and the stern of the boat was completely off, and we pulled around the starboard quarter and we went by where she was blown off and we took and laid there. Just as we started to slack off the submarine broke surface right abeam of us, but she come up about a mile off. It was the first time I had seen her. She started shelling the ship and the first four shells were short, because she was too far off and the range was too great. She had a four-inch gun and a three-inch gun, and they kept moving in and firing all the time until they got right up on her, and they started to work.

They started and they took and raked No. 1 hatch. That was where we had the dynamite and that 50 calibre anti-aircraft ammunition, and then after they shelled that for a while they moved to No. 3—they didn't touch No. 2, but they moved to No. 3. That is where we had the highly inflammable gasoline and various accessories for planes and tanks, and after they got going good in there and got a fire started in there, they moved back to No. 4 hatch. They stayed in that position but they shifted the guns. Then they blew up the deep tank, the fuel oil tank; they knew where everything was. I think only one shell hit the engine room.

It took about an hour, between an hour and a quarter and an hour for the vessel to sink. I saw her go down completely. We were about a quarter of a mile off and No. 3 boat was alongside of the submarine. She had an injured man in her, one of the gunners had an injured hand, and they gave him a package of medicine. After she shelled the ship, after she shelled her for about a half hour, then she went by the stern and cruised around and came back up again, and then she left that 3-inch gun, the aft gun, have a little target practice. The 3-inch gun fired about twelve or fifteen rounds, and the ship was settling all the time, and then the submarine went back and stayed in its original position until the ship sank. After they had shelled her there and had her afire, the ship was lying down by the stern. Then the submarine came from this position amidships where she had been shelling her and moved around the stern right by our lifeboat, and then she cruised over here (indicating), and came back by here again, and then they let the after gun, the 3-inch gun, have a little fun with her, and fired 12 or 15 rounds at her, and then the submarine went over and stayed in its original position until the vessel sank, and after the vessel sank it went back to where the second mate's No. 3 boat was.

Of course, the boat was plainly marked "Thomas Mc-Kean, Baltimore," but the submarine wanted to know where it was from, and I believe they told him. The submarine gave No. 3 boat some kind of sleeping potion for the man that was hurt and some first aid equipment. We saw him for over two hours, because he talked with the second mate in No. 3 boat and then he proceeded southeast and he was still afloat, still on top of the water, when he went over the horizon.

There were three naval men on watch in the pill box on the starboard quarter and after the explosion we did not see any of these three men. There was another man, one of the crew, whose name was Russell Funk, a wiper, who was sleeping on No. 5 hatch. He was injured very severely, and he died and we buried him at sea. A sailor from No. 3 boat picked him up from off the deck and put him in the lifeboat. I can not tell you the name of that sailor, but he was a Canadian. He is a naturalized American citizen now. I can not say definitely whether this man Funk was dead when he was put in the lifeboat. There was also a gunner stationed in the pill box on the port side aft, and he was blown completely overboard, but he swam back to the ship to help out. He later got into No. 2 boat, the first mate's boat. He was cut around the head very badly and also on his left leg, and he had lacerations and abrasions all over his body. He was taken care of in the boat and he was left in Norfolk at the Naval Base. There were a few others who received small cuts and abrasions, and there was one other gunner who had his left hand severely injured, and it was that man to whom the man on the submarine gave some aid. That man was in No. 4 boat. I understand all of the other men have been accounted for.

The ship was equipped with guns forward, amidships on both sides, and on the stern. The guns were all manned by a Navy crew. There were fourteen gunners and a Lieutenant junior grade, on board. I can not give you any definite information as to how these guns were manned at the time of the submarine attack. After the sub had left and the ship at that time had completely gone out of sight, she was sunk, we took and pulled over near the second mate's boat to check up on how many men he had on, and how many were injured. So he said, "I think I got a dead man here, Captain," and everybody was a little bit upset about it, so the skipper said to me, "Chief, you had better look at him."

So I asked them what tests they had made to find out whether he was dead, and after they had told me what they had done I said, "All right, did you burn his feet with a cigarette butt?" They said, "No," I said, "All right, let's try that." We tried that. I put my finger on his pulse to try to get any reaction, but got none, and I watched his eyes, and then we burned his finger tips, and there was absolutely no sign of anything in his eyes or anywhere else, and you could see that rigor mortis had already started to set in. So we took the hooks out of the lifeboat that he was in and took the hook out of our lifeboat, which was No. 1, and we took the after hook out of No. 3 boat and made a couple of lanyards out of No. 7 thread line that we had in the boat and secured the hooks to his ankles and dropped him overboard.

We took an account of the men again, and the Captain said, "All right, now, we are here on the chart." All of the boats were equipped with charts, each boat had a sextant and necessary equipment with regards to water and food and medical equipment, each of them had everything, and the captain said, "All right," and he told the three mates, "Here we are, we are about 66 east and 20 north." So he said, "All right, we will have to make it southerly as much as we can to land in the Islands," because it was a westerly set there, which was swinging us to the westward, and there was an easterly wind there all the time—I think they call it Trades.

We started, we got under way, we got the sails rigged in each of the boats and we started off. No. 3 boat was equipped with a motor with a tank of gas and all ready to go. It was not equipped with a regular trysail, it just had a squaresail, and then it started to drag behind after the three of us got started—that was No. 1, 2, and 4— No. 3 had the motor. So after they started dropping back the captain said, "We better get back and see what is the matter with them." So we dropped back and asked them what seemed to be the trouble, and they said they could not get the motor started. The motor had been tested out the day previously and found to be in working order.

So I transferred from the skipper's boat, No. 1, to No. 3 boat and wanted to know what the trouble was. Well, they wanted to know where the battery was, and different things. So I turned on the ignition and got gas in the carburetor and spun the engine and it went off. Then the captain gave the second mate, who was in command of No. 3 boat, Mr. Foster, instructions each nightfall, no matter which boat fell behind, he was to use his engine and consolidate all of the boats at sunset.

The first evening at sunset, around 7:30, the third mate's boat, which was No. 4, and the second mate's boat, which was No. 3, had dropped behind. The second mate took the third mate's boat in tow and all of the boats were consolidated that first evening around ten o'clock. The Captain wanted to know how they were making out in regard to smokes, and some of the boats were short of cigarettes, and we had the case the Captain gave me to throw in the boat, so we divided up the cigarettes. The same orders were in effect to continue to make as much south as possible on account of the westerly set, and then any boat that was lagging, the motorboat was to pick up.

Forty-eight hours after the sinking of the vessel all the boats were in sight. No. 3 boat, No. 4 boat, were plainly visible by both Nos. 1 and 2, right after sunrise, which is approximately around 4:30. At noontime boat No. 1, the second day out, and Boat No. 2, were running within a mile or so of each other. Boats No. 3 and 4 were over the horizon, you could not see them. Well, we held a consultation at that time to go back for those two boats—that is, the Captain did—to see whether they were in difficulty or not, but it was decided to keep sailing until nightfall, that is, Nos. 1 and 2 boats did, they decided to keep sailing until nightfall, that is, before sunset to see whether the motorboat would come along with the other boat in tow.

That night a heavy squall came up, a heavy northeast wind and rain and the skipper thought to go back to look for the other boats would be foolhardy and would jeopardize the men we had in our boats. We had 29 men in those two boats. Well, we lost the mate's boat that night, some time around midnight. The mate's boat was No. 2. And the following morning, with a heavy northeast sea running, we were out of contact with the mate's boat. We are still hauling to the south as much as possible and steering a course of south by west, making it southerly as much as possible on account of the westerly set. So approximately 24 hours afterwards, around eight or nine o'clock in the morning, the lookout on our boat, No. 1, spotted a sail aft. So when we came up on the crest of a wave everybody looked and we could make out the mate's boat by the way he had her rigged. That was No. 2 boat.

All that day he was within sight of us. That night we lost him again, the following morning at approximately 9 o'clock, 9 or 10 o'clock, a United States plane sighted us and took and dropped down a message for us to hold our course we were steering, south by west, and they would contact the shore and send out aid. We sailed that day until five o'clock approximately. A big bomber came out, it was an amphibian, and looked us over. In about a half hour afterward a cutter appeared over the horizon and it came alongside and picked us up some time between five and six in the evening.

That was on Friday afternoon or Friday evening. I do not know the day of the month. We were four days out that morning. It was July 3rd when we were picked up. It was a mine sweeper, No. 58, which picked us up and landed us at St. Thomas around three o'clock in the morning of July 3rd.

When we got aboard the cutter, everybody was checked off in regard to their name and next of kin and given whatever comforts that they could. We were brought from the cutter and they got some soup and a light meal for us at the gas station, or rather the submarine barracks—it was a submarine base where we landed at—and were given a place to sleep. Night before last at Norfolk, the agent of the Calmar Line there, Mr. Smith, told me that one boat had landed at San Kitts, which was evidently the second mate's boat, because I could check it by the number of men in it, and the other boat landed in San Domingo. That was the third mate's boat. That would be No. 4 boat.

When we landed on the cutter, the crew of No. 2 boat, in charge of the mate, were already on board the cutter. They had been picked up two or three hours previous. We were transferred from the submarine base at St. Thomas to San Juan by the Coast Guard Cutter "Unalga," and landed on the dock there and put aboard the Navy Transport which brought us to NOB, Norfolk. That is the Norfolk Operating Base. They fed us there in the afternoon. That evening around nine o'clock we were transferred by the agent from the Operating Base to a hotel down in Norfolk. We got the hotel ourselves. He gave us money for transportation up to here. I received no injuries.

I lost everything I had on board. I had a brand new outfit and I didn't get anything off of the ship except what I had on my back. I had no shoes on even. I as well as every one in my department, made out a list of the lost personal effects, and these lists were turned over to the captain.

The total number of men we had on board were 59, four of them were passengers, technicians. I think they were airplane technicians. I do not know their names, but they were being sent to the Near East. There were fifteen gunners, including Lieutnant Slack. All of the rest of the men on board were members of the crew.

The "McKean" was an oil-burner, her horsepower being 2500, with two B & W boilers, rated at 4200 horsepower.

All appliances were in excellent shape for a new ship. That applies to the time of the torpedo attack, and I think this ship was a tribute to the people who built her. The ship between perpendiculars was 450 feet long, with a beam of about 60 feet. Her tonnage was 8010—that is, her carrying capacity was 8010 tons. She was a Liberty type of vessel. We did not push this ship at any time, and at the time of the submarine attack I should say we were running about 10½ knots.

I did not save any of the engine room log books as I had not time. I was concerned with getting the men off more than with saving log books, and I did not save any of them, although I understand that the Captain saved his.

End of Chief Engineer's Statement

The above is a typical sailor telling his story exactly the way a sailor tells it. The story begins when he reports aboard the ship and he accounts for every port she visited and every time she anchored or got underway again. No fiction writer could duplicate his description of the torpedoing. Very few would think of having a Chief Engineer go back down below for a last look around while the ship is sinking and being abandoned, just to see what damage had been done to his bailiwick. And very few real engineers would be able to resist the urge to do exactly that. A good novelist could easily make a chapter out of the Chief's terse statement about the radioman who went back—"but he didn't want to jump."

His description of the manner in which the sub shelled the ship, and his conclusion that the Germans knew exactly what was in each hold in typical of what many sailors thought at this time. However, Loewe's encounter with the "McKean" was by pure chance and he certainly knew nothing about how she was loaded.

I don't know why it's important to tell how they rigged the dead man for burial, using "No. 7 thread line," but no seaman would omit this detail from his tale.

I'm sure that when the Chief was starting that engine for No. 3 boat, he must have made comments which would be worth handing on to posterity, about the intelligence of the fifteen swabs who couldn't even find the battery. You can almost see him spit when he says, "So I turned on the ignition and got gas in the carburetor and spun the engine and it went off." I'm surprised he doesn't add, "What the hell else could it do, and why couldn't one of those fifteen helpless lugs have done the same thing?" Naturally, he takes occasion to say that this piece of equipment in the engineer's department had been, "tested the day before and found to be in working order."

He winds his statement up as any Chief Engineer would by explaining why he couldn't save his papers, inferring somewhat testily that he was busy with more important matters while the Captain was loading archives into the boat.

ROLAND L. FOSTER, JR.,
Second Officer

Made the following statement:
I live at 831 Fairfax Avenue, Norfolk, Virginia, I have been going to sea since 1936. I hold a second officer's license which I have held since February, 1942. The "Thomas McKean" was the first Calmar Line boat I

123

ever worked on. I joined her as second officer at Baltimore on May 26, 1942. I went on her in the shipyard and was on her during the trial trip. I was on her when she went down to Wolf Trap for DeGaussing and from there to Norfolk for DePerming. From Norfolk we proceeded up the Chesapeake Bay, through the C. & D. Canal to Philadelphia where we started to load cargo. From Philadelphia we went to New York where we finished loading cargo.

On the morning of June 21 we left New York in convoy. That night we anchored in the Delaware Breakwater, and left early the morning of the 22nd still in convoy for Norfolk, where we arrived 10 P.M., June 22nd, and we anchored. The convoy was dispersed at Norfolk, and on the early morning of June 23rd we left Norfolk bound for Trinidad. Everything went well until the morning of June 29th when we were attacked by a submarine. I think our position at the time of the attack was approximately 22.10 North Latitude and 60 West Longitude. My watch was from 12 to 4. By my watch the attack took place at 7:29. I was asleep in my room and the explosion woke me up. I jumped up right away and looked at my watch and it showed 7:29. Well, the first thing I did was my license was laying on the corner of the desk and I grabbed it and my life preserver and rushed out on deck to my lifeboat station, No. 2. That is on the starboard side aft, and I released the strap around it that holds it on to the side of the ship. By that time the A.B. and the boatswain were up to take the falls, and I went on the bridge to get my sextant and chart, and then I came back and they had the boat waterborne when I got back. When I went on the bridge I told them to lower away, and I went to get my sextant and chart and when I came back I got in the lifeboat and we took a wounded man in the boat at that time and we shoved off from the side of the vessel at 7:36.

Everything was orderly and there was no confusion and everybody went to his boat station. Each officer and the captain got away in his respective boat and it was pretty generally true that there was no confusion, although I did have one man more in my boat than was supposed to be in that boat, but I transferred 2 men

124

later to No. 1 boat, the mate's boat. I started out with fifteen, including the engine wiper. The wiper was buried at sea and two men were transferred to the mate's boat, which left No. 3 boat with twelve men in it, four of whom were passengers.

The man who was buried at sea was a wiper by the name of Russell Funk. One of the passengers told me that he was sleeping back aft where the explosion occurred and that the wiper was sleeping back aft also, and that the wiper had been injured by the explosion. He was brought up to my boat by some of the other Navy crew that was back there and they just dropped him on the deck and went on to their boat. He was dropped on the deck by my boat and they went to their boat. The wiper was still alive when he was placed in my boat, and I gave him medical attention and was still working on him when he actually died. He died within about an hour after the explosion, or an hour and a half, and not very long after he was placed in my boat. He died right after the submarine went from alongside my boat, which I will describe hereafter.

This wiper was hurt internally but I did not know it when I was working on him. He had wounds to the face and neck and legs that I was treating. I forget what I washed them with, but it was an antiseptic, and I put on clean bandages which was all I could do. He never really talked any, but he did some mumbling. He was in considerable pain. There was some fellow hurt in the third mate's boat, a gunner. I saw him in Miami the night before last, and his hand was healing all right. I do not know anything about the other gunner who I have heard was cut across the forehead. I never even heard about that casualty until I heard one of the boys speak of it here a little while ago. . . .

We had conducted boat drills on this vessel and there was no reason why everything should not have gone along in an orderly fashion, as it did go.

When I first saw the submarine it was 7:45. That was the first time I saw him. Whether he had been on the surface before that or not I could not say. The second engineer said he saw him before we left the deck of the vessel, but I did not see him. When he surfaced we were between him and the ship. We were in his line of gunfire. He waited for us to row our lifeboat out of the way before he started firing, and the first shell hit very close to our lifeboat and fell in the water, and that was the only shell that missed in the entire firing. The fellows in our lifeboat counted thirty-nine other shells, which were fired in three periods.

After the second period of firing he came alongside my lifeboat and he came up and the commander of the submarine hollered through the megaphone, "Please come alongside," in English. That is all the commander said, and then his interpreter, I can not say what he was, he only had on shorts and had a big red bushy beard and no other indentification, no indentification as an officer at all. I do not know what he was. All I know is he was the interpreter and he asked us whether we were an American ship and I said, "Yes." He wanted to know what kind of an American ship and I said, "An American merchantman." And he said, "Gut," in German, and he wanted to know if there was anything he could do for us. He gave us first aid bandages for the wounded man. He wanted to know where we were bound, and before I had a chance to say anything, some member of the lifeboat crew, or a passenger, one or the other, said, "Trinidad," and that is all that was said about that.

Then he said, "You are carrying munitions? Yes?" And then he looked at every one of us in the lifeboat with that wicked eye he had, as much as to say that none of you had better say "No" to that, and I would say approximately thirty of those shells were fired at the hold where the munitions were in, and that looked to me suspicious, but maybe it was not. And I asked him what was the course to the nearest land; and he understood me to say I wanted him to tow me to the nearest land. I said, "No." He said, "No, we can not do that. We haven't got the time." I said, "I didn't say that, I said the nearest course to land." He said, "Steer mit the wind." He turned around to the commander and he said, "He says he is going ashore, he says he is going ashore." He shouted it out the second time. I am sure they were Germans, mostly young. They had a very large submarine. I read in the paper this morning where some other fellow said it was 250 feet and I would say it was about 200. She was very maneuverable, and I would say it would do 22 knots. She had a Swastika and a German ensign, and she also had a lioness painted on the side of the conning tower. This lioness was standing on its hind foot, I believe its left one, and in its front paw it had a big hammer, and in its tail it had a torch. They were all the markings on there. Her paint looked very good. Some of the fellows were very sun tanned and the majority looked like they had been faring pretty good in those islands down there.

It was very nice weather that morning. The rest of the trip, it went on well because we got in all right, but we had very rough weather and we landed at the northern-most tip of Anguilla, British West Indies, on July 5, at 11:10. We were not picked up. Our provisions were all right, but the water was not good. Our keg of water was sour. It was a new ship and the water had not been changed in the keg, and I heard the Trail Master of the ship tell the mate to change the water four or five times, because the water was going to be bad if he didn't. We drank it, but I thought it would make us all sick.

On July 2nd we were spotted by a PBY Naval Patrol plane at 9:05, and he dropped us some food rations and pemmican and malted milk rations and he circled us for quite a long time and he went out of sight to the south-west and we never saw any more of him and never heard any more from any other naval vessels. The mate's boat seemed to sail faster than the skipper's or the third mate's either, and this motorboat, she just was not equipped for sails. She had no place to step a mast, but we did rig it with rope yarn, and what rope we had in the boat. I cut a place in one of the thwarts, one of the seats in the lifeboat for the mast to sit in. We only had one mainsail and we made a jib out of the distress flag.

During the first day they sailed right away from me. We tried putting the boats together and it would not work, and the Captain said that at night to tie the boats up together and we would be all together every night, and I did that once during the day, towed them all up together and at nightfall I rounded them up again, and each time they sailed away from me. No one said nothing

127

to me about coupling my boat to their boat because they knew I couldn't sail.

Well, the next morning I did not see the skipper's or the first mate's boat, but I did see the third mate's boat. I started up the motor and ran up to the third mate and he got a line ready for me to tow him on, and when I got even with him I could just see the mate and the captain sailing together. He got his line ready to tow and I told him I was not going to tow any more, I was going to sail because if I did this twice more all of the gas would be gone and if a squall would come up and blow my sails away, where would I be. I did not run the motor any more until July 4th. I did not have any navigation books. I had a sextant. I was only able to get a latitude each day at noon and on July 4th I figured I was sixty miles north of the British West Indies, and I started the motor and I ran it from then until dark that night and the next morning I sighted land and we started the motor again and ran on in. All told, I ran the motor about fifteen hours, I guess.

I landed at Anguilla, which is the northernmost island in the British West Indies. From there they sent us in a schooner to St. Kitts. There the British authorities took charge of us. We went to the Government hospital there for about three or four days—I won't say for certain— and then they got in touch with the American consul at Antigua. We were sent again by schooner to Antigua, which took about 54 hours altogether to get down there. At Antigua we were put up in a hotel there until we could get in touch with the company and they made arrangements to get us back by Pan-American. We were flown to Miami and came up from there by plane.

Nobody in my boat was injured by this experience. Some of them got sunburned, but they got over it all right.

I did not sustain any injuries.

I made out a list of my personal effects before the vessel sailed and I gave it to the captain. I saved my sextant, which I had on my list, but that is all I saved.

As to the lifeboat, I turned it over to the British authorities at Anguilla.

End of Second Officer's Statement

Notice in the above statement the things that a sailor-man grabs first when he gets jarred out of his bunk by a torpedo explosion—his license, and then a life preserver. This ship may be on the way to the bottom but to get a job on the next one he's got to have that license.

Note also that by this time the U-505 has a lion rampant painted on the conning tower.

There is one feature of this statement particularly worthy of notice and comment. Foster was second mate of the "McKean," but after his ship got sunk was skipper of No. 3 lifeboat. In speaking of what happened on the "McKean" he always says, "We left New York. . . . we were attacked. . . ." In telling the tale of the lifeboat he says, "I started out with 15 . . . I was 60 miles north . . . I landed at Anguilla." This is characteristic of seafaring men. In speaking of events on a voyage, everyone in the ship except the skipper says we did so and so. The skipper says I did so and so, or if telling what another ship did will say he instead of she (meaning the skipper of the other ship). Usually around the bar of an officers' club, with everyone in civilian clothes you can sort out the skippers just by listening for the pronouns they use.

This is not because of any egotism on the skipper's part. It's simply a custom of the sea, stemming from one of the elementary facts of life at sea. There is no other job in the world where one man has unquestioned authority and responsibility so firmly fixed on his shoulders alone. He can get plenty of advice, but, in theory at least, he must reject all the bad advice. The skipper makes the final decisions, holds the sack and sweats out many a night watch wondering whether he is right or wrong.

If he loses his ship he will have to say "I" when he testifies at the court martial, even though disaster was the fault of his subordinates. So why shouldn't he say "I" when astounding his listeners around a bottle. In Foster's case, he automatically shifts from "we" to "I" as soon as the ship goes down and he becomes a Captain, even though his command is only a lifeboat.

Foster had one important command decision to make, when the third mate's boat demanded a tow from him. The skipper had given him instructions about towing the day before, but meantime had sailed off and left him. Foster was senior to the third mate, so in naval parlance he was now the senior officer present and as such exercised his prerogative to decide he would not tow No. 3 boat.

Foster did a good job with his command. The nearest land to the scene of the sinking was Anguilla. He sailed directly to it in seven days. No. 4 boat wandered off to the west and took nine days to reach San Domingo.

Note also that Foster is a man that Diogenes would be proud of—at the end of his statement he tells his owners that although he expects to be reimbursed for most of his personal stuff, he did save his sextant!

Contrast the salty informality of the above two reports with the following official report from the U. S. Consul at Ciudad Trujillo to the State Department.

Ciudad Trujillo, D.R., July 17, 1942

No. 0026

Subject: Destruction by Enemy Action of the *S. S. Thomas McKean* of the Calmar line

The Honorable
    The Secretary of State,
        Washington, D.C.

Sir:

In amplification of my cable no. 327 of July 10, 1942, concerning the destruction by enemy action of the steamship *Thomas McKean* of the Calmar Line. I have the honor to submit certain additional information concerning the incident.

The *Thomas McKean* was a ten thousand ton freighter on her maiden voyage carrying a valuable cargo of food, general supplies, aviation gasoline, and 11 airplanes bound for Trinidad, Capetown, and further undisclosed destinations. The attack on the vessel took place at 7:25 a.m., June 29 last. At that time the vessel was approximately 500 miles off the coast of Trinidad, about 60° west and 23° north. The submarine fired a torpedo without warning which hit aft, putting the stern gun out of action and killing instantly three naval gunners; Bragg, Anthony, and Allen. The ship was abandoned within ten minutes after the torpedo attack, but in this short space of time a wireless call for help was sent. Four lifeboats were launched.

The last men to leave the vessel were naval gunners Coxswain Albert H. Rust, Roy Adams, Dorsey Lee Grave, and Jack Hannan. The latter was suffering from split fingers on his left hand and from shock. Although the ship was flooding rapidly, the gunners took time to carry an unconscious merchant seaman to safety with them. The conduct of these four men, who range in age from 17 to 19 is highly deserving of commendation not only for their calmness in action but for the example which they gave to the merchant seamen. The condition of the vessel after the first torpedo explosion made it impossible for any of the defensive armament to be brought into use.

The submarine, which was painted white, surfaced shortly after the men had abandoned ship and from a position 4,000 yards off the stern of the *Thomas McKean* proceeded to sink the vessel by gunfire. In all 57 shells were fired by the submarine and the *Thomas McKean* sank in approximately one hour and twenty minutes. Following the sinking of the *Thomas McKean* the submarine approached the lifeboats and an officer asked the men in English whether they needed medical aid, food or directions. The survivors replied in the negative. The men in the lifeboats gained the impression that the submarine commander knew the destination of the *Thomas McKean* since he asked no questions in that regard.

The lifeboat which brought the 14 survivors of the *Thomas McKean* to the Dominican Republic was in charge of Third Officer William S. Muci, apparently a very able and well-qualified officer. The men were in the lifeboat nine days before reaching the Dominican coast, and, for the reason that the compass of the lifeboat was broken, Muci was obliged to navigate by the stars. Although the lifeboat was new, when the men attempted to use the oars the oar locks broke. When they attempted to mend the oar locks with the tools that were in the lifeboat the tools broke. Had it not been for the fact that the lifeboat was equipped with a sail, their ordeal would have been much more difficult. A few hours after the sinking of the *Thomas McKean* a wiper from the ship's crew died and was buried at sea by his companions. Unfortunately, it has been impossible to fully identify this man, whose first name was Russell.

On the fourth day of the lifeboat journey, an airplane circled the boat, dropped food by means of a parachute, and indicated to the men that they should travel in a westerly direction. The survivors were convinced that they would be rescued shortly after this occurrence and drank all of the remaining supply of fresh water on board. For the next five days they had to depend on such rain water as they could catch in blankets, etc., for drinking purposes. On the ninth day land was sighted near Miches, Dominican Republic, where the men finally came ashore.

Third Officer Muci and the rest of the men were unanimous in their gratitude and praise for the efforts made, on their behalf by the Dominicans in Miches, a small community. They were given food, clothing and a place to sleep in the local jail. Since there were no criminals being detained, they had the jail to themselves.

Communications between Miches and Ciudad Trujillo are difficult and for this reason the men were obliged to remain there for two days before arrangements could be made to bring them to the capital. With the cooperation of the Dominican authorities, a coast guard vessel brought them from Miches to Sabana de la Mar where they were met by a Dominican Army bus on July 10 and brought to the capital on the same day. Three ladies of the American community, one a trained nurse and two others experienced in first aid, also met the survivors at Sabana de la Mar and brought the wounded gunner immediately in a private car to a hospital in Ciudad Trujillo. The lifeboat in which the men made their voyage is in the custody of the Dominican Coast Guard authorities in Sabana de la Mar.

As reported in my cable no. 330, on July 13 last all the survivors of the *Thomas McKean* were repatriated on that date by two ferry command Army planes with the exception of the naval gunners who departed today on a United States Coast Guard vessel in accordance with arrangements made by the Naval Attache. I am grateful to the Department for the prompt and efficient arrangements which were made for the repatriation by air of these survivors.

As of possible interest to the Department there is enclosed herewith a translation of a communication from the President of the Town Council of Miches which was given to Third Officer Muci to deliver to me, and a copy of my reply thereto. There is also enclosed a list of the survivors from the *S. S. Thomas McKean* landed in the Dominican Republic.

Respectfully yours,
A. M. WARREN

Enclosures:
1. Letter as stated
2. Reply to 1.
3. List of survivors

BLB:mk
711-Thomas McKean

Enclosure 1 to dispatch no. 0026 dated July 17, 1943, from the American Legation at Ciudad Trujillo, D. R.

Translation: SLM

Dominican Republic
Town Council
of Miches

Miches, D.R.
July 10, 1942

From: President of the Town Council of Miches
To: Consul of the United States of America, Ciudad Trujillo, District of Santo Domingo
Subject: Attentions to the Survivors of the Merchant Ship "Thomas McKean"

In the name of this town which has had the satisfaction of being able to give hospitality to these patriotic men who are fighting for the Right and for the Liberty of The Democracies I am happy to salute you with the Faith that this nation, under the wise direction of our President, Generalissimo Dr. Raefael L. Trujillo, co-operating with yours, will happily achieve the Victory.

With respectful salutations,
(signed)
Ismael D. Adams
President of the Honorable
Town Council

Enclosure No. 2 to despatch no. 0026 of July 17, 1942, from the American Legation at Ciudad Trujillo, D.R.

Ciudad Trujillo, D.R.
July 14, 1942

The Honorable Ismael D. Adams,
President of the Town Council,
Miches, Dominican Republic.

Dear Mr. Adams:

I am very grateful for your kind letter of July 10 last which was delivered to me by Mr. William Muci, Third Officer of the *S. S. Thomas McKean.*

All of the survivors of the *Thomas McKean* have spoken in the highest terms of the many courtesies and kindnesses shown to them by you and the people of Miches.

It is most gratifying to have this additional proof of the solidarity of the Dominican people with our common cause and I share with you the hope and faith that our two countries will achieve the victory for which we are fighting.

Sincerely yours,
A. M. Warren

Enclosure No. 3 to despatch No. 0026 of July 17, 1942 from the American Legation at Ciudad Trujillo, D.R.

1. William S. Muci, Third Mate
2. Tom Clark, Oiler
3. Frank A. Snyder, Ordinary Seaman
4. Russell Nelson Ham, A. B. Seaman
5. Paul McCastline, Water Tender
6. Eldred Harrington, Seaman
7. Luther Gothers, Messboy
8. Jesse Rumble, Third Engineer
9. Oscar Thompson, Oiler
10. Albert Brooks, Cook
11. Coxswain Albert M. Rust, U.S.N.R.
12. Roy Adams, U.S.N.R.
13. Jack Hannan, U.S.N.R.
14. Dorsey Grave, U.S.N.R.

So much for the survivors of the "McKean." Comparatively speaking, they had an easy time of it. They were only 240 miles from land when they got sunk, two boats were picked up within four and a half days, one got ashore in seven, and the last after nine days. This was a picnic compared to the crazing thirsty hell that many others went through.

Only four lives were lost in this sinking out of a total of fifty-nine. But some inkling of the slaughter among ships then going on can be gained from the fact that this was the second time within six weeks that the Chief Engineer had been sunk. The reader will also note that there is no statement from Captain Respess of the "McKean." As related by the Chief Engineer, he was picked up by the Coast Guard cutter safe and sound, but on his way back to the States on another ship, he got sunk again and was drowned.

Chapter

9

END OF CARIBBEAN CRUISE

GETTING BACK to the U-505, two kills in rapid succession started visions of sugar plums dancing in all heads again. They now had six sinkings totalling 40,300 tons. Two more of similar size would put them over the 50,000 mark, win Loewe an Iron Cross First Class and give Iron Crosses Second Class to many of the crew. With six more weeks to prowl in an area where ships didn't even zigzag, this should be a cinch. If they could economize on torpedoes by using their deck gun as they had on the "McKean," it was even possible they might stretch their tonnage close to 100,000.

Some peace loving citizens will say that it must take a brutal and calloused type of man to think simply in terms of statistics on tonnage sunk, when the lives of human beings are involved. This is a smug and mistaken way to look at it. All it takes to make the indignant and peaceful citizen think the same way is to find himself placed in a similar set of circumstances. The U-boat crews were average human beings no different from you and me. They were products of our western civilization whose destiny on this earth put them in a spot which demanded that rational human beings become ruthless about certain things. You can't conduct submarine warfare in a kindly humane manner any more than you can blast a sleeping city off the map benevolently. We found that out in the Pacific where American subs following the same ground rules as the Germans, rolled up some impressive statistics.

We don't change the character of our men overnight when war breaks out. We just change our scoring system for what is good and bad. In accordance with long established custom among civilized nations and with full approval of courts, churches and governments, certain rules of conduct are temporarily suspended in wartime. Acts which society usually calls by unpleasant names and punishes severely may become praiseworthy acts for the duration. Deeds for which a citizen might ordinarily be criticized, and maybe even hung, are rewarded with medals.

So far, the U-505 had sunk over 40,000 tons. In doing so she had killed perhaps several dozen men and left about 300 more to make their way to land, if they could, in open boats and rafts. But that was incidental, merely one of the loose ends in the normal way that nations work out their differences. The duty of a U-boat crew was to sink ships. What happened to the little men who ran up on deck after the explosion, scrambled into boats and rowed away while the ships were sinking, that was a problem for the survivors to work out with their destiny. When the U-boat crew got home from that cruise, if they did, they would be just as kind to their wives and children as they had been before.

So, after her second kill the U-505 continued happily on her journey looking forward to a busy time and a rich haul. But it didn't turn out that way. They spent the next month prowling through the Caribbean seeing nothing but airplanes apparently flown by dopey pilots who were just out for the ride. They crash dived for planes thirty times but only had bombs released at them once, and then not accurately.

The contempt in which they held our planes at this time is clearly shown in their war diary. They seldom spent more than one hour out of twenty-four submerged even though they were averaging one sighting per day! Our flyers in the Caribbean, when they happened to see a submarine, would scatter a few depth bombs around, note that the submarine had disappeared and fly back to base grinning from ear to ear to boast of their sinking.

It was for this reason that we set up Assessment Boards in Washington and London to analyze all attacks on U-boats and decide which ones had damaged submarines and which ones had merely shaken up the fishes.

The most hard-hearted and cynical bunch of skeptics that I have ever known sat on these boards. They wouldn't believe their own grandmother under oath unless she was able to produce oil samples, photographs of thirty identifiable Teutonic types in the water, and the skipper's pants.

Like the umpire in a baseball game their word was final. Their decisions often infuriated us who were fighting the Battle of the Atlantic and left us weeping into our beer at the Officers' Club between cruises and muttering "we wuz robbed." But at the end of the war when we got into the German Navy archives we found that they had been uncannily right most of the time.

These board members had good reason for their skepticism—and they weren't necessarily calling you a liar when they reduced your claim of a sure kill to "possibly minor damage." The very nature of anti-submarine warfare is such that the boys working at this trade will always firmly believe that they are doing better than they really are.

When a surface ship drops depth charges on a submerged sub, the ocean reverberates with echoes of the explosion for a long time and it is impossible to ping again for some minutes. Meantime, a skillful sub skipper, who was merely shaken up by your attack, may give you the slip and get away. A depth charge must explode very close to a submarine to crack the tough pressure hull. But any destroyer skipper who had a good solid sonar echo when he dropped his charges, had all the dials on his attack director screaming "Fire" at him, and who never got another echo off that sub, is going to swear that he made a kill—especially if the sub ejected oil, garbage and maybe an old pair of pants from its stern torpedo tubes right after the attack.

Aviators have been held up to scorn as being flagrantly over-optimistic in their claims. In general they were, but in anti-submarine warfare there was much more excuse for it than in the bombing of surface targets where the "wild blue yonder" boys claimed any bomb that landed in the outlying suburbs of a big city was a direct hit on the city hall. Whenever an airplane dropped a bomb within half a mile of a surfaced submarine, the sub naturally pulled the plug and "sank" forthwith to a safe depth. When the flyer returned from

138

that hop and swore that he had "sunk" the submarine, he was merely stating the facts truthfully as he had observed them.

The Assessment Board had to sift the facts, with the above and many other things in mind, and determine whether the intrepid birdman had really killed the sub or had merely frightened him into submerging. Photographs of fifty Germans clinging to bits of oil-soaked wreckage were the best evidence. Pictures of a salvo of depth charges exploding close aboard a sub on both sides were the next best. A huge oil streak that kept spreading hours after the attack was sometimes good enough. The noise heard by listening gear when a hull was being crushed by water pressure a minute or so after the attack carried a lot of weight. Many U-boats went to the bottom in very deep water with all hands, leaving no evidence whatever behind until a day or so later when oil began seeping to the surface. The Board had to score these attacks, as well as the ones in which the photographs showed the submarine with its stern end sticking straight up out of the water and the crew plunging overboard. In both cases the U-boat was dead, but in the first one the evidence of death was inconclusive. At the end of the war we found that the Board's crystal ball had been a lot more accurate than any of us who were sinking subs would believe it was when these chairborne bureaucrats were rejecting claims that we "knew" were true. The Board only allowed me ten sure kills, although I still claim eleven.

During the next month while Loewe ranged from one end of the Caribbean to the other, crossing and recrossing the regular traffic lanes, the Yesterday, Today and Tomorrow routine could have been even further simplified by eliminating Yesterday. There was no use remembering Yesterday, because luck was always bad, or rather they had no luck whatever, good or bad. Tomorrow, of course, always promised to be better.

Little incidents assume great importance at a time like this. One morning there was a muffled explosion behind one of the diesels. The man on watch spun his throttle closed and the chief engineer was soon squirming his way through the crates of canned provisions stored between the diesel and the pressure hull, to find out what was ailing his engine. He finally traced the explosion to a case of canned frankfurters which couldn't stand the tropic heat plus that of the diesel engine.

This casualty placed a command decision squarely in the skipper's lap. Ordinarily a U-boat would run out of food before she ran out of fuel. When preparing for a cruise, every nook and cranny of the boat was stuffed with provisions after she got her torpedoes and other war supplies aboard. Her stay in the operational area was planned on the basis that she had food for ninety days aboard.

Napoleon said that an Army travels on its belly. So does a U-boat. When a whole case of frankfurters explodes, it upsets a lot of carefully laid logistic plans. Loewe's command decision was a clear cut but touchy one, profoundly affecting every man in the boat. Should he eat up this case before it spoiled—feeding his boys nothing but frankfurters as long as they lasted—or should he heave the offending hot dogs overboard and cut short his operations by a week? He decided, as any good military man would, to stuff his men (and himself) with frankfurters for a while.

Being a smart Captain who kept his crew briefed on the overall strategy of the war, Loewe got on the public announcing system and gravely explained this decision to all hands. He said, "Enemy flyers can't drive us home by the explosions of their powerful bombs, I'll be damned if I think we should be driven home early by the explosion of a case of our own canned goods." The crew all nodded reluctant agreement, each man ate a couple of fathoms of hot dogs in the next week, and probably had a family spat next time a frankfurter appeared on his table at home.

Perishable items, like eggs, had to be eaten up early in a cruise. The U-boats put to sea with the passageway through the boat cluttered with crates of fresh eggs. By the end of the first couple of weeks, the crew all had a belly full of eggs, and had eaten their way into a little more elbow room in the passageway. While the eggs lasted, the messenger on watch used to turn over each crate once a day, the crates all being marked with a circle on the side that should be up on even numbered days, and an "X" on the side for odd days. I am told that this procedure postpones the day when the eggs begin tasting like moth balls. Whether it does or not, it adds an extra little chore to keep the boys busy when nothing much is happening during the first ten days or so of a cruise.

Loewe relates in a letter to me that when they shoved off on this Carribbean cruise there was a shortage of coffee, so they were given a large supply of tea to make up for this. This led to an unforeseen burst of indignation from his crew the first time tea was served. It seems that when a young sailor drew the assignment as cook on a U-boat he was given a ten-day course ashore on how to keep hungry sailors well fed and happy. But you can't impart all the secrets of the culinary art to a willing amateur in ten days and evidently one secret overlooked at the school was how to make tea.

Shortly after arrival in the Caribbean, Loewe's young cook dumped several pounds of tea in a big pot and boiled the hell out of it the same as if it had been coffee. The indignant howls of protest from the crew when they took their first swig of this poisonous brew brought Loewe scrambling out of his cubbyhole to the mess room to stop a riot.

Loewe says in his letter, "Since my mother was Dutch, I had learned how to make tea as a child and was able to correct my cook's education. I must have done it well because the crew seemed to like tea—prepared my way." I doubt if many readers have ever imagined that one of the duties of a U-boat skipper fighting the Battle of the Atlantic, was to teach young sailors how to make tea!

Loewe relates another little incident of this voyage. One day while cruising on the surface, a messenger came scurrying down to his cabin with a request from the watch officer, "Permission to change course and get some turtle steaks." He had sighted a school of huge sea turtles basking in the sun, and though it would be easy to bag a couple of these proverbially slow leviathians. Loewe promptly granted permission and scrambled up on deck followed by all hands not on watch, to see the fun.

The watch officer stationed a couple of men up in the bow with long handled nets, slowed to creeping speed, and conducted his approach on the school of turtles as carefully as if he were Prien making the firing run on the "Royal Oak." But this naval engagement, like the Battle of Jutland, turned out to be indecisive. When the battle was over, U-505 retained control of the seas, as did the British after Jutland—but they got no turtles.

Loewe's action report to me says, "Turtles are phlegmatic animals which will let you get close to them but become suspicious when you poke nets at them. We soon found the turtles could submerge just as well as we could!"

To help keep the boys amused Loewe sometimes got up contests among the crew. These were simple affairs in which luck usually played at least as big a part as skill, like guessing the number of dried peas in a five pound bag, or working a series of riddles each of which had a dozen plausible answers but only one of which had been pre-designated by the Captain as the official one. They ran checker tournaments for the championship of the boat. Another contest was guessing the last two numbers that would appear on the revolution counter at the precise moment of noon.

These contests aroused great interest, because of the prize that Loewe put up, which caused each man to try as hard as if he were competing for an Olympic medal. The prize was that the skipper himself had to stand the winner's next watch.

It isn't every skipper that could put up a prize of that kind. To do it you've got to know just about all there is to be known about a submarine, because there's no telling whose watch you will have to stand. It may be the cook's, a lookout's, a throttleman's, a radioman's, or the watch officer's orderly. It's a good bet that when Loewe fell heir to a technician's watch the man involved stayed close to the skipper while he was standing it—not because he was afraid that Loewe might goof, you understand, but because in case of an alarm the monkey business would have to stop and the skipper would be needed elsewhere. Even so, Loewe made character with his crew by showing them he could do the job of any man in the boat.

After twenty-three days of futile prowling following the sinking of the "McKean," a puzzling entry appears in the war diary of the U-505: "JULY 22 7:25 A.M. Sighted sailing ship bearing 30°, course West. Three masted schooner 'Roamar' from Cartagena with Colombian flag. As he did not stop for my warning shot I sank him with 22 rounds from my 10.5 cm gun. Size 400 BRT. 9:00 A.M., she sank."

"She sank." So far as the war diary is concerned, that's the end of the story. . . . But this ending leaves a number of questions to be answered. In the first place, the shelling of this harmless little sailing ship seems completely out of character for Loewe. When he sank large steamers he always waited, after his first torpedo hit, and gave the ship a chance to lower her boats before firing his second shot. In every case where the ship was unescorted and got off no SOS, he approached the life boats after the sinking to see if he could give them medical supplies, provisions or advice on the course to nearest land. Why did he klobber this small schooner after one warning shot? Why is there no mention whatever in his log about the fate of the crew?

And why didn't the schooner heave to after the first warning shot? It was impossible for her to outrun the U-boat. It was suicide for her to do anything but luff up and douse her sails. There is no logical explanation for what she did except panic. She had a native crew who knew nothing about the customs of war at sea among civilized nations, and they probably were paralyzed with fright, didn't know what to do, and so did nothing.

Even so, it's difficult to see why Loewe lowered the boom on her with his second shot. If she had been a submarine trap she wouldn't try to run away from him. The script for mystery ships called for them to stop, lower boats, and send off the "panic party" leaving the ship ostensibly abandoned. The sinking of this 400 ton spit kit plying between two Caribbean ports could obviously have no effect on the outcome of the great Battle of the Atlantic. Why did Loewe waste twenty-two rounds of ammunition on her and risk disclosing his position, possibly bringing aircraft and destroyers down on his neck?

There is little use speculating and philosophizing about things like this thirteen years after the event. It's just one of the messy little incidents of a global war which are important only to the men concerned in them. Looking back on it now, it is easy to say that this four-hundred-ton schooner could have been spared from the grand total of over twenty million tons sunk, without affecting the final result. But the Germans can also point to some hospitals and churches we blew up in Dresden and say the same thing.

Actually, I can't say that I blame Loewe for sinking her. She might have been a submarine trap. About a year later, when I commanded a jeep carrier task group, I met several majestic old full-rigged sailing ships off the Azores. I had a sentimental attachment for these wonderful old ships that link present-day sailors to their adventurous ancestors. But I gave all these seagoing heirlooms a thorough casing, had my planes photograph them from all angles, and examined the photos with a magnifying glass looking for suspicious radio antennas, oiling connections, or concealed hatches and sideports. I will admit, however, that while doing this I felt just a little bit as if I were peeking under my grandmother's skirts, counting the ruffles on her pantaloons and accusing her of robbing poor boxes.

But, looking at it from Loewe's point of view, three masted schooners that put to sea when a world war is in progress should have a skipper who isn't panicky, and should hire extra hands to be on deck at all times ready to douse sail and heave to the instant a warning shot crosses their bows. If they don't, they can expect to get klobbered and to have the second shot explode in the middle of the crew's bunk room.

Whether the U-505 was justified in sinking the schooner or not, the U-boat's luck changed from that day forward. Far be it from me to say that this was because she had sunk the "Roamar." But many "superstitious" sailors will shake their heads and say, "It's bad luck to sink a sailing ship."

Sailors are supposed to be notoriously superstitious and to believe in all sort of omens religiously. When you get down to brass tacks, these so-called superstitions are fundamentally religious in nature. They are an admission that man doesn't run this Universe to suit himself and that his plans are subject to veto by a Higher Power. Sailors instinctively understand this and believe in God because they have a better chance than men who stay ashore to observe and think about the handiwork of God.

They see the daily miracles of sunrise and sunset and understand the Power that regulates them better than the scientists do. The scientists can "explain" the whole thing in terms of Newton's Laws and show you that there is no miracle to it at all, the sun can't help rising and setting. But sailors who know nothing about Newton's Laws are wiser than the scholars who expound laws which sailors can't understand. They go beyond the mathematics of the sunrise and see in it the hand of the One Who created these laws of mathematics as well as everything else.

They rub elbows with God's power and majesty in the storms at sea, and when the ocean worships God by raising great sweeping mountains of water that dwarf in power and majesty anything we see ashore, they get drenched to the skin in worship.

During the night watches when the sky is clear, sailors gaze out into the depths of the starry universe in which we live. Each night they see how perfectly all parts of creation fit together. They see how harmoniously the whole magnificent machine operates everywhere except on this puny planet where man can interfere.

Men who live close to these wonders every day on a tiny ship, absorb and learn some things that smarter men may miss in the strife and turmoil of life ashore. They know instinctively that we and this universe were created by a Supreme Being, more powerful than the effect which He created, and not simply by the haphazard operation of the laws of probability.

Sailors often speak of "good luck," but when they do they do not mean gambler's luck controlled by the laws of probability. When a sailor speaks of good luck, he means God's blessing, and there is certainly no better luck you can enjoy than that.

Whether it is proper to say that the U-505 ever enjoyed good luck in this sense may be debatable. To get an impartial judge for this debate you would have to reach far out into the starry night, beyond the limits of our solar system. But, however that may be, the U-505 had nothing but bad luck after sinking the "Roamar."

Her first bit of misfortune was that Loewe got sick and had to request permission to curtail his stay in the operational area. As a matter of fact he had been sick for several days before the "Roamar" sinking and perhaps this explains it. U-boat HQ granted permission to return and ordered a new skipper to relieve Loewe as soon as they arrived in Lorient.

This was indeed a stroke of bad luck for the U-505. Loewe had been a good skipper. He was considerate of his men, he had confidence in them and they trusted him. Until he sank the "Roamar" the U-505 had been quite successful and success is the one thing above all else that creates high morale and a happy ship. Now the U-505 would have to go through the ordeal of breaking in a new skipper, and only time would tell whether he brought good luck or bad aboard with him.

On the way back to Lorient, the U-505 had a chance encounter with another U-boat bound for the Caribbean. On 20 August, they exchanged recognition signals with U-214, and since they were returning from patrol early and had extra supplies left, they took time out from their return voyage to go alongside U-214 and, as recorded in their war diary, to give their friends two cases of tea. (Maybe Loewe's tea wasn't as popular with his crew as he now claims it was.)

On August 25, Loewe arrived back in Lorient having been out for 79 days. This time they had seen six targets and sunk three—counting the "Roamar." They had seen thirty airplanes but only one had seen them. Their cruising record was 12,842 miles on the surface and 498 submerged.

The U-boats were still able to operate as surface vessels. But it is worthy of note that on her first cruise the U-505 travelled forty times as far on the surface as she did submerged, on her second the surface travel fell to only twenty-five times as much.

The comment of Doenitz's staff officers on this cruise was as follows: "Mission prematurely ended because of sickness of Captain. Took advantage of few chances of attack during time of almost total traffic stoppage. The sinking of the Colombian schooner had better been left undone."

Two days after arrival in Lorient, Loewe had his appendix removed. He spent the rest of the war on shore duty with Admiral Doenitz's staff.

Chapter

10

CSZHECH TAKES COMMAND

A NAVAL change of command ceremony is a simple, straight-forward affair. The crew lines up on deck in dress uniform and the departing Captain takes position in front of them with the new one. The old skipper reads the orders relieving him of command and says whatever he thinks he should to the men who have served him during his stewardship. The new skipper reads the orders placing him in command, salutes his predecessor and says, "I relieve you sir."

That's all there is to it. The instant the words, "I relieve you sir," are spoken, complete responsibility for that ship is transferred from one man's shoulders to the other. From here on, whatever good the ship does reflects credit on the new skipper—whatever bad, reflects blame. If he is built the right way he will be smugly modest in accepting credit, but will also step forward and take the rap when something goes wrong, even though it was something over which he had no control. After all, the skipper is supposed to have control.

The change of command ceremony is held at an all hands muster because the transfer of authority involved is of such vital importance to every man on board. The orders which this new man will issue can mean life or death to the whole crew. This man will be the chief executive of their country's government when the ship goes to sea and each individual in the crew owes him unswerving obedience. To make sure there can be no mistake about who this man is, he gets up in front of the crew, lets them take a good look at him, and displays the credentials of his authority. Kapitän Leutnant Cszhech relieved Loewe early in October, 1942.

Cszhech came to the U-505 with a good reputation and an impressive record of combat experience. In fact, he had a great deal more wartime submarine service behind him than Loewe. He had been first watch officer for a year in the U-124 under Mohr, and the U-124 was a number to conjure with around Lorient in 1942. She was one of the ace U-boats, had already sunk 100,000 tons, and anyone who had served his apprenticeship in her certainly ought to know his business.

But although the transfer of authority from the old skipper to the new becomes final and complete in one instant, transfer of the crew's loyalty is not quite that simple. Usually the crew starts off with a respectfully hopeful attitude toward the new man. For the time being they will take those gold stripes that he wears at their face value. They want to believe in the new skipper and be proud of him, and will give him the benefit of the doubt until he gives them reason to do otherwise.

But this isn't by any means the belligerent loyalty they give a proven skipper. A sailor from a good ship brags about my Captain as if he owned a big piece of the skipper and you can start bloody fights along the waterfront by making slighting remarks about a captain who has taken his boys safely through some tough jams and has left his claw marks on the enemy. The new skipper doesn't inherit that kind of loyalty at the change of command ceremony. He has to earn it, the same as his predecessor did.

Cszhech took over command with a somewhat tolerant and condescending air toward his new crew. After all, he came from the U-124, which in one two-week period had sunk more tonnage than this crew of newcomers had sunk in two complete war patrols. Of course, Mohr, skipper of U-124, got the credit and the medals for that performance, even though it was he, Cszhech, who had trained that crew, and who, in his own opinion, had been the mainspring of the whole boat. Several times Mohr had passed up chances for attacks which he, Cszhech, would have seized. He felt that if Mohr had been a little more daring and had followed his advice, U-124 would have rolled up an even higher score. Now, with his own command, Cszhech would be able to give his initiative full play . . . and Mohr might find out things did go well, as they used to in U-124.

There is no exact parallel for the process that takes place on a ship after a change of command. It's almost as

148

if the head were amputated from a living body and a new one grafted on without killing the body. If the old and new skippers are of similar temperaments, the change may occur smoothly and the severed nerves and blood vessels will grow together again. The test comes the next time they go into action and if the operation has been successful, the ship performs as she did under the old skipper.

But if the two men are radically different in character, some major upheavals may occur. An ace U-boat can become a "clunker" over night if she acquires a weak sister in command. If a "clunker" gets a hot-shot skipper aboard, the change in the opposite direction begins immediately. The word gets around, "No more foolishness—this man means business." In the first week a few heads will roll, the slack rigging is set taut, and the former weak sister is a fighting unit.

A crew's judgment of a wartime skipper is completely objective. If he gives them something to brag about without getting them hurt too badly, he is affectionately called the "Old Man" and you had better not say anything against him no matter what kind of an SOB you think he is. If he doesn't, he's not considered much of a skipper no matter how he may pamper the boys trying to get in their good graces.

The U-505's reaction to the new skipper was good. All hands knew that in the U-124 Cszhech had seen much more action than they had in the U-505. They expected great things of him.

But Cszhech had seen all his action as first watch officer, *not* as skipper, and this can make a big difference. The skipper is the man to whom everyone on the boat, including the first watch officer, looks in wide-eyed admiration after they get out of a bad jam safely. He is the man whose eyes they avoid, but who can feel the accusing glances on the back of his neck when things go wrong.

A top-notch first watch officer under an ace skipper can be an utter flop when he moves up to the number one spot. Making the life and death decisions yourself is a different thing from just seeing to it that they are carried out after the Old Man has made them. So, although the U-505 accepted Cszhech on his reputation, time and some successful operations were the only things that could confirm this judgment. Until they had been under fire together everyone on the boat would have some reservations, and would be just a little more formal in speaking to the new skipper than he had to the old. A few common adventures were necessary to remove the barrier between them.

Cszhech knew that big successes were expected of him, both by the high command and this new crew because of his service in the famous U-124. He intended to produce them.

When the U-505 sailed from Lorient on October 4, 1942, bound again for the happy hunting ground in the Caribbean, she had an important new piece of equipment aboard. It was a radar detector, called "Metox," designed to give warning of any active radar set operating in its vicinity. This equipment picked up any radar pulse that bounced off the sub's hull and showed it as a dancing blip on the trace of a scope down in the radio room. It was intended primarily to warn of approaching aircraft, which previously could only be spotted visually by the bridge lookouts. This gadget gave all hands a new sense of security because bridge lookouts didn't always see approaching aircraft in time for a crash dive to get the boat out of danger, particularly on overcast days. Every boat has a few eagle-eyed lookouts who spot everything that comes along, but they can't be on watch all the time. Now the U-505 wouldn't have to worry too much any more about who was on lookout watch. This new electronic marvel could "see" even through clouds, and would not get dopey toward the end of a long watch, or indulge in day dreams about a gal back in Lorient.

Cszhech took the boat through the Bay of Biscay, running surfaced all night and submerged during daylight. Twice during the third night out, the Metox gear detected aircraft which the bridge lookouts neither saw nor heard before the "Crash Dive Alarm" was sounded from the control room below.

Five days out of Lorient Cszhech figured he was in the clear. From there to the Caribbean he ran surfaced around the clock except for an hour or so of diving drills each day to check his new crew and keep them on their toes. On the trip across the Atlantic they sighted only a Portuguese schooner and two Spanish ships.

Half way across the Atlantic, a significant incident showed how adjustments must be made to a new skipper. One morning the leading chief requested permission from the watch officer to set up the picnic table for lunch on deck. Next time Cszhech came up to the bridge the watch officer referred this request to him and while the skipper was turning it over in his mind, the watch officer unwisely added, "Kapitän Loewe used to permit this, sir."

That settled the matter then and there. "Nein," snapped Cszhech. "Captain Loewe is no longer commanding this ship. When you ask me for decisions, I do not wish to be told how you used to do things before I came."

At this time Loewe's crest of a lion rampant was still painted on the conning tower. That afternoon Cszhech had it painted out. A few days later the watch officer sighted a school of turtles. He ignored them and the turtles continued their siesta undisturbed.

Another incident confirmed to the crew that the new regime was indeed different from the old. Willi Bunger (the "Ostrich") had been studying hard, devoting all his spare time to qualifying himself for promotion to petty officer. En route to the Caribbean he took his test and passed it with flying colors. In due course his petty officer's warrant was presented to Cszhech for signature.

"How many vacancies do we have for this rating in our allowance now?" asked Cszhech.

"None, Herr Kapitän," replied the executive officer.

"None?" said Cszhech. "So if we promote this man we will lose him for a recruit as soon as we get back from this cruise?"

"Yes, Herr Kapitän."

"Nein," said Cszhech. "I'm not running a kindergarten to train men for other boats. Hold this till later." There was no doubt in anyone's mind now that they had better not use past precedents on the U-505 in drawing conclusions about the future.

The first chance of the new skipper and old crew to size each other up in action came a month after leaving Lorient, just as they arrived in their assigned area east of Trinidad. On November 7th, around 3:00 P.M., Cszhech gave chase to a smoke trail and soon found it led to an

151

unescorted freighter. Four hours later he had worked his way ahead into position to shoot.

With his eye glued to the periscope, Cszhech called out his final orders for a double shot from the bow tubes. "Target speed 12, depth setting 4 meters."

The first watch officer set these figures on the attack director and passed them by voice tube to the forward torpedo room. Soon the dials on the attack director indicated that the torpedo room crew had set their eels as ordered and confirmation came back over the voice tube, "Speed 12, depth 4."

"Fire," barked Cszhech and punched his stop watch as he felt the jolt of the tubes discharging. After thirty seconds he could see by the wakes of the torpedoes in the periscope that he had overestimated the speed and led her too much. This was a bad beginning for the new captain fresh from the famous U-124.

"What speed did you tell them?" he demanded of the first watch officer.

"Twelve knots, Kapitän."

"Dammit, I told you ten," snarled Cszhech. "Prepare to fire tubes three and four, target speed ten. . . . one-zero."

"Aye aye, sir. Speed ten—one-zero," said the W.O.

Two minutes later two torpedoes hit the steamer, both forward of the stack. (Even ten knots was a little on the high side.) The war diary reads: "Two mast high black splashes, no fire on deck. Life boats set out. Steamer immediately down by the bow. Aft section out of water. Steamer sinks. Did not send SOS. Left her to sink and departed. Estimated size 5500 BRT."*

Now the U-505's total tonnage was 46,200, and they could hardly help going over 50,000 on this cruise. Success covers a lot of minor sins in a skipper, and Cszhech had now given them a success. He was not a pleasant man to live with, and nobody would ever get beat-up along the waterfront for making slighting remarks about him, but that was incidental so long as he kept on sinking ships.

---

* Cszhech was a lot more cold-blooded about survivors than Loewe had been. He simply steamed off and left them without even getting the name of the ship.

His second chance came the very next morning. At 8:30 he sighted another smoke trail and chased it until 1:30 P.M. He had a difficult time getting into firing position because the ship was escorted by aircraft until about noon. Quoting from the war diary: "Freighter with two tall masts—zigzagging without plan. [The navigator of the U-505 kept a careful plot of all zigs and zags, and was convinced that he had analyzed the plan and could predict future zigs and zags but Cszhech disagreed with him.] 1323 double shot tubes 5 and 6. Missed. One minute after firing steamer zigged 50 degrees away from me. Probably a chance tack. Because of position astern second shot impossible."

There was furtive discussion of this attack afterwards throughout the boat. Half the crew believed that if Cszhech had followed the navigator's advice on the zigzag he would have known the ship was due to zig fifty degrees to port before the torpedoes could get there. The navigator, of course, kept his mouth grimly shut. The other half of the crew thought Cszhech had pulled a "Totem Pole," stuck his periscope up too far, had approached so fast that it threw up a conspicuous plume of spray, and that the steamer had seen it just in time to turn away. This school of thought pointed out that the steamer held to a course directly away from the U-boat for a solid hour after the attack and therefore must have seen the periscope. Both schools found the Captain to blame for the escape of this ship which would have put them over the 50,000 mark for Iron Crosses.

For the next three days Cszhech patrolled back and forth 150 miles east of Trinidad. There was an RAF base at Trinidad so airplane alarms were frequent. There were eight alarms, two from actual sightings by lookouts and six from dancing blips on the scope of the Metox gear. In these three days, U-505 spent about eighteen hours submerged. Once when the blip caused her to crash dive before any lookout had seen the plane, Cszhech remarked sarcastically to the watch officer, "I don't see how you people survived with these lookouts when you didn't have Metox." The watch officer stared straight ahead, bit his tongue and said nothing.

On the morning of November 10th, Cszhech's number

came up. The sky was about half covered with white clouds, the bases being at one thousand feet, with bright sunshine and good visibility in between. This was what Loewe used to call perfect air surprise weather, and in such weather he always ran with decks awash so he could crash dive in a few seconds if necessary. Cszhech was running in normal surface trim. When the first watch officer pointed to the low clouds and inquired if Cszhech wished him to double the lookouts, the skipper brushed off the suggestion impatiently. A skipper in his first command is apt to be embarrassed when someone else suggests something he should have thought of himself. To justify his hasty decision he added, "With more lookouts it would take us longer to submerge—and we now have Metox."

Half an hour later the Metox gear showed a clear scope. Suddenly, at 1014, a twin engine Lockheed dove out from the base of a nearby cloud heading right at them. A lookout sighted him only five hundred yards away just as four cylindrical objects dropped off the wings. "Alarm! *Flugzeug!*" he screamed and ducked down behind the bridge spray shield. The watch officer and other lookouts whirled around and looked aft just in time to get the blast of an explosion from a direct hit full in the face. There was a blinding flash of flame, a stunning shock, and a few seconds of the unearthly din from steel plates ripping themselves apart while three other bombs exploded in the water close aboard.

Down below, the accustomed quiet hum of the boat was shattered by a tremendous KERBLAM! The steel framework of the submarine and the bones of the crew vibrated in unison for a short period, while the pressure hull rang like a gong hit by a great hammer. "BO-I-I-I-INN-G!" This contact explosion on bare metal staggered the boat as if she had smashed into a stone wall.

On deck three lookouts struggled to their feet just in time to hear a WHOOMP in the water off the starboard bow and to glimpse, through the billowing smoke, an airplane crashing into the sea a hundred yards away with a great white splash. The plane had come down too low and been destroyed by the blast of its own bombs. The lookouts gripped the coaming and goggled at the carnage aft, blood streaming down their faces. The watch officer and one lookout lay in bloody heaps on the deck.

The whole after deck was a shambles. The anti-aircraft guns had disappeared bodily. Pieces of jagged metal were still dropping into the sea all around, raising little plumes of water. Acrid choking fumes from the explosion hung over the bridge and a huge pillar of black smoke rose from the flaming wreck of the airplane. Two bodies floated face down in the water near the plane.*

Before the fumes could dissipate, Cszhech scrambled out of the hatch to the bridge and surveyed his wounded boat. The first glance told him he no longer had a combatant ship. Whether he still had a submarine which could resurface again if she once submerged, remained to be seen. The boat, from the conning tower aft was a junk heap of bent jagged plates and twisted pipes all tangled up in a rat's nest of metal. Both engines were stopped and the sub was coasting to a stop about two hundred yards from the column of black smoke marking the spot where the plane crashed. Cszhech's first concern was to keep his smashed boat afloat.

"Report condition of boat," he bawled down the hatch. ". . . All hands not needed below, on deck."

When the sailors scrambled out of the hatch and saw the carnage aft, their eyes nearly popped out of their sockets.

"Get down there and heave that junk over the side," barked Cszhech. As the men jumped down off the bridge and began tugging at the wreckage, the reports were coming up from below—"Forward torpedo room undamaged. . . . Acid spilled in Battery Room. . . . All sound and radio gear out of commission. . . . Main Control Room—unable to dive. . . ."

---

* When I came across this incident in the U-505's war diary, it occurred to me that this might be the only record of what happened to this aircraft and might clear up a minor mystery for the RAF. I sent the information in to London and received a letter of thanks from the Admiralty. The U-505's war diary had supplied final details on a plane and crew which had been listed for twelve years simply as "missing, fate unknown."

At this point the chief engineer's head appeared in the hatch. "I'm out of commission, Captain," he said. "Port engine is hurt bad and full of water. I need at least ten minutes to check the starboard one before I try to kick her over again."

"Very well, take all the time you need, Chief—but get her going as soon as you can . . . send hacksaws and torches up here," said Cszhech coolly. There was no use getting excited and yelling at people now.

Lying dead in the water on the surface, the boat was in a desperate situation and everyone knew it. Every man had an equal stake in getting her clear for diving again, knew what had to be done, and yelling at them wouldn't help them to do it.

"Clear that rubbish away from the starboard engine's induction and exhaust," Cszhech said quietly, and then called down the hatch, "Send four men up when you can spare them to take wounded below."

For the next hour the men on deck worked desperately with hacksaws, crowbars and cutting torches, clearing away the junk and dumping it overboard, as a surgeon cuts the ragged flesh away from a great open wound. The whole wooden deck aft and all its gingerbread supporting structure had to be cut free and shoved over the side, exposing the pressure hull and the various nerves and blood vessels that ran along the outside of it. Many of these had to be amputated and plugged off. So far as anyone could see, the pressure hull had not been punctured, but the great pool of oil forming around them on the surface showed that the fuel tanks had been. Probably some of the ballast tanks were too, but the boat was at least ten tons lighter now with guns and upper deck gone, so a few extra tons of water in the after tanks wouldn't sink her.

After forty-five minutes the starboard diesel let out a few muffled coughs and started up again. As the sub got underway and limped off in the direction of France, she was still in a desperate fix. Lorient was almost 4,000 miles away. Unable to submerge, the boat was a sitting duck for any airplane that came along—and it was quite likely planes would soon be out looking for their crashed comrade. But at any rate, U-505 was now putting distance between herself and the RAF base in Trinidad. It was

11:00 A.M. as they crept away to the northeast leaving a telltale oil streak behind. There were ten hours of daylight left.

The most urgent job was to restore the boat's ability to dive. The openings through the pressure hull for the port engine had to be blank flanged. The induction and exhaust for the starboard engine needed numerous patches to make them watertight. Broken air lines had to be replaced, and jammed valves and vents had to be freed. All hands turned to on this task, knowing that whether they got back to the Fatherland or not depended on how well they did it.

At 2:30 P.M., a flying boat appeared on a course that would bring it within five miles of them. There was practically nothing they could do that would have any effect whatever on their fate now.

Everyone knocked off work, scrunched down to make himself inconspicuous, and all eyes remained riveted on that airplane. Cszhech changed course gradually to keep the stern of the boat pointed directly at the airplane, thus presenting the smallest and most easily overlooked silhouette to her. . . . But that goddamned oil trail was impossible to miss! Nevertheless, the plane missed it!

Many survivors of ordeals in lifeboats told of seeing airplanes appear, raising their hopes of early rescue, only to fly on out of sight while the men in the boats send agonized prayers to heaven. In this case, some prayers went up too, but they pleaded that the plane would keep going—which it did! An hour later the same plane, evidently searching for the one that crashed, appeared on its return leg and again failed to see the crippled U-boat.

By two-o'clock the next morning blank flanges had been installed in the intake and exhaust pipes for the port diesel, the holes in the outboard connections of the starboard diesel had temporary patches installed that should hold for a shallow dive just deep enough to get under and out of sight. Although one bomb had hit squarely amidships, a careful check of the pressure hull showed no holes. The blast had expended itself in wrecking the superstructure. At 2:00 A.M., they battened down the hatches and cracked the inlet valves to flood the ballast tanks gradually, and take her down in easy stages, double checking every step in the process for any untoward developments. As she went under all hands held their breath and all who could crowd into the control room watched the hand on the depth gauge to see if it stopped at twenty meters . . . or kept on going into eternity.

It stopped at twenty, and Cszhech kept it there until three the next afternoon. By the time he surfaced again many internal pipes and fittings had been repaired and he could make ten knots on the starboard engine. Now his main concern was to stop the oil leak which was leaving that trail behind him. He spent the rest of the day getting that fixed and putting as much distance as he could between his stern and the coast of Trinidad. In another day he would be out in the broad Atlantic where aircraft couldn't reach and would be able to lick his wounds and repair his damage in comparative safety, provided he wasn't unlucky enough to be seen by a fast warship. In that case, he would scuttle the boat, abandon ship, and rely on the British to observe the Geneva Convention and rescue his men.

He was still in a tough spot but he didn't have to go all the way back to Lorient before he got help. Doenitz took good care of his men, and never hesitated to divert nearby boats to the assistance of one that got hurt. Within a few hours of Cszhech's first damage report to Doenitz, orders were cracking out to three nearby U-boats to rendezvous with him and supply him with spare parts and medicines. One of these had a doctor aboard who could tend to his wounded. Meantime, U-boat Headquarters demanded details of the men's injuries and radioed back suggested courses of treatment for two of them who were still semiconscious and in serious condition.

During the next week they got morphine from the U-105, spare parts from the U-68, fuel and medical advice from the U-462. On advice of the doctor on the refueler, the injured watch officer was transferred to the U-462, where he could be given better care. By this time they were well clear of the South American coast, their boat's wounds were reasonably well healed and they squared away on the course for Lorient.

During the twelve days that had elapsed since the bombing, all hands had been so busy repairing the boat to get her out of danger that they had had little time to think. Now came a long period of routine cruising with little else to do but think. Cszhech began to feel the eyes looking at him when his back was turned, and to notice how they were hastily averted when he turned around. No one spoke to him now except when necessary to answer his questions. If he struck up a conversation it was a stilted one that kept going only as long as he forced it. It was obvious that his men were ill at ease with him and, of course, the reason was that he had brought them bad luck. He spent long hours on the bridge by himself, staring into the sea ahead, resentment at his misfortunes gnawing at his vitals.

One day in the conning tower thumbing idly through the quartermaster's note book in which rough notes are made about events as they occur, to be transcribed later in the official log, he noticed a page in the back of the book, on which some sort of a tally was being kept. There were bunches of four vertical marks with a horizontal mark through every group of four to keep the count by fives. He noticed that the marks were arranged in three groups. The first group had twenty-four marks in it, the second thirty, and the third eight. The name Freetown was written over the first group, Karibik over the second, and Trinidad over the third. Cszhech, without giving the matter any real thought realized that this must be a record of the number of times that some recurring event had happened on each of the three operational missions so far. While speculating idly on what this might be, he noticed some doodles drawn on the far side of the page. Opposite Freetown and Karibik, there was a lion rampant clawing an airplane apart. Opposite Trinidad was a mouse slinking way, looking back over his shoulder with his tail between his legs, pursued by a swarm of airplanes.

Cszhech tensed suddenly and the blood rushed to his head. This tally was the number of aircraft sightings on each cruise the U-505 had made so far. There had been fifty-four under Loewe and no harm done. There had been eight under him. Loewe's name meant "Lion" and the paint was hardly dry over his insignia on the conning tower!

For some moments Cszhech struggled with himself to

avoid exploding and making an embarrassing scene. Finally he ripped the page out of the book, clambered up to the bridge, tore the paper into small pieces and flung it over the side. When he went below again his jaw was set and his face pale. The bridge lookouts looked at each other questioningly, shrugged their shoulders, and said nothing.

After two days of internal boiling over this incident, Cszhech sighted a smoke trail and saw a chance to redeem himself. It proved to be an unescorted freighter on a course passing fairly close to him. It was an hour after sunset so he lay in wait on the surface and passed the word, "Target in sight, stand by for double shot from bow tubes."

It was obvious immediately that this was a great boost in the crew's shattered morale. One more normal sized ship would shove the boat's total tonnage over the 50,000 mark and mean Iron Crosses Second Class for some of them after all. The attitude of the crew changed immediately from stolid indifference—almost sullenness—to eager anticipation. Eyes which hadn't sparkled since the bomb hit, showed the old time flashes now as the crew readied the tubes for firing. At 9:30 Cszhech fired a double shot from tubes one and two and all hands held their breath as the stop watches ticked off the running time. Nothing happened.

Cszhech had paralleled his victim's course to keep his firing position just in case he did miss. "Stand by three and four," he ordered, and twenty minutes later he fired another double shot. Again they both missed. The steamer was still unaware of his presence but was making twelve knots against his best speed on one engine of eleven. Cszhech hung on desperately, and his stern tubes being out of commission, reloaded his bow tubes, dropping slowly behind all the time. A half hour later he missed with his fifth shot, and finally an hour after that, fired a sixth futile shot at extreme range which also missed.

Cszhech notes ruefully in his war diary that some of these shots, "May have run erratically or been duds on account of bomb damage." He also logs an occurrence which was misinterpreted by the crew. He states, "The last shot exploded after nineteen minutes run." Some of the crew said sixteen months later, when interrogated by

U. S. Naval Intelligence Officers, that this last shot curved back and hit the U-505 but failed to explode. They claimed to have seen the dent in the side when the boat was dry docked in Lorient. Of course, a dent in the side might be explained by one of those near miss bombs, but a recurving torpedo could do it too, if the exploder mechanism had failed.

The upshot of this well-meant attempt by Cszhech to raise the crew's morale, was to sink it even further in the depths. This failure certainly wasn't Cszhech's fault, unless you trace it clear back to the bomb hit which made the torpedoes run erratically, or say that he was foolish to fire torpedoes which he knew might not run straight. But the worst fault any skipper can have in the eyes of a wartime crew is to be unlucky. Napoleon is alleged to have sacked a Marshal of France with an outstanding professional reputation simply because he always had bad luck. Cszhech had now clinched his reputation as being unlucky with the crew of the U-505.

After they had limped into Lorient, on 12 December 1942, Admiral Doenitz's staff put the following comment on the war diary: "Mission broken off because of extremely heavy bomb damage. . . . The air attack came as a surprise without any warning from the Metox. The electronic detection device must never lead to relaxation of the lookouts on the bridge.

"The toughness and stamina of the Commandant who tried to attack despite his heavily damaged boat should be specially mentioned."

This pat on the back for the six futile torpedo shots did wonders for Cszhech's own morale. But it did nothing to restore his standing with the crew.

On that cruise Cszhech steamed 10,250 miles on the surface and 626 submerged. Loewe went forty times as far on the surface as he did submerged on his first cruise, and twenty-five times as far on the second. On this cruise the ratio was sixteen to one. Although the Allies were still losing the Battle of the Atlantic they were beginning to gain back some of their lost ground.

Chapter

11

LORIENT

FROM LORIENT, where the U-505 spent the next six months, Doenitz directed the far-flung operations of his whole U-boat fleet. Each morning at his headquarters in a villa on the outskirts of town, he held a staff conference at which the night's incoming dispatches were analyzed and digested, and the great grid chart of the Atlantic was brought up to date. The staff went over every detail of the previous day's operations and revised plans for the current day's work if necessary.

The huge chart of the Atlantic Ocean, ruled off into numbered squares six miles on a side, showed the location of all U-boats and the latest reported positions of enemy ships and convoys. Junior officers measured off distances and senior ones framed dispatches to boats in position to intercept worthwhile targets. Intelligence reports on prospective convoy sailings were weighed and scouting lines of U-boats were formed across the expected sailing routes. Sinkings reported the previous day were totalled, added to the grand total of tonnage sent to the bottom so far, and the names of ships sunk were checked off in Lloyd's register. Questionable tonnage claims were discussed, checked against the register, and decided. The exchange rate for the previous ten days was brought up to date and boats in unproductive areas might be shifted to better ones.

Ominous little red flags were put up on the grid chart at the last reported position of U-boats which hadn't been heard from recently. When a red flag had been up for a week, headquarters would call the boat periodically for several days. If no answer came back, the duty officer removed the red flag, and boat, from the master grid chart and corrected the flotilla roster. Next morning Doenitz would be notified, telegrams would go out to relatives of the crew, and the personal effects would be removed from the storage locker in the U-boat barracks, inventoried, and shipped home.

At these conferences staff officers reported items of interest culled from the war diaries of recently returned boats, and skippers just back from a war patrol gave Doenitz the highlights of their cruises. The Admiral was no mere figurehead at this headquarters. He personally interviewed every returning skipper and kept the whole Battle of the Atlantic at his finger tips.

All information of any kind, technical, tactical, or strategic, which had any bearing on the Battle was funneled into this headquarters where it was carefully sifted and evaluated. Every significant trend in the statistics of ships sunk vs. U-boats lost (exchange rate) had to be explained to Doenitz by the staff experts. As soon as they knew what caused a trend they took action if the trend was favorable to keep it so, if unfavorable to change it back.

If one U-boat skipper was consistently more successful than others working under similar conditions, the staff would study his methods to see how he differed from the rest. It usually turned out that the big factor in outstanding success was the personality of the skipper, and the staff couldn't do much about that. But study of Kretschmer's methods had a lot to do with going to the wolf pack technique, and, even though no skipper came close to Kretschmer's total, the wolf pack tactics took a terrible toll of Allied shipping.

With access to the vast fund of up-to-date data available in headquarters, staff experts could usually put their fingers on necessary changes in tactics even before most of the U-boat skippers, who knew only what happened to their own boats. These staff officers, and Doenitz too, were all former U-boat officers themselves and knew the business from the point of view of the skipper at the periscope. In tactical and strategical matters they were tops and their answers to a U-boat skipper's problems were efficient and practical. If anything, these staff officers were too practical and not scientific enough.

When the long haired research experts in Berlin asserted that aircraft radar was a scientific impossibility, they believed it longer than they should have. It was Doenitz's staff officers who finally learned from their own

163

analyses of war diaries that aircraft radar was an accomplished fact for the Allies. Even then, they had trouble ramming this fact down the throats of the skeptical scientists and forcing them to produce radar detectors for the U-boats.

At Doenitz's villa there was a constant two-way stream of radio traffic, information coming in from all over the Atlantic and orders going out to the boats at sea. I am amazed at some of the things for which U-boats in operational areas broke radio silence and reported to headquarters. Doenitz took a "calculated risk" on the incoming radio traffic and decided it was more important for him to get information than it was for his boats to keep radio silence at sea. Almost daily he arranged ocean rendezvous between U-boats to transfer spare parts for machinery, or to have home bound boats with extra fuel or torpedoes transfer the excess to boats remaining in the area, or to transfer a sick man to the nearest boat having a doctor aboard. He even held radio musters of his boats at times when he suspected trouble—ordering all boats to "report position and successes." It was by such a muster that he learned he had lost his three great aces, Prien, Schepke, and Kretschmer, early in March of 1941.

When a boat in distress sent an SOS, Doenitz never failed to send nearby boats to her assistance. He was cold blooded in his orders that they were not to jeopardize their own safety by rescuing Allied survivors, but he took long chances to save his own people.

Most naval men will agree that the outgoing stream of radio traffic from Doenitz was necessary. But some of us think he miscalculated the risk in breaking radio silence and required his boats to do too much transmitting.

Every time a ship at sea touches a radio key, she pinpoints her position to an alert enemy with a good direction finder network. Maybe Doenitz was forced to discard radio silence because he had no air arm. If he had gotten any help from the Luftwaffe, much of the radio traffic from boats at sea could have been eliminated. But Goering, head of the Luftwaffe, was contemptuous of navies and wouldn't send *his* planes out to sea searching for convoys to help Doenitz roll up a score. If the boats had kept radio silence, Doenitz wouldn't have known what was going on at sea until they returned to Lorient—when it would have been too late.

At any rate, one effect of all this radio traffic was to make U-boat crews feel close to headquarters. They all knew that when and if they got in trouble an SOS to Doenitz would bring immediate help. This is important in an organization like a U-boat fleet, in which morale often affects results more than technical matters do.

Doenitz himself was a sour looking character, resembling Calvin Coolidge, but, like Coolidge, he had a sly sense of humor. They say he had an oil seascape hanging in his headquarters with nothing but white-caps visible in it. When visitors asked him what the picture represented, he replied, "The fleet passing in review in 1955." When they said, "But I don't see any ships," his answer was, "There are hundreds of them—submarines cruising in submerged formation." (Note: in 1955 NATO started reorganizing a new German navy.)

From this headquarters in Lorient, Doenitz kept his fingers constantly on the pulse of the Atlantic Ocean. The Grand Admiral ran the show and knew his business and took care of his people. All hands in the U-boat fleet swore by him and considered him a great leader.

But the citizens of Lorient had every reason to hate him, his U-boats, and every thing connected with them. Their presence in Lorient changed a happy, peaceful community into a brawling, boisterous hotbed of intrigue, espionage, hate and murder, in which families were disrupted and the only friends you could really trust were those in the graveyard.

Until France collapsed, no enemy soldier had set foot in Lorient since before Napoleon's time. It had been a quiet little community of shipwrights and fishermen, centering around some of the finest shipbuilding ways and best marine repair shops in France. Far removed from the cockpit of Europe where the wars are fought, for centuries its inhabitants had been peaceful, industrious, thrifty and God-fearing people.

The first year of World War II affected them little. Even when the phony war exploded into a real one, all the battles were fought far to the east. The surrender of France, instead of bringing peace, plunged the whole Biscay coats of France deep into the maelstrom of war. During the phony war, and even during the invasion, it had been "business as usual" for the shipbuilders, fishermen and citizens of the Biscay ports. Maybe business was even a little better than usual. But when France collapsed, the grim facts of life in a global war were finally brought home to them and ground into the souls of all inhabitants. For the citizens of the Biscay ports, "Peace" was a will-o'-the-wisp, leering and mocking at them while the rest of France did enjoy peace, of a sort. The German Navy, hemmed in for the first year of the war in bases on the North Sea and Baltic, immediately took over Brest, Bordeaux, Saint Nazaire and Lorient. Lorient's fine shipyards and spacious harbor close to the Atlantic hunting ground, made it an ideal submarine base. But its selection by Doenitz for his HQ brought down a terrible curse on the peaceful inhabitants of the little town for the next three and one-half years.

Garrison troops swooped down on their city, billeted themselves on the community, and set up a military government. Their behavior toward the inhabitants was "correct," but this is a relative term and its meaning depends on whether you are doing the behaving or submitting to the behavior of conquerors. When a conqueror takes over a town which has spent a thousand years developing its way of life, he simply issues an order telling the people which old customs and institutions they shall abolish and which new ones they shall adopt. The citizens who are able to adjust themselves to this over night, get along as best they can with the new regime. Those who can't, get shot.

Right behind the garrison troops, heavy antiaircraft batteries rumbled into place in concentric rings around the town. This gave the citizens a temporary sense of security which was soon dispelled. Other things moving in after the AA batteries provided magnets to attract RAF bombers and make the nights hideous for the next three years, despite the powerful ack-ack batteries.

Thousand of expert U-boat mechanics from Germany swarmed into the shipyards and began converting them into U-boat repair yards. Engineers erected huge concrete structures along the east bank of the river. These bomb-proof U-boat pens had reinforced concrete roofs fifteen feet thick. The aircraft bombs that soon showered down on them did no more harm than fire crackers. But hundreds of bombs intended for the shipyards or U-boat pens blasted ugly scars all over the town.

By 1942, Lorient was the greatest U-boat base the world has ever seen, and a totally different town from what it had been for several hundred years. Battered by RAF bombs, its swollen population of civilians, soldiers, technicians, collaborating French floosies and their camp followers, was a simmering brew of arrogance, intrigue, deceit and hate. Lording it over all the rest were the thousand or so of Doenitz's swashbuckling U-boat sailors for whom the whole thing existed.

While their U-boats were in port being readied for the next patrol, these battle hardened conquerors had nothing to do but "rest." Resting was a strenuous business, both for them and the local and imported whores. Most of them, knowing how uncertain their future was, lived as hard and fast as possible during each visit to Lorient. For Doenitz's bully boys between cruises it was, "Eat, drink and be merry, for tomorrow . . . you may be in the mud at the bottom of the sea."

It wasn't necessary to go to Paris for wine, women and song. Local cafes, bars and sporting houses offered adequate facilities for as wild a binge as anyone could want, even if it might be his last one on earth. Professional prostitutes led busy lives and a thrifty gal who worked earnestly at her trade, could lay up quite a nest egg for her post-war life.

Life was hard for the local maids who wished to remain virtuous. They had to be very strong characters indeed to do so. Everything was rationed and plain hunger drove many of the weaker girls to the easy life. A young Frenchman thinking of matrimony had little to offer a nice girl except a chance to share his hardships and privations. The German conquerors controlled everything and could offer many tempting inducements, including food—as much as a hungry girl could eat. Some local gals sold their virtue almost for physical self-preservation.

In an occupied town, "correct" behavior means that physical rape is frowned on. But mental and economic pressures, plus hunger, are normal incidents of war. The military authorities were tolerant of U-boat sailors blowing off steam after a hard patrol, and leading local gals astray. They gave them the benefit of the doubt in cases where there was dispute about what kind of persuasion may have been necessary.

The citizens whose daughters were being despoiled were not tolerant. Their hate was a terrible, vengeful one. Some opportunists among the local citizens, thinking the Germans would certainly win the war, collaborated wholeheartedly with them, and paid savage penalties to their neighbors when the Nazis lost. Most citizens submitted to the occupation sullenly, but with the necessary minimum of outward respect and obedience.

Beneath the surly submissive surface, boiled a venomous hatred which flared out occasionally in the activities of the underground. These activities were many, far reaching and mostly death-dealing. There were secret Maquis killers who shot German sailors in the back and then disappeared till the war was over, into Southern France. There were spies and saboteurs of many kinds. Every local citizen was a potential enemy of the Germans, and it was almost an impossible job for the military government to separate the "good" from the "bad." About all they could do was to shoot suspects regularly enough to deter the fainter hearted citizens from getting too far out of line.

Despite the most rigid checks by the Gestapo on the French shipyard workers, underground agents actually wormed their way into the yards where the U-boats were readied for their next cruises. These seeming collaborators, ostensibly working for the Germans, slipped little bags of sugar into the lubricating oil tanks of U-boats. The sugar dissolved into the oil and those U-boats came limping back to Lorient with their engines in sad shape. The underground agents made sound looking welds on pressure fittings that would give way when the boat went deep. Some skippers who didn't take their boats down to maximum depth on trial runs, are on the bottom of the ocean now with their whole crews because these welds gave way under attack. Workmen drilled small holes in the tops of fuel tanks and plugged the holes with stuff that was soluble in salt water. A few days after this boat went to sea, the plug would dissolve and the boat would leave a tell-tale oil streak behind her when she submerged. There was a certain kind of grease you could smear on the gaskets of pressure fittings that would cause salt water to eat away the rubber gaskets.

The Frenchmen who did these things took a desperate chance. The penalty for being caught was death. If a sabotaged boat didn't come back, that was fine. But if she did manage to limp back in, the men who worked on her were in trouble, and the Germans didn't waste too much effort in legal proceedings to pick out the right workmen to shoot. They were apt to execute all suspects in order to be sure that impartial justice was done. Thus the activities of the underground agents imperiled their friends who might be neither saboteurs nor collaborators, but simply citizens trying to stay alive. Sometimes a collaborating French workman would squeal on a saboteur. But when this happened word usually got back to the underground and soon there would be two new graves in the cemetery.

The underground agents ranged from the parish priest who hid fugitives overnight without being too inquisitive about what they were fleeing from; to the call girl who wangled vital information out of the U-boat sailor she slept with and passed it on through devious channels to London. One such channel led from the madam of the leading whore house, to the butcher, to the Mother Superior of the convent, to her brother who ran a clandestine radio station. Some loose-mouthed buckaroos and their shipmates are drowned now because they told an extra good sleeping partner little things which filled out a jig-saw puzzle for the intelligence experts, enabling them to predict a sailing date or pin-point an operating area.

In a sense, some of these gals were valued compatriots of high ranking officers sitting in London and Washington on assessment boards to analyze the results of attacks on U-boats. A tipsy love-making sailor, after his ardor begins to wane, is apt to get sentimental about a pal whose boat got sunk and who will never again enjoy such pleasures as he just has. This can provide information that an attack far out in the North Atlantic, which was given a preliminary assessment of "minor damage" should have been scored as a kill. It takes all kinds of characters to make up a wartime intelligence service and spying produces strange bed fellows—and board members. I feel the least we can do for the gals who supplied valuable information to us is to list them as "hors de combat." They helped us to win the war.

At times it was hard to tell whether the townspeople of Lorient hated the Germans or the British most. The RAF came over frequently at night and scattered bombs around all over the place. If they had done any harm to the U-boat pens, most of the townspeople could have forgiven them for an occasional stray blockbuster in the middle of town. But after it became apparent that the only damage being done was to the town, the townspeople were pretty bitter about it, some directing their bitterness toward the British, some toward the Germans. Many reasoned that their own country had been defeated and surrendered, and they had a right to be left in peace now.

Community life was chaotic and families were often split into factions with lethal designs on each other. Many of the old folks, knowing the best part of their lives was behind them were content to live what was left to them in whatever way was the easiest. They had no further interest in the war, one way or the other, after France collapsed. They knew France was dying and hoped to live out their own lives in peace before she did.

The younger generation took sides violently. Some through hatred of the British or for other reasons, became full-fledged collaborators. A collaborator's brother or sister might be an active member of the underground. This situation eventually produced at least one permanently empty space at the family table.

Often members of the same family joined the underground for very different reasons. One might go to avenge the death of a brother killed by the Germans and to prepare himself to assist in the rebuilding of France after the war. Another might join the communists and go underground to prepare for tearing down the old regime after the war. While her brothers in the underground were plotting to kill Germans ashore, a sister might be in bed with one of them wheedling information out of him that would bring about his death at sea.

French public officials and military officers were in a very difficult position. They had been officials of the legal government of France which surrendered to the conquerors and was officially collaborating. They had to at least go through the motions of collaboration or be thrown out of their jobs and put behind barbed wire. If they collaborated too convincingly, they were storing up vengeance at the hands of their countrymen, if and when Germany lost. If their cooperation became too lukewarm, the Germans might suspect them of "treason" and shoot them. There were cases where officials became double agents and worked efficiently for both sides until they could make up their minds which side would win.

In this situation, probably the only people in Lorient who really trusted each other were the U-boat sailors and many of them destroyed each other unintentionally with their wagging tongues.

Even the priests were caught on the horns of a dilemma. Their first loyalty was to their flock, but to stay free so they could serve their parishioners, they had to go through the motions of collaboration. They hated the godless Nazi system, but they also hated the godless Reds whom the Nazis were killing far to the east. The padres were preaching a religion of brotherly love in a community where the dominating motive for everything was hate. Many of their parishioners were in the underground and, as men of God, the padres couldn't advise or condone out-and-out murder.

As the U-boat fleet grew in size, more and more Germans and hangers-on swarmed into Lorient and soon the town was overrun with them. U-boats were either sailing or returning from a mission every day. Either event called for about a week's binge by her crew on the waterfront.

When young men, who have just reached their manhood, are about to sail on a cruise from which they may never come back, some feel urged to test out and demonstrate their manhood while they can. On the last night in port a few may drop into church for a quiet word with God. But it doesn't take long to tell Him what they want to say . . . and that last night is a long one. Most U-boat

171

sailors found other places than the church for their last night's meditations.

Lusty youths just returning from ninety days at sea usually bypassed the church and proceeded direct to their favorite whore house to verify the recollections of the way things were three months ago.

It was easy to differentiate the celebrating crews and pick out those who were about to sail. Those who had just come back knew they had some weeks of life they could count on. They got drunk, but they were relaxed, hilarious drunks. Those about to sail were only sure of a few more days on this earth. They were intensely serious drunks, and disappeared upstairs with the gals more often than the others.

It was impossible to keep secrets in a base such as Lorient. The whole life of the town revolved around the operations of the U-boat fleet and everyone in town rubbed elbows with the U-boats one way or another. The shipyard workers, of course, got right down inside them. Tradesmen delivered food to the boats, and any fool could tell from their grocery orders when a boat was about to sail. A brass band met boats returning from a successful cruise and the boats came up the river proudly displaying pennants with the names of their victims printed on them for anyone to see. Bartenders, waitresses, and gals of the evening took intimate parts in the continual round of arrival and departure binges. Anyone who kept his ears open after the first five or six rounds of drinks, could pick up many items of secret official information.

You can never keep that sort of information from becoming known in the base city itself. Even in one of your own ports, confining this knowledge to the local citizens is a difficult job. In a hostile port, it is a very tough job indeed. The Germans didn't succeed very well in their censorship attempts. From an operational point of view, Doenitz gained a great deal by moving his bases six hundred miles closer to his hunting grounds. From a security point of view, he lost.

Into this devil's brew at Lorient the U-505 was plunged for six months following her return from the Caribbean in December, 1942. It was during this six months, while the

U-505 lay idle, that the tide of battle turned against the U-boats with crushing finality.

The year 1942 had been a year of overwhelming victory for the U-boats. Counting sinkings from all causes, 1570 Allied ships, totaling 7,697,000 tons had gone to the bottom. Churchill says of this period, "The Battle of the Atlantic was the dominating factor all through the war. Never for one moment could we forget that everything happening on land, sea, and in the air depended ultimately on its outcome and amid all other cares we viewed its changing fortunes day by day with hope or apprehension."

For the Allies, 1942 was a year steeped in apprehension as the awful destruction at sea mounted. But toward the end a ray of hope appeared. Although the shambles on the shipping lanes continued, the exchange rate dropped from forty to one in the first quarter, to ten to one in the last. This was the sign that the flood tide had reached high water stand and was about to turn.

Turn it did—with dramatic suddeness. When the U-505 limped in to Lorient to be repaired, the U-boats were riding the crest of the wave and Doenitz had only lost 86 boats in the whole preceding year. Before the U-505 was ready for sea again, he had lost 150 more. In May, June and July of '43, the Allies rocked him back on his heels by destroying 73 of his submarines at sea. During these months the exchange rate was two to one!

This stunned the U-boat High Command. By the end of June, losses had mounted till the odds were heavy against any sub returning safely from a sortie into the Atlantic. Doenitz was losing U-boats and their trained crews faster than he was getting replacements for them.

There is a limit to the casualties that any military organization can stand and still keep its fighting morale. Most armies, when losses approach twenty per cent, pull the units concerned out of the firing line to rest and be reorganized. Doenitz's losses were over fifty per cent. It speaks highly for the discipline and morale of his men that they still obeyed him when an operation order directing a U-boat to sail was practically a death warrant for the whole crew.

At the end of June, Doenitz had to call a halt. He pulled his U-boats off the heavily protected North Atlantic shipping lanes and redeployed them to quiet areas. There would be few targets to shoot at in these areas but at least his trained crews could stay alive and lick their wounds while his staff and the experts in Berlin searched frantically for ways to put them back in action.

This withdrawal from the North Atlantic was Doenitz's retreat from Moscow. His U-boat flotillas never recovered the initiative. The Battle of the Atlantic went on for two more bitter years in which 506 Allied ships of 2,500,000 tons, and 518 German U-boats were sunk. But it was a grim, losing battle for the U-boats from that point on. The exchange rate fell to less than one to one!

The Allies broke the back of Doenitz's fleet in the middle of 1943, and thereafter the once feared U-boats were hunted down and killed methodically and relentlessly. In 1942, the cry, "U-boat in sight," struck terror into the hearts of all merchant sailors. In 1943, it was like the "Tally Ho" of the hunt to Allied aviators and destroyer sailors. The prowling arrogant wolves from the Night of the Long Knives became slinking fugitives creeping beneath the seas submerged even at night. The nature of these prowlers required them to operate as surface ships if they were to do their jobs of destruction. But simple self-preservation made them stay submerged most of the time except when a run-down battery forced them to surface furtively and recharge as quickly as they could.

German accounts of the war still blame the debacle on a new type of Allied aircraft radar for which they were not ready. But that was only part of the story. Had the sudden turn of the tide been due to only one new development, Doenitz's experts might have produced a technical device to counter it. But actually there were many Allied developments that all came to a head at once. The new radar was only one. Others were: better weapons for destroying subs, huge numbers of new long-range aircraft rolling off the U.S. production lines, the new jeep carrier hunter-killer groups, bombing raids on the U-boat building yards and finally, the massive production of U.S. shipyards. All these things coming at the same time simply overwhelmed the U-boats.

If any one factor was more decisive than the others, it was the amazing expansion of the U.S. shipbuilding industry. In the first three months of the phony war our shipyards were practically idle. By the middle of 1943, they were producing 1,000,000 tons per month. Hitler's "experts" had scoffed at a fantastic guess by Doenitz that by an all-out effort we might build a maximum of 8,000,000 tons per year.

The whole economy of the U.S., its industry, and most of its citizens were involved one way or another in this herculean effort. Finished ships put to sea in 1943, which had been almost entirely buried in the ground among the ore deposits of the Mesabi range in Minnesota when the war began. We dug the ore out of the ground, hauled it to Pittsburgh, made it into steel, and rolled the steel into plates, bars, and beams. All over the country we manufactured steam and electric machinery, boilers, pipes and valves, shafts, propellors, anchors and chains, radio and electronic equipment. All this stuff, tailored to fit the places where it had to go, in many cases by workmen who had never seen salt water, was brought together in the shipyards and assembled into seaworthy ships by workers, many of whom were high school gals. This miracle of production, coupled with our new military developments, is what won the Battle of the Atlantic.

There were also a number of important technical developments on our side. Until early '43, shore-based aircraft in Iceland, Greenland, Newfoundland, and England, straining to their maximum range had left a mid-ocean gap where the wolf packs were comparatively safe. Now, new types of planes rolling off the production lines in the U.S. in large numbers were closing this gap.

German scientists had dropped the ball badly on radar. Despite constant warnings and pleas from Doenitz early in the war, the German long hairs had smugly assured him that aircraft radar was technically impossible, and that his submarine skippers who were attacked by aircraft on dark nights were imagining things. By 1943, the "experts" knew they had been wrong and had

175

hastily equipped the U-boats with a primitive radar detector. But the Allies came out with a new short wave length radar that baffled the outmoded detectors and caught the U-boats flat-footed again. We also had developed new and better weapons for killing U-boats after we found them.

Finally, a new deadly enemy to the submarines was just getting into the battle—the jeep carrier Hunter-Killer Group—which put mobile air bases all over the Atlantic and closed the mid-ocean gap.

None of these technical developments alone would have turned the tide of battle. But all of them coming to a head at once early in 1943, dropped the boom on Doenitz. Actually, it cut the head off Nazi Germany's offensive out in the Atlantic Ocean and made a Nazi victory impossible after July '43. But the body continued to thrash around in a death struggle that Hitler refused to recognize until two years later in early 1945, when he committed suicide and dumped the mess into the lap of the man who had almost won the impossible victory for him, Grand Admiral Doenitz.

Doenitz, with his finger constantly on the pulse of the battle, sensed the turn of tide even sooner than his superiors did. He pulled his U-boats out of the North Atlantic and deployed them to what he thought would be comparative safety west of the Azores, where they might intercept some Gibraltar-bound convoys. But while they were basking in the sunlight there and relaxing, the jeep carriers "Bogue," "Card," and "Core," tore into them in a daylight Allied version of the Night of the Long Knives and sank two dozen surprised U-boats in a couple of months. After the jeep carriers appeared on the scene, there was no place for the U-boats to hide except deep down in the ocean's depths. There were no more "mid-ocean gaps."

From here on in, the Battle of the Atlantic was a different story. The exchange rate for the rest of the war was less than one to one—Davy Jones' accountants at the bottom of the sea checked off more U-boats settling into the mud than they did Allied ships.

Doenitz tried desperately to save the battle which was by now hopelessly lost. Ships were pouring down the building ways in the U.S. twice as fast as he had ever been able to sink them.

He belatedly equipped his subs with radar detectors which his scientific "experts" had assured him would not be needed. They did more harm than good. By this time the air was full of Allied aircraft and every time one of his U-boats surfaced, he could almost be sure of picking up some sort of a radar indication and being forced to crash dive. As a result, the U-boats spent most of their time submerged.

The World War II U-boat was primarily a surface vessel which could accomplish little of military value if it had to stay underwater using up the vital charge in its battery. To overcome this handicap Doenitz started fitting all his U-boats with schnorkels so they could at least run almost fully submerged on their diesels without using up the battery on which their lives depended when the chips were down. He also rammed through the development programs for the type XXI and XXIII U-boats with huge storage batteries and high submerged speeds. He developed the Walther cycle boats, the first true submarines which never had to come up to recharge batteries. But these things came too late to turn the tide in World War II.

From May 1943 on, the exchange rate remained at less than one to one. The United States supplied England with the food it needed, got its armies and air forces over seas, and in 1944 invaded Normandy. After the middle of 1943, the war at sea was won and the Battle of the Atlantic became a mop-up job. But lest you get the impression that it was a picnic, from July '43 to the end of the war, remember that the Germans sank ships totalling two and one-half million tons.

After the slaughter of U-boats in early '43, Hitler told Doenitz to keep on fighting because the U-boats tied up huge naval forces and reduced the RAF bombing effort on German cities. Doenitz passed this idea along to his U-boat crews and by doing so probably shook their morale instead of helping it. This idea of tying down Allied forces by an offensive threat was a far cry from the Night of the Long Knives, and gave the U-boat crews an excuse for being over cautious. If their mere presence at

177

sea was all that was required, why stick their necks out attacking anything but sitting ducks?

Chapter

12

SUICIDE

SUCH WAS the situation toward the end of June, 1943, when the U-505 was declared ready for sea again. By then only one-third of her original crew was left on board, the rest having been transferred to other boats while she was being repaired. Of these, about half had been killed in the terrible retribution which the Allies were then exacting out in the Atlantic. Still on board were the four leading chief petty officers and a dozen plank owners who had put her in commission. All the original officers were gone.

The U-505 was scheduled to sail on July 1, and on the night of June 30, the crew made a final round of the bars and bistros in Lorient to bid adieu to their friends. U-boats always sailed in the late afternoon and everyone could get good and drunk the night before sailing knowing they would have all the next day to sober up.

The U-505's crew put on the customary binge on June 30. Theirs was even more frenzied than most departure parties because everyone who had spent the last six months in Lorient knew better than the usual transients how heavily the dice were loaded against them. Since January they had said *auf wiedersehen* to several dozen crews that didn't come back. Now it was their turn to go out and act as decoys to keep RAF bombers away from Germany. It was late that night before the last of them got to bed. At noon the next day all hands mustered on board the U-505, bleary eyed but ready to go to sea for ninety days.

Cszhech, with a bad hangover himself, took his boat down the river that evening and headed out into Biscay. He started this cruise with mingled emotions. A lot of his friends had disappeared forever into Biscay during the past six months. In a way, he was lucky to still be alive. But meantime, others of his contemporaries had come back with good scores, been decorated, promoted, and assigned to shore duty. He had fallen behind them and now he must try to catch up after the tide of battle had definitely turned. But there was no use brooding over his bad luck. This was his fate and he just had to make the best of it. He was bound for the Azores where the opposition would not be too heavy and there were still some targets for a skillful skipper to sink. He took a last look over his shoulder as the French coast dropped out of sight and thought, "If I'm lucky, I'll be assigned to shore duty next time I step off onto the dock."

He was back on the dock within twenty-four hours with a long list of minor discrepancies in the shipyard repairs and one major one which couldn't be fixed at sea but wouldn't take long at the dock. U-boat headquarters had a crew of experts on the dock to meet him. They made short work of his discrepancy list, freed the jammed valve on one of his ballast tanks and had him ready to sail again by the next evening.

Some of his boys got in another last fling ashore that night, repeating the same ritual as the night before. Like the U-boats at sea, the madams, gals, pimps, and bartenders of Lorient were on a Yesterday, Today and Tomorrow routine too. One night was the same as another to them. They had already forgotten they had said goodbye to these same men the night before. They said it all over again with equal fervor.

Next evening, July 3rd, the U-505 sailed again, this time in company with four other outbound U-boats, and an escort of seven motor torpedo boats to furnish anti-aircraft protection until they reached water deep enough for them to submerge.

The change in the tide of battle that had occurred in the past six months is graphically shown by the U-505's war diary for the first five days out of Lorient. While trying to get across Biscay to Cape Finisterre, she spent only about twenty per cent of the time on the surface. She averaged twenty hours out of each twenty-four submerged. Her distance run on the surface was only twice that submerged—quite a change from Loewe's first cruise when the surface distance was forty times the submerged run!

After four days of this Cszhech got impatient and decided to make a break for the open sea. It was a clear day with excellent visibility so he should be able to sight any aircraft in time for a crash dive. He surfaced at noon on July 8 and boiled along at eighteen knots until one p.m. when he submerged again feeling that he had stolen a march on the enemy.

It would have taken him at least twelve hours to run eighteen miles submerged. This sprint on the surface in broad daylight put him half a day's run closer to the comparative safety of the broad Atlantic. Fifteen minutes after submerging, all hands in his crew were still grinning at each other like a bunch of small boys who had just raided a candy store when hell broke loose around them.

Six stunning blows slammed into the hull in rapid succession, knocking men off their feet, smashing lights, and jarring great flakes of paint off the bulkheads.

The watch officer and Cszhech had been flung against opposite sides of the conning tower. They remained braced there staring at each other silently, waiting for the battering to stop. Some seconds after the sixth explosion had died away, the watch officer inquired incredulously, "Destroyers?"

"Nein," said Cszhech, "There were no destroyers in sight fifteen minutes ago. It's an airplane."

"But how could he see us down at forty meters?"

"These new listening buoys that they drop into the water . . . they have a microphone and a radio that broadcasts our propellor noises and. . . ." There were four more crashing explosions much too close for comfort but not quite as close as the first ones.

Cszhech dropped down into the control room. The grins were gone from the crew's faces now and all eyes stared at him questioningly—big with fright. "All stations report damage," he ordered.

The reports showed no serious structural damage had been done and the engines were still OK. But the Metox and listening gear were completely out of commission.

180

Loss of the listening gear was a very serious matter indeed. A submerged U-boat without listening gear knows nothing about what goes on in the ocean around it except, of course, when the explosion of depth charges serves emphatic notice that bad things have been going on.

"You hear nothing whatever?" demanded Cszhech of the sound operator.

"Nothing Kapitän . . . the whole set is dead."

"Silent speed," said Cszhech to the man on the engine-room telegraph, and then to the depth control man, "Hold her at forty meters." For the rest of the afternoon the crew tiptoed through the boat as she crept along 240 feet below the surface at one knot, gradually putting distance between herself and the scene of the previous attack.

There is little that a skipper can do in a situation like this to influence events. Unable to hear or see, he just has to trust to his luck. When the situation gets that tough, a show of nonchalance by the skipper does a lot of good. After a couple of hours of creeping, Cszhech said to the first watch officer, "I don't think any more planes are coming out. Just hold everything as it is now. I'm going to take a nap. . . . Call me at 6:00 P.M.

For the next few hours Cszhech lay in his bunk wide awake braced for the next series of explosions, but with the curtain drawn so no one could see. Reassured by the knowledge that the skipper had turned in, many of the crew grabbed off a nap they would have missed otherwise.

Meantime, Cszhech kept turning over in his mind the chain of events leading up to the attack, and always came to the same conclusion—he must be leaving an oil trail on the surface. That attack had been too accurate to explain by sonobuoys alone. . . . A sonobuoy only tells the plane there is a sub within a mile or so of the buoy. But a sonobuoy, plus a telltale oil slick would pinpoint the submerged sub. If he was leaving an oil slick he was in a desperate siuation—blind and deaf himself, but plainly advertising his own location, at least in daylight, to aircraft and surface vessels alike. He decided to surface after dark, check for oil leaks and then make up his mind whether to keep going or head back to Lorient.

At 8:00 p.m., before it was dark enough to surface, he got sudden and emphatic confirmation that, despite his forty meter depth and creeping speed, something was indeed revealing his location. A salvo of nine depth charges made the ocean quake like a bowl of jelly. As the thunder subsided and he realized that he still wasn't hurt Cszhech barked, "Full speed on electric motors. . . . Fire decoys!"

He now had fifteen minutes when reverberations of the sea would make it impossible for destroyers to use their sonar gear, and if luck was still with him the enemy might concentrate on the decoys instead of the U-505 when the rumblings died down. Fifteen minutes later six more depth charges exploded, but further away than the others. Apparently the decoys had worked. This gave him another fifteen minutes to run at high speed, and when this reprieve expired there were nine more explosions plainly audible to all in the boat but obviously aimed at the chemical bubble which the decoys had made a couple of miles astern.

Cszhech settled down to creeping noiseless speed again for an hour during which time all was quiet. Evidently the destroyers, or aircraft, or whatever they were that had beaten that chemical bubble to pieces were satisfied that they had destroyed a submarine. With his sound gear inoperative, the only way Cszhech could find out what was going on was to come up to shallow depth and stick his periscope up. An hour and a half after the attack he poked up his scope cautiously and took a look.

There were three destroyers sniffing around the ocean a mile to the north of him. The sea was glassy calm, and a quick swing of the periscope astern confirmed that the boat was indeed leaving a conspicuous oil trail behind her. But it was nearly dark now, and if those destroyers were convinced they had destroyed him, they might not pay too much attention to a little stray oil on the surface in the area of the "kill." This would just add weight to their claims for a kill and a medal for their skippers. Cszhech went back down to forty meters and crept toward the coast of Spain.

A few hours later he entered Spanish territorial waters where he surfaced and ran east the rest of the night under the lee of the coast, taking stock of his situation. It would be humiliating to limp into Lorient again and his pride made him want to go on, but common sense told him not to. That oil leak was a conspicuous one and could not be fixed at sea. Without radar or sound gear he couldn't accomplish much anyway even if he went on. And finally, Doenitz had stressed the need for caution and preserving his trained crews until the new types of U-boats were ready. Cszhech decided to go back.

He hugged the Spanish and French coasts close into the beach, lying on the bottom during daylight and surfacing for a few hours sprint each night. Oil came up when he sat on the bottom, but a stationary oil puddle in these waters, where there were lots of fishing boats wasn't as conspicuous as a moving streak out in the middle of Biscay. On July 14, he tied up again in Lorient.

The dockyard found, in addition to the troubles Cszhech reported, that all the gaskets on the vent valves had been eaten away by some corrosive substance and there was a hole the size of a lead pencil drilled into one of the underwater oil tanks. It was two weeks before they got these things fixed, repaired the radar and listening gear, and pronounced the boat ready for sea again.

During July, thirty-seven U-boats failed to return from the operating areas. Fourteen of these had been killed in the Bay of Biscay, and every one of the skippers was a personal friend of Cszhech.

On the first of August, U-505 sallied forth again but was back in again the next day. There were ominous noises when they dove deeper than fifty meters, sounds as if the joints in the hull were coming apart or a ballast tank were being crushed. There were also noises of water coming in somewhere. They could find no leaks but every time they went down to fifty meters the noises began again, indicating at least that something was being strained close to the breaking point.

For two weeks the shipyard checked the hull rivet by rivet and joint by joint. They could find nothing wrong but Cszhech and all his men swore they had not imagined these noises. The shipyard sent them out again on August 15, and exactly the same noises were repeated. This time Cszcheh took her a little deeper and when he surfaced, found the main air injection had been crushed in and was full of water. At least this would prove to the dockyard skeptics he hadn't been dreaming about the noises. They were back in the dockyard again on August 16th, for another week to repair the injection.

They went out again on August 22nd, and came back in again as usual the next day. This time they found the vent gaskets eaten away the same as they had been on their first cruise. The gaskets had been OK when they sailed the day before. The dockyard inspectors smelled a rat and half a dozen French laborers who had renewed these gaskets were arrested on suspicion of sabotage and shot.

On September 18th, the U-505 took her fifth departure from Lorient in the two and a half months since her overhaul had been "finished." She was getting to be a joke along the waterfront now. The departure binges of her crew came so close to each other that sometimes the men hardly had enough money on the books to get properly drunk again . . . . and departing U-boat crews certainly couldn't get credit from the bartenders or gals.

This time when the U-505 sailed, the engineering officer from Doenitz's staff sailed with her to observe her trial dives. Cszhech took this as a not too veiled hint that the high command were beginning to think that he got discouraged too easily and magnified his difficulties. With the Staff Engineer breathing on the back of his neck, Cszhech ran through his test dives and as usual found a lot of small things wrong.

But staff officers who are fighting the war in a swivel chair are the same in all navies. This one minimized the difficulties and pointed out that they could all be repaired at sea during the first week of the cruise. So he patted Cszhech on the back, wished him luck, transferred from the U-505 to a motor torpedo boat and headed back for Lorient at a high rate of speed. Cszhech submerged and set course for Cape Finisterre again.

This time he made the transit of Biscay even more cautiously than he had before. He never came up except to charge batteries and for about ten minutes in the morning to grab a quick sextant altitude of the sun and

184

verify his run. He averaged less than three hours a day on the surface and in the first four and one-half days covered only 200 miles surfaced and 131 submerged. The joint British-U.S. air patrol over Biscay was getting more effective every day.

During these four days, thanks to the ingenuity of the four chief petty officers in the original crew, the men of the U-505 had fixed most of the discrepancies which the staff engineer claimed he could fix over night.

Near midnight on the fifth day out, the U-505 surfaced to recharge batteries, but as she was breaking surface she got radar warning of nearby aircraft and had to crash dive again immediately. There was no reason why this should cause her to blow any fuses. A sub is always ready to crash dive when she surfaces. But this was the first time U-505 had had to crash dive on this cruise, and in her haste to get down she overloaded her main ballast pump. Some fuses which should have blown didn't and as a result, the armature of the main ballast pump went up in acrid electrical smelling smoke. The pump became a piece of useless junk.

Cszhech spent the whole night trying to figure out some way of repairing that pump at sea. His war diary records that he considered requesting another outbound boat to bring out a spare armature for his pump, transfer it to him in a safe place at sea, and thus avoid another return to Lorient. Although installing the big armature at sea would be a very difficult job, it was physically possible to do it. But there were no safe places at sea for surfaced U-boats, and it would be suicide for him to go on without this pump. True, he didn't need it for shallow dives, but the way the war at sea was going now now, any U-boat had to be ready to go to a hundred meters at any time, and had to be able to get up from there fast to give the crew a chance to scuttle and get overboard if deep submergence didn't shake off the pursuers. That main ballast pump was vital. So Cszhech turned back for the sixth time and crept into Lorient on the 30th of September.

In the ninety days since his boat had been pronounced ready by the dockyard and scheduled for operations on 1 July, he had spent twenty days at sea and seventy

185

alongside the dock. During these ninety days, seventy-one submarines commanded by his flotilla mates had been sent to the bottom by the Allies. One hundred and fifteen Allied ships, totaling over one-half million tons had been sunk by Cszhech's comrades in the U-boat flotilla, but the U-505 had done nothing except wear a path in the channel in and out of Lorient. Cszhech was not anxious to see any of his contemporaries when he came in this time, although he had no choice about returning and it wasn't his fault.

But when a boat is lucky the skipper often gets a medal which he didn't really earn. By the same token, if a boat is unlucky, the skipper has to take the rap for things over which he had no control. The most damning charge you can bring against a military man is that he is unlucky. As he was bringing the U-505 back to Lorient again, Cszhech, in the silence of the conning tower could sense this charge being preferred against him by all the men in his crew, who no longer looked him in the eye when they spoke to him.

As the sub came in to tie up to her usual dock in the shipyard, the French underground got in a shrewd blow at the Captain's morale. Painted in large white letters which could not be seen by anyone standing on the dock, but which couldn't be missed by anyone on the deck of a U-boat coming alongside the dock, was the legend, "U-505's Hunting Ground."

Fixing the motor was a major job that took ten days even in the shipyard. Cszhech spent most of this time brooding over his series of failures. He had been fully justified every time he turned back and no one could have done any different. But his contemporaries now were beginning to treat him rather patronizingly, almost as if he were a cripple who wasn't to be blamed for his infirmities, but who was not the same as other men. When he joined a circle of them at the club there was an embarrassed lull in the conversation. He took to solitary drinking and avoided the company of his friends.

The night before he was to sail on his seventh attempt to get out, he was seated in a booth at a waterfront cafe with a gal of the evening getting drunk. In the next booth, separated from them only by a thin partition, was a noisy group of U-boat sailors hashing over recent events. Cszhech was listening in absent-mindedly.

At this stage of the war there were no successes to brag about and most of the talk was about recent losses and boats reported missing.

U-68 and U-515 sail tomorrow," said a voice on the other side of the screen, "And the way things are going now at least one of them won't come back."

Another voice challenged this statement, "Both have good captains—Henke and Lauzemis—they will be back."

"Many just as good as they are haven't come back . . . the odds are two to one against anybody now."

There was a lull in the conversation while that ominous statement sank in. Then a joker trying to relieve the tension said, "At least we've still got one ace who will always come back."

"Who?" demanded several voices.

"Cszhech."

The blood drained from Cszhech's face, he clamped his jaws together and tightened the grip on his glass. As a roar of derisive laughter from the other side of the screen greeted this quip, Cszhech sat staring at his glass and squeezing his grip tighter until his knuckles were white and the sinews of his wrist stood out like steel wires. The glass shattered in his hand, cut into the flesh, and for several seconds more he squeezed the broken pieces. Then he flung the fragments against the wall, threw some money on the bloody table, and reeled out into the night.

Back at the dockyard a hospital corpsman picked pieces of glass out of his hand, bandaged it up and told him it would heal in about a week. The wound to his soul was a mortal one. When he sailed the next day nothing in this world could have induced Cszhech to return from that cruise prematurely.

He literally crept out of Biscay. To insure against being spotted from the air he stayed submerged twenty-two hours out of every twenty-four. He had to surface for a minimum of two hours each day to recharge his battery and during these two hours he ran wide open putting about thirty-five miles behind him. But at creeping speed submerged for the other twenty-two hours he only covered about the same distance, so his daily run averaged about seventy miles. He crossed Biscay so slowly, keeping radio silence, that U-boat Headquarters sent him a message when he was ten days out, asking if he hadn't forgotten to report reaching the Atlantic. He replied that he had not—and continued at creeping speed.

In the early evening of their fourteenth day out, the U-505 was cruising slowly at forty meters when the sound room reported, "Screw noises at medium distance." Meyer, the first watch officer, notified the Captain and got ready to come up to periscope depth and have a look.

As Cszhech climbed up the ladder to the conning tower, favoring his injured right hand, he inquired nervously, "What is it Meyer? What is it?"

"Sound room can't tell yet," replied Meyer. Then nodding at the periscope he asked, "Shall I bring her up to shallow depth so you can see, Captain?" This was the natural reaction of any U-boat man in these circumstances. A submarine's sensitive listening gear would nearly always pick up propellor noises much further away than a surface vessel could hear the echo of a ping from her sonar gear. The sub therefore always had the big advantage of surprise on her first attack, and to a normal skipper any screw noises were a challenge to a battle, with the opening odds heavily in his favor. But Cszhech was not normal now.

"No," he said, "Hold her at forty meters. This must be a destroyer."

Meyer thought it strange his captain made up his mind so quickly that this was a destroyer rather than a merchant ship and that he had no intention of attacking. But Meyer obediently passed the word below, "Hold her at forty meters."

"What do you hear now?" demanded Cszhech on the voice tube to the sound room.

"Twin screws making 180 RPM . . . diesel engines . . . approaching rapidly," came the answer from below.

"Another submarine?" asked Meyer.

"No," said Cszhech. "There are no other submarines near us. This is a Britisher, just as I thought."

"Maybe he won't find us, Captain," said Meyer. "We can't even hear his sonar pings yet."

"He will find us," said Cszhech, a hunted look coming over his face. "I know he will find us."

Soon a report came up from the sound room, "Bearing holds steady—he is heading right at us."

Cszhech cast a furtive look, like a cornered animal, at his first watch officer.

"Shall I change course ninety degrees, Captain?" suggested Meyer.

For some seconds Cszhech made no reply. Finally he said, "Very well, Meyer. . . . But it won't do any good—we can't escape."

"Left full rudder, said Meyer to the helmsman, wondering what had come over the Captain, "Steady on course 180."

Cszhech stared at the dial on the bearing indicator from the sound room as if he were looking at a ghost. "The bearing remains steady," he said in a hollow voice, "He knows where I am."

"Not yet, Captain," said Meyer. "We don't hear any pings yet."

Almost immediately the sound room called up, "Hear pings now on same bearing as screw noises—approaching fast."

Cszhech shot an accusing glance at his first watch officer as if to say, "I told you so," but took no other action.

"Shall I go deep, Captain?" asked Meyer.

"It's no use, Meyer," said Cszhech despairingly. "We can't get away . . . they have caught us again . . . my luck is bad."

By now everyone in the boat could hear the propellor noises without benefit of listening gear. "Shall I sound the alarm, Captain?" asked Meyer with his hand on the button.

For perhaps half a minute Cszhech made no reply. He stood there in the conning tower as if in a trance, clenching his fists so tightly that he split the scabs on his right hand. "No," he said, "Everyone knows now anyway. . . ."

A minute later all hands heard the tempo of the screw noises change, indicating that the destroyer was slowing so she could hear better in the final stage of a carefully calculated attack. There was no doubt whatever now that the destroyer had them pinpointed. As the destroyer neared the firing point, Cszhech seemed to shrivel within himself as if he knew the battle was hopeless. Screw noises were very loud now and all hands braced themselves knowing that the climax was close at hand.

"Destroyer is firing depth charges," said the sound room.

Cszhech stared at the gauges like a man who was already in another world and said nothing.

"Right full rudder," said Meyer on his own iniative.

For fifteen seconds everyone in the U-505 held his breath and prayed silently as the depth charges were sinking. They all knew now from experience that a depth charge attack was a terrifying experience but that unless the charges were set to explode at exactly the right depth, they might come out of this with just another bad shaking up.

The charges were set almost exactly right, and the rippling salvo of explosions gave the U-505 the worst jarring she had ever received, even including that direct hit by the aerial bomb.

Oberleutnant Meyer says that the first depth charge smashed the lights, and a few seconds later, while the other depth charges were exploding all around him, he heard an explosion which seemed to be from an extra close depth charge and saw a flash of flame in the conning tower. He thought the flame came from an electric switch. He smelled pungent smoke which might have been from burning insulation. In the darkness his Captain slumped against him and fell to the deck.

There was no time to investigate what had happened now. The skipper had apparently been knocked out by being slammed against the periscope. But the boat was in a desperate situation and until Cszhech came to again and could resume command, it was up to Meyer to take over.

"One hundred meters," barked Meyer, "Full speed—fire decoys." Then he yelled down the hatch to the control room, "Come up here and get the Captain. He is knocked out." He concentrated on the gauges again while they lugged the Captain below. "Left full rudder," he said to the helmsman.

As the boat circled to the left, Meyer noted that they were still at forty meters and at creeping speed. He stuck his head down the hatch and yelled, "Achtung! Full speed! One hundred meters! What the hell's the matter down there?"

The men were all huddled like sheep around the Captain, who was stretched out on the floor plates. One of the chief petty officers looked up at Meyer with despair in his eyes, pointed his forefinger at his temple and moved his thumb like the hammer of a revolver. At this same moment Meyer saw the pool of blood on the deck of the conning tower with the Captain's Luger lying alongside it. Cszhech had shot himself!

Meyer leaped down into the control room, saw at a glance that Cszhech was done for, and then faced what were now his crew. This was a change of command ceremony to put the new skipper's soul to the acid test. Cszhech had quit—deserted under fire. The destroyer was circling to make another attack.

Discipline, based on regulations, went overboard when the Commanding Officer pulled the trigger of that Luger. Meyer's gold stripes meant nothing now. Why should these men obey a junior with less experience than the man who had just deserted them? What happened now would depend on Meyer the man, not Oberleutnant Meyer. The whole Officer Corps of the Kreigsmarine was discredited in the minds of those terrified men standing on the brink of eternity.

"I am in command now," said Meyer to his dazed men, "Go back to your battle stations."

No one moved. Meyer reached up into the conning tower, got the Captain's gun, cocked it, toyed with it for a moment looking around the circle of faces and then tossed it onto the chart table.

"Anyone who wants to die—help yourself," he said. "The rest of you do as I say and I'll get you out of this. . . . One hundred meters—full speed—fire decoys."

No one was ready to die. The gun lay there untouched.

Some men went slowly back to their stations and began executing his orders. Others hesitated, motionless. Panic was very near.

Willi Bunger (the "Ostrich") broke into uncontrolled sobbing. Meyer slapped him across the face, shoved him toward his battle station, and said, "Get going son, you're not old enough to die yet." Willi pulled himself together, took his battle station, and all the others did likewise. "The worst is over—we will escape," said Meyer coolly.

"Steady as you go," he called to the helmsman. "Fire two more decoys."

"What shall we do with him, Captain?" asked one of the chiefs, nodding at Cszhech's body, as the men resumed their duties.

For the leading chief to call him "Captain" at this moment meant more to Meyer than a direct commission from *der Führer* himself.

"Lash him up in a hammock, put a weight at his feet, and I'll put him overboard when we have time," replied Meyer.

In the face of mortal danger some men come apart if responsiblity is suddenly thrust upon them. Others exceed anything they have ever done before. Meyer carried out his promise to his men and got them out of the jam. The destroyer was fooled by the decoys and for the next fews hours the U-505 heard depth charge explosions receding farther and farther astern as the destroyer blasted away at phony echoes from chemical bubbles.

At six bells of the mid watch, Meyer surfaced. They carried Cszhech's body up on deck and committed it to the deep beneath the eternal stars.

This whole eight hour period is tersely recorded in the war diary of the U-505 as follows:

1952 Propellor noises in medium distance.
1954 Piston engine noises.
1956 Sonar noises.
1958 Wabos—very close. (Note: Wabos, depth charges)
1958 Kommandant ausgefallen. (Literally, "Captain fell out of ranks")

2100   Kommandant tot. (tot, dead)
        First Watch Officer Meyer assumes command.
0406   Captain's body overboard.

Above is the whole story so far as the official log of the U-505 goes. "Kommandant ausgefallen." "The king is dead—long live the king." Note that although Meyer took over at 1958 and saved the boat, he doesn't officially record assuming command until an hour later when Cszhech dies!

So, after putting Cszhech overboard the U-505 headed back to Lorient again, Oberleutnant Paul Meyer, Commanding.

They got back in on November 7th. Meyer made his report to Doenitz and was "absolved of all blame."

That's all he ever got out of this operation—absolved of all blame! He had saved a U-boat from certain destruction under almost impossible circumstances, after the regular captain had quit under fire and blown his brains out. He had preserved a trained crew for Doenitz and had restored respect for authority in a group of men who had just seen the highest authority there is at sea fail them shamefully. The first watch officer's reward was, to be "absolved from blame."

The only way I can explain this is that Doenitz considered the incident had to be hushed up to avoid dishonoring the Officer's Corps and damaging the morale of the surviving U-boat crews. Meyer's outstanding conduct could not be recognized without publicizing Cszhech's cowardice, so Meyer stayed on as first watch officer of the U-505 and got nothing to show for what he had done—except his own life, and the lasting respect of some fifty men, who had felt the long finger of death tap them on the shoulder, hesitate and be snatched away by Meyer.

Chapter

13

THE S.S. "CERAMIC"

NOTE: I do not claim historical accuracy for the incidental
details of this chapter. There was only one survivor of the
"Ceramic," Sapper Munday, and I have not interviewed him.

This account of the sinking is reconstructed from the War
Diary of the U-515 of which I have a copy. The main facts
—time and place of sinking, number of torpedoes fired, time
the ship took to sink, state of the wind and sea etc., are as
recorded in the U-515's war diary.

Incidents on the "Ceramic" and U-515 are related as they
often were in similar cases and may have been in this case.
                                                    —D.V.G.

WE COME NOW to a minor incident in the Battle of the
Atlantic which must be told in some detail as it has a
bearing on the U-505 story. In the master table of statistics kept in the British Admiralty, the following item
appears:

Date	Place	Ship	Remarks
Dec. 1942	Near Azores	SS Ceramic	Missing

In the war diary of the U-515, now reposing in the
Admiralty archives, the following appears:

Date	Position	Event
7 Dec. 1942 0100	40°-50′ N 39°-55′ W	Sank SS Ceramic, 18,800 BRT. Rescued one soldier.

The "Ceramic" was a passenger ship built in 1913 for
the Shaw, Savill and Albion Line. She spent a long and
useful life on a regular run between England and Australia
via the Cape of Good Hope. When war broke out she was
too old to justify conversion to a troop ship, and even

during a world war some civilians must travel back and forth between Australia and the home country. So the "Ceramic" stayed on her regular run.

She was one of the few ships that did work at their peacetime trade, and thousands of civilians at both ends of her run had urgent, legitimate reasons for taking passage in her. Getting on her civilian passenger list was a difficult, tedious business involving a long wait and much red tape. She was not a troop ship but she did carry miscellaneous military people and naturally they had priority. Civilians needed affidavits from England and Australia, and had to explain all the facts of their cases to different officials whose duty it was to listen to hundreds of heart-breaking stories and select the most deserving applicants. Every time the "Ceramic" sailed, she left many aching hearts behind to sweat out the long wait for her next trip. One plea always hard for the officials to deny was that of a mother and her children, caught on a visit to England when war began, asking to be reunited with their daddy in Australia. So the "Ceramic" always carried many women and children.

The "Ceramic" sailed from England on her final voyage late in November, 1942, with convoy ON-149, carrying about four hundred military personnel and civilians on official business, plus one hundred women and children. The convoy was bound for Canada and the "Ceramic" would break off and proceed independently after clearing the submarine-infested waters around England. Convoys such as this one were given an anti-submarine escort of a dozen destroyers or corvettes, and usually had one or two cruisers to beat off attacks by surface raiders. They sailed northwest out of the Irish Sea and passed within range of the shore-based aircraft in Iceland. As long as possible, the RAF gave them continuous air cover.

No Allied ship was really safe at sea during the grim year of 1942. But ON convoys were at least as safe as any.

We can imagine wide-eyed youngsters huddling around their mothers on the main deck of the "Ceramic" as ON-149 sailed, asking all sorts of questions about the armada of ships, destroyers, and air escorts. "Mama, is the war over for us now? . . . Are all these ships going to Australia? . . . Is that a battleship, Mama? . . . Will we see any submarines? . . . Will Daddy be on the dock to meet us?"

What fun it must have been for most of these kids each day when they had to put on life preservers during abandon ship drill and line up alongside their assigned lifeboat, pretending they were ready to climb aboard and be lowered away. No doubt the more adventurous were disappointed when only the sailors in the boat's crew were allowed to get into the boat. I'm sure dutiful mothers did their best to impress the children with the importance of these drills and at the same time to conceal from the little ones the deadly fears that were in their hearts. I'm sure that while they were going through the war zone, each mother made her youngsters stay within sight all day long, and tucked them in at night with a fervent prayer that nothing would happen while they slept.

This shipload of humanity had little to do with the war, except that most of the people on board were trying to get as far away from it as possible. The "Ceramic" herself was just a nice old lady following a well worn path from England to Australia and back, taking no part in the battle and doing exactly what she had done for twenty-nine years. Although the Navy had put a three-inch gun on her stern when war broke out, she was about as belligerent as the ancient char-women who scrubbed floors in the Admiralty, and could affect the tide of battle in World War II just about as much. That three-inch gun could only shoot astern—a rather strong indication that their Lordships in the Admiralty felt that when she encountered battleships, she should entice them into a running fight rather than slug it out yardarm to yardarm.

The North Atlantic in December is cold and blustery, but the run past Iceland was uneventful. By the time the "Ceramic" was southwest of Greenland, skies were bright, the weather mild, seas calm and no submarines had been sighted. England, with its hunger diet, wailing air raid sirens and hideous nights of terror, was a long way astern and out here at sea the world seemed saner.

Off Cape Farewell at the southern tip of Greenland, the "Ceramic" changed course sharply to port heading south and bent on full speed, while the convoy stood on toward Canada. As they parted company, the convoy commodore and the skipper of the ancient liner exchanged identical blinker messages, "Good Luck." Soon the forest of masts in the convoy dropped below the horizon to the northwest and the "Ceramic" was on her own.

She was in reasonably safe waters now. She would run south till she passed the Azores and then head for the Cape, keeping far to the west of the usual shipping lanes. The U-boats' hunting ground was off Freetown, where convoys run close in to the coast. But she would pass Freetown far off-shore and wasn't likely to encounter any subs out in the South Atlantic.

As she took departure from Cape Farewell she was heading for the Cape of Good Hope, and I'm sure that faith and hope became stronger in the hearts of all on board as they drew closer to it.

Loading up a ship with civilians, women, and children and sending her on a 12,000 miles voyage unescorted most of the way, is what military men call a calculated risk— when they get away with it! They had gotten away with this trip by the "Ceramic" several times. She could make seventeen knots so a submerged U-boat had no chance of getting a shot at her unless she happened to run almost over the U-boat. A submarine on the surface might catch her, but if she saw the sub in time she could make a long race out of it, get off warning signals and probably stay out of range from the U-boat's gun till help arrived. Besides, she had that gun of her own. She was well protected in the convoy during the early and most dangerous part of the voyage . . . and, finally, she had to sail. You simply can't cut off all passenger traffic to Australia for five and one-half years.

At sunset on December 6, the "Ceramic," four hundred miles west of the Azores, boiled along on course southeast bucking a choppy sea in a restless empty ocean. The sky was overcast, and a spanking southwest breeze was threatening to make up into a gale, keeping most of the passengers below decks. On the bridge the Captain squinted at the sky and said:

"We're getting a good break on the weather this trip."

"Yes sir," said the mate, "It'll be black as the inside of a hold under that overcast tonight."

"And if this wind freshens up any more no sub would

be on the surface even if he could see," added the Captain.

"Right you are, sir."

But even as they spoke a baleful eye on the other side of the horizon to the west was focussed on the masts above them, and a submarine, running at high speed on the surface, obscured from them by the curvature of the earth, had settled down on a course that would intercept the "Ceramic" about midnight.

By ten that night when the watch passed the word, "Four bells and all's well," the children had said their prayers and been tucked into their bunks. A few passengers still lingered in the salons but the increasing motion of the ship had sent most of them off to bed too. The night was even blacker than the Captain had predicted and the wind was still rising. At this time the submarine to the west was ten degrees forward of the "Ceramic's" starboard beam and had closed to ten thousand yards. The thrashing of the "Ceramic's" screws was plainly audible in the submarine's sensitive listening devices. The U-boat's skipper, coached by his sound operator exactly where to point his powerful night glasses, could see her blacked-out shape well enough for his purpose.

Two hours later eight bells had sounded, the mid-watch had just come on and nearly all passengers were sound asleep, when the "Ceramic" shuddered as if she had hit a submerged rock. All sleepers awoke instantly, not knowing why, and sat up in their bunks while the ship still quivered from the blow—which might have been from a big wave. For ten awful seconds of suspense in the darkened cabins there was no sign of anything wrong, except the decreasing beat of the vibration from the "Ceramic's" engines. Then the silence was shattered by the clanging of the alarm, each stroke of the gong's hammer pounding directly on the hearts of all on board. Panic is only a few seconds away at a time like this but it takes more than what had happened so far to release it. The ship had simply quivered, the throbbing of the engines was decreasing, the heart beats of all hands were racing. But there was no real cause for alarm yet—except the clanging of those gongs.

This couldn't be another drill—not at midnight! Lights popped on in the cabins behind shielded ports, children looked into their mother's eyes to find out what it all meant, saw fear written there and their own little faces became grave. Then stewards, trying to keep their voices from quaking, were passing the word, "All hands fall in at your lifeboat stations immediately."

Men, women and children scrambled out of their bunks, pulled on shoes without lacing them, threw on overcoats, grabbed life preservers and started hurrying through the passageways to the upper decks. Lights still burned brightly in the passageways and salons.

When the people got on deck the inky blackness blinded them. For some minutes, until their eyes refocussed, they saw nothing. Women with children clinging to them groped their way along the deck. Few knew it yet, but that deck led from there to eternity! They were feeling their way through the darkness down the exit passageway leading out of this world. The wind, now nearing half a gale, moaned through the upper works ominously. There was no outward panic . . . just stark, numbing, unbelieving fear. The ship began to wallow in the trough of the sea, but as yet there was no sign on the upper decks that she was badly hurt—no fire, no wreckage, no wounded crying out. It seemed incredible that anything serious could be wrong with the stout ship that had brought them all through safely so far.

On the bridge the Captain got the chief engineer on the phone, "What do you say, Chief?"

"We're finished Captain," came the answer. "The starboard engine room has had it. Water rising fast in the port and I've got to abandon it. Get your boats out while you can." The wind moaned louder in the rigging.

"God have mercy on us," said the Captain despairingly. "Pass the word 'Abandon Ship.' . . . Get those boats clear of the side as soon as they hit the water."

As the awful word "Abandon Ship" was swept along the decks by the mournful wind, it was so fantastic that many simply couldn't believe it. It seemed absurd to lower boats on a night like this. It was bad enough just to be at sea on a big ship in this kind of weather; leaving the ship in those tiny open boats would be suicide. The ship was still firm under the passengers' feet, her steel plates brushed the wind aside and her hull rode the seas steadily, supporting the passengers safely forty feet above the waves. Many refused to get into the boats, sobbing and pleading with the ship's officers to wait awhile.

At 0021 another heavy blow as if from a giant sledge hammer struck the "Ceramic" and there was a muffled rumbling inside her. The Captain, knowing that to remain blacked out could serve no further purpose, flashed the deck lights on now. To the people on deck, this showed no visible proof that the ship was badly hurt. Many of these people had lived through the blitz in London and that latest jar to the ship was nothing like as terrifying as a near miss exploding half a block away. Maybe some poor men down in the engine room had been killed, but up here on deck everyone was still safe. The seamen all knew when the lights flashed on that this was indeed the end.

"All hands in the boats," came the cry along the deck. "Last call before we lower away." This brought stark reality home to the dazed undecided passengers. Now they had to make up their minds whether to get into those tiny boats where their chance of survival seemed one in a million, or to stay with this still solid but certainly doomed ship. The only choice seemed whether to drown in a large group with the ship or to drown in small groups out there in blackness. Many chose to stay with the ship.

The "Ceramic's" crew of veteran seamen lowered a dozen crowded boats into the water safely before the first casualty occurred. As the next boat started down, the forward fall jammed and the after one slipped off the cleat. The boat hung up vertically by the bow and spilled men, women and children into the stormy water thirty feet below. The first screams heard that night came from these unfortunate people . . . but they were soon drowned out.

As boats got into the water safely and careened clear of the ship, they were swallowed up in the darkness. Those on deck watching them disappear into the gale still felt they had chosen the lesser evil in staying aboard. If the huddled humans in the pitching, spray-drenched boats were still able to think, they probably regretted not having stayed behind. Not much was said in the boats. There was an occasional muffled sob as the people hung onto the thwarts and stared back at the lights on the deck of the huge ship that loomed above them and rode the sea so steadily.

At 0040 a third torpedo crashed into the already mortally wounded "Ceramic." It was just a question of time before the gallant old lady would go down, but an implacable enemy out there in the darkness was getting impatient. Now the "Ceramic's" last electric generator coasted to a stop, all lights dimming slowly and finally going out. The "Ceramic" was dead . . . but her corpse still floated.

By now those left on board knew the end was close at hand. But there was nothing to be done, except to make their peace with God and hope He would be merciful when they appeared before Him. In many ways, death came more mercifully during the air raids in England. When a blockbuster hit a residential district, the lives of men, women and children were snuffed out in a flash of flame. But it was all over in a moment. The survivors knew before their ears stopped ringing from the explosion that they were still alive and their minds were sorting the new problems of life out of the rubble. On the deck of the "Ceramic," you knew you could *not* survive, and there was no use planning beyond the end of another hour.

There were few children left on board to await the end. Almost all mothers had clung to the last straw of hope, loaded their youngsters into the boats and climbed in with them, knowing in their hearts they were just prolonging the agony. Though the life boats bobbed around crazily, they remained afloat with their cargoes of humanity. But the nearest land was four hundred miles and the wind whipped sheets of spray off the tops of the waves which were getting bigger.

At one o'clock, a quartermaster on watch on the bridge, struck two bells, as he always had at this time, during thirty years of faithful seafaring service. Some of those huddled in the darkness on deck began to think that maybe a miracle was occurring. In the past hour three torpedoes had hit, but the gallant old "Ceramic" still floated. Maybe the sub would go away now . . . and maybe the "Ceramic" would remain afloat. The dirge that the wind was playing in the rigging increased in pitch.

At 0102 a fourth torpedo hit the "Ceramic" and broke

her back. A big ship doesn't suddenly snap into two pieces like a stick of wood when she breaks her back. It takes time—perhaps twenty or thirty seconds. She jack-knifes in the middle, the bow and stern rising out of water and the midship section going under. This happens ponderously with the tempo of a heavy roll from port to starboard. It is accompanied by the unearthly noise of steel plates tearing apart, being crumpled like tissue paper, of internal explosions, escaping steam, and loose gear in the ship smashing down across the slanting decks. For the second time this night screams filled the darkness.

In less than half a minute the bow and stern of the "Ceramic" floated alongside each other at a forty-five-degree angle with a jumbled mass of humanity clawing at the decks as they slid down into the sea. In a few more seconds the two broken pieces of the ship sank gurgling into the depths leaving behind on the wind-whipped water a welter of wreckage, life rafts, and struggling humans.

Of the 650 souls on board the "Ceramic," perhaps only twenty had been killed by the torpedoes. Another twenty had drowned when the life boat hung up at the davits. Perhaps a dozen were crushed inside the ship when she broke her back. About a hundred more were dragged down in the suction when the broken fragments of the ship went under. When it was all over, about five hundred were still alive, half of them in a score of bobbing lifeboats, and the rest paddling around in the oil-covered, wreckage-strewn sea. All knew in their hearts that the end of their lives was at hand but couldn't help struggling to postpone the end a few more minutes. There was a deathly silence broken only by the wailing of the wind and of children. The tiny island of Flores in the Azores was four hundred miles to the east.

We flash back seven hours now and shift to the bridge of the submarine U-515, Kapitän Leutnant Werner Henke, Knight's Cross with Oak Leaves, Commanding. Henke, an efficient and ambitious U-boat commander is damning his luck at being in transit out here in the empty ocean when he knows that many juicy convoys are converging on Gibraltar to support the invasion of Africa which started just a month before. As Henke sweeps his eye around the sharp and empty horizon, he thinks bitterly of how some of his rivals and comrades will be piling up big scores now simply because they were assigned to good areas, whereas, he, Henke, through no fault of his own, is out here where there is nothing. In another couple of hours it will be dark and even if there were any steamers out here he might not see them.

Suddenly a flaw in the horizon catches his eye as it sweeps around. When he concentrates on it he can see nothing, but when he puts his ten-power glass on it, his heart skips a beat. "Achtung," he barks, "Alarm. . . . Top masts in sight." There are two tiny spars sticking up over the horizon, well separated as on a long ship, broad on the port bow.

"I thought I saw something, Kapitän, and was just about to report to you," said a lookout apologetically.

Henke was too engrossed to reply.

He observed the bearing carefully for two minutes and noted it remained nearly constant. This meant he was already on a good intercept course. "Estimated distance sixteen sea miles," he barked down the hatch—"All engines full speed—come right 30 degrees." Running at nineteen knots he would be able to hold his present favorable position forward of the steamer's beam, while he slowly converged on her after dark until close enough to fire torpedoes.

Down in the diesel room the machinist's mate on watch spun his throttle wide open and remarked to his oiler, "Ach, maybe if we sink this one we can live with this man." "Ja," said the helper, "he is very severe when we have no success."

On the bridge Henke had soon solved the enemy speed as being seventeen knots—no zigzag. "It's probably a fast convoy," he thought, "And pretty soon I'll see the escorts' masts coming up over the horizon." By sunset it became apparent that no escorts' masts were going to appear, but two more of the steamer's did, indicating she was a big one. She was running independently, relying on her speed to escape attack. Henke estimated her at 20,000 tons, probably carrying troops to Egypt via the Red Sea and Suez.

As it grew darker Henke drove in on the surface at high

speed, gaining bearing ahead of the "Ceramic" and working carefully into position by eye and by sound bearings of the "Ceramic's" screws. In a few hours he would be in perfect position for a close range shot at this juicy target. Henke's trained mind dropped into the groove worn by many previous attacks. His only thoughts now were target, angle, course, speed, depth setting, and the number of torpedoes to fire, weighed against his own position, course and speed.

All six of his torpedo tubes were loaded and ready. A fat target like this one, probably loaded to the gunwales with troops, certainly justified a spread of four torpedoes to allow for errors in estimating enemy course and speed. But Werner Henke didn't make such errors. With arrogant confidence he ordered, "Stand by for double shot. Tubes one and four. Keep other tubes ready."

Henke never questioned his first judgement that this was a troop ship—and it probably wouldn't have made any difference if he had. By this time the rules of Prize Warfare had gone down the drain and both sides sank enemy ships without warning whether they were war vessels, cargo, troop, or passenger ships. By midnight the U-515 was in position to shoot, 1200 yards on the "Ceramic's" starboard bow, giving the torpedoes a perfect ninety-degree track angle.

In the forward and after torpedo rooms the expert crews made final settings on the "eels" as Henke announced them over the battle circuit. "Depth setting 6 meters, gyro angle zero, ½ degree spread." The chief torpedomen personally checked each setting, reported back to control, "Ready," and stood by with stop watches to check the time of the explosions against the known running time of the torpedoes to the target.

At 0001, Henke, with his eye glued to the attack periscope in the conning tower, gave the order, "Achtung. . . . Fire one. . . . Fire four."

In the forward torpedo room there were muffled coughs inside tubes one and four and the chief torpedoman punched his stop watches. All hands waited tensely, listening while the sweep second hands of the watches counted out the sands still remaining in the hour glass of

Father Time for the "Ceramic." Henke kept his eyes glued to the periscope.

At 0003-½, there was a light tick on the U-515's hull from the shock waves of an underwater explosion, followed a split second later by a rumble heard throughout the boat. Cheers went up in the forward torpedo room and the chief, glancing at his watch, reported over the battle circuit, "Number one hit, sir." Henke, peering through the periscope, saw no indication that anything had happened to the "Ceramic." His torpedoes were set to run deep and the explosion had been swallowed up inside the "Ceramic."

The sound operator in his cubbyhole just abaft the torpedo room, with the sensitive underwater phones clamped to his ears sang out, "Number four hit but did not explode." The chief relayed this message to conn while the crew of tube one looked smugly at the crew of tube four, who looked miserably at the chief and braced themselves for a tongue lashing.

In a few minutes the Captain's voice came over the loudspeakers, "Target is stopping. . . . Set target speed zero. . . . Target angle ninety degrees. . . . Depth four meters." The readjustments on the next torpedo were quickly made.

For the next ten minutes Henke used his engines skillfully to hold the boat in position for the next shot, if one were necessary. The sub rode up and down with the seas, the blacked out target clearly visible in the periscope, lying to but apparently unhurt. At 0018, Henke gave the order, "Achtung—fire two." at 0020-½, the tick followed by the muffled roar came back and the chief sang out, "Number two hit, sir."

The lights came on along the "Ceramic's" deck and Henke could now see a dozen boats being lowered, but was too far away to make out any details. He waited twenty minutes more until the boats were clear and gave the order, "Fire three." When this torpedo exploded, the "Ceramic's" lights went out, but the dark shape of her hull still riding on an even keel was plainly visible in the periscope. "There's something wrong with these damned torpedoes," muttered Henke. "Port engine ahead full speed, starboard engine back one third," he barked.

Keeping the periscope trained on the target, Henke turned his boat carefully on her heel and drew a bead on the "Ceramic" with his after tubes. One hour after his first shot he fired tube five, and two minutes later he let out a yell of triumph, "Gott, she's breaking in two!"

Turning to his radio operator, Henke asked, "Did she get off an SOS?"

"Yes, Kapitän," said the radioman. "SS Ceramic, 18,800 tons, but there is heavy static tonight and I doubt if anyone heard it. . . . Shall I send another for her?"

"Nein," replied Henke. "Bridge watch on deck," he ordered, and led the way up the conning tower hatch himself. A half gale was blowing now, but the U-boat with all ballast tanks blown out rode lightly up and down with the waves like a cork. Occasionally a sea broke across the weather deck, but the bridge was dry, except when a sheet of spray slapped the men's face like a whip.

"Engines ahead one-third," said Henke. Cruising slowly through the darkness he could hear faint cries in the water as he neared the spot where the "Ceramic" went down. The people in the water heard his motors and were trying to attract his attention. He still thought he had sunk a troop ship. When the cries were close aboard on both sides he said, "Turn on the searchlight."

The first thing the searchlight picked up on the starboard side was a woman clinging to a piece of wreckage with her right hand and clasping the body of a child with her left.

"Train right," said Henke to the searchlight operator.

The searchlight swung thirty feet across the oily water and spotlighted a group on a raft. Henke put his glass on them and saw one man, five women, and several children.

"Train right," he said.

The search light swung round again. It swept over several oil soaked globs in the water. You couldn't tell what sex they were because the figures were black with oil and nothing but the whites of eyes showed up in the searchlight.

The light stopped on a piece of wreckage with a lone figure hanging onto it. Henke put his glass on it and decided it was a man. "All engines stop. Come right twenty degrees," he ordered. "Two men get up on the bow to heave a line.'

As U-515 coasted to a stop alongside this piece of flotsam, the sailors on the plunging fo'c's'le heaved their line and soon hauled aboard Jonathan Doe, 70 years old, whose last kin in England had been killed in a bombing raid six months previously, and who was on his way to join his great grandchildren in Australia.

The two sailors helped the exhausted old man across the heaving deck and up to the bridge. Henke addressed him in English. "Where were your troops bound for?"

"Troops?" said Jonathan Doe, "We were not a troop ship, we were a passenger ship bound for Australia."

"So-o-o," said Henke, "No troops at all?"

"There were soldiers and sailors on board, going home to see their families,' said the old man.

"But most of the passengers were civilians?" asked Henke.

"That's right."

"Where is the ship's Captain?" asked Henke.

"I don't know, sir."

"Put him back in the water," said Henke after a pause. His men did as he had ordered. While this interview had been going on with the U-515 dead in the water, a dozen humans had swum alongside, seized the beading around the edge of the heaving deck, and were hanging on pleading for rescue. Eight men, a woman and two sturdy youngsters were slammed against the side by each wave and were alternately submerged and lifted out of the water as the sub rode up and down with the sea.

"Half speed ahead,' said Henke, and as the sub gathered headway, three of the men lost their holds and disappeared in the darkness astern. Eight people still hung onto their only hope for life.

"Full speed ahead," said Henke. At sixteen knots they all washed loose except one sailor, the woman, and one teen-aged boy, all on the starboard side. They hung on for dear life. After he saw that he couldn't shake them off, Henke said to a seaman, "Go down there and get those people clear of the side." The seaman did as his captain had ordered.

Down in the starboard engine room the machinist's

mate and the oiler looked at each other quizzically as their engine seemed to falter for half a revolution, but then resumed its regular rhythm.

"Propeller hit a piece of wreckage," said the machinist's mate.

"Yeah. Lots of it around here. Hope we didn't hurt the wheel." The machinist's mate put his hand on the crank case for a few seconds, feeling for any strange vibration. "No harm done," he said.

Meantime, in the searchlight probing the darkness, a dozen lifeboats and scores of crowded rafts were visible, in addition to hundreds of heads alongside pieces of wreckage. Henke hailed three life boats and asked for the Captain, but all denied that he was aboard. Pretty soon the light settled on a raft with three figures on it, obviously men. Henke stopped his submarine about ten feet away from it and hailed, "Who are you?"

"Merchant seaman Jones," came the first answer.

"Doctor Smith," came the second.

"Sapper Munday, Royal Engineers," came the third.

"Heave him a line," said Henke, and Sapper Munday was dragged aboard.

Henke noted that he was wearing a British uniform. "You are a soldier?" he asked.

"Yes sir," said Sapper Munday, "Of the Royal Engineers."

"Take him below," said Henke. "Engines ahead full speed."

The other occupants of the raft had meantime swum over to U-515 and had dragged themselves aboard the after deck and collapsed, lying face down on the gratings.

"Stand by to dive," ordered Henke.

Three lookouts plummeted down the hatch. The lookout for the after sector paused for a second, nodded his head aft and said, "Kapitän—there are two men on deck. . . ."

"Get below!" said Henke, and followed him down himself, slamming the hatch a few seconds before the U-515 submerged and departed from the scene.

The rest of that night Henke tossed in his bunk down in his cabin amidships, alone with his conscience. He assured himself that his conscience was clear, and it was—

at least so far as his official orders were concerned. U-boat captains had been authorized by Admiral Doenitz since 1940 to torpedo enemy ships of all classes, except hospital ships, without warning. And besides, this one was armed—he had seen the gun on her stern. He was certainly in the clear on that, although he wished he could forget the pleas of the children that still rang in his ears. So far as rescuing survivors was concerned, there could be no blame put on him—Doenitz had plainly said, "Don't ever endanger the safety of your boat to rescue survivors." A U-boat is jammed to capacity with its own crew of sixty aboard. The only way he could possibly have rescued a couple of hundred survivors would have been to take them on deck—and then he would have given up his ability to submerge and been a sitting duck for RAF aircraft. The "Laconia" incident had shown that this was foolhardy. Planes bombed any submarines they saw, not stopping in the heat of battle to count the people on deck or check their identity cards to make sure they weren't friends.

Of course, some of the scenes he had witnessed and the pleas he had heard would be etched into his brain the rest of his life. But war is a ruthless business, you've got to be tough to win, and his conscience was clear. So Werner Henke rolled over in his bunk, but couldn't sleep well that night or a couple of nights thereafter.

As the U-515 slunk away from the scene of the disaster, at least four hundred people were still alive. Had the weather been moderate perhaps fifty or so of those on the rafts might have survived for several days and might have been sighted by passing planes or ships. The lifeboats could have sailed to the Azores in about a week and over half the two hundred and fifty people in the boats would have survived that ordeal.

But that night the wind increased, and next day it blew a whole gale. Huge breaking rollers swept majestically across the surface of the sea. When they broke, they flung lifeboats end over end, spilling the occupants into the boiling waters and smashing the capsized boat down on top of them. By sunset, December 7, there were no survivors of the "Ceramic" except Sapper Munday.

At noon of December 7, Henke wrote in his log the

seaman's terse description of a howling gale: "Wind NW, Force 10, Sea 8 (very rough), rain and hail. . . . Submerging on account of weather."

When Henke returned from that cruise, he made a full report of the "Ceramic" incident and turned in Sapper Munday to verify his tonnage claim. Admiral Doenitz approved what he had done and credited Henke with twice the "Ceramic's" tonnage toward another oak leaf because she was a troop ship. Sapper Munday was sent by Doenitz to Berlin and handed from one agency of the Nazi party to another, where they did various things to him which I have no way of knowing about.

Early in 1943, Sapper Munday spoke on a radio broadcast from Berlin and gave the first news that the British had of the "Ceramic's" fate. This news made the British very angry and, as will appear later, started an ominous chain of events for Henke.

A year and a half later in April 1944 this chain of events came to a new head when my hunter killer group sank the U-515 just a few hundred miles from where she sank the "Ceramic."

As will be related in due course, the circumstances of the U-515's sinking, in which we rescued Henke and most of his crew, played a key role in starting another chain of events that finally put the U-505 alongside the Museum of Science and Industry.

Chapter

14

LANGE

ON NOVEMBER 18, 1943, Oberleutnant Harald Lange reported aboard the U-505, read his orders to the crew, and took command. He was stepping into a tough spot.

His crew's morale, ground thin and brittle by six months of continuous failures, had been completely shattered by the brutal shock of having their captain desert them in battle. By now the U-505 was known throughout the Second Flotilla as an unlucky boat, the most damning label you can hang on a ship.

This crew should have been broken up and distributed among a dozen other boats. But in war time you can't always adopt the best solution to problems like this. Shaking down a new crew would put the U-505 out of operations for at least three months. The next best solution was to hand pick the new skipper. Lange was specially selected by U-boat headquarters as being the kind of a man who could handle the tough problem in leadership that they were dumping in his lap.

In technical knowledge he was fully qualified, having commanded a similar type boat. But much more important, he was a more mature man than most current U-boat skippers. He was a Reserve Officer who in peace time had been first officer on a merchant ship. He had learned to handle men without benefit of rigid military discipline by winning their confidence and exercising leadership. Not being a professional naval officer, he was perhaps more tolerant of human frailties than a regular might be, although he didn't pamper his men and insisted that important things be done exactly right. But he understood what this crew had been through, was informal in his dealings with them, and made allowances in small things. He was a "big brother" type, which was exactly what this crew needed if it were to be kept together.

The boat sailed for her first cruise under Lange on Christmas Day, 1943. The one thing Lange needed from Santa Claus more than anything else was some sort of a success to take the curse off their long series of failures. His luck was good, and within three days he had it.

On December 28, there was a battle out in Biscay between some British cruisers and a group of German motor torpedo boats and destroyers in which one of the German ships got sunk. The U-505 heard gunfire from this battle about sixty miles away in her sensitive underwater microphones. At sunset she got orders from U-boat headquarters to pick up survivors.

Although Biscay was now a dangerous place for surfaced U-boats at night, Lange ran surfaced at full speed for five hours to reach the scene of battle and remained surfaced all night searching the area. At 5:00 A.M. he found seven life rafts lashed together and hauled aboard thirty-three survivors from the destroyer T-25, including her skipper.

As the crew of the U-505 dragged the crew of the T-25 out of the water, their morale got just the kind of shot in the arm it needed. They saw gratitude and admiration shining from the eyes of a group of their peers. After six months of constant failure, failure so conspicuous that their U-boat comrades were avoiding them along the waterfront, the U-505's crew suddenly found themselves heroes in the eyes of the surface Navy.

These thirty-three unexpected guests recorded their thanks in the U-505's guest book, now on exhibit in the Museum as follows:

31 December 1943

In August of this year the crew of the destroyer T-25 was able to pick up a large part of the crew of the U-106 about 13° W.

On 28 December 1943 the crew of the U-505, belonging to the same flotilla as the U-106, nearly at the same place picked up a part of the crew of the T-25.

The T-25, with flag flying, sank in an encounter with a heavy and a light British cruiser. We are grateful to our rescuers of the U-505 for all their good fellowship and we are thankful that a kind fate will enable us to start very soon on another mission against the enemy. Let us hope that we shall soon succeed in forcing him to his knees.

In this hope we wish the U-505 lots of luck and a safe return.

[signed] WIRICH V. [illegible]
Lieutenant Commander,
Commanding Officer, T-25."
[Signatures]

Btsmt. Wagener (boatswain)
Mech. Mt. (A) Heidtmann (mechanic)
Mtsmt. Timm (boatswain)
Masch. Ob. Gefr. Wendler (machinist)
Matr. Ob. Gefr. Voss (seaman)
Strm. Gefr. Wallbraun (quartermaster)
Willi Buerger

Gefr. Kurt Wissner (seaman)
Matr. Gefr. Arthur Biewald (seaman)
Matr. Gefr. Heinz Frenzel (seaman)
Matr. Ob. Gefr. Guenther Waschult (seaman)
Kurt Pfleider
Fk. Gefr. Wrede (radioman)
Matr. Ob. Gefr. Weme (seaman)
Masch. Gefr. Karnauke (machinist)
Masch. Gefr. Brausdorf (machinist)
Fk. Ob. Gefr. Liebau (radioman)
Fk. Gefr. Handt (radioman)
Matr. Obergefr. Joseph Friedl (seaman)
Kadett (See) Daedtow (midshipman)
Kadett (See) Scheel (midshipman)
Masch. Gefreiter Gettschling (machinist)
Masch. Gefr. W. Jallasch (machinist)
Masch. Gefr. Prediger (machinist)
Wolfgang Panzer
Mech. Gefr. (1) Wittenberg (mechanic)
Mtr. Ob. Gefr. Hermann Stimbach (seaman)
Masch. Gefr. Kurt Hoecker (machinist)
Masch. Gefr. Hans Goebelt (machinist)
Masch. Gefr. Ewald Jellonek (machinist)
Seekadett Heinz Keller (midshipman)
Masch. Gefr. Paul Grosser (machinist)

The U-505 welcomed these torpedo boat sailors literally with open arms. Naturally, they were pleased to help shipwrecked comrades in distress. But the real godsend was that this finally took them off the hook as the weak sisters of the Second Flotilla. They could look any of their friends in the eye now and tell them to go to hell.

But as the boat put into Brest with her survivors on New Year's Day, 1944, her bad luck struck again, and something happened to one of her main propulsion motors. All the war diary says about this is: "0935. Fire in electric motor because of inrush of water and resultant short circuit. 0945 put out fire with extinguishers."

This burned out a main propulsion motor and laid her up in the dockyard again for another two and one-half months. But, at any rate, this time they were in Brest, not Lorient. They had no bad reputation to live down here, and their rescue of the T-25's crew gained them some stature.

On March 16, 1944, the U-505 sailed from Brest for Freetown on what was to be her last voyage as a German U-boat. This time she finally got out of Biscay. She spent twelve days doing it, running 228 hours submerged and 60 surfaced. Contrast this with her first trip to Freetown under Loewe just over a year before. On her first twelve days of that trip she ran submerged 34 hours and 258 surfaced. This tells an eloquent story of how the tide had turned in the meantime. Submarines were no longer prowling surface raiders that submerged occasionally. They were underwater fugitives that popped up for brief periods when they hoped the coast was clear.

Early in April, the U-505 passed close to the U.S.S. "Guadalcanal" and her task group which I commanded. We were hunting for U-boats coming out of Biscay, but we didn't see U-505 and she didn't see us. A few days later, on April 9 and 10, we sank two boats from the U-505's flotilla in the area she had just passed through. But her number wasn't up, yet.

Proceeding south and starting with Freetown on April 24, she reconnoitered every harbor along the Ivory Coast as far east as Grand Bassam. She looked in at Monrovia, Harpers Village, Port Bouet, and Grand Lahou, but saw nothing. Returning west she took station off Cape Palmas and spent the rest of her time patrolling back and forth there across the route from Cape Palmas to the Cape of Good Hope. All she saw there were three neutral steamers, some fishing vessels, and one large British passenger steamer probably home bound from Australia on the "Ceramic's" former run. She gave chase but the liner was too fast and got away. From examination of his war diary, I would say that Lange patrolled diligently, in fact aggressively, but there just wasn't much traffic there any more. The Mediterranean was open to Allied shipping now and Freetown was practically out of business as a shipping center.

Lange's diary records several serious machinery breakdowns during this period which could have justified a return to base. But he repaired them at sea and remained in his operational area. Maybe he figured he was better off near Freetown than he would be in France at this stage of the war. And besides, Doenitz himself had said it was important to keep boats at sea and pin down Allied anti-submarine forces.

While patrolling off Cape Palmas he ran at periscope depth in daytime and on the surface between sunset and sunrise. He only had to crash dive to get away from airplanes nine times in about a month. Three times his lookouts actually sighted aircraft. Six times his Naxos gear gave warning before any plane could be seen. No aircraft sighted him, and no bombs were dropped near him.

On May 24, the U-505 departed from the Cape Palmas area homeward bound. She was returning empty handed, but so were most of the U-boats these days. At least, after six months of continuous failures, she had now completed a war cruise and her people would get credit for ninety days frontline service when they got back. She was no longer a barnacle on the pier in Lorient. She was back in good standing as an operational unit of the Second Flotilla.

For the next six days Lange proceeded north hearing and seeing nothing until the night of May 29, at 10:16 P.M., when he had to crash dive for a Naxos warning. This was the beginning of a series of such warnings which did him more harm than good. It seemed that from here on almost every time he came up to recharge his battery, he would get a Naxos warning from the radio room. Often Naxos "saw" aircraft and cried "wolf, wolf" when the planes were much too far away to be any threat. But the Naxos didn't specify how far away they were and there was nothing that a prudent skipper could do but crash dive. Lange's battery got more and more anemic because the Naxos wouldn't let him stay surfaced long enough to recharge it.

On May 30, the following entries appear in the U-505's war diary:

Date and Time	Account of Position, Wind, Weather, Sea, Light, Visibility of the Atmosphere, Moonlight, etc.	Events
30/5/44	East of the Cape Verde Is.	
0002	EK 1462	Crash dive. Naxos warning.
0045		Surfaced.
0102	EK 1462	Crash dive. Naxos warning. Warnings come in with staccato effect. Immediately after the dive nothing to be seen at periscope depth. Bright moonlight.
0301	EK 1462	Surfaced. Still blowing tanks.
0312		Crash dive! Naxos warning. The radar operator is obstinate; I cannot believe that it is a plane from the continent since at a distance of 180 m. from the base it could scarcely maintain contact here for 5 hours. Will surface again once more after two hours—after the moon has set.
0400	EK 1435	
0534	EK 1438	Surfaced. Dark night with bright stars. Warning at once. A/A guns manned. Warnings increasing rapidly from signal strength 3 to 4 and 5. Warning stops for a short time, then suddenly roars loudly in again. After blowing tanks, went off at high speed. Steered deceptive courses in NW part of square.
0540	EK 1435	Two distinct receptions in Naxos gear and Wanze! Both

		very loud, at times stopping.
0540		Believe there is now a third radar being heard in the receiver.
0549	EK 1435	Crash dive. Submerged to A-10. No bombs. I suspect carrier A/C—Possibly a carrier search group. Nothing in hydrophones. Determine to set off eastward toward the coast. On opposite courses to those steered for deception.

So the U-505 took an eighty-four mile jog due east toward the coast of Africa for forty-two hours to get out of the way of an aircraft carrier task group which the skipper thought was breathing down his neck.

This marks the beginning of a strange series of mistakes by Lange and by the only carrier task group that was anywhere near him, which was mine. When Lange was making his detour toward the African coast, I was just starting on his trail and thought I was three hundred miles from him. Actually, we were twice that distance apart, but he thought I was right on top of him. Maybe I smelt something in the air that night. Lange certainly smelt me for the next five days, although at this time I was taking a bath at least once a month whether I needed it or not!

Lange's Naxos kept seeing planes for the next five days which he assumed to be carrier-based planes but were not mine at all. All this time he was crossing under the air lane from South America to Africa and there was a constant stream of Air Force transports shuttling back and forth over this route that couldn't hurt him even if they wanted to. Those planes were perfectly harmless as far as U-boats were concerned. Most of their pilots wouldn't know a submarine if they saw one and the unarmed planes couldn't do anything about it if they did.

But all planes look alike on a radar scope at night. Every time Lange came up to charge batteries, a little dancing blip popped up in the Naxos scope and down he went again. I have been grateful ever since to my comrades in arms of the Air Force for this accidental assist

217

they gave me. It harried Lange and kept him short of volts and air.

When Lange started his eighty-mile jog toward the African coast because he thought I was on top of him, I was 600 miles to the southwest. None of my airplanes had yet been within 500 miles of him—nor had any planes except that harmless stream of transports overhead. In fact, it wasn't until thirty-six hours later that I shifted from a general patrol, looking for any sub that came along, to a specific search for this one in particular on which I thought we had a definite lead.

By noon of May 31, Lange was in trouble. All those Naxos warnings the night before had prevented him from getting any charge in his battery during darkness. It was about to poop out on him—in broad daylight. He surfaced for three quarters of an hour, ran at full speed and jammed enough juice into it to last him till dark.

Around eight o'clock that evening Lange records, "Heard six aircraft depth bombs in the far distance." (My task group dropped a depth charge pattern on a "possible" sound contact at this time, but we were 550 miles away. If it was our depth charges he heard, "In the far distance" is a classic understatement!) He surfaced at midnight and stayed up for six hours, getting a full charge in his can before another Naxos warning drove him down. Just before submerging he changed course north to parallel the coast again.

At noon on June 1, I was 420 miles southwest of U-505, blithely confident that I would nail him either that night or the next. Lange, north bound about sixty miles from the coast, was creeping along submerged waiting to see if that carrier task group which had been "on top of him," had gone away. He surfaced near midnight that night but crash dived an hour later (Naxos again). He came up again at 0330 but was driven down again in sixteen minutes.

The following entry appears in his war diary: "June 2—0330: Continuous night patrols—here under Cape Blanco!" (Note: The astonisher—"!"—is Lange's, not mine. At this time we were still 280 miles southwest and none of my planes had yet been close enough to him to be any threat.)

At 0315 the night of June 3, the war diary records: "Heard one A/C depth bomb in the far distance." (At this time my planes were bombing around a noisy sonobuoy at least sixty miles away.) Lange tried to surface again at 0710 but another Naxos warning drove him down before he could even start his diesels. He got no juice back in his can at all that night.

Since 0330 on the night of June 2, he had been driven down every time he stuck his conning tower up. Before he could get the boat aired out and the battery charged, he was down below again using up more air and battery.

By 1338 of June 3, he had spent forty-five and a quarter hours out of the previous forty-eight submerged. His battery was nearly flat again. The air in the boat was rotten and decaying. The crew was getting dopey. Once again he was forced to risk a daylight surfacing. It was a clear day with no clouds, and gambling on the vigilance of his lookouts, he surfaced for two hours and two minutes in the middle of the afternoon—and got away with it!

When I first noted from the war diary that he had run on the surface for that long, just sixty miles east of my task group, my only comment was, "Well, I'll be damned!"

I had based all my operations on the assumptions that U-boats were submerged all day long, and all but about two hours of the night. I had been flying only token patrols in daylight and saving my main effort for after dark. In this I was right ninety-nine per cent of the time, and Lange's war diary for the whole cruise proves it. But on June 3, the U-505 and I steamed on converging courses for two hours in broad daylight almost elbowing each other across the horizon and neither one of us detected the other! I'm glad we didn't now, because had my planes caught him on the surface that far away (as they should have) I doubt that we would have captured him. You can't send a boarding party from a carrier based airplane!

Lange stayed up no longer than he had to that afternoon—just long enough to give the boat a good airing, top off his compressed air tanks, and store up a little juice. He was up again soon after dark to get back on his regular night recharging routine. He stayed up for over four hours, gave everybody a good whiff of fresh air and didn't submerge until 0213, June 4.

Twice during that night my planes missed him by fantastically close margins. At 2200 when he was surfaced, one plane passed within six miles of him, forty-five miles northeast of the task group. Our aircraft radar was supposed to be good for at least ten miles on a surfaced sub. His Naxos was good for several times that far, and God knows it had apparently been picking up even the seagulls for the past week. My plane's radar didn't see him—he didn't see us! According to her war diary this was the first completely "quiet" night the U-505 had experienced for a couple of weeks.

About 0230, another of my planes flew smack over the spot where he had submerged only a few minutes before! Neither one saw the other. He just happened to submerge because he had got his business finished minutes before my plane would have certainly spotted him.

I have plotted this final night's operations out very accurately, using his war diary and my logs. Everyone who looks at this plot notes the two missed contacts by my planes, and sees our tracks converge to a point the next day, just shakes his head and mutters "It doesn't seem possible." We both blundered along practically within hailing distance all night and stumbled over each other at noon the next day!

When he submerged just in the nick of time at four bells of the mid watch, Lange had a well charged battery, a good belly full of fresh air, and had apparently shaken off the aircraft carrier which had been "right on top of him" a few days before. He and his crew settled down on their homebound course for a quiet and relaxed Sunday.

They had just piped down for their noonday dinner on Sunday, June 4, when the sound operator picked up propeller noises. His set wasn't working well and these noises sounded like they were far away. It was 1110 my time, 1210 Berlin time, which the U-boat was keeping.

Lange came up to periscope depth to have a look, expecting perhaps to see masts over the horizon and possibly to get in a shot at a merchant ship. Instead, a terrifying sight confronted him. There were war ships all over the ocean, with three destroyers converging on him at high speed, one nearly on top of him, and planes diving at him. He had stuck his head into a hornet's nest.

"Take her down," he barked and the depth control men wrestled with their big wheels in the compartment below. Lange was in a desperate fix. Obviously he had been spotted and would be depth charged within seconds. He had gotten a quick glimpse of a carrier and two destroyers in the distance. Six warships and God knows how many planes were on top of him. It would take a miracle to come out of this alive.

If he went deep immediately, the first depth charge attack from these destroyers might smash him so he couldn't surface. In the undisturbed water their first attack should be pretty accurate. It was better to ride out the first storm of explosions at shallow depth where tons of sea pressure would not be helping the explosions to crush his hull and where he would have some chance of surfacing if they did smash it open. If he survived the first attack then he might go deep under cover of the disturbed water. He held her at shallow depth and maneuvered violently to confuse sonar indications.

In a few seconds all hands, without benefit of ear phones, heard the throbbing of propellers passing right over them. They braced themselves and prayed. Nothing happened. Perhaps half a minute later, all hands heard sounds which they described later as like a cable dragging across their hull. (Note—this was from aerial machine-gun bullets hitting the water right above them.)

Since no depth charges had been fired and the water was still undisturbed, Lange still couldn't go deep. He squirmed and twisted, fired decoys, and cut loose with a desperation acoustic torpedo, aimed at nothing. . . . For some minutes the expected attack didn't come. With its defective listening gear the U-505 could only tell that destroyers were still nearby, but not how near.

The sound man reported a muffled series of rippling thuds. That would be a destroyer's Y guns arching her depth charges into the air. All hands braced themselves again for the explosions. Lange got set to go deep under cover of the disturbed water, if he survived the explosions that disturbed the water.

For what seemed like hours but was only two minutes nothing happened. The destroyer had evidently been sucked in by that decoy and had fired hedgehogs instead of depth charges at it.

There was another series of muffled thuds. "Right rudder," said Lange, trying to get out from under whatever they were dropping on him now.

Seconds later the whole ocean exploded around them in the most shattering convulsion any of them had ever felt. At least one of the charges in this salvo must have been only inches outside lethal range. All U-boat sailors who felt closer ones have probably been on the bottom of the sea for the past 12 years.

The lights went out, the rudder went over to hard right and jammed there, the boat rolled over on her beams and dumped the crew down on what should have been the starboard vertical bulkhead. Mess tables, crockery, and junk, showered down on top of them in the darkness.

As they were picking themselves "up"—or whichever way it was—someone in the after torpedo room yelled, "Water is coming in!" That meant the end for the U-505. All hands scrambled out of there, slammed the water tight door behind them, and ran forward to the control room shouting that the pressure hull had been split.

Lange had little choice of what to do and only seconds to make his choice. If the after torpedo room was flooding, there was no chance whatever to save the boat. Unless he could blow her to the surface immediately, she would sink taking all hands down with her. Even if the torpedo room were not flooding, his brutally battered boat had a jammed rudder and with that armada of ships and planes above him, further resistance would be foolhardy.

When a battle is hopelessly lost it is the captain's duty to save the lives of his men. When the eyes of sixty men, who have served you well, who trust you, and are on the brink of eternity look at you in extremis saying, "What now, my captain?" this is a heavy responsibility.

"Blow all tanks," Lange ordered. "Abandon and scuttle the boat."

Trembling hands spun valves by feel in the eerie darkness of the control room. The dim emergency lights came on, and the boat rolled slowly back upright. Pleading eyes focussed on the depth gauge to see if they were going up, to meet whatever awaited them up there, or down into oblivion. . . . They went up!

As the conning tower broke surface and before they could even get the hatch open, a grisly tattoo began beating on the hull—machine-gun bullets!

The captain is always the first man out of the hatch when a sub surfaces and just as Lange emerged, a 40 mm shell burst right next to him knocking him unconscious with severe wounds in the face and legs.

As others scrambled out of the hatch, they ducked a torrent of hot steel and plunged into the sea as fast as they could make it overboard. Two men picked up their captain and lugged him overboard to safety with them. Before all hands got up from below, the hail of bullets ceased, and the last few men had time to drag rubber boats out of their stowage places on deck, inflate them, and heave them overboard.

All this time the sub was running at six knots on the surface, making a tight circle to the right, and sinking further and further down by the stern. As she circled she drew the line of fire away from the men who had gone overboard and only one man was killed by all that gunfire. It was Gunner's Mate Fisher, a "plank owner" who had put the boat in commission. He was lying face downward alongside the conning tower hatch—the only German left aboard.

In a few minutes the fifty-nine survivors were clinging to the rubber boats, and Lange, boosted into a raft and conscious again by now, led his crew in three cheers for their "sinking" U-boat.

Thus ended the career of the U-505 as a man-of-war in the Third Reichskreigsmarine. Soon American destroyers hauled her crew out of the water, bandaged their wounds, gave them dry clothing and made them prisoners of war.

A week later in U-boat headquarters at Lorient, a familiar label went up alongside the U-505's name, "Overdue—presumed lost."

Chapter

15

HUNTER-KILLER TASK GROUP

WE NOW CHANGE to the Allied side of the battle and watch the rest of this story from the bridge of a jeep carrier operating in the U.S. Atlantic Fleet. In January 1944, at Norfolk, Virginia, I was given command of a hunter-killer task group made up of the small escort carrier U.S.S. "Guadalcanal" and her four escort destroyers. Groups such as this one were used to keep air cover over areas beyond the reach of shore-based aircraft. After these groups made their appearance in the Battle of the Atlantic, there were no more mid-ocean gaps and a sub might be attacked by aircraft anywhere at sea.

In addition to being Task Group Commander, I was also the Captain of the "Guadalcanal," a Kaiser-built prefabricated carrier of 11,000 tons commissioned only three months previously in Astoria, Oregon. On the "Guadalcanal" we had just finished our shakedown period working our way to the Atlantic via Panama and doing everything we could think of to make sailor men out of our crew of young farmhands, shoe clerks and high school boys, eighty per cent of whom had never seen salt water before. It had been a busy time.

When my crew were assembling before commissioning, we gave each new man who reported the following memo:

1. The motto of this ship will be "Can Do," meaning that we will take any tough job that is given to us and run away with it. The tougher the job, the better we'll like it.

2. Before a carrier can do its big job of sinking enemy ships, several hundred small jobs have got to be done and done well. One man falling down on a small job can bitch the works for the whole ship. So learn all you can about your job during this pre-commissioning period. Pretty soon we will be out where it rains bombs and it will be too late to learn.

Note: This ship will be employed on dangerous duty. We will either sink the enemy or get sunk ourselves depending on how well we learn our jobs now and do our jobs later.

ANYONE WHO PREFERS SAFER DUTY SEE ME AND I WILL ARRANGE TO HAVE HIM TRANSFERRED.

D. V. GALLERY,
Captain, U.S.N.

On the day of commissioning, we lined up on the flight deck in our best blue uniforms. Father Weldon said a prayer, I read the orders, and we hoisted the colors. I then made a short speech reminding all hands that we had just become the custodians of a name that was enshrined forever in American history. We would have to do great things to live up to what the Marines had already done in making this name immortal.

Next day Father Weldon, with my hearty approval, started a custom which I feel had an important influence on our subsequent career. He and I had both read battle reports from the Pacific telling of ships on which the Chaplain said a prayer over the loud speakers just before going into battle. Father Weldon and I agreed it was poor psychology as well as rather shabby theology to wait till you were looking down the enemy gun barrels before asking for God's help. We decided to ask for it every day as a matter of ship's routine.

From then on each morning at eight bells, right after colors, the boatswain's mate passed the word, "Attention to morning prayer." All hands would knock off whatever they were doing, uncover and face the bridge for a few moments while Father Weldon said a nonsectarian prayer to which Protestants, Catholics, Jews or Moslems could all say "Amen," simply reminding God that we needed His help and would be grateful for it that day. There are no atheists in the combat zones in wartime so our gerenal prayer was accepted by everybody in the spirit in which it was made: "We will do the best we can, please God help us."

These three things: the "Can Do" motto, the custodian of a great name, and faith in God, were what put life and purpose into that ship. Looking back now twelve years later, I think I can say we did live up to the name on our stern. I know, better than anyone else that we were a very lucky ship. But . . . we asked for God's help every day. We got it. . . .

During our shakedown cruise we had splattered some salt water on our eager-beaver crew and I had occasionally made some comments in seafaring language which couldn't be repeated at the baptismal font of a church. But by the end of it we were a reasonable facsimile of a fighting ship, except we hadn't yet been within 3,000 miles of a fight.

When we shoved off from Norfolk in January, 1944, on our maiden cruise, we were a cocky but unproven outfit. Like Doenitz's new U-boats, the big thing we needed was a victory to confirm that we were an effective fighting unit. We on the "Guadalcanal" were all sure that we were a great bulwark to the western world against Hitler's attempt to wrest freedom of the seas from us. But to the rest of the U.S. Atlantic Fleet we were just a big question mark. We had made it from Astoria to Norfolk without getting sunk; now we were going out where they played for keeps and the penalty for making small mistakes could be all hands getting both lungs full of salt water.

We drew our first blood within two weeks. On January 16, several hundred miles west of the Azores, we had a flight of eight "turkeys" out scouring the ocean on all sides of us. They were scheduled to land just before sunset. At this period, as the reader knows, U-boats seldom surfaced during daylight hours, but we had reason to believe that in this particular area and at this particular time, we might find something.

We found plenty. About twenty minutes before sunset two planes on their return leg to the ship spotted a group of three surfaced U-boats. It was a refueling operation in which a "milch cow sub" supplied oil to boats of the U-505 type. There was a solid overcast that day making it easy for my boys to approach unseen. They caught the cow with one of her calves sucking eagerly on the six-inch, hundred-foot-long rubber teats from her ample fuel tanks, and the other waiting its turn a few hundreds yards away. They barged in on this little domestic scene like a couple of hawks in a chickenyard and plastered depth charges all around the two subs that were encumbered with mooring lines and hoses so they couldn't submerge quickly. When the depth charge plumes subsided there was junk all over the ocean and about thirty Germans swimming around in a huge puddle of oil. All three subs had disappeared and until we got back from that cruise we thought we had certainly sunk two of them.

A month later the experts on the Cominch Assessment Board told us we had sunk the refueller (U-544) and badly damaged the one alongside her (U-129) which managed to limp home. The other one (U-516) got away. The credit line for this information probably belongs to some gal in Lorient who may have a lot of serious sins to answer for at the Last Judgment and may need all the character witnesses she can get when she appears before the heavenly throne. If so, I will be glad to testify in her behalf—if I am available in the heavenly area.

Jubilant cheers went up all over the ship when the loudspeakers from CIC announced we had just blasted two subs to the bottom. Now we were full-fledged, combat seasoned members of the Atlantic Fleet team. But the day's work wasn't over yet. We still had to get those eight planes on deck before it got dark.

As soon as we got word of the kill we recalled all planes. But curiosity is a strong human emotion, this was our first kill, and that oil puddle with the Germans paddling around in it was only 40 miles from the ship. I had detached a destroyer to pick up survivors, but every one of our pilots felt it was essential to the war effort for him to fly over there and take a gander at the scene. We put out some peremptory orders on the radio to "get the hell back here and land." But the boys later claimed there was a lot of static.

At this stage of the war we were all still primarily daytime pilots in the jeep carriers. Even on the big carriers in the Pacific, night flying was regarded as a hazardous business to be undertaken only by a few highly trained specialists. Landing on a jeep after dark was perhaps three or four times as difficult as landing on a

227

big carrier, because of the tiny deck, greater motion of the ship, and slower speed. By the time my pilots came wandering back from their rubberneck trip the sun had gone down, and under that solid overcast darkness was rapidly closing in on us.

The first four lads got aboard OK, but the fifth one landed too far to starboard and wound up with his right wheel down in the galley walk-way and his left wing and tail sticking out over the deck, fouling the landing area. We still had three planes in the air and the darkness was getting blacker every minute. I had a feeling then and there that we "had had it."

Ordinarily, getting the plane back on deck and out of the landing area should have been about a five minute job. But we were a new ship, the pressure was on us for the first time and we got butterfingered. After we had fumbled around for about ten minutes, the plane suddenly took a sickening lurch, swung its left wheel over the coaming of the flight deck and came to rest nose-down in the walk-way with its tail now sticking out at right angles across the deck into the landing area. My farmer boys messed around with it for five more minutes, getting nowhere, and then I said, "The hell with it—shove it overboard."

This was easier said than done. We heaved and we hauled, we grunted and we cursed, we pried with 4 x 4 beams, we pumped hydraulic jacks, and we even rammed into it with tractors. We couldn't move that damn plane. Like Uncle Remus' tar baby, it just sat there and wouldn't budge.

Finally, in desperation, I went ahead full speed on the engines, jammed the rudder hard over left, and whipped the ship into a tight turn thus listing her ten degrees to starboard to help jettison the crash. We still couldn't budge her.

By this time it was pitch dark and my boys in the air were getting low on gas. We couldn't fool around any longer. You don't like to turn on the lights when you know for sure there is at least one undamaged sub within a few miles of you. But sometimes you have to stick your own neck out for the boys who are sticking theirs out executing your orders, and you've got to have light to land on a jeep carrier at night. We lit the ship up like a waterfront saloon on a Saturday night and I made the following pitch to the boys in the air by radio phone:

"That tail doesn't stick out very far into the landing area. If you land smack on the center line your right wing will clear it. So just ignore that plane on the starboard side. . . . come on in and land."

Three very dubious "Rogers" came back out of the darkness.

For the next half hour those three lads made the most hair raising passes I've ever seen made at a carrier's deck, except maybe for dive bombing attacks. Our landing signal officer gave them wave-off after wave-off trying to get them to settle down. It was easy enough for us on deck to make believe that wreck wasn't there but the boys in the air just didn't have enough imagination. They kept edging over too far to port coming up the groove.

Finally, one of them reluctantly drifted over pretty close to the center line and the LSO gave him a desperate "cut," even though he was way too fast. He hit wheels first, bounced into the air, rolled over on his back and plunged into the sea to port. A plane guard destroyer fished all three men out of the water unhurt.

That was enough of that business. We turned on the searchlights of all ships, pointed them down at the water and ordered the other two planes to ditch alongside destroyers. The "cans" fished everybody out of the water, we blew out the lights, and got the hell out of that area.

What I went through that night was a miniature preview of something that happened to Admiral Mitscher in the Pacific a few months later. On the night of the "Marianas Turkey Shoot," Mitscher got caught with several hundred planes in the air after dark, and half of them wound up in the water. That was the night he gave the famous order, "Turn on the lights." When I heard about this some months later, I knew just exactly what had gone through his mind that night. But I never could see why the feature writers made such a fuss over the decision to turn on the lights and I doubt if Pete Mitscher could either. It was just one of those things that had to be done.

When something like this happens, the comment down

in the crew's bunk room that night is, "Boy-oh-boy, the Skipper sure loused it up tonight." Tomorrow you may stumble across a great success which was really none of your doing, and be a great hero in the bunk room that night. But tonight you are the lug who couldn't get a crashed airplane out of a catwalk and had to land two others in the water.

(Incidentally, the destroyer I sent back to look for those Germans in the oil pool didn't find any. With another sub nearby he couldn't very well turn on search lights, and men fighting for their lives in a cold, oil-covered ocean don't live long anyway.)

On the way back to Norfolk from the hunting ground, I made sure that never again would our flight deck be tied up by a plane in the cat-walk. We had a damaged turkey that would ordinarily have to be turned in for overhaul when we got back and I figured that a few more bumps and bruises on this turkey for the overhaul people to fix wouldn't overtax the war effort of the United States. We used the cripple as a guinea pig learning how to get wrecks out of the cat-walks.

We rolled it carefully over to the edge of the deck, eased one wheel down into the cat-walk, and held a stop watch on the deck crew while they wrestled it back up on the flight deck. When they got so they could do this in five minutes we eased both wheels into the cat-walk and cracked a big black whip over the boys until they could get it out of there in four minutes. After they became real experts and could throw up sheer legs, rig blocks and tackle, knew where to put jacks on 4 x 4 levers, or to use just plain manpower and could clear any wreck in three minutes, our battered airplane wasn't worth overhauling. So I said to the boys, "Start her with a run from the other side of the deck next time and see if you can get rid of it."

By this time the boys were sick and tired of dragging that airplane in and out of the cat-walks. All hands gathered around, put their backs into it, and had her making knots by the time they got her to the opposite deck edge. But the decrepit clunker just dropped both wheels into the cat-walk and stuck there. From the bridge I could almost imagine that poor old turkey looking back over its shoulder at me reproachfully. The boys had to drag it out and try again.

The plane became an albatross around the necks of the whole flight deck crew. Try as they would, and believe me they tried real hard, they just couldn't get up enough speed to heave it plumb overboard. The day before we got in to Norfolk I finally let the boys jack it overboard giving it a proper burial at sea with appropriate ceremony. Meantime, my lads had become outstanding experts in the Atlantic Ocean on how to get airplanes out of the unusual places that pilots sometimes park them in.

When we shoved off on our second cruise in March, I had made up my mind to do some experimenting with night flying. All jeep carrier skippers had been toying with the idea of flying around the clock and everybody knew we had to come to it eventually. Some ships had launched planes at midnight with enough gas to stay up and land after sunrise. Others had installed extra gas tanks so they could take off at sunset, stay up all night, and land at dawn, even though the planes could carry no weapons with this load. But this was just sticking our toes into the cold water tentatively. Somebody had to take the plunge of simply ignoring the darkness and scheduling operations around the clock.

The skipper who broke the ice would have to risk the necks of his pilots finding out how thick the ice was, and knowing that he would be running no physical risks himself. He also knew that he would be subjected to much smug criticism in high places if he failed, because the high command had not been willing to go on record and demand night flying. Besides, after you have spent twenty-five years in naval aviation and have attended the funerals of many good friends, you don't like to order the younger pilots to do things you haven't done yourself. For these reasons no skipper had yet undertaken full-fledged night operations. At it turned out later, this wartime generation of naval aviators could do lots of things we old timers had never done.

As we left Norfolk, I got the pilots together and explained what I had in mind to them. I wanted to operate around the clock during the next full moon, feeling our

231

way along as the moon waned to see if we could eventually work into pitch dark operations. They all took it in stride and said they would like to try it. They were a lot more confident about it than I was.

Our hunting area this time was between the Azores and Gibraltar in the well travelled lane used by U-boats creeping out of Biscay. There were plenty of U-boats coming out of Biscay, but in the first part of the cruise, flying mostly in daylight, we didn't see any. Checking back on war logs now, eleven years later, I can show you one night when a sub outbound from the Bay of Biscay on her way to Freetown, went almost between my legs when I had all my planes on deck. She was the U-505, but her rendezvous with us in the book of fate was set for about two and a half months later.

The fact that we patrolled over this area for about a month asking for trouble but not getting any shows how the U-boats had been beaten down by this time. Just a year before, any U-boat skipper would have rubbed his hands in glee at the prospect of getting a potshot at an aircraft carrier. Now, they avoided us.

Early in April, as the moon got bigger, we started getting our feet wet on our night landing program. It was scary business, we went at it gingerly, but it worked out well.

At sunset on the evening of April 8th, we launched four "turkeys" to patrol an area extending one hundred miles on each beam and sixty miles ahead. Our planes were all equipped with radar enabling them to spot objects on the surface of the sea below. However, the radar was not accurate enough to conduct an attack blind—you had to see the target visually before you could hope to straddle it with depth charges. And besides, a radar simply tells you there is "something" down there in the blackness—whether it is a Portuguese fishing trawler, an Allied ship running without lights, or a German submarine, is up to you to find out. You can do this either by dropping flares, which warns the sub to submerge, or if you're lucky and the moon is just right, you can approach so you see a silhouette in the silver path of the moonglow on the ocean. Tonight we would have a full moon.

After we launched this first flight we had a casualty on the flight deck which put two of our seven arresting gear cables out of commission. We would have to land the first flight with only five cables working, and I decided that in view of the highly experimental nature of our night landings, I would cancel further flights that night unless we definitely found a sub on the first flight. At midnight with a bomber's moon lighting our decks, we landed our first flight and passed the word, "Secure operations till sunrise."

I was down in Combat Information Center with the operations officer, combat intelligence officer and CIC officer waiting to quiz the pilots about any unusual happenings when the flight landed. The last pilot came in with a tense look and his eyes bugging out.

"Cap'n," he said, "I almost got him!"

We all looked up from the chart table a bit startled, "Wh . . . Wh . . . what do you mean!" I said.

"That submarine," he replied. "He barely got under in time to get away after I identified him.".

We all did a double take, and I said, "What submarine?"

"Didn't you get my radio an hour ago?" the land demanded.

I glared accusingly at the CIC officer and he shook his head. "Check with communications right away," I said.

After fifteen seconds of tense silence the report came over the voice tube, "Nothing whatever from Four Sail 8, sir."

"Captain, I sent it an hour ago and my radioman says they 'Rogered' for it," protested the pilot.

"We'll go into that later," I said. "Now let's get the dope on what happened." In brief, the lad had picked up a radar blip forty miles on our port quarter, had maneuvered around to get down moon from it and had sighted a small silhouette when only a quarter of a mile away from it. By the time he could be sure it was a sub, it was too late to drop depth charges so he whipped around in a flipper turn for another run, but when he completed his circle she was gone.

"You're sure it was a submarine?" I asked.

"Absolutely certain—I looked right down the conning tower hatch and saw lights inside as I went. . . ."

"How certain are you of the position?" I demanded.

"If you'll give me about two minutes to work it out, I'll give you a real good position on it."

"Okay, get busy," I said, and then turning to the operations officer, "Prepare to launch another flight immediately and have a second group of four ready to back it up."

In fifteen minutes we had four "turkeys" back in the air proceeding to the spot where the sub was last seen. I headed the whole Task Group over there so other planes would have less distance to fly if we regained contact. At 0130, April 9, two and a half hours after the first sighting, a "turkey" pilot caught the sub on the surface again fifteen miles from the first spot. But night bombing on a pinpoint target is a difficult business. My pilot reported, "All depth charges fell short—estimate no damage—Sub has submerged again."

Now we had confirmation of the first sighting, a new fix on it, and the Task Group was rapidly closing on it. The sub wouldn't get much of a charge in his battery tonight and would have to come up tomorrow. He should be a dead duck within twenty-four hours unless we muffed the ball.

We had one more sighting by our planes that night as the U-boat kept trying to come up and charge his battery. This time I was only fifteen miles away from him, and peeled off three of my destroyer escorts to be over the spot at dawn and try to root him out by sonar. An hour after sunrise they had him on sonar and the ocean rumbled and shook from depth charge explosions.

But even a surface ship with a solid sonar echo can't be sure of a kill every time. A depth charge must explode almost in contact with the tough pressure hull of a sub to get a kill. It takes some seconds for a depth charge to arch through the air and more seconds to sink through the water to its set depth, during which time a skillful sub skipper may maneuver out from under it. If he chooses to go down to say five hundred feet, he has quite a few seconds for his evasive maneuvering. If you miss him once he has that fifteen minutes reprieve

234

during which he doesn't have to creep silently but can run at high speed while the ocean is reverberating and disturbed water conditions give your sonar phony echoes.

This chap that we were after was obviously a tough customer who knew his business. Three times during the morning my tin cans got him on sonar and dropped several full patterns of a dozen depth charges around him. Each time when the ocean quieted down again the destroyer's sonar men could hear telltale noises which indicated a U-boat was fleeing for its life somewhere in the nearby depths. Each time the cans went into our prearranged expanding search pattern and regained sonar contact. After the fourth attack a lot a garbage and oil came up to the surface, but this was an old familiar stunt by this time in the war, and we paid no attention to it. We could still hear the desperate thum . . . thum . . . thum of propellors running very deep.

This submarine we were after gambled on staying deep. About 1300, our destroyers were pinging on him again. One took station about half a mile from him and coached another into firing position. Sonar loses contact on a deep submarine when you are nearly over it and the firing ship, if relying on its own sonar, would make the last minute of the approach blind. We had already found out for sure that if you gave this guy half a minute, it was too much.

At 1410 the "Pope" dropped a depth charge pattern and half a minute later the U-boat skipper down at six hundred feet was slammed against the steel walls of his conning tower and knew that the jig was up. "Blow all tanks," he ordered. "Prepare to abandon ship and scuttle."

At 1417 the submarine surfaced within a hundred yards of the "Pope," "Flaherty," "Pillsbury" and "Chatelain." I could see him from the bridge of the "Guadalcanal" five miles away. There was no way of knowing that he had surfaced in extremis to abandon ship and scuttle. A deadly rattle snake had just reared his head from the depths—ready to strike, as far as we knew! So we let him have it. All destroyers opened up with everything they had in their lockers, depth charges, torpedoes, four-inch guns, and 20 mm AA guns. All indications were that the U-boat was structually sound and was quite capable of firing a salvo of six torpedoes from her bow and stern tubes. In such a situation, you don't count the number of men who pop out of the forward and after escape hatches and dive over the side before issuing the order to cease fire. You watch the snake to see if you have broken its neck.

Four minutes after the U-515 surfaced, she slowly reared herself straight up in the air her stern going down and her bow pointing into the sky with white water pouring out of all the vent holes in the gingerbread around her pressure hull. I suppose a literary man might say she looked like a cobra rearing its head to strike. But on the bridge of the "Guadalcanal," my seafaring exec, yelled, "Thar she blows . . . and sparm at that!"

We fished forty-five survivors from this U-boat out of the water and hauled them aboard the "Guadalcanal." From some of the first we learned that her number was U-515, which meant nothing whatever to me except another U-boat. I directed the boys to bring the skipper up to the cabin when and if they got him.

Soon my chief master-at-arms and his number one helper escorted a husky, blond, eagle-eyed character, clad in U.S. GI dungaree pants and a dry sweat shirt, into the cabin.

"This is the Captain, sir," the CMAA said.

It was hardly necessary for him to say this. The man had a commanding personality and I knew the instant he came in the cabin that he was the skipper. He looked like an All-American halfback whose team had just lost a close game and who was beaten but unashamed. I found out later that he was one of Doenitz' aces and though his crew respected his ability as a U-boat skipper, they hated his guts. They said he took unnecessary chances because he wanted an Oak Leaf for his Knight's Cross and they blamed the loss of their boat on his reckless confidence that he would sink the "Guadalcanal" (getting double tonnage credit) before we got him. They were also bitter because for two years he had frozen promotions on his boat to prevent any of his hand-picked crew from being transferred to other boats when they were promoted.

"Your name?" I asked.

"Henke," he said, continuing in English as good as mine, "Werner Henke, Kapitän Leutnant, Kreigsmarine, and gave his serial number.

"The number of your U-boat?" I asked.

Henke stood mute.

"It was U-515," I said, and the look in his eye admitted it.

"How long were you at sea this cruise?" I asked.

Henke made no answer.

"You sailed from Lorient ten days ago," I said. It didn't take a crystall ball to figure that one out. Lorient was the Nazi main sub base in Biscay; every time we had sighted him he was on a southwest course away from Biscay; and it took eight or nine days to creep out of Biscay now that the RAF and U.S. Navy's Patrol Wing 7 were patrolling over it around the clock.

Henke shrugged his shoulders as if admitting it but said nothing. All this time he had a beaten but defiant look in his eye. Now the look began to harden.

I started to ask another question, "How many ships . . ."

He interrupted, "Captain, I have a protest to make!"

Caught off guard I said, "What is it?"

"You violated International Law and the Geneva Convention," he said.

"How?"

"You killed many of my men while we were trying to surrender."

The answer to that one was easy. I said, "I had no way of knowing whether you were trying to surrender or to torpedo my ships. As soon as we were sure you were harmless we ceased firing and we have rescued forty-five of your men."

"But you killed ten," he said—"in violation of the Geneva Convention."

Henke knew as well as I did that several times wounded U-boats had surfaced to allow the crew to escape and with their dying gasp had torpedoed the ship that had done them in. I've often wondered whether in this situation the survivors from opposite sides should negotiate a truce after their ships go down or should keep on fighting in the water. But there was no point in continuing

237

this argument any further. "Take him below," I said to the MAA.

Some of our skippers in the Battle of the Atlantic treated rescued U-boat captains as guests, and since they themselves lived in the sea cabin near the bridge when in dangerous waters, they turned over their own main cabin to the captured U-boat skipper. I didn't go along with this idea and figured it was better for all concerned to treat U-boat survivors as prisoners of war regardless of rank.

On the "Guadalcanal" we put all officers, including the skipper, in the brig (ship's prison) and separated the enlisted men into groups. We kept all non-rated men in one compartment and all petty officers in another. These three groups could never communicate with each other so they had no chance to give each other pep talks on security, or to hatch any plots to overthrow the government of the United States, or of the U.S.S. "Guadalcanal"—especially the "Guadalcanal."

So Kapitän Leutnant Werner Henke, Kreigsmarine, just awarded the Knight's Cross of the Iron Cross, was incarcerated in the brig. His cell there was bigger than his "cabin" on the U-515, the air was better, and the food that my chief master-at-arms brought him was at least as good as what he had been eating on his own ship.

Next day the master-at-arms brought word up to me on the bridge that Henke would like to see me. "What for?" I asked.

"Something about the Geneva Convention," said the chief.

"Oh, that again," I said, "Okay, bring him up to the cabin after we land the next flight."

When Henke was escorted into the cabin he had lost some of the beaten air of the day before. He registered an official beef against being quartered in the brig and quoted what he claimed was the Geneva Convention to me, saying that under its terms he was entitled to an officer's stateroom and should be allowed to eat in the officers' mess.

This wasn't too hard to answer either. I didn't have my copy of the Geneva Convention handy, but I explained to him that regardless of what the Convention said, we were still in the war zone and had to be practical. I couldn't give him an officer's stateroom without putting one of my own officers out of his bunk, which I didn't proposed to do.

"But the Geneva Convention says . . ." he began.

"Besides," I interrupted, "Many of my officers and sailors are of Jewish or Polish ancestry. They might not be very polite to you if I gave you the freedom of the ship."

"According to the Geneva Convention, it is your duty to protect your prisoners."

By this time I was getting a little burned at being lectured on how to run my ship. The next thing I said was just a shot in the dark, on a completely unpremeditated impulse, "Captain, we are going to refuel in Gibraltar about ten days from now. If you don't like the way I'm treating you, I'll be glad to turn you and your crew over to the British. Maybe they will treat you better."

There are several things about this statement of mine which literal-minded people may criticize now. In the first place, we weren't going anywhere near Gibraltar. In the second place, if we had, the whole British Mediterranean Fleet couldn't have taken Henke and those prisoners away from me—I was bringing them home for proof!

My statement had an even greater effect on Henke than I had expected. The beaten look came back into his eyes and he said quickly, "Captain, it isn't that bad. I can put up with this treatment for a few more weeks. I withdraw my protest."

So Henke went back to the brig and requested no more audiences with me.

A few days after this interview, my chief master-at-arms, who had been listening just outside the cabin during this discussion with Henke, came up to me on the bridge with a very interesting story. (Remember that up to this time none of us on the "Guadalcanal" had ever heard of the "Ceramic.")

It seems that Henke, knowing that the war was over for him, that he would survive it and could look forward to sitting out the rest of it in comparative comfort in the U.S., had done some reminiscing with my MAA. The chief was a sharp operator and had wormed his way into Henke's confidence by assuring Henke that I was a son-of-a-bitch, that all my men would like to shove me overboard, and he personally hated me. This had relaxed Henke so that he did a little talking. The story that the chief brought up to the bridge, given to him by Henke himself, was as follows:

"Just before the U-515 sailed from Lorient, the BBC had beamed a propaganda broadcast at the U-boat bases, saying they had learned that it was the U-515 that sank the "Ceramic." (Obviously they learned this from Sapper Munday's broadcast.) They went on to say they had also learned that after the sinking the U-515 had surfaced and had machine-gunned survivors in the water. Therefore, the broadcast continued, if anyone from the the U-515 ever fell into their hands, they would try them for murder and hang them if convicted."

I don't know what prompted Henke to tell this story to my CMAA, except that the chief had established pretty friendly relations with him . . . and maybe something was preying on Henke's mind. He, of course, denied that there was any truth in the part about machine-gunning survivors, and may have told the story to put the British in a bad light. The British now deny that they ever made such a broadcast, but can offer no explanation as to why Henke, in 1944, should make up such a story. Personally, I take no stock in the part about machine gunning lifeboats, but I do believe the British broadcast such a story.

Anyway, this tale gave me food for thought. I had already found out that Henke did not enthuse when you suggested to him that he might go to England. I began to wonder just how far I could push the idea of sending him there.

After weighing a lot of pros and cons, I decided to try a shenanigan. I had a message to the "Guadalcanal" written up on an official dispatch blank purporting to come from CinC, Atlantic Fleet, saying: "BRITISH ADMIRALTY REQUESTS YOU TURN OVER CREW OF U-515 TO THEM WHEN YOU REFUEL GIBRALTAR. CONSIDERING CROWDED CONDITION YOUR SHIP AUTHORIZE YOU TO USE YOUR DISCRETION."

I also drew up a statement on legal paper with the ship's seal on it ready for signature by Henke:

"I, Captain Lieutenant Werner Henke, promise on my honor as a German officer that if I and my crew are imprisoned in the United States instead of in England, I will answer all questions truthfully when I am interrogated by Naval Intelligence Officers.

Signed

Kapt. Lt.

Witness:
D. V. Gallery, Capt, USN
J. S. Johnson, Cdr, USN"

Sizing up all the angles on this shenanigan before going into it, the chance of success didn't seem very good. But it was one of those deals where you have nothing to lose and might come out way ahead if it worked. The worst that could happen would be for Henke to spit in my face and tell me to go to hell, which wouldn't affect the outcome of the war one way or the other. If it worked, something pretty good might come of it.

I sent for a large scale anchorage chart of Gibraltar, drew some lines on it as if I were studying the best approach to the anchorage, and left it lying on the table with parallel rulers and dividers on it where Henke would be bound to see it. I sent for Commander Johnson to come up to the cabin as a witness and explained the pitch to him. Then I had the chief master-at-arms bring Henke up from the brig and handed him the phony dispatch.

His face fell when he read it. A cornered look came back into his eyes and he said, "Why do they want me?"

I shrugged and said, "I don't know."

"The Geneva Convention . . ." he began.

"Wait a minute," I said, "The U.S. and England are allies, you can be legally imprisoned in either place."

After a long pause he looked at me rather pathetically and said, "Well, Captain, I suppose there is nothing you can do about it."

"Yes there is," I said. "That dispatch allows me to use

my discretion. If you make it worth my while, I'll keep you on board till we arrive in the U.S."

"What do you want me to do?" asked Henke.

"Just sign this," I said, pushing the prepared statement across the table and laying a pen down alongside it.

Henke read the statement carefully twice, thought it over for a while and then said, "Captain, you know I can't sign that."

"It's up to you," I said. "Sign and you go to the United States. If you don't sign, then you and your crew go to England."

Henke was a courageous and tough man, as proved by the decorations he wore. But I had put him in a hell of a spot. Finally he looked at me and I could sense that here was one professional military man baring his soul to another whom he respected even though an enemy. "Well, Captain, what would you do if you were in my position?" he asked.

I answered him truthfully and said, "if I were convinced that my country had lost the war and that I could help my crew by signing—I would sign."

Henke and I stood on opposite sides of the table for a few minutes without saying a further word. It was like a scene from a movie. I knew nothing of the real story of the "Ceramic" at the time, but I'm sure now that all the harrowing details with which he was so familiar ran through his mind again. He knew that no impartial court would punish him for what he had done. He believed a British court-martial would hang him. Finally he picked up the pen, signed the paper, looked at me defiantly, and went back to the brig.

I then circulated a photostat of the agreement which the Captain had signed among the petty officers and non-rated men in the two prisoner compartments, and put a similar proposition to them. . . . Sign and you go to the United States—refuse and you go to England. The proposed agreements for the crew went into much more detail as to what they would say than did Henke's. But they all knew the skipper's signature and there could be no doubt that he had agreed to talk. Every man in the U-515's crew signed, promising to tell all he knew.

Upon arrival in the U.S., Henke reneged on his agreement as I knew he would, saying quite correctly that it had been obtained under duress and false pretenses. But his crew, isolated from him and from each other, never knew this. They figured, "The skipper is talking—why shouldn't we?" When interrogated by our anti-submarine experts they sang like canary birds and our ONI people made quite a haul.

Now that the war is over and we've had time to forget, some bubble-headed people may say that I was guilty of using dishonorable tactics on Henke. However, I fed him well, gave him a comfortable bunk to sleep in, used no rubber hoses or drugs on him, and put him ashore in the United States alive, healthy and mentally undamaged. When I think of Buchenwald and Dachau, and of the brainwashed debris of humanity that the Communists have sent back to us from Korea I roll over and go to sleep with a clear conscience in spite of the finale to this episode which I could not foresee.

When Henke reneged on his agreement which all his people carried out as best they could, our intelligence experts decided to hold him to the terms of the agreement. They told Henke, "Either you talk, or you go to England." When he still refused they made preparations to send him to Canada for further transfer to England. The day before he was due to be shipped to England, Henke was pacing the exercise compound of the prisoner's camp. It was broad daylight, there was a high barbed wire fence all around the compound, and even if he got over it there were armed sentries outside the fence. Henke's mind must have gone back to the "Ceramic." The BBC broadcast about it, which the British now claim is a figment of his imagination, apparently was too much for him.

· He waited till a sentry was looking right at him and then started climbing the high wire fence that separated him from this world and eternity. "Halt" cried the sentry, who didn't know Henke from dozens of others in the camp.

Henke kept on climbing despite two more hails.

The sentry let him have it. When you squeeze the trigger of a submachine gun you can't just put one well aimed bullet in the leg of a fleeing prisoner. You blast a dozen or so slugs in his general direction. Several of the sentry's bullets hit Henke and killed him.

What is the moral, if any, of this grim tale about Henke and the "Ceramic"? A pat answer would be, "He who liveth by the sword shall perish by the sword." That seems to dispose of Kapitän Leutnant Henke quite neatly. But it is much too pat and simple.

Henke's torpedoing of the "Ceramic" and leaving the survivors to drown seems ruthless and brutal, but our own submarine skippers in the Pacific operated in the same way. They had to, just as Henke had to. That's the only way you can wage war with submarines.

I'm sure that if the Allies had lost the war I could have been hung on Henke's accusation that I ruthlessly killed his men when they were trying to surrender. Maybe he could even have convinced a Nazi court-martial that I brainwashed him and violated the Geneva Convention with that shenanigan I worked on him.

If there is any moral at all to this tale, it is one that we refuse to admit in this country—that war is a grim business.

When we hauled the survivors of the U-515 out of the water and aboard the "Guadalcanal" we were smack in the middle of the U-boat lane leading in and out of Biscay and had another moonlight night coming up. Our first night of round the clock operation had hit the jackpot so we repeated the same program the next night.

Again it paid off. At the crack of dawn on April 10 (Easter Sunday) a group of three turkeys got a radar contact and, carefully maneuvering to approach from the west, they made out a surfaced sub against the anemic light of dawn in the east.

They caught the U-boat flat-footed. Her lookouts didn't see them boring in from the dark hemisphere of the sky and apparently either her Naxos gear, or its operator slipped a cog. At any rate, the first warning her lookouts had of my planes screaming down at them was a hail storm of fifty-caliber bullets bursting on them. Three planes roared over, seconds apart, sowing a field of depth charges all around the sub and circling back to fire streams of high explosive rockets. That U-boat never had a chance. It was a götterdämmerung sunrise for the handful of lookouts on deck to see it. For the rest of the crew it was the same fate they had been bringdown on merchant sailors for three years . . . sunk without warning!

When the third plane swooped over for his rocket attack the sub was gone and my boys could see nothing in the blackness below. They marked the spot with flares, circled, and informed us by radio that they had chalked up another kill.

As the light in the east grew stronger, objects took shape in the dark water below. For a while they thought we had another whole crew in the water. But by the time the sun peered over the rim of the world to say, "Good morning and Happy Easter," they found only three human heads in the middle of a huge spreading pool of oil, surrounded by a welter of rubbish, wooden boxes, and torpedo air flasks. My lads dropped rubber boats, we took a careful bearing on the planes by radar, and headed over that way at full speed to rescue seamen in distress.

When we got there three hours later, only two men were left. One of these was dead, but the other, although badly wounded was hanging onto a rubber boat with one hand and holding up his shipmate with the other. They were from the U-68, a number which together with the U-515 appears often in the U-505's war diary.

Later I tried to pull what I now feel was my only really unethical shenanigan of the war on this sole survivor of the U-68. I thought I might get something out of this lad by telling him his skipper had slammed the hatch on him and the other lookouts and had submerged and abandoned them, whereas I had gone out of my way to rescue them.

After he recovered enough to walk, I had him brought up to the cabin, sat him down, and tried to question him. I gave him a pitch about his captain deserting him when the going got tough, whereas I had stuck my neck out to save him. He listened respectfully and made no comment. Then I asked him some questions he had no right to answer, but which in that particular part of the

Atlantic Ocean at that particular time, I was very curious about.

I'll never forget how this gaunt kid, who was not yet sure he was going to live, looked me smack in the eye and said, "Captain, I am a German soldier."

He then added to the interpreter that our attack had torn the U-boat in two, so his captain obviously hadn't abandoned him. He went on to say that even if the U-68 had escaped from our attack it was the captain's duty to submerge and sacrifice the lookouts to save the rest of the crew.

I asked this man no more questions, but had him taken back to sick bay and we restored him to good health. I suppose he is back in Germany now. I'm sure that under similar circumstances a communist brain-washer, confronting a prisoner still shaken by a terrible experience, would not have been as chicken-hearted as I turned out to be. I believe that if I had snarled at this man and threatened him, he might have broken. But I'll never know and I'm glad I won't. I can still look myself in the eye in the morning when I shave—if I had broken him, I don't think I could.

This man's name was Kastrup, a lookout on the U-68. If he gets to be the head man in Germany later on in this century, I will not be surprised. If he does, the power politicians in this world will get no place trying to bluff him.

Coming back from the cruise with two pelts in our belt, at a time when U-boats were hard to find, one thing was obvious. Our night flying experiment had paid off and blazed a trail that we had to follow each time we went to sea thereafter. In a twelve-hour period we had sunk two ace U-boats which, as we found out later, between them had sunk 55 ships, totalling 250,000 tons.

But looking back on the U-515, another idea kept cropping up in my mind all the way home—an idea that had originated under the Aurora Borealis up in Iceland almost two years ago. . . "Why not try to capture the next one?"

Why not? After all, the U-515 was one of the ace boats of the German submarine fleet. Henke was a brilliant skipper and a realistic, tough minded, military man. He fought skillfully as long as he felt he had a chance. But when he knew the jig was up, he blew his tanks, came up to the surface and gave his crew a chance to save their lives before scuttling his boat. He didn't shoot at me with either guns or torpedoes after surfacing because he had waited till he knew that he was finished before surfacing.

The more I thought about this the more significant it became. At this stage of the war, if a U-boat surfaced during an attack it probably meant that he thought he was finished and was coming up simply to give his crew a chance. But a skipper who was hounded and battered might surface prematurely before his boat was actually fatally wounded. After all, we had thrown everything but the galley ranges at U-515 before she up-ended and sank. For a while I thought we were going to have to ram her to put her on the bottom. . . . Suppose we hadn't been quite so bloody minded about sinking her. Suppose we had sent a party of stout hearted characters over there, to go aboard and make a survey of the situation after the Germans had shoved off. . . .

Maybe they would have reported back to me, "This sinking isn't really necessary."

All the way back to Norfolk a fantastic idea kept thrusting itself forward and would not be swept under the rug.

Chapter

16

CRUISE TO CAPE VERDE ISLANDS

BEFORE SHOVING OFF on a cruise, hunter-killer groups always held a departure conference attended by the skippers of the ships in the Task Group, and by numerous kibitzing "experts" from the staffs of CinCLant, ComAirLant, Anti-SubLant, and Cominch from Washington. At our conference in Norfolk before the next cruise, we ran through the usual routine items, clearing up questions about the communication plan, methods of reorienting our screen when turning into the wind for flight operations, the search plans we would use both for air and surface operations, etc., etc. The kibitzers all nodded approvingly as we settled the usual problems according to the book.

Finally, I took the floor and told the boys what I had been thinking about. I said that this time, when and if we brought a sub to bay within gun range, we would not klobber it forthwith as we had the U-515. Instead, we would assume he had surfaced for the sole purpose of saving the hides of his crew and intended to scuttle as soon as the crew got overboard. When he surfaced we would therefore cease fire with ammunition that could do serious structural damage to the boat, such as depth charges, torpedoes or rockets. We would blast away briskly with small calibre antipersonnel stuff in order to expedite the German's abandon ship drill, keep them away from their guns, and encourage them to get the hell off of that U-boat so that we could put an inspecting party on board. If this party, after a diligent survey, closing scuttling valves, disarming booby traps and doing whatever else such a party might have to do, believed we could keep her afloat, we would pass them a tow line and bring the sub back to the United States.

When I finished outlining this idea there was a silence in which a flake of falling dandruff would have made an audible thud. Then I went on to review our experience with the U-515 and to point out that even after the Germans went overboard, convinced that she was sinking, we expended a lot of armor piercing ammunition on her before she went down. She probably was finished as a submarine when she came to the surface, but maybe if we hadn't cooperated with the Germans by hammering her to pieces she might have survived as a surface vessel. I could see several of my destroyer skippers glance at each other and indicate agreement with me on this. I also saw one of the kibitzers in the back of the room glance at a cohort and make circular motions with his forefinger pointing at his head, indicating he thought I had barnacles on the brain.

I continued, "I want each ship to organize a boarding

party and keep a whale boat ready to lower throughout the next cruise. Also keep your tow line where you can get at it in case we need it. Any questions?"

What questions can they ask you in a spot like that? Your own subordinates aren't going to pipe up and say, "Are you nuts, Commodore?" Some of the kibitzers seemed to be toying with this idea but didn't quite have the nerve to do it. There being no questions the meeting adjourned.

As we cleared the Virginia Capes the next day, I sent the Task Group a signal reminding them that I expected each ship to have a boarding party organized and ready in case a situation came up where we might use it.

I'm sure that most of us in the Task Group had our tongues in our cheeks when we organized those boarding parties. Even now I'm not sure whether I had mine there or not. Some people may say this was an example of sound imaginative planning, but I feel it's more accurate to call it "wishful thinking." I think most of the boys who were named for the boarding parties figured, "What the hell, this will never come off—I might as well get credit for volunteering." But whatever their reasons, we got plenty of volunteers. We organized the parties and were ready when opportunity hammered on our door the next time.

Our night flying experiment on the previous cruise had paid off so well that this time we made the plunge into full scale round the clock operations. On the way to the hunting grounds we checked out all the pilots in our new squadron for night take-offs and landings. We started with a full moon and flew every night, watching it get blacker and blacker as the moon waned. At the end of two weeks the boys were making good landings in the pitch dark. We smashed up some of our airplanes learning how to do this, but didn't hurt any of our people.

You can't just issue an order to your pilots to go out and do this kind of flying. You have to sort of talk them into it and persuade them it isn't as dangerous as they know it is. The main reason why we were able to get our pilots into the right frame of mind was that we had made three notable rescues on previous cruises, and the

249

boys felt that if they got in trouble we would go all out to help them.

One was the night we had to turn on the lights. I don't like to think of that one even now, because it was our own incompetence that caused it. But anyway, we washed out four airplanes that night and didn't lose a pilot or an aircrewman. Pilots and aircrewmen take notice of things like that.

On the previous cruise, while we were disposing of U-515 and U-68, one of our turkeys had a complete radio failure in the middle of the night and missed the Task Group on his return leg from his search sector. It was a black night with a layer of cloud extending from 1500 to 2500 feet. Above that layer were the stars—below it was inky darkness.

When our lad failed to check in from his return leg on time and we couldn't raise him by radio, we assumed he had a radio failure. We pointed a big searchlight up in the sky and broadcast instructions to him in the hope he could receive even if he couldn't send. In about fifteen minutes it was apparent that this wasn't going to work. He was either in the water or was very badly lost by now. He still had gas for two more hours so we decided to play it on the basis that he was in the air trying to find his way home, and would follow the standard instructions for just this sort of emergency. He did! He climbed through the overcast, got up around 10,000 feet where we could see him on our radar over a hundred miles away and circled there. As soon as we spotted the circling blip on our radar, we banged off a couple of other turkeys to find him and lead him home.

He had wandered so far afield that he was almost out of gas when our "guardian angels" got to him. As the early light of dawn was breaking in the east they closed in on him, and nudged him around to the homeward course, a few minutes before his engine quit. He spiralled down through the overcast and made a good ditching in the rough sea with our other two turkeys giving us a running account of what was happening. Meantime, we had the whole Task Group headed that way at full speed. After the plane went in, all three men climbed out of it, inflated their rubber boat, got into it and settled down to wait. We were eighty miles away, so one plane stayed under the overcast to keep the tiny raft in sight and the other climbed up through the clouds periodically so we could see him on the radar and talk to him. Every four hours we sent out another pair of turkeys to relieve the watch and make sure we didn't lose track of that little raft in the broad Atlantic. Just before lunch the turkeys relayed a message to us from the raft, "Please save chow for crew of turkey number six." We saved it for them! They were back on board safe and sound early that afternoon.

In the third rescue episode, we had launched a plane on a black night; he checked out by radio on his initial search leg, and then suddenly disappeared from our radar screen a little sooner than he should have. This, in itself, was no cause for alarm. Maybe he had encountered low clouds, decided to stay under them, and had therefore disappeared behind the curve of the earth before we expected. But my young radar operator in CIC had a hunch and stuck to his guns on it. He put his pencil on a spot on his scope and said, "Cap'n, I think that plane just now went in the water here."

"Call turkey number four and see if he's all right," I said to the watch officer.

"We just completed a radio check with him a minute ago, Cap'n," said the watch officer, "He's Okay."

"Captain, I think he's in the water," insisted the radarman.

"Call him again," I said to the watch officer.

There was no answer to our call.

We headed over to the mark on the radar scope, and half an hour later we spotted flashlights on the water and hauled three of our boys back aboard.

Their altimeter had been set wrong by a thousand feet. It was a pitch black night and the pilot flew into the water on instruments, thinking he was a thousand feet above it. Many readers will ask how they can make such mistakes, but most aviation accidents are caused by "pilot errors" such as this. Alert, young, highly trained flyers occasionally dope off and make mistakes just as their elders do.

When our three lads fought their way out of the
251

wreckage of that turkey and joined hands with their heads just out of water in the inky blackness, they had little hope of survival. They figured since they had just completed a radio check a minute before the crash we wouldn't miss them for at least an hour and a half during which time we would be steaming away from them. They figured we wouldn't be looking for them until daylight and then wouldn't have any idea where to start looking. They were the most surprised shipwrecked aviators in the Atlantic Ocean that night when we hauled them out of it half an hour after they crashed. They spread the word among their friends, "This ship takes care of its people."

Rescues such as these inspire confidence in your pilots. On account of them we were able to persuade our pilots on later cruises that our night flying program was a reasonable one.

By the time we arrived at the hunting grounds about one-third of our airplanes were hangar deck lilies because of injuries received in line of duty during the training period, but the boys were landing aboard on black nights as if they were owls. I figured that flying all night long with two-thirds of our planes we could accomplish a lot more than we would by simply boring holes in the air flying all of them, but only in daylight.

For the next three weeks we scoured the area around the Cape Verde Islands keeping four turkeys in the air around the clock and having no trouble, except we couldn't find any submarines. We patrolled across the route from Biscay to the U-boat hunting ground at Freetown where we knew there were U-boats going back and forth, but all we could find were whales, porpoises and Portuguese fishing smacks, plus an assortment of electronic gremlins and false alarms.

We prowled through our assigned area with the carrier three thousand yards behind a bent screen of five destroyer escorts, using our airplanes to scour the ocean for about a hundred miles on each side of our base course and a hundred and sixty miles ahead. With four turkeys you could, during a four hour flight, cover an area of roughly 20,000 square miles. In round numbers, this is one-third the area of the New England states, and you would expect to find plenty of action in an area that big.

But hunting subs is a dull, tedious business ninety-nine per cent of the time. Your planes patrol back and forth, back and forth, combing the same area time and time again. The first time you send a flight out in the hunting area you hang around the radar scope in CIC expecting every minute to get a contact. You always feel gypped and think they sent you to the wrong area when the first flight sees nothing. You become more and more convinced of this as successive flights go out and return with nothing to report. But, of course, the fact that you have combed an area over and over without finding any submarines doesn't mean there are no subs there. Aircraft can't find a submerged U-boat even with radar, and at this stage of the war the U-boats were submerged most of the time. Our destroyers could find them submerged with their sonar gear, but the maximum range at which we could get an echo off a sub was about 2,000 yards. Even with five destroyers sweeping a path ahead of us all day long we only searched 3,600 square miles with sonar—about three per cent of the area the planes covered. For the destroyers to find a U-boat, we had to run right over him, and the submarine, with his sensitive listening devices, would hear us coming perhaps an hour before we stumbled over him. During this hour the sub could do several things, depending on what sort of a man the skipper was. She could go deep and perhaps hide under a layer of cold water which our sonar wouldn't penetrate. She might put on a burst of speed and run out of our path if the skipper didn't mind using up his battery. If he were a real tough skipper he might even run head on at our screen, hoping to break through and get a shot at us before we got him.

Our planes could only spot U-boats when they were surfaced. One of the hardest ideas to sell to a young turkey pilot who is just going out on a four hour night patrol is that there really are submarines in an area his pal has just finished patrolling without finding anything. He resents being sent on what he thinks is a wild-goose chase even after you explain that you think the subs were submerged when his pal searched the area.

There can be three or four U-boats in a 20,000 mile area that you are patrolling constantly and you may never see them. If they happen to be lucky and pop up to recharge their battery five minutes after your plane has flown over them, they probably have two hours during which they can remain surfaced safely. The only way you can guarantee that there are no U-boats in an area like that is to keep every square mile of it under continuous surveillance for about thirty-six hours. By that time any sub in the area would be forced to come up and recharge his battery. But a jeep carrier task group cannot keep the whole area covered all the time. Actually, at any given instant our four night-flying turkeys would have about six per cent of our total area on their radar scopes. By sweeping this six per cent back and forth at 150 knots for four hours, we stood a good chance of finding any U-boat that surfaced for as long as an hour, but we couldn't be sure of doing it.

Even when our plane's radar picked up a sub ten miles away, that didn't mean school was out by any means. The business was just beginning. Usually a sub would get early warning of our plane's approach and crash dive. By the time the plane got to the spot he would be gone. In such cases the plane circled the spot and reported by radio. Our radar on the ship would pinpoint the circling plane and we would detach three destroyers to proceed there at full speed and start an expanding sonar search from the point of submergence. We could have destroyers on top of any point in our area within six hours and then if we played our cards properly we should have a kill within twenty-four hours. The sub's submerged speed is low and he only has juice in his battery to cover about sixty miles. If he runs wide open he will use up his battery before he goes more than about ten miles. If he creeps, he can drag it out to maybe thirty hours and cover sixty miles. At the end of that time he is plumb out of volts and oxygen for his crew, and he must stagger to the surface and take a couple of hours to shake the cobwebs out of his head and get juice back in his battery.

Knowing these facts of life about submarines, the proper procedure after you made a sure contact was obvious. You concentrated your air search in a circle of an eighty mile radius centered on the point of submergence. Next time he came up to charge batteries and get a whiff of air, you should spot him and drive him down again. Your destroyers start another expanding search around the new point of submergence and you reorient your air search. The noose is tightening now. He pops up and down again several times but each time you fence him in a little closer until finally the destroyers or planes, or both, get him at the end of his rope and klobber him.

The plane's weapons are 50-calibre machine guns, rockets, depth charges, and torpedoes. The destroyer's are guns of various calibres from three inch down to 20 mm., torpedoes, depth charges, and hedgehogs. These last are small weapons, thrown ahead, that look like potato mashers. You shoot a couple of dozen of them a hundred yards or so ahead of you at the spot where you think the U-boat is. If one of them touches the sub as it sinks past him it blows a hole in his pressure hull. If they just miss the sub nothing at all happens. In this respect they differ from depth charges which are much bigger, are set to go off at a certain depth, and which tear hell out of the ocean whenever you fire them. If you miss with hedgehogs you can make another attack immediately because there were no explosions and your sonar still works in the undisturbed water. If you miss with depth charges the sub has about 15 minutes to get away from you before the ocean quiets down enough to use sonar again.

But after a salvo of ash cans explodes all around him, maybe it takes the skipper's nerves that long to settle down too. While they are still agitated he may do something foolish. So the standard procedure at this time was to fire a salvo of hedgehogs as you approach the sub and if you got no explosion as you continued your run, to plant a garden of ash cans around him.

In perhaps half the sub killings during the Battle of the Atlantic, the whole action was fought without either side actually seeing the enemy. The battle begins with a radar blip or a sonar contact on the Allied side, and a hydrophone or Naxos warning on the German side.

An hour or so later it ends with a blazing surface ship upending and sinking, or a great puddle of oil spreading out across the ocean with pieces of submarine junk in the middle of it.

This is a tremendously exciting game which may go on for twenty-four hours. Sleep is just out of the question till the game is over because the jackpot is a lot of lives, including your own. If you had a submarine to begin with and if you play the game the way I have indicated, you will wind up with one submarine credited to your account in the official statistics of the war.

The only hitch to all the above is that right at the beginning the Task Group Commander has to make a difficult command decision on which the whole business hinges. You seldom get a clear-cut sighting and know for sure that you've got a submarine. You get indirect evidence such as a radar blip, a sonar echo, or propellor noises in an aircraft sonobuoy. The Task Group Commander doesn't usually get even these first-hand. He gets a second- or third-hand report of what someone else is seeing or hearing and he has to decide whether the little blip that one of his airborne radarmen claims he saw on his scope was a submarine or something else. If it was a submarine, the Task Group must drop everything and proceed as described above until they have killed the sub. He has no right to leave that area until he has disposed of that "known" submarine. But if the blip was something else and he decides it was a sub, then his Task Group is out of the war for three or four days, jousting with windmills.

There are perhaps a dozen "something elses" that can give you convincing blips for a few seconds on a radar scope. There are "ghosts," which are simply the electronic version of gremlins. There are bits of small floating rubbish which occasionally present just the right surface to a probing radar beam and send back a strong echo for a minute or so, and then don't happen to synchronize that surface with your beam for days. There are the goddamn balloons that submarines used to turn loose, anchored to a piece of driftwood with strips of tinfoil dangling from the balloon. When you pick up one of these phonies on a radar scope, anybody who is skilled in the art of anti-sub warfare and is an expert on electronics will swear that you have a submarine periscope on the screen. So you chase the bastard all night and when dawn breaks just as you are closing in for the the kill, you see this silly booby-trap bobbing around betwixt wind and water leering at you. The real bad part of it is, your people all see it too, and you can almost hear them saying mentally, "Hmmm . . . the Old Man ain't as smart as we thought he was." Of course, if the Old Man is really smart, he notices during the night that this "periscope" is moving exactly down wind, at a few knots less than the speed of the wind. So he calls the "attack" off before dawn breaks, and thus saves himself much face.

There are many natural noises that come out of the sea which sound a lot like submarine noises. When an eager young pilot drops a sonobuoy at the spot where a radar blip has disappeared and hears such noises coming back up out of his sonobuoy, you'll never convince him that he didn't have a submarine. If he has been patrolling long enough with nothing happening, he can sometimes imagine noises where there are none. In fact, I used to say that after about a month of fruitless patrolling a pilot could hear brass bands playing "Deutschland über Alles" on a sonobuoy if he tried hard enough.

I know from experience that this business of deciding how to evaluate a radar blip was by far the toughest decision that a hunter-killer Task Group Commander had to make. You stand in the middle of CIC with all your experts around you and the lad who made the contact in front of you. You listen to his story, you get the advice of the experts, and then all eyes bore into you as you make up your mind. The radarman is always sure he had a sub, otherwise you wouldn't be holding the conference. The experts are never sure of anything, and, if they are real experts, can phrase their advice in such a way that they will be right no matter how the thing turns out.

But "time's awasting," and finally the Old Man has got to make up his mind. I've taken part in many of those midnight conferences, winding up with a dozen pairs of eyes looking at me respectfully while they all thought

I was logically analyzing the various factors and arriving at a shrewd and penetrating answer. Actually, what I was doing was mentally flipping a nickel.

Many people think that the outcome of the wars of this world are decided by military geniuses. In my life-time of over thirty years of active duty in the Navy, I haven't met a single "military" genius. I've met some stuffed shirts who thought they were geniuses, but who couldn't punch their way out of a wet paper bag, unless they had several thousand eager young Americans helping them. I know and have served under men like Admirals King, Halsey, Nimitz, and Ingersoll, who were our top naval leaders in World War II. They are all great men, but I would say their outstanding characteristics were that they were fine seamen, knew their weapons systems, and inspired confidence in their subordinates. They surrounded themselves with good men, gave their subordinates authority to act, went to bat for them when they were right, and were cold-blooded about getting rid of incompetents. They had the guts to make weighty decisions and accept heavy responsibility.

But all these characteristics, except the knowledge anybody can acquire by spending his life at sea, are found in leaders of industry as well as military leaders. The identifying characteristics of a military genius is that his battles turn out the right way. A learned strategist who loses a battle because of an earthquake is not a military genius. A bull in a china shop who wins a battle through simple good luck may go down in history as a genius. In the middle of 1940, right after the fall of France, Adolph Hitler was the greatest military genius that had ever lived up to that time. If he had dropped dead when his Wehrmacht was at the gates of Stalingrad in 1941, he would have a permanent place in the history books as the greatest conqueror who ever lived.

Many bubble heads, including some military men, will disagree with my statement that success is the only test of "genius." But it's a solid fact of life as we live it on this earth, just as victory in battle is. What difference does it make now if General Grant was plastered every afternoon by four o'clock, and General Lee was a learned gentleman who could hold his liquor and knew more military strategy when he had a bad hangover (if he ever did) than Grant knew when he was sober (if he ever was)? Lee surrendered to Grant and that settles that.

The big difference between civilian tycoons and military geniuses is that in civil life the leaders are making important decisions all the time. In military life you make them only in war time. In a peacetime military career some men reach the top by evading all difficult decisions on the theory that if you never do *anything* you won't do anything wrong. This policy often brings mediocre characters to the top in peacetime who have to be weeded out when the shooting starts. Had King, Halsey, Nimitz, or Ingersoll, been in command at Pearl Harbor on December 7, 1941, I'm convinced the Jap attack would have failed. But it took a war to bring them to the top.

But if they had been at the top before war started, maybe the whole subsequent history of the world would have been changed. In view of the divided sentiments in this country before we got klobbered, an unsuccessful attack might not have aroused us to the fighting pitch that Pearl Harbor did. We might have remained neutral while Hitler and Stalin killed each other off. Whether mankind is better off now because we did get caught with our pants down at Pearl Harbor is too big a question for me to comment on at this time.

Let's get back to the Cape Verde Islands in the spring of 1944. On May 30, 1944, after three weeks of fruitless operations, we had to leave the area and head toward Casablanca for fuel. Our route north followed the lane to the Bay of Biscay, and we had a report of a U-boat homeward bound along this route so we centered our operations around him.

He was supposed to be about three hundred miles north of us and we planned to run right smack along his track passing directly over him on June 2, if our information was accurate. For the next four days we got many indications that there might be a submarine nearby. We heard strong transmissions on the U-boat's radio frequency. We had disappearing radar blips at night. Some of our pilots thought they heard submarine propellor noises on sonobuoys. We were sure we were close to a sub, but it seemed to be a very cautious one who stayed submerged most of the time, and who could detect our radar about as far as we could detect him.

We had several of those midnight conferences in CIC trying to decide whether disappearing radar blips were submarines that had seen us coming and submerged, or merely one of the many "other things." On the night of June 2-3, we ran over his reported position. Around 1:00 A.M., our conference "experts" decided we had him cornered. We had just had a disappearing blip and a noisy sonobuoy at the spot where the blip disappeared. Our pilots were so sure of the indications that they dropped a lot of high explosive and we took the Task Group over to the spot expecting the sunrise to reveal a big oil pool and a lot of junk. The sunrise revealed nothing. But soon after, my chief engineer, Earl Trosino, came up to the bridge with a long face and said, "Cap'n, we've got to quit fooling here and get in to Casablanca; I'm getting down near the safe limit of my fuel."

We resumed course North, leaving the reported position of the U-boat astern of us. By this time I was thoroughly convinced that we had spotted our prey the previous night, driven him down before he had finished charging his battery, and that one more night in the area would cook his goose. He *had* to come up again soon, and I was sure we would find him on the surface in bad shape if we stuck around one more night.

I argued with Trosino all day about fuel and, finally, late in the afternoon, I browbeat him into admitting that *maybe* we had enough fuel for one more day's operations, provided I was willing to arrive in Casablanca with tanks practically dry. This is, of course, a foolish thing to do because you never know what may come up in a global war and you should always leave yourself a little leeway on fuel. A belligerent Captain can always intimidate his chief engineer into conceding that he has a little bit of extra fuel stashed away for emergencies and I was dead certain by this time we would get a kill from one more night's operations and decided to shoot the works.

We turned south at sunset, and worked back over the same area all night, keeping the air full of planes. We drew a complete blank, and at sunrise I headed for Casablanca badly worried whether we would make it or not.

Of course, I could always radio in for a tug, but this would gain me a place in naval history comparable to that of the foolish virgins in the Bible!

This was a Sunday morning, and when Trosino gave me his fuel report right after sunrise, he said rather solemnly. "You better pray hard at Mass this morning Cap'n, you used more oil than I figured on last night."

Chapter

17

THE CAPTURE OF THE U-505

THAT MORNING at breakfast, my orderly brought me the ship's Plan of the Day. This is a routine mimeographed sheet, drawn up the day before, setting forth the operations we think we will conduct the next day and containing various official announcements of interest to all hands. I noted one item somewhat wryly. It was a list of names entitled, "Final Crew For Captured U-boat."

We had been revising our original boarding party almost daily for the past three weeks to get the best qualified people for a prize crew. We had plenty of eager volunteers for this duty who had never seen a submarine, except the U-515, but we wanted men who had some knowledge we might put to use, men who knew something about diesel engines, storage batteries, or had served in submarines. But now, right after this notice that we had finally made up our minds was posted on all bulletin boards, we were abandoning the hunt. There might be some caustic comments about this in the bunk room that night. "Ah well," I thought, "maybe we will have better luck on the trip back to Norfolk." But in view of what happened within a few hours, this plan of the day caused my crew to credit me with an infallible crystal ball from then on.

Incidentally, we did find one man on the ship who had served in a U.S. submarine and who immediately became our submarine "expert." He had been a yeoman on an

S-boat, and could tell us anything we wanted to know about the paper work or filing system on a submarine!

Right after attending Mass that morning on the hangar deck, I was up on the bridge, seated in the skipper's chair overlooking the flight deck. It was a beautiful, clear day, with a light breeze and medium sea. We had only two fighter planes aloft maintaining a token patrol, because we figured our only possible target was out of range far astern of us. I was still fuming over the "fact" that we had let him get away from us.

Suddenly, at 1110, the squawk box on the bridge blared forth, "Frenchy to Bluejay—I have a possible sound contact!" (Frenchy was the U.S.S. "Chatelain" Commander Dudley Knox. I was Bluejay.)

This was nothing to get excited about yet. We had been getting possible sound contacts for the past months on whales, layers of cold water, and other natural phenomena in the sea. But you always treat a "possible" as the McCoy until you find out otherwise.

"Left full rudder," I said. "Engines ahead full speed." Then grabbing the mike of the "Talk Between Ships" radio, I broadcast, "Bluejay to Dagwood—take two DE's and assist Frenchy. I'll maneuver to keep clear."

This told the screen commander (Commander F. S. Hall) that it was his party from here on. An aircraft carrier right smack at the scene of a sound contact is like an old lady in the middle of a bar room brawl. She has no business there, can contribute little to the work at hand, and should get the hell out of there leaving elbow room for those who have a job to do. As we gained sea room to the west, I banged off a couple of turkeys to lend a hand if they were needed, but warned the pilots, "Use no big stuff if the sub surfaces—chase the crew overboard with 50 calibre fire."

As we veered off to the west, "Pillsbury" and "Jenks" raced over to help "Chatelain" which had picked up her contact so close aboard that she ran smack over it before she could make up her mind what it was. She now announced, "Contact evaluated as sub—am starting attack," and wheeling around under full rudder, she maneuvered into firing position again. She made a complete circle pinging away on her contact, straightened out and fired a salvo of twenty hedgehogs, which arched up in the air and splashed into the water like a huge handful of rocks one hundred yards ahead where the sonar was pinpointing the as yet unseen sub. All eyes locked on the spot and we ticked off each second after the splashes. When the count reached ten, we knew there would be no explosion and began to doubt that "Chatelain's" contact was really a sub.

"Pillsbury" and "Jenks" were now prowling warily within hailing distance of the "Chatelain" and probing the contact with their sonar. If this was a sub and if "Chatelain" missed again, they would pounce on it and plaster it themselves.

Suddenly our two fighter planes circling over the spot like hawks, opened up with their machine guns, blasted a few bursts of 50 calibre into the water about one hundred yards from where the hedgehogs hit and yelled over the radio, "Sighted sub—destroyers head for spot where we are shooting!"

The "Chatelain" heeled over again under full rudder and headed for the bullet splashes where the pilots saw the dim shape of the completely submerged sub—trying to go deeper. At 1121, 11 minutes after the first sonar echo, "Chatelain" fired a spread of twelve six hundred pound depth charges all set to explode shallow.

From the carrier a few seconds later, we saw the ocean boil astern of the "Chatelain" and felt it quake as a dozen geysers spouted into the air from the underwater explosions. As the great white plumes were subsiding, Ensign Cadle in one of the circling "Wildcats" shouted, "You've struck oil Frenchy, sub is surfacing!"

At 1121½ on June 4, 1944, one hundred fifty miles west of Cape Blanco, French West Africa, the U-505 heaved itself up from the depths and broke surface seven hundred yards from the "Chatelain"—white water pouring off its rusty black sides. Our quarry was at bay.

When a cornered sub first breaks surface, you can never be sure whether he came up to abandon ship and scuttle or to fire a spread of torpedoes and try to take some of our ships to the bottom with him. "Pillsbury," "Jenks" and "Chatelain" cut loose with all the guns they had, and for about two minutes, 50 calibre slugs and 20 and 40 mm. explosive bullets hammered into the conning tower and tore up the ocean around it. Our fighter planes sent streams of hot metal ricochetting across her decks. Fortunately, all the three-inch stuff we fired missed, as did a torpedo fired by "Chatelain" when she thought the sub was swinging around to bring her own torpedo tubes to bear.

As the sub ran in a tight circle to the right, small crouching figures popped out of the conning tower and plunged overboard. While these men were leaping for their lives amid our hail of bullets, I broadcast to the Task Group, "I want to capture that bastard, if possible."

After about fifty or so men had gone overboard, Commander Hall, at 1126, ordered, "Cease firing"—and the ancient cry, "Away all boarding parties," boomed out over modern loudspeakers for the first time since 1815. The "Pillsbury's" party, led by Lieutenant (jg) Albert David, had already scrambled into their motor whale boat and the boat plopped into the water and took off after the sub, which was still circling to the right at five or six knots. As that tiny whale boat took off after the circling black monster, I wouldn't have blamed those men in the boat for hoping that maybe they wouldn't catch her. The Nantucket sleighride they might get if they did overhaul her would top anything in Moby Dick! But cutting inside the circle the gallant band in the boat drew up alongside the runaway U-boat and leaped from the plunging whale boat to the heaving, slippery deck. As the first one hit the deck with the whaleboat's bow line, it looked for all the world like a cowboy roping a wild horse. I grabbed the TBS and broadcast, "Heigho Silver—ride'm cowboy!" —not a very salty exhortation but readily understood by all hands.

On deck was a dead man lying face down with his head alongside the open conning tower hatch, the only man killed on either side in this action. He was Hans Fisher, one of the plank owners of the U-505 who had been aboard since commissioning. David and his boys now had a wild bull by the tail and couldn't let go. They were in charge of the topside of this submarine, but God only knew who was down below or what nefarious work they were doing. Somebody had to go below and find out.

No one in that boarding party had ever set foot on a

submarine of any kind before—to say nothing of a runaway German sub. Anyone who ventured down that conning tower hatch might be greeted by a blast of gunfire from below! Even if abandoned, the ship might blow up or sink at any moment. That sewerlike opening in the bridge leading down under the seas looked like a one way street to Davy Jones's locker for everyone in the boarding party.

Lieutenant David, Arthur K. Knispel and Stanley E. Wdowiak, jammed all these ideas into unused corners of their minds and plunged down the hatch (David told me later that on the way down he found out exactly how Jonah felt on his way down into the belly of the whale).

They hit the floor plates at the bottom of the ladder ready to fight it out with anyone left aboard. But the enemy had fled for their lives and were now all in the water watching the death struggle of their stricken boat. My boys were all alone on board a runaway enemy ship with machinery humming all around them, surrounded by a bewildering array of pipes, valves, levers, and instruments with German labels on them. They felt the throbbing of the screws still driving the ship ahead and heard an ominous gurgle of water coming in somewhere nearby. This was a new version of the "Flying Dutchman," even more eerie than the old sailing ship with all sails drawing and not a soul on board.

But the submarine was all theirs. All theirs, that is, if they didn't touch the wrong valve or lever in the semidarkness of the emergency lights and blow up or sink the boat. David yelled up to the boys on deck to tumble down and lend a hand while he, Knispel and Wdowiak ran forward for the radio room to get the code books. They smashed open a couple of lockers, found the books and immediately passed them up on deck, so we would have something to show for our efforts in case we still lost the boat.

Some readers, knowing that all naval code books have lead covers to make them sink, will ask why didn't the Germans throw these code books overboard? But why throw a code book overboard from a submarine which you are abandoning in over a thousand fathoms of water, thinking she will be on the bottom in another couple of minutes? Nothing had gone overboard except the crew and we now had in our possession one U-boat, complete with spare parts and all charts, codes and operating instructions from Admiral Doenitz. It would be the greatest intelligence windfall of the war, if David could keep her afloat.

It seemed doubtful that he could, because the sub was now in practically neutral buoyancy, was riding about ten degrees down by the stern and was settling deeper all the time.

One of the first to plunge down the hatch in response to David's call from below was Zenon B. Lukosius. As soon as Luke hit the floor plates he heard running water. Heading for the sound he ducked around behind the main periscope well and found a stream of water six inches in diameter gushing into the bilges from an open sea chest. By the grace of God the cover for this chest had not fallen down into the bilges where we wouldn't have been able to find it, but was lying on the floor plates. Luke grabbed it, slapped it back in place, set up on the butterfly nuts and checked the inrush of water. By this time the boat was threatening to up-end like the U-515 any minute. If she had, she would have taken the whole boarding party with her. Luke got his little chore done just in the nick of time. Another minute might have been too late.

Luke told me later that while he was jamming that cover back in place, he was too busy to be scared. But when he tore his Mae West life jacket on a sharp projection in the conning tower, that really shook him— because he didn't know how to swim.

The sub was now so low in the water that the swells breaking across the nearly submerged U-boat were beginning to wash down the conning tower hatch. David ordered the man left on deck to close the hatch while he and his men continued their work below. The main electric motors were still running and driving the sub in a circle at about six knots.

Meantime, I had reversed course, got back to the scene of action and sent over a whale boat with Commander Earl Trosino and a group of our "experts" in it. They arrived aboard the sub literally "with a bang." A swell picked up their boat and deposited it bodily on the deck of the sub, breaking the boat's back and spilling the occupants on deck unceremoniously. This blow from above caused some concern even to David and his stout-hearted lads below, who at this time were engaged in ripping electric wires off things which they thought were demolition charges.

When Trosino and his crew scrambled up to the bridge, they couldn't get the conning tower hatch open. It was stuck as if fastened from the inside, a partial vacuum inside the boat holding it down so the boys couldn't budge it. The circling U-boat was constantly passing Germans in their rubber boats and Mae Wests, so Trosino's boys grabbed one, hauled him aboard and asked him how to open the hatch. The German showed them a little valve which let air into the pressure hull, equalizing the pressures inside and out and enabled them to get the hatch open.

"Thanks Bud," said Trosino, and shoved him overboard again.

Trosino then scrambled down the hatch and took over command from David in the same spot where Oberleutnant Meyer had assumed command after Cszhech ran out on him. No other U-boat ever had so many changes of command under fantastically improbable circumstances!

I cannot speak too highly of the job that Trosino did in keeping that sub afloat. He too had never been aboard a submarine before. But he had spent most of his life at sea as a chief engineer in Sun Oil tankers. He is the kind of an engineer who can walk into any marine plant, whether it is installed in the "Queen Mary" or a German U-boat, take a quick look around the engine room and be ready to put the blast on any dumb cluck who touches the wrong valve at the wrong time.

He spent the next couple of hours fighting to keep the sub's head above water. It was touch and go whether he would succeed or not and they had to keep that conning tower hatch closed. A lot of the time Trosino was down in the bilges under the floor plates tracing out pipelines. Had the sub taken a sudden lurch and up-ended herself, as it was quite probable she would—Earl wouldn't have had any chance whatever to get out. I recommended him for a Navy Cross when we got back to Norfolk. All he got was a Legion of Merit. He did this job in the wrong ocean! But that Legion of Merit is worth more than some of the Navy Crosses they were handing out in the Pacific at this time.

Trosino got the right valves closed and didn't open any of the hundreds of wrong ones. While he was doing this, Gunner Burr went through the boat looking for demolition charges. Our intelligence reports told us we would find fourteen five-pound TNT charges placed against the hull, several in each compartment. We had no information on their exact location or how the firing mechanism worked. Gunner Burr found and disarmed thirteen while Trosino was bilge diving. They found the fourteenth in Bermuda three weeks later! The Germans had been so sure when they abandoned ship that this sub was on the way to the bottom within minutes, that they hadn't set the firing devices! This information is worth only a raised eyebrow now, but when Burr, Trosino, David and their boys were aboard that first day, the knowledge that there was an unlocated demolition charge raised the hackles along all their spines.

Shortly after Trosino got aboard, the "Pillsbury" came alongside to pass salvage pumps over and take the sub in tow. Her skipper didn't allow for the fact that submarines have large flippers sticking out from the bow under water on both sides. The sub's port bow flipper cut a long underwater slice in the "Pillsbury's" thin plates as she came alongside, flooding two main compartments and making it necessary for the DE to back off and fight to keep herself afloat.

Trosino reported that as long as the sub had headway, she rode about ten degrees down by the stern. But when he slowed her down, she lost the lift of her stern diving planes, settled to a steeper angle and submerged the conning tower hatch. The "Pillsbury" reported a DE couldn't do the towing job, so I headed over to take her in tow myself. As we drew near, Trosino pulled the switches and stopped the sub.

Working fast, we laid our stern practically alongside the nose of the sub, threw over a heaving line with a messenger line and an inch-and-a-quarter wire towline bent on.

As the lads on the heaving, slippery deck of the sub were struggling to secure the towline, with four loaded bow torpedo tubes of the submarine practically nuzzling my after end, I said a fervent prayer. "Dear Lord, I've got a bunch of inquisitive lads nosing around below in that sub —please don't let any of them monkey with the firing switch!"

When the tow line was secured, we eased ahead, took a strain, and got underway again with the U.S. colors proudly flying over the swastika on a boat hook planted in a voice tube on the U-505's bridge. As we gathered speed the stern came up and they could open the hatch again. I cracked off an urgent top secret dispatch to Cin-CLant and Cominch, "Request immediate assistance to tow captured submarine U-505." That dispatch really shook the staff duty officers back home. At first they didn't believe it and demanded a recheck on the decoding—but lost no time getting necessary action underway in the improbable event that it was true.

It soon became apparent that although we had our bronco roped, she wasn't broken to the halter yet. She sheared way out on our starboard quarter and rode out their listing to starboard and stretching the tow line as taut as a banjo string. Her rudder was jammed hard right. But I couldn't do anything about that now—I had four planes in the air that were getting low on gas.

So, hauling our non-cooperative prize behind us, we swung into the wind and landed our planes. With that sub dragging its heels back there I could only make about six knots so the pilots didn't have much wind across the deck for landing. But everyone seems to rise to the occasion at a time like this and they made it look easy— so easy, in fact, that I launched a couple more. Our speed and maneuverability was seriously restricted by the tow, making us a sitting target for any other sub that came along, so I figured we *had* to keep our planes aloft.

Meantime, the "Pillsbury" had been wallowing astern of us, struggling to stay afloat. She now flashed a message that two main compartments, including one engine room were flooded to the water line, but she hoped to get underway again in a couple of hours on one screw. I detached the "Pope" to stand by her, the other three DE's formed a screen around us and we dragged our prize off at six knots. Next day knowing that the "Pillsbury's" skipper would be worried about a board of investigation when he got home I sent him the following signal: "This is for your files regarding damage done to your ship this cruise. This damage was done executing my orders and I assume responsibility." Commander Casselman of the "Pillsbury" still thinks I'm a nice guy.

Now I was in real trouble on fuel. One thing was for sure, I didn't have enough left to make Casablanca with that U-boat in tow. I was bashful about sending an official dispatch admitting I had made the unpardonable blunder of stretching my fuel supply too far. If I had stopped to think about it, I would have realized that at this point I could have admitted almost anything, including membership in the communist party, and no one would have given it a second thought. Finally, I swallowed my pride and sent a dispatch suggesting I head for the nearest friendly port, Dakar. CinCLant promptly vetoed this and said, "Further orders coming soon."

Sunset was approaching so we now battened the sub down for the night and brought our boarding parties back to the ship. Trosino informed me he thought she would stay afloat. He also reported that he thought the after torpedo room was flooded but couldn't be sure because the water tight door was dogged shut and he didn't want to open it for fear of flooding the boat. He also said there was what looked to him like a booby trap on the main dog. He had been so busy over there he hadn't noticed that the rudder was jammed but said he could get it amidships for me next morning.

Shortly after sunset the "Flaherty" announced she had a disappearing radar blip and "Chatelain" chimed in with a "Possible sound contact." The only thing I could do was pray and stick on a few extra turns to get the hell out of that area quicker. I must have put on too many because at midnight the tow line snapped and we spent the rest of the night circling the sub under a full moon and rousing our two-and-one-quarter-inch wire up on deck to put over in the morning.

During the night we got orders from CinCLant to take our prize to Bermuda. (Dakar was full of spies and if we had gone in there, news of the capture would have reached Germany before our anchor's splash subsided.) Admiral Ingersoll diverted the fleet tub "Abnaki" from an east bound convoy to take over the towing job and also the oiler "Kennebeck" to refuel the task group.

Next morning we got the big tow wire rigged and when Trosino came back from the sub he reported he had put the rudder amidships, using the electric controller in the conning tower. But as we gained headway again, it became apparent that the rudder hadn't moved at all. The electric rudder *indicator* in the conning tower had come back amidships, but the rudder was still hard right. We would have to get into the after torpedo room and hook up the hand steering gear to move it.

I had been itching to get aboard that craft myself and the booby trap on the torpedo room door gave me the excuse I wanted. I was an ordnance post-graduate and knew as much about fuses and circuitry as any one on board, so I had designated myself as officer-in-charge of booby traps in the capture plans. Trosino and I took along four helpers and went over to investigate.

As we drew alongside the heaving U-boat, riding with its bow out of water, the stern clear under, and seas breaking over the conning tower hatch, I wasn't so sure I had any business being there. After we had scrambled up on the bridge and I could see that we had to close the conning tower hatch behind us after we went down to keep the seas from coming in after us, I could think of a dozen more important things I should have been doing at this time . . . this trip wasn't really necessary! But the skipper can't back out when he has gone that far. Down the hatch we went, this being the first time *I* had ever been on a submarine. Trosino was a veteran by now, so he led the way aft. The battery was practically flat and the lights burned very dimly. The boat was way down by the stern and wallowing heavily. The air stunk. That trip through the control room, diesel engine room, and after motor room, seemed endless. As we went further and further aft, I suddenly remembered that one way of correcting trim in a sub was to have men move to the high end of the boat, and here were four of us trooping aft to the heavy end of a boat that was teetering on a knife edge!

But we had passed the point of no return on this junket when we went down the hatch. You do your best to look calm, cool, and collected, and to tell yourself, "You can't live forever anyway."

At the after bulkhead of the motor room, Trosino put his flashlight on an open fuse box and said, "There she is, Cap'n." There were a dozen exposed fuses in the box and many wires leading in and out. The cover of the box opened downward and was lying across the main dog of the watertight door to the torpedo room. To move the dog you had to close the cover of the fuse box. This had the makings of a booby trap and closing the cover might complete a circuit that would blow us all up.

But I didn't think so. This was an improbable place for a booby trap—the Germans obviously hadn't expected us to board their ship, so why set booby traps? It looked to me as if that cover had been jarred open accidentally after the door was dogged shut. A close scrutiny of the wiring and circuits revealed nothing suspicious.

You can't hem and haw over a question like this very long when you are twenty-five feet under water in a wallowing submarine, and one nice thing about fiddling with booby traps is that you find out right away, after you have sprung one, whether your calculations were right or not. I eased the cover shut and nothing happened.

Now for the door. Three of us braced our backs against it so we could get it closed again if water started squirting out, and we moved the main dog carefully till we had just cracked the hatch. No water. We swung the door open and scrambled aft to the hand steering gear. In half a minute we had it hooked up and moved the rudder back amidships. As we gave the wheel its final spin, I said, "Let's get the hell out of here." There being no objections —out we went, everybody trying his best to walk up that long slanted passageway nonchalantly. The salt fresh air smelt mighty sweet as we clambered out into the sunlight on the bridge.

While we were below, my lads on deck had been busy with a paint brush. In big red letters across the face of the conning tower they had emblazoned the name "Can Do Junior." My crew always called the "Guadalcanal" the

"Can Do." Everyone in the task group has referred to the U-505 ever since, as "Junior."

The sub towed properly now and we proceeded at eight knots for our rendezvous with the "Abnaki." On June 9, 1944, we turned our tow over to "Abnaki" and refueled the task group from the "Kennebeck." Then we formed a screen around the "Abnaki" and "Junior" and headed for Bermuda, 2500 miles away.

Ever since we opened that booby trap, Earl Trosino had been after me to let him start the sub's diesels and bring her in triumphantly under her own power. I wish now I had let him do it. But at the time I was afraid that if we got fancy and tried to start the engines somebody might open the wrong valve and sink the boat. I hereby apologize to Trosino and his brave lads for underestimating them. I'm sure after all the other improbable things they did, they would have brought her in with colors flying.

Trosino did one thing that some of my submariner friends still seem skeptical about when I tell it. At the end of the second day, there wasn't enough juice left in the sub's battery to run a bilge pump. By this time Earl had figured out how to pump out the after ballast tanks and bring the boat up to an even keel if he had power to run the pump. But I wouldn't let him start the diesels so he couldn't charge the battery in the usual way. (Note: Each of the sub's main shafts has a diesel engine on one end, the propeller on the other, and an electric armature in the middle. When you charge the battery, the diesels turn the propellers and the armature as well, which then acts as a generator and puts juice back in the battery. When cruising submerged you unclutch the diesels and your storage battery supplies juice to turn the armature and propel the ship.)

Trosino figured out how to set the switches so the armature would generate juice if something turned it. Then he disconnected the clutches joining the heavy diesel engines to the propeller shafts and asked me to tow at ten to twelve knots that night. I did, and dragging the sub through the water at this speed with the big diesels disconnected made the propellers windmill in the water. This made the main shafts turn and the armatures had no way of knowing that they weren't being turned in the usual manner. They obediently made juice and recharged the battery. Next morning Earl was able to run a ballast pump and bring the boat up to full surface trim.

By this time we had all prisoners from the sub aboard the "Guadalcanal"—fifty-nine out of a crew of sixty. Oberleutnant Harald Lange was badly wounded and I went down to see him in sick bay. Because of his wounds he hadn't seen our people get aboard his boat and he thought his order to scuttle her had been carried out. He wouldn't believe we had her in tow until I sent over to the sub and got a picture of his family off his cabin desk. This convinced him, and he said over and over again, "I will be punished for this." I tried to cheer him up by pointing out that Germany was losing the war and that a new regime would replace the Nazis. He kept shaking his head and saying, "No matter what happens, I will be punished."

Maybe he was right. I have had some letters from Lange since the war, and reading between the lines I can see that he may be blamed for things which were not his fault. So far as I know, no legal action has been taken against him by the German government, but perhaps other former U-boat skippers exclude him from organizations to which he should be welcome. If so, this is a grave injustice, in my opinion.

Lange was the victim of circumstances. He did exactly what several hundred other U-boat skippers did when they thought the end was at hand and surfaced to give their crew a last chance to survive the war before scuttling their boats. Perhaps a dozen or more of these boats could have been captured if we had been prepared to send off boarding parties. I still think I could have towed the U-515 home if I had exercised proper foresight before she surfaced. Kretschmer, the greatest ace of them all, was captured with most of his crew, and his U-boat lay helpless on the surface with two British destroyers close aboard for much longer than it took us to get aboard the U-505.

I am told that various false stories have circulated in Germany that the U-505 surrendered. She did not surrender any more than several hundred other German subs that did the same thing surrendered. If there is any discrimination against her crew in Germany now, it is wrong. In my opinion, the man responsible for her capture was Cszhech. That crew should have been broken up and spread around among a dozen U-boats as soon as she came in from the cruise on which Cszhech ratted on his men by committing suicide. Lange inherited an impossible situation. He and his men, like most other U-boat sailors, were conscientious men who did their duty, were worthy opponents who almost beat us in a fair fight, and should be treated as such now.

On June 19, 1944, we escorted the "Abnaki" and U-505 into Bermuda with the traditional broom hoisted at our main truck. A delegation of experts from Washington swarmed aboard the sub and we turned our fifty-nine prisoners over to the Commandant of the Naval Operating Base, Bermuda. They were imprisoned there in a special camp all by themselves till the war was over, when they were returned to Germany.

Some people, waxing enthusiastic about this capture, say that the ability to read German naval codes from then on shortened the war by several months. I doubt this. The invasion of Normandy began two days after we got the U-505, and once the U.S. Army got ashore in France, the duration of the war was in their hands, so long as the Navy kept them and the Air Force supplied with the stuff they needed. The Navy could still prolong or even lose the war by losing control of the seas, but it couldn't do much to speed up the tempo of operations ashore. The capture did save seamen's lives by providing complete technical data on German subs and new developments, such as the acoustic torpedo.

The big thing we got out of it was the ability to read the German naval codes. We got the current code books, the cipher machine, and hundreds of dispatches with the code version on one side and German translation on the other. Like all military services, the German Navy changed their code about every two weeks, so enemy cryptographers wouldn't be constantly working on the same system. But the key to the routine changes was in the code books. We read the operational traffic between U-boat headquarters and the submarines at sea for the rest of the war. Reception committees which we were able to arrange as a result of this eavesdropping may have had something to do with the sinking of nearly three hundred U-boats in the next eleven months.

This brings me to what I think is the most remarkable part of this whole improbable episode. It was very important to prevent knowledge of this capture from reaching Germany. If it had, the Germans would have heaved all the old code books overboard, changed their whole system, and issued brand new ones, which are always kept ready for issue in just such an emergency. While towing the sub to Bermuda we carefully explained this to all hands in the task group and directed them to tell no one, but no one, what had happened on this cruise.

We had about three thousand young lads in that task group, all of whom had seen the whole thing happen and who came back from that cruise just bursting with the best story of their lives. But they knew they shouldn't tell it. I am very proud indeed of the fact that the Germans never found out we had this U-boat till the war was over. The boys did keep their mouths shut.

I think this speaks very highly indeed for the devotion to duty and sense of responsibility of the average young American wearing bell-bottom trousers. When I read the headlines these days about atomic secrets leaking from high level sources and important government officials popping off with top secret stuff just to get in the headlines, I feel even prouder of my lads in Task Group 22.3. As long as we continue to raise kids like those, the country will survive despite the bureaucrats and politicians.

While lecturing the boys on the importance of keeping the capture secret, I also laid down the law on souvenirs. I pointed out that there's no use having a souvenir unless you can show it around and brag about it and that regulations required all captured equipment to be sent to Office of Naval Intelligence in Washington. "So," I said, "If anyone has picked up a souvenir, turn it in to the exec's office tomorrow and no questions will be asked. But we will lower the boom on anyone found with souvenirs after tomorrow."

Next day the Exec's Office was inundated with the damnedest collection of stuff you've ever seen—Lugers, flashlights, cameras, officers' caps, German cigarettes, etc.,

etc. It was incredible that while struggling to keep a sinking U-boat afloat, the men whose lives were in danger could find time to accumulate all that junk.

I knew that the boys would all rather have turned in their right arms than these souvenirs. So, in accordance with the regulations, we tagged the souvenirs with the names of the "owners" and told the boys that (according to the book) at the end of the war the Office of Naval Intelligence would return them. Most of us, including me, were naive enough to believe this! But nobody ever saw their souvenirs again. After peace broke out the Washington bureaucrats absconded with them.

Checking back on this capture now, it seems that the U-505 and my task group simply had a rendezvous set up for us in the book of destiny and that there was no avoiding it. The U-505 was never where I thought she was until the moment she popped up almost under foot. I was searching the wrong areas all the time, except that last night when my planes must have missed her by inches once, and by seconds another time.

Plotting my own track that night and the courses flown by my planes against the track given by the U-505's war diary, it is apparent that we should have spotted him about ten o'clock. One of my planes passed within six miles of him when he was surfaced recharging his battery. My radar operator should have picked up a faint blip on his scope but he didn't. By the same token, the sub's Naxos operator should have picked up our plane's radar, but he didn't, although apparently he had picked up every other airplane within miles of him for the past two weeks. Two hours later, and only five minutes after the sub finished recharging and submerged, another one of my planes passed smack over the spot where he had just gone down.

I suppose I can say that at any rate, I was right in my decision to turn back and search that area again. But I was right for the wrong reason. I had turned back because I was certain we had made contact with him the night before. Actually, he had not been in our search area at any time the night before, and our contacts had been phonies.

So it is apparent now that this whole business hinged

on the fallible workings of two men's minds—mine and Lange's. Working on false premises, both of us made decisions which combined to bring out an extremely improbable result. Had either of us decided to do things just a little bit differently from what we did, the result would not have come about.

What causes such things as this to happen? I don't know of any way to explain it except to say, "Maybe our daily morning prayer had something to do with it."

It's no good to say it was all a matter of chance. If it had been, I should have made at least one "correct" decision instead of the series of wrong ones I did make, and one correct decision would have upset the apple cart completely.

Naturally the advance planning that we did on this thing belongs on the credit side of the ledger. So also does the venture into night flying, although in the final analysis the only real effect it had on this operation was to hold us in the area for one more night. Had we found the U-505 at night, there would have been no possibility of capture—that boarding idea was improbable enough in broad daylight, it was impossible at night.

This whole operation is an example of the fact that a military commander controls events only up to a certain point. He can anticipate certain things, perhaps even set the stage for them to happen, and can be ready to cash in on them if they do happen. But whether they will happen or not depends on many things over which he has no control. One is what goes on in the other commander's mind and another is what goes on in his own. Both of these mental processes are subject to influence from above, or by Divine sufferance, from below. I am not trying to say that we have no control over our destiny on this earth. But I do say that in many things we control it only up to a certain point. Beyond that point nebulous things which occur inside men's brains decide the issue. In this particular instance, I speak from first hand experience when I say the stuff that ran through my mind for a week or so was all wrong, but the final result was very good. . . .

The only moral I can see to all this is to plan your operations carefully, get the best advice you can from experts, fix it so that if certain things happen, you will not be caught flatfooted, and then, rely on the motto we have stamped on all our pennies—"In God We Trust."

Chapter

18

CHICAGO

AFTER GERMANY surrendered, the U-505, manned by an American crew and cruising under its own power, made a war bond tour of the Atlantic and Gulf coasts. When the Pacific war ended, she tied up at the Navy Yard in Portsmouth, New Hampshire, to await final disposition. She was not decommissioned or mothballed. The American crew simply closed the valves, pulled the switches, hauled down the colors, and walked ashore—taking with them all souvenirs such as name plates, gauges, and small pieces of equipment that weren't double riveted to the hull. For the next nine years the U-boat lay alongside the dock in Portsmouth and rusted.

At the end of the war, all German naval vessels and submarines still afloat were divided among the four so-called great powers. England, Russia, the United States, and France, each got a dozen or so U-boats under an agreement whereby all these craft would be sunk in deep water or scrapped within two years. As the two year limit approached, we got ready to carry out our agreement and word reached me that the U-505 was to be taken out with the surrendered U-boats and sunk.

I immediately objected on the ground that the U-505 was not included in the Four Power Agreement, which applied only to U-boats surrendered at the end of the war. The U-505 had not surrendered, she was captured in battle on the high seas. She was therefore, U.S. property with no strings attached and we could keep her as long as we wanted.

I had no immediate plans in mind for the sub at this time, but my boys had gone to a lot of trouble to prevent that U-boat from sinking off the coast of Africa, and I took a dim view of scuttling her now. Government bureaucrats always like to have some precedent or a piece of paper to justify what they are doing and there were no precedents for this case. But I raised such a fuss that the Navy Department finally changed its mind rather dubiously and vetoed the scuttling order.

Some years later, after the sub got to Chicago, this question of the Four Power surrender agreement came up again. Molotov visited the Museum of Science and Industry while passing through Chicago on his way to the tenth anniversary celebration of the U.N. at San Francisco. While looking at the U-505, he was heard to ask an aide, "Do you think they really captured her?" The aide simply shrugged.

Molotov obviously didn't believe we had captured her and the implication was that he thought this was one of the subs turned over at the end of the war which we should have sunk. Mr. Molotov figured he had stumbled on a little item he could file away for future reference. At an opportune time, he could make one of his sweeping accusations of bad faith and cite this submarine as an example. Major Lohr, President of the Museum, sent the State Department a telegram about this incident and I am told Secretary Dulles straightened the little squarehead out on the facts of the case.

After the reprieve on the scuttling order, my brother, Father John Ireland Gallery, had an idea about a possible use for the U-505. He was a naval reserve chaplain and had helped fight the Battle of the Atlantic with the Navy's Patrol Wing 7, which played a big part in the air offensive over the Bay of Biscay. Father John observed that there were monuments all over the country for the land battles in every war that this country has fought, but naval memorials were few and far between. Father John asked himself, "Why not bring the U-505 to Chicago and make it a memorial to the thousands of seamen who had lost their lives in the two great Battles of the Atlantic? These were two of the crucial battles in our history, and what could be a more appropriate monument to these battles than one of the very submarines around which the battles centered."

One day, while visiting the Museum of Science and

Industry near his parish in Chicago, Father John mentioned this idea to Major Lenox Lohr. The Major lit up like a Christmas tree, pushed a button, and told his secretary to bring in the Museum's "submarine file." In this file there were letters going back twenty-four years asking the Navy Department to give them an obsolete submarine for display at the Museum. The Major explained that when Julius Rosenwald endowed and established the Museum back in 1926, he specified he wanted it patterned after the Deutsche Museum in Munich. This Museum was filled with modern exhibits featuring the technology of the age in which we live and the two principal attractions were a full scale model of a coal mine and an actual submarine hauled out of the water and installed alongside the Museum.

The first exhibit installed in the new Museum of Science and Industry at Chicago, was an accurate replica of a modern coal mine. It has been a feature attraction ever since. The Museum, located five hundred yards from the shore of Lake Michigan, had been trying unsuccessfully for twenty-four years to get a submarine.

The Major, who is one of the country's greatest showmen, realized immediately the possibilities of the U-505 for the Museum. This wasn't just any old submarine. It was a historic trophy, the first enemy war ship captured in battle on the high seas since 1815. It could fulfill the founder's dream, but on a bigger scale than Rosenwald had visualized. The Major and Father John agreed that afternoon that they would get a project started to bring the U-505 to Chicago and install it alongside the Museum.

This was easier said than done. It involved acquiring title to the U-boat, making it seaworthy, towing it to Chicago, dragging it out of the water and hauling it across the busiest thoroughfare in the city to the Museum, restoring it to presentable condition, and installing it as a permanent addition to the Museum's main building. Offhand, this looked like an expensive project—and the Museum had no funds for it. Most people with whom the Major and Father John discussed the project agreed that it was a "good idea," but were not anxious to do anything about it. No such project had ever been undertaken before, and there were many difficulties involved.

In 1948, most people wanted to forget war rather than erect war memorials. As one critic expressed it, "If you get it here it will just be another cannon on the courthouse lawn."

But, in the course of a couple of years, a few real enthusiasts for the project were found and the idea began to take root. Alderman Clarence F. Wagner got the City Council to pass a resolution asking the Navy Department to give the U-boat to the Museum. Colonel McCormick of the *Chicago Tribune* threw his considerable weight behind it and for the next several years the *Tribune* ran stories periodically about the project and printed editorials favoring it.

Negotiations to secure title from the Navy Department took some time. The Navy was anxious to get this rusty elephant off its hands and would gladly have sunk it in deep water if they could have done it while nobody was looking. But a resolution by both Houses of Congress was necessary before they could give it away. It took two years to get the Congressional resolution because eighty days had to lapse after it was introduced, before Congress could vote on it, in order to allow other interested communities, if any, to put in their bids. No other communities were interested, but the first session of Congress to consider the matter adjourned eight days too soon and another eighty day waiting period was necessary at the next session. Finally we got Congressional approval and the Navy Department drew up legal papers for the transfer of title.

The first draft of these papers contained a clause typical of the stuff you run into whenever government lawyers get their fingers into the pie. It specified that in case of war, the Museum undertake to return this vessel on demand to the government in the same condition in which it had been turned over to them! I had some fun needling the legal beagles about that one. We finally ridiculed them into reluctantly omitting the clause.

The law says that when an obsolete naval vessel is given away, the recipient must take it over at no expense to the government. The Navy Department interpreted this clause literally and informed the Museum the U-505 would become their property alongside the dock in Ports-

282

mouth, and the Museum would have to pay for all repairs necessary to make her seaworthy. I got a sharp rap across the knuckles from the Department for trying to get Senator Dirksen to persuade the bureaucrats that their estimates on these repairs were a little on the high side and that it would be good training for the Navy to tow it to Chicago for us. As a matter of fact, I eventually had more trouble getting that sub from Portsmouth to Chicago than I did getting her from Cape Blanco to Bermuda.

Early in 1953, Mayor Kennelly of Chicago, appointed a committee of leading citizens to take charge of this project, raise the necessary funds, and bring the U-505 to Chicago. Heading this committee as honorary chairman was Mr. Ralph A. Bard, formerly Undersecretary of the Navy. Robert Crown and Carl Stockholm, active members of the Navy League, served as cochairmen. Estimates of the amount of cash necessary to do the job ranged all the way from $50,000 to two million. It's difficult to estimate a job that has never been done before and which involves taking a strange craft like a submarine out of its element and putting it in a park a thousand miles inland. The committee set a goal of $250,000 to be raised by its 100 members making personal solicitations.

Despite the fact that this project had been a *Tribune* baby for years, all Chicago papers got behind it and the cooperation of news media, press, radio and TV for the next year and a half was unprecedented in the history of the city. The U-505 became a household word and the project a civic enterprise in which everyone was interested.

The committee eventually raised $125,000 in cash and obtained a similar amount in free services from civic minded corporations. This was peanuts in view of the unprecedented publicity given the project. Had the project been put in the hands of professional fund raisers, I'm sure they could have collected several million. But we didn't need that much and the committee insisted, as a matter of principle, on keeping the fund raising on a strictly amateur basis. There was no cut for any professional fund raisers and every cent collected went into the project.

There was one contribution to the fund that just about floored me. It came from Steve Leo, who had been the head man in public relations for the Air Force when I was on duty in Washington after the war. This was during the big inter-service rhubarb about unification and Steve and I used to burn the midnight oil trying to dream up ways to make each other unhappy. Despite this, we were good personal friends and occasionally used to have lunch together in the Pentagon's high-brass dining room just to see everyone goggle and do a double take when two nefarious characters like us sat down together publicly.

As a gag, more than anything else, I sent Steve one of our circulars about the fund drive and pointed out to him that it would be a fine example of unification at work if he contributed to this project. I expected a somewhat flippant reply.

When a letter came back enclosing a check for $250.00, I almost fell out of my chair. Herewith is the letter that accompanied it:

Dear Dan:

Enclosed herewith my contribution to the U-505 Fund.

I trust that this project will be the beginning of a world wide movement to put all naval vessels in their proper place, namely alongside of inland museums!

> Best regards,
> STEVE

Two incidents in connection with the free services are typical of the way the whole community got behind this project. One day I got a phone call from a Mr. Leonard Grosse, whom I didn't know from Adam at the time. He announced that his business was making bronze memorial plaques and said, "It seems to me you are going to need some plaques for the sub at the Museum, aren't you?" "Yes," I said rather guardedly. "Well, I can make you some nice ones," said the voice. So far this seemed like a straight pitch for some business by a man who was alert enough to spot a possible need for his product when he saw it. I replied, "That's fine, we will keep you in mind . . . but those things are expensive, aren't they?" "These won't be," said Grosse, "I want to give them to you." This came out of a clear sky, entirely on Mr. Grosse's own initiative. He presented the Museum with plaques that would have cost close to $5,000.

The other incident concerned getting the use of a floating drydock to lift the U-505 out of the water and put it on the beach. There was only one floating dock in the Great Lakes big enough to do this job. It belonged to Great Lakes Dredging and Dock Company. Some of the Great Lakes Company engineers were leary of this haul out job, didn't want to have anything to do with it, and informed our chief engineer, Mr. Seth Gooder, that their drydock wasn't big enough. Seth and I got the dimensions of the dock, calculated its displacement and lifting power and knew it was big enough.

One day Seth and I called on Mr. William P. Feeley, head of the company, to talk him into participating in our project. He was a poker-faced gentleman who sat back and listened for a long time saying nothing and indicating nothing. I gave him an earnest pitch about the civic aspects of the project, benefits to the school kids, etc., and then Gooder went through all the engineering angles proving mathematically that his drydock could handle this job. When we got through I felt it had all been a waste of time and we had made no impression. Mr. Feeley sat in silence at the head of the table for a few minutes and then fixed a cold eye on us and said, "Just what sort of a proposition did you want to make to us for the use of our drydock?"

I figured we had lost the battle and there was no use wasting time beating around the bush. I said, "Mr. Feeley, we would like to borrow your drydock for six weeks." Mr. Feeley didn't bat an eye, "Okay," he said, "you can have it."

The American Shipbuilding Company of Cleveland and the Fitzsimons and Connel Dredging and Dock Company were equally generous in furnishing special equipment and services.

The committee was very fortunate indeed to secure the services of Mr. Seth Gooder, as project engineer. Mr. Gooder had been one of the leading civil engineers of Chicago for many years and had done some big jobs, including moving large churches, and the whole grandstand of the Cubs' ball park. He had just retired from active practice and found time heavy on his hands. He took over the engineering of this project, at no fee, and gave it his full attention for a year and a half. His services were irreplaceable at any price. It might have been possible to hire the best engineers in the city to do this job, but you can't hire the enthusiasm and personal interest that Gooder gave to it. He made complete engineering studies of every possible way of getting the submarine out of Lake Michigan and alongside the Museum. The South Shore Drive, which runs between the Museum and the lake shore, handles 80,000 cars per day, and getting the U-boat across or under, this drive with the shortest possible interruption of traffic was the prime consideration. Various schemes for squeezing it under a low bridge into a shallow lagoon near the Museum were discarded because we might damage the bridge. The safest and best method seemed to be the straightforward one of beaching it on the shore of the Lake and hauling it across the drive in the same way that houses are moved. The sub drew nine feet of water and to beach it the keel had to be lifted about four feet above lake level. She weighed about eight hundred and fifty tons and this weight had to be lifted thirteen feet above its normal position when waterborne. When it looked like we couldn't get the floating drydock, Gooder drew up plans for improvising a floating dock, if necessary, by sinking a gravel barge under the U-boat and raising it with the sub sitting on top. Early in 1954 Gooder had all his plans ready and the Portsmouth Yard pronounced the submarine seaworthy and ready for her last voyage.

On May 14, 1954, the U-505 started her journey to Chicago via the St. Lawrence River, Welland Canal, and the Great Lakes. She was towed by the tug "Pauline L. Moran" to Lake Erie where the Coast Guard cutter "Arundel" took over.

I rode the tug "Pauline L. Moran" while going from Cornwall to Cardinal on the old St. Lawrence waterway, and had the unforgettable experience of listening for two days to a couple of real old salts trying to snow each other under with yarns about their experiences in forty years of seafaring. The "Moran" skipper and the Canadian pilot had spent their lives at sea, and both were crusted with salt. When you get two characters like that together on the bridge of a tug, each one feels duty bound to outdo the other one with his tales of nautical adventure. When they've got a Rear Admiral, U.S. Navy, standing behind them and listening, in addition to the personal challenge offered by the other's exaggerated tales, each one feels that his professional standing is at stake. In this case, a salt water man was defending his breed of sailors against a character, who although he might be a pretty good seaman, was after all just a river man.

It had never before been my privilege to listen to such a series of colossal tall tales as these two exchanged with perfectly straight faces. No matter what sort of epic one related, the other could top it. While they were doing this, we were clawing our way up the St. Lawrence towing the sub alongside in a current which often was as high as eight knots. The channel was winding, the stream was full of strong eddies, and every now and then a large ship coming down stream would careen around a bend ahead and sweep down at us sidewise.

Time and time again I held my breath in such situations, expecting some frenzied maneuvering on our part to avoid collision. The two old salts seemed to regard these things as minor distractions. Getting the tow safely to its destination was just an incidental job that either one could do with his eyes shut—but not with his mouth shut while the other was along. The really important work of the day was the reminiscing. They went right on relating their sagas until disaster seemed imminent, when the pilot would say apologetically, "Come left a little," the tub skipper would flip his wheel a few spokes, and the tale would be resumed right where it had been interrupted, while the down bound steamer swept by a few yards to starboard.

Earl Trosino, who kept the U-505 afloat off Cape Blanco was along on this cruise too. He is chief engineer of a Sun Oil Company tanker, and the company generously loaned him to us for this trip. It was quite fitting that Trosino, who was mainly responsible for saving the U-505 off Cape Blanco should be her skipper on her final voyage to Chicago.

In June the U-505 arrived in Chicago and received the biggest civic welcome ever given on the water front. She was met by a fleet of several hundred yachts out in the

Lake, escorted to the harbor, saluted by the fireboats, and received at the Michigan Avenue bridge by the Mayor and a huge crowd.

Following the reception, the U-boat spent the next six weeks at Calumet Harbor getting ready for the hauling out job. She had to be drydocked to remove ninety tons of ballast from her keel, and then transferred from the American Shipbuilding Company's 800-foot graving dock to the Great Lakes Company's floating dock. After she was safely ensconced in the floating dock with her keel four feet above water level, a steel cradle was built around her to take her ashore and carry her to the Museum. When this cradle was completed, hydraulic jacks boosted the cradle under the sub and then lifted the submarine and cradle high enough to insert several hundred two inch steel rollers between the cradle and the railroad rails which had been placed on the floor of the floating dock. When the jacks were let down and removed, she was ready to roll.

Our main concern now was weather, and not entirely local Chicago weather, but weather all over Lake Michigan. We were not worried about a steady blow of any kind. A northeast gale can cause surf on the Chicago side of the lake much too heavy for any beaching operation, but steady gales can be predicted. We only needed about four hours to get the U-boat ashore from the drydock, and we wouldn't start beaching operations till we were sure that none were coming for at least twelve hours.

What we were worried about were small, violent thunderstorms anywhere in the Lake, which produced a phenomena called a seiche. A seiche is a surge of water caused by sudden changes in barometric pressure such as occur in line squalls. Such a change can start a great surge of water out in the Lake which rolls out, expanding in all directions, toward the shore. The wave produced may be only a few inches in height but over a mile from one crest to the next. When it reaches the beach its action is entirely different from that of the ordinary wave which lasts for a few seconds and is gone. When a seiche surges in, the mean level of the Lake rises for a period of five or ten minutes rather than seconds and if it happens to be reinforced by reflected surges, and if the contour of the beach traps the water, the Lake can rise four or five feet in extreme cases as if the tide were coming in. Exactly this happened the day the U-505 arrived in Chicago and seven fishermen were swept off a pier in Lincoln Park and drowned. One or more small seiches occur almost every day in Lake Michigan. The mean level of the Lake goes up and down at least as frequently as does the sea level in a tidal port, but the variations are almost completely unpredictable. A big seiche at the wrong time, just as we got the U-505 half way ashore, would, of course, produce spectacularly embarrassing results.

While work on the cradle proceeded at Calumet City, a nine-foot channel was being dredged five hundred feet out into the Lake from the beach alongside the Museum. At the inshore end of this channel we built a pier about fifty feet out from the beach capable of carrying a thousand tons, and laid rails on it to receive the cradle and submarine.

On August 13, two tugs brought the floating dock up from Calumet City, eased it up the nine-foot channel and nosed it against the pier. The height of the rails on the pier and in the dock matched to within a sixteenth of an inch, but while we were hooking up the cables to haul the sub ashore, a small seiche lifted the drydock four inches too high and eased it down where it belonged again in a period of twenty minutes.

But the Lake behaved itself after that one little seiche and the sub came ashore without incident soon after dark on Friday the 13th of August.

Seth Gooder had to do some expert juggling of water ballast to keep the drydock on an even keel during the beaching operation. As the submarine inched forward onto the pier, water had to be admitted to the tanks of the dock just fast enough to compensate for the weight being transferred to the beach. It was like walking a tightrope with a thousand-ton weight.

On the night of September 3, they closed the Outer Drive at 7:00 P.M., we laid railroad rails across the pavement and the sub was dragged across the drive at an average rate of about eight inches per minute. Fifteen thousand people stayed up till 4:00 A.M., watching the U-boat creep across the drive. Every one of these citizens knew a better way of doing the job than the way we were doing it. There were many arguments that night among the sidewalk superintendents, and the only thing they all agreed on was that they wouldn't do it our way. A large sign on the Outer Drive warned motorists, "Drive Carefully—Submarine Crossing." The Drive was open for normal traffic again in time for the morning traffic rush. The U-boat still had three hundred yards to go and a sixty-seven degree turn to make before it reached its final berth, but from here on it was a straight house moving job.

After the submarine was installed on its concrete foundation at the Museum, holes were cut in her port side and two covered passageways were built connecting her to the Museum. Visitors now enter the U-boat aft, walk forward and return to the Museum through the forward passageway. The U-boat in anchored to the foundation amidships, but the bow and stern rest on rollers. Temperature variations between winter and summer can cause the length of the boat to vary three inches, which would crack a concrete foundation if she were securely anchored.

The Secretary of the Navy came to Chicago for a large banquet in the Museum and a preview of the submarine the night before the dedication ceremony. His son, Ensign Heyward Thomas, was in the engine room of the "Guadalcanal" the day we captured the U-505.

On September 25, 1954, the U-505 was dedicated as a memorial to the 55,000 Americans who have lost their lives at sea. Admiral Halsey made the principal address, Arthur Godfrey was the master-of-ceremonies, and Bishop Weldon of Springfield, Massachusetts, Chaplain of the "Guadalcanal" when we made the capture, gave the invocation. Mr. William V. Kahler was chairman of the dedication committee. About a hundred members of the task group were on hand for the ceremony, including Captain Trosino and all nine surviving members of the "Pillsbury's" original boarding party. About 40,000 Chicagoans gathered under the trees in Jackson Park to witness the rites.

As I met the various lads in the task group, most of whom I hadn't seen in eleven years, I soon learned exactly what to expect in the way of greeting. After the customary polite preliminaries had been disposed of, each of them would look at me sort of quizzically and say, "Cap'n— where the hell is that Luger you made me turn in and were going to get back for me?"

All I could do was mutter some profane comments on the ONI characters who let us down.

The sub has proved a great drawing card at the Museum. During the first year it was on exhibit, attendance at the Museum increased twenty per cent over the previous record breaking year. A total of 2,400,000 people came to the Museum, of whom 569,349 went through the sub. Many more would have done so except that only so many can get through it at a time.

But Major Lohr, being the smart showman that he is, refuses to herd people through the sub. He says he would rather give people time to look around and digest what they are seeing, even if this means he has to turn some away at the end of the day.

Of the 569,349 visitors the first year, 228,414 were youngsters. Organized classes from 3,000 schools located in twenty-two different states came to the Museum and went through the sub and saw the movies made by our combat photographers the day we captured her. All these youngsters lived through a few moments of high adventure and took away a lasting memory of one of the epics in our naval history.

The Museum has done a wonderful job of restoring the boat to its original condition. Major Lohr is a perfectionist who will never be satisfied with it. His hobby is restoring old machines to operating condition and the U-505 gave him something he could really get his teeth into. Every week some new piece of equipment is put back in working order. Often it's a piece that looked perfectly OK before, to anyone except the Major, who wants things not only to look right, but to work properly too. He has even fired up the diesel engines and kicked them over under their own power. The sub is actually cleaner, more presentable and in better condition today than it was when we took it away from the Germans.

NOTE: In May 1967 the total number of visitors to the U-505 reached 7,800,000. It averages 600,000 a year, which is all they can handle.

Chapter

19

EPILOGUE

NOW THAT THE war is over and some of the fires of hatred
have died down a little, perhaps I can say a word of
recognition for the U-boat sailors who fought us almost to
a standstill in submarines similar to the U-505. A total
of seven hundred eighty-one German U-boats were destroyed during the war, including twenty-nine still listed
simply as "missing, fate unknown." Seventy per cent of all
the officers and men who served in the U-boat fleet went
to the bottom of the sea with their boats. This is an
almost incredible casualty rate. In the Pacific the personnel loss rate for our submarines was only one-third as
great. Well trained military outfits have cracked and
mutinied in the face of much less. It takes a high calibre
of leadership in the officers' corps, good discipline and
high morale to keep on fighting despite such brutal losses.
It's too bad such valor was wasted in an evil cause.

Twenty-eight thousand German sailors rode their U-
boats down to Davy Jones's locker. I helped send several
hundred on their way there and didn't lose any sleep over
it at the time. So far as I was concerned, there was no
malice in what I was doing—except when some U-boat
skipper made a monkey out of me by outwitting me. I
was just discharging an official duty the same as the U-boat
sailors were. Speaking as a professional fighting man
myself, I must admit that those men fought well, and
observed the code laid down by civilized nations to govern
the organized murder that we call war. I have nothing but
reluctant respect for the courage and patriotism of the
U-boat crews in executing the orders of their Nazi masters, even when the odds against them became hopeless.
In fact, I look on this U-boat in Chicago as a memorial,
of a sort, to our misguided enemies whose devotion to
duty deserved a better cause.

It's an ironic proof of war's futility that now, only eleven years after VJ Day, we are wooing the Germans and Japs, and arming them to help protect the western world against our former allies, the communists. Hitler's ghost must cackle sardonically over that one!

Now that we face an evil worse than the Nazis, this submarine in Jackson Park should remind us that men will fight well even for bad causes, and that we can't depend on winning simply because we are right. The U-505 is also a peculiarly appropriate warning that it is folly to stake our security on international agreements, because if solemn treaties had been worth the paper they were written on, it would be impossible for that submarine to be alongside the Museum today. Commerce-raiding submarines were abolished by international agreement long before the U-505 was built. The fact that it *is* there in Jackson Park now should be a permanent object lesson to us that international pacts based on good faith and morality have a way of coming apart at the seams when a shooting war starts and man suspends the operation of the Fifth Commandment, for the duration. Perhaps the best advice ever given to this country was Theodore Roosevelt's, "Speak softly but carry a big stick."

After World War I, all great nations agreed that the submarine was an uncivilized weapon which should be outlawed—just as we all now agree the atom bomb should be. But to outlaw an effective and useful weapon requires more mutual confidence and trust than civilized nations have ever had in each other. The great maritime nations who had little to gain and much to lose from unrestricted submarine warfare against merchant vessels were perfectly willing, between wars, to declare this form of warfare uncivilized and to ban it. But they wouldn't outlaw submarines completely because they might want to use them against each other's war ships next time they had to settle their differences in the traditional way employed by the human race ever since Cain settled his with Abel in the Garden of Eden. With this in mind, the great powers, including the United States, foisted off on a gullible world the London Treaty of 1930, saying that if submarines were ever used against merchant ships again, they would follow the Rules of Prize Warfare.

These rules, drawn up originally in the days of sailing ships, were as obsolete in 1930 as sailing ships, and everybody who agreed to them knew this. Nevertheless, the United States put its signature on this pious hokum, and (like everybody else) kept right on building submarines.

This hypocritical stuff went down the drain during the first week of World War II. The Germans sank the "Athenia" and the British armed all merchantment, ordered them to report submarines by radio, and to ram them—things which were impossible in the good old days of sail when Prize Rules originated. Before long, both sides threw the book away and went to unrestricted submarine warfare the same as in World War I, each side piously claiming it was simply retaliating against the other.

When the U.S. got into the war, our submarines in the Pacific operated the same as the Germans did, and sank six million tons of ships. We torpedoed without warning and left survivors to their fate. That's the only way submarines *can* operate. Admiral Lockwood, who commanded our submarines in the Pacific, tells the story with a few words in the title of his book, *Sink 'Em All.* Naval officers were not at all surprised by any of this. War is a brutal business and no amount of wishful thinking by bubble-headed statesmen between wars will make it otherwise.

When the statesmen louse up their job so badly that they have to have the military men pull the chestnuts out of the fire for them, a lot of innocent bystanders are going to get hurt. When nations, by mutual consent, decide to ignore the commandment "Thou shalt not kill," it is very difficult for the military leaders to restrict the killing to just the right people.

You might think that since our submarines fought the same way the Germans did, we would sweep the question of Prize Warfare under the rug after the war and say no more about violation of the laws of war at sea. Our naval officers were perfectly willing to do this, but our statesmen and lawyers were vindictive. When the war was over, they insisted on trying the German Admirals Raeder and Doenitz at Nuremberg as war criminals for permitting their submarines to do exactly what ours did. A justice of

294

our Supreme Court prosecuted them and tried to hang them. To our eternal shame, we convicted the German Admirals of violating the laws of war at sea and sentenced them to long terms of imprisonment: Raeder to life; and Doenitz to ten years.

This kangaroo court at Nuremburg was officially known as the "International Military Tribunal." That name is a libel on the military profession. The tribunal was not a military one in any sense. The only military men among the judges were the Russians. Some military titles are listed on the staffs of the secretariat and prosecution counsel, but these belong to a lot of lawyers temporarily masquerading in uniform as military men.

Nuremberg was, in fact, a lawyers' tribunal, although I can readily understand why the legal profession is ashamed to claim it, and deliberately stuck a false label on it.

I'm glad our real military men had nothing to do with the travesty on justice that the lawyers and "statesmen" conducted at Nuremberg. Raeder and Doenitz simply did their duty to their country in World War II, trying to straighten out the mess that their politicians got them into as all military men are sworn to do. Our politicians and lawyers set a rather stupid precedent when they tried these officers for carrying out the orders of their own misguided politicians.

Actually, the decision to court-martial the German military brass was on par with the "unconditional surrender" blunder, which prolonged rather than shortened the war. From now on, Nuremberg gives enemy military leaders good reason for fighting to the last bullet and dying in the trenches rather than trying to negotiate surrender of a hopelessly lost cause. There certainly is no use in surrendering if you know you will be hauled up before a kangaroo court and hung, as most defendants were at Nuremberg.

After all, Doenitz did surrender six days after he stepped into Hitler's shoes following the paperhanger's suicide. He couldn't have surrendered any sooner without leaving millions of Germans in East Prussia to the mercy of the Red savages.

Even today, few people realize that the German Navy, in the last days of the war, evacuated several times as many refugees from East Prussia as the British Navy took out from Dunkirk. As soon as Doenitz got his people to safety in West Germany, he surrendered . . . but one of the charges on which our Supreme Court prosecutor tried to hang him was that he prolonged the war!

Had the German people seen fit to try their own military leaders for losing the war, I might go along with that. Or if our statesmen had insisted on hanging the Nazi politicians and had felt that a mock trial was necessary before doing it, I could see some logic in that. But our politicians and lawyers were undermining their own authority when they convicted the German generals and admirals. After all, one thing the much maligned military brass must do, in a democracy as well as a dictatorship, is to swallow their convictions, if any, and do as they are told by the politicians.

I have no sympathy for the sadists who operated the death camps at Buchenwald and Dachau. They should have been shoved into their own death chambers and liquidated quietly by the first military commanders to lay hands on them while the rest of us looked the other way. I even approve of their final hanging. But I do not approve of the baldfaced hypocritical hocus pocus by which our statesmen try to justify it legally. The mass murderers at the death camps operated on the basis that might was right, and so did we when we hung them.

At Nuremberg, mankind and our present civilization were on trial, with men whose own hands were bloody sitting on the judges' seats. One of the judges came from the country which committed the Katyn Forest massacre and produced an array of witnesses to swear at Nuremberg that the Germans had done it. Maybe crimes of such magnitude as those charged at Nuremberg should be left to the Last Judgment for punishment.

The outstanding example of barefaced hypocrisy at Nuremberg was the trial of Admiral Doenitz. We tried him on three charges: (1) Conspiring to wage aggressive war; (2) Waging aggressive war; and (3) Violation of the laws of war at sea. Even the loaded court at Nuremberg acquitted him of the first charge, but convicted him of the other two. How in the name of common sense a military officer can wage any kind of war except an aggressive one without being a traitor to his country, I'll never know. I took an oath when I entered the U.S. Navy almost forty years ago, to defend the United States against all enemies —and there wasn't anything said about doing it in a non-aggressive manner. I'm surprised that the Reds in Korea didn't hang all U.S. prisoners, quoting Nuremberg as a precedent, instead of just brainwashing them and sending them back to us for punishment. If the Nuremberg evidence had shown that Doenitz waged a non-aggressive war, the German people themselves would have been entitled to hang him.

Doenitz's conviction on charge three—violation of the laws of war at sea—was an insult to our own submariners. Admiral Doenitz requested early in the trial that our own Admiral Nimitz be summoned as a witness in his defense to testify about how our subs operated in the Pacific. Our Supreme Court prosecutor had to hem and haw and to back water fast when that hot potato was tossed at him. Admiral Nimitz (God bless him for the honest seafaring man that he is) finally submitted a sworn statement, answering questions put to him by Doenitz's counsel and said that our submarines in the Pacific waged unrestricted warfare the same as the Germans did in the Atlantic.

Despite this, we convicted Admiral Doenitz on the charge of violating the laws of war at sea. If the old gentleman ever gets out of jail, I hope I never meet him. I would have trouble looking him in the eye. The only crime he committed was that of almost beating us in a bloody but "legal" fight.

Doenitz's conviction for violating the laws of war in carrying out the orders of his government, raises a serious question. We have just promulgated a Code of Conduct for our fighting men, designed to steel them against brainwashing if captured, and thus to protect them from prosecution in our own courts for improper conduct while prisoners of war. Perhaps, to protect our soldiers from prosecution by tribunals like Nuremberg, we should amend the oath of allegiance they take when they enter the service. After what we did to Doenitz, maybe we should add a proviso to the oath saying, "Before carrying out the orders of my superior officers, I will check to insure that they are compatible with our international commitments, the Charter of the United Nations, etc., etc."

The only precedent set at Nuremberg in which I take any stock at all is that they didn't hang any admirals!

The Nuremberg trials placed a solemn stamp of approval on a code of war at sea which we not only didn't follow ourselves in World War II, but which may embarrass us in the future. We are, at present, busily engaged in building atomic submarines designed to remain submerged for weeks at a time. It is absurd to think that these submarines will expose themselves on the surface to follow the archaic code of sailing ships, which we confirmed as being the law of war at sea for the atomic age when we threw Doenitz in jail.

Lest there be any mistakes about how I feel on this matter, I hasten to say I am not in favor of actually trying to follow Prize Rules with atomic submarines. I'm in favor of denouncing pacts which can't be followed in war time and of announcing what everybody knows anyway: that in case we are attacked, we will defend ourselves with every weapon in our arsenal.

According to newspaper reports, the Russians now have a trained fleet of four hundred operating submarines. I don't think this fleet is seven times as dangerous as the fleet of fifty-seven with which Hitler started the war, because, in my opinion, the Russians are a little bit stupid on the starboard side. But if the Russians ever get a fleet of four hundred atomic subs—or even fifty-seven—we will bitterly regret having opened this Pandora's Box of the atomic submarine.

The atomic sub is a greater threat to us than to the Russians, because we are much more dependent on our seaborne imports, and our coastal cities are more vulnerable than theirs. Even if we have complete control of the air we could still be grievously hurt by submarines which our aircraft could never see. We must not allow newer things, such as intercontinental jet bombers and push-button missiles to obscure the fact that sea power is one of the keystones of our nation's greatness and strength.

The U-505 will be alongside the Museum for many years to come, perhaps over a hundred if it isn't blasted to atoms by a hydrogen bomb in the meantime. It should serve as a constant reminder to us that seventy per cent of the earth's surface is salt water, and the United States owes a great deal to the sea which carried our ancestors to freedom and a new way of life on a virgin continent, was the bulwark that protected us when the country was young and weak, and gave us access to the markets and resources of the world to make our industry thrive and grow.

In both World Wars, after bloody battles against submarines, the sea was the great military highway over which we deployed our military might to fight the enemy a long way from our home shores. Now that we are the world's greatest industrial nation, the sea's highways bring in the strategic raw materials needed to keep the wheels of our mighty industry turning.

All over the country there are monuments to the land battles of the wars we have fought. The Unknown Soldier has a tomb at Arlington; there are many soldier's memorials and national cemeteries throughout the land. But there are no tombstones on the sea. Ironically, the best known naval memorial is the capsized hulk of the U.S.S. "Arizona," resting on the bottom in Pearl Harbor—a symbol of naval disaster.

In the two great Battles of the Atlantic, 9,935 ships, totaling 34,540,000 tons, went to the bottom. Fifty-five thousand of our soldiers, sailors, airmen and merchant seamen have gone down to unmarked graves defending our freedoms at sea. What more fitting memorial could they have, and what more appropriate symbol is there of our victory at sea than an enemy U-boat itself, beaten in mid-ocean battle, towed across the Atlantic, and installed in the mid-West, a thousand miles from salt water?

Even in the atomic age, the submarine is still the greatest threat to our control of the seas. This captured submarine at the Museum of Science and Industry is a tribute to the heroism of our Navy men, a memorial to the dead, and a stern reminder to the living that control of the seas, so vital to our existence, has been purchased at great price. It should also remind the red commissars who dream of world-conquest, that dictators Hitler and Napoleon very nearly conquered the world, but failed because they couldn't control the seas.

APPENDIX

Atlantic Fleet

Admiral R. E. Ingersoll CinC

Task Group 22-3

Captain Daniel V. Gallery, U.S.N.

U.S.S. Guadalcanal CVE-60 (Flagship)
Captain Daniel V. Gallery, U.S.N.

VC Squadron 8
Lieutenant Norman D. Hudson, U.S.N.

Escort Destroyer Division 4
Commander Frederick S. Hall, U.S.N.

U.S.S. Pillsbury DE-133
Lieut. Comdr. George W. Cassleman, U.S.N.R.

U.S.S. Pope DE-134
Lieut. Comdr. Edwin H. Headland, U.S.N.

U.S.S. Flaherty DE-135
Lieut. Comdr. Means Johnston, Jr., U.S.N.

U.S.S. Chatelain DE-149
Lieut. Comdr. Dudley S. Knox, U.S.N.R.

U.S.S. Jenks DE-665
Lieut. Comdr. Julius F. Way, U.S.N.R.

MERCHANT SHIP LOSSES AND U-BOATS SUNK

1939

Month	Number	Tonnage	U-Boats Sunk
September	29	152,040	2
October	21	104,712	4
November	22	57,173	2
December	23	103,496	1
	95	417,421	9

1940

Month	Number	Tonnage	U-Boats Sunk
January	24	101,869	1
February	21	110,372	5
March	13	39,302	0
April	19	74,838	7
May	77	273,219	1
June	125	471,496	0
July	98	381,967	2
August	88	394,010	3
September	90	442,634	0
October	97	442,452	1
November	91	376,098	2
December	79	357,314	0
	822	3,465,571	22

1941

Month	Number	Tonnage	U-Boats Sunk
January	75	320,048	0
February	100	401,768	0
March	139	537,493	5
April	154	653,960	2
May	126	500,063	1
June	108	431,037	4
July	43	120,975	1
August	41	130,699	3
September	83	285,752	2
October	51	218,289	2
November	34	104,212	5
December	187	485,985	10
	1,141	4,190,281	35

1942

Month	Number	Tonnage	U-Boats Sunk
January	97	415,741	3
February	130	652,516	2
March	225	794,689	6
April	127	666,814	3
May	149	704,673	4
June	170	823,656	3
July	127	613,641	12
August	124	665,633	9
September	114	567,327	10
October	100	632,720	16
November	135	812,867	13
December	72	347,628	15
	1,570	7,697,905	86

1943

Month	Number	Tonnage	U-Boats Sunk
January	50	261,359	6
February	73	403,062	19
March	120	693,389	15
April	64	344,680	15
May	58	299,428	41
June	28	123,825	17
July	61	365,398	37
August	25	119,801	25
September	29	156,419	9
October	29	139,861	26
November	29	144,391	19
December	31	168,524	8
	597	3,220,137	237

MERCHANT SHIP LOSSES AND U-BOATS SUNK
(Continued)

1944

Month	Number	Tonnage	U-Boats Sunk
January	26	130,635	15
February	23	116,855	20
March	25	157,960	25
April	13	82,372	21
May	5	27,297	23
June	26	104,084	25
July	17	78,756	23
August	23	118,304	34
September	8	44,805	23
October	4	11,668	12
November	9	37,980	8
December	26	134,913	12
	205	1,045,632	241

1945

Month	Number	Tonnage	U-Boats Sunk
January	18	82,897	12
February	26	95,316	22
March	27	111,204	34
April	22	104,512	57
May	4	17,198	28
	97	411,127	153
GRAND TOTAL	4527	20,448,074	783*

* Includes U-505 and U-570.

NOTE: The above figures are from Churchill's books. The total given in Admiral King's final report to the Secretary of the Navy is: Total tonnage 23,351,000. Differences are due to Churchill not counting ships of less than 1,000 tons and to different methods of expressing tonnage (net tons, register tons, gross tons, etc.).

Statement of Commanding Officer of U-505

On June 4th about 1200 I was moving under water on my general course when noise bearings were reported. I tried to move to the surface to get a look with the periscope. The sea was slightly rough and the boat was hard to keep on periscope depth. I saw one destroyer through West, another through Southwest and a third at 160 degrees. In about 140 degrees I saw, far off, a mass that might belong to a carrier. Destroyer #1 (West) was nearest to me, at about ½ mile. Further off I saw an airplane, but I had no chance to look after this again because I did not want my periscope seen. I dove again and quickly, with noise, because I couldn't keep the boat on periscope depth safely. I suppose that I must have been seen by the airplane because if these heavy boats are rolling under the surface they make a large wake.

I had not yet reached the safety depth when I received two bombs at a distance and then close after them two heavy dashes, from depth charges perhaps. Water broke in; light and all electrical machinery went off and the rudders jammed. Not knowing exactly the whole damage or why they continued bombing me, I gave the order to bring the boat to the surface by pressed air.

When the boat surfaced, I was the first on the bridge and saw now four destroyers around me, shooting at my boat with .50 caliber and anti-aircraft. The nearest one, in now through 110 degrees, was shooting with shrapnel into the conning tower. I got wounded by numerous shots and shrapnels in both knees and legs and fell down. At once I gave the order to leave the boat and to sink her. My chief officer, who came after me onto the bridge, lay on the starboard side with blood streaming over his face. Then I gave a course order to starboard in order to make the aft part of the conning tower lee at the destroyer to get my crew out of the boat safely. I lost consciousness for I don't know how long, but when I awoke again a lot of my men were on the deck and I made an effort to raise myself and haul myself aft. By the explosion of a shell I was blown from the first antiaircraft deck down onto the main deck; the explosion hit near the starboard machine gun.

I saw a lot of my men running on the main deck, getting pipe boats (individual life rafts) clear. In a conscious moment, I gave notice to the chief that I was still on the main deck. How I got over the side I don't know exactly, but I suppose by another explosion. Despite my injuries I somehow managed to keep afloat until two members of my group brought me a pipe boat and hoisted me into it; my lifejacket had been punctured with shrapnel and was no good. During all this time I could not see much because in the first seconds of the fight I had been hit in the face and eye with splinters of wood blasted from the deck; my right eyelid was pierced with a splinter.

When I sat in the pipe boat I could see my boat for the last time. Some of my men were still aboard her, throwing more pipe boats into the water. I ordered the men around me to give three cheers for our sinking boat.

After this I was picked up by a destroyer where I received first aid treatment. Later, on this day, I was transferred to the carrier hospital and here I have been told by the Captain that they captured my boat and prevented it from sinking.

Harald Lange
Oberleutnant z. See d. Res.

U-505 COMMITTEE MEMBERS

Ralph A. Bard, Honorary Chairman
Robert Crown, Carl Stockholm, Co-Chairmen

Ex-Officio Members

William G. Stratton, Governor of Illinois
Everett M. Dirksen, United States Senator
Paul M. Douglas, United States Senator
Martin H. Kennelly, Mayor of Chicago

Robt. McCormick Adams
Charles W. Allen
Ralph L. Atlass, Jr.
A. G. Cox Atwater
Charles W. Becker
Louis J. Behan
Carl A. Birdsall
A. Andrew Boemi
P. F. Brautigam
Mark A. Brown
Maurice F. Brown
Fred J. Byington, Jr.
John L. Clarkson
Edward D. Corboy
Thomas A. Dean
John L. Donoghue
William W. Downey
Alex Dreier
Brian J. Ducey
T. M. Dunlap
T. J. Ellerthorpe, YNC,
USN
Lee Ettelson
John W. Evers
Harold S. Falk
John D. Farrington
B. T. Franck
James B. Forgan
Jack Foster

Philip Furlong
Reverend John I. Gallery
Arthur Godfrey
David N. Goldenson
Seth M. Gooder
James R. Graham
Leonard H. Grosse
Cornelius J. Hagan
Morton Hague
George S. Halas
David L. Harrington
Edward A. Hayes
Frank A. Hecht
Maurice L. Horner, Jr.
Oscar Iber
James A. Jennings, Jr.
Fred A. Joyce, Jr.
William V. Kahler
L. B. Kidwell
J. B. Kolko
Francis H. Kullman, Jr.
William A. Lee
George W. Lennon
Louis E. Leverone
Major Lenox R. Lohr
D. M. MacMaster
William Maloney
John J. Manley
J. L. McCaffrey

Joseph J. McCarthy
F. B. McConnell
James G. McDonald
John F. McGuire
Dr. L. Robert Mellin
Gerhardt F. Meyne
Edward F. Misewicz
Raymond T. Moloney
Vice Admiral Francis P. Old, USN (Ret)
Lieutenant E. W. Oliphant, USNR
Rudolph F. Onsrud
W. A. Patterson
Harold E. Peterson
Ben Regan
Rear Admiral James M. Ross, USNR
Willard M. Rutzen
Brigadier General E. H. Salzman

Philip B. Schnering
Rudolph A. Schoenecker
Gilbert H. Scribner
Sherman H. Serre
James G. Shakman
Rear Admiral D. F. J. Shea
Arnold Sobel
John L. Spiczak
Russ Stewart
Arthur Sullivan
Patrick F. Sullivan
Hamilton Vose, Jr.
Basil L. Walters
William P. Whalen
John A. Wheeler
Roger Q. White
Thomas F. White, Jr.
Lawrence H. Whiting
Edward Foss Wilson
Frank H. Yarnall

Robert McCormick Adams
Advocate Printing Co.
Aero Club of Michigan
Mrs. Weston Afferbach
E. J. Albrecht Company
Charles W. Allen
Allen-Bradley Company
Allis Chalmers Mfr. Co.
Allstate Foundation
Amalgamated Society of
  Machinists of Chicago
American Can Company
American Community
  Builders, Inc.
American Furniture Mart
  Bldg. Co., Inc.
American League Baseball
  Club of Chicago
American Molded Products
  Co.
The American Ship
  Building Co.
American Steel Foundries
A. Harold Anderson
C. K. Anderson Co.
Anson & Gilkey Company
Appleton Coated
  Foundation, Inc.
Appleton & Cox
Appleton Wire Works
Henry W. Armstrong
Arrow Plating Co.
H. Leslie Atlass
R. L. Atlass, Jr,
A. G. Atwater
Avenue Bar
Sewell Avery
N. W. Ayer & Son, Inc.
Bachner Die-Mold &
  Machine Corp.

Badger Meter Mfg. Co.
Balaban & Katz Corp.
Dr. Frederick B. Balmer
Ralph A. Bard, Honorary
  Chairman
J. M. Barker
T. H. Barth
Bartholomay & Clarkson
B. M. Baruch, Jr.
Charles W. Becker
The Bederman Foundation
Louis J. Behan
Bell Aircraft Corporation
Beloit Iron Works
R. F. Bensinger
John J. Bergen & Co., Ltd.
Paul E. Berry
Berteau-Lowell Plating
  Works, Inc.
Big Ben Petroleum
  Products Co.
Binks Mfg. Co.
Carl A. Birdsall
Bismarck Hotel Co.
Roy A. Blomquist
Morton Bodfish
A. Andrew Boemi
Chauncy B. Borland
Bowey's Inc.
Bowman Dairy Co.
Brad Foote Gear Works,
  Inc.
Robert A. Brandt, Jr.
P. F. Brautigam
Briggs & Stratton Corp.
  Foundation, Inc.
Bronze, Inc.
Brown & Bigelow
Isidore Brown
Mark A. Brown

M. F. Brown
Donald Buckingham
Ralph Budd
Kenneth F. Burgess
O. W. Burgess
Fred J. Byington, Jr.

Calumet Shipyard &
  Drydock Co.
Geo. M. Campbell
George A. Canning
Capitol Wood Works
Cardwell Westinghouse Co.
Alfred T. Carton
J. I. Case Company
Thomas G. Cassady
Central Steel & Wire Co.
Chain Belt Foundation, Inc.
Charmin Paper Mills, Inc.
Checker Taxi Co.
Chicago-American
Chicago Bears Football
  Club, Inc.
Chicago Board of Trade
Chicago Building Trades
  Council
Chicago City Bank & Trust
  Co.
Chicago Daily News
Chicago Duluth & Georgian
  Bay Transit Co.
Chicago Extruded Metals
  Co.
Chicago Newspaper
  Publishers' Assn.
Chicago Park District
Chicago Sun Times
Chicago Tribune
Chicago Wilmington &
  Franklin Coal Co.
Chippewa Paper Products
  Co., Inc.

Cirque Club
Cities Service Oil Co.
City of Chicago
City National Bank & Trust
  Co.
Philip R. Clarke

In Memoriam—
  Warren Thomas Clark
  Sophia Symington Clark
  John Burlingame
    Halladay
  Emma Clark Halladay
John L. Clarkson
Cleveland Diesel Eng. Div.,
  General Motors Corp.
A. J. Clonick
L. L. Colbert
The Columbia Malting Co.
Commonwealth Edison Co.
Concora Foundation
Consumers Tire & Supply
  Co.
Continental Can Co.
Continental Grain Co.
Continental Motors Corp.
Cook County Council,
  American Legion
Benjamin O. Cooper
Corbett Clinic
E. D. Corboy
H. Corman & Co.
Cornell Paperboard
  Products Co.
Cosmopolitan National
  Bank
Lewis N. Cotlow
Alfred Cowles
William D. Cox
Frederick C. Crawford
Albert J. Crowe & Son

Arie Crown Memorial
Fund
Robert Crown, Co-
Chairman
Curtiss Candy Company
Cutler-Hammer, Inc.
Cyclone Fence Dept., Am.
Steel & Wire Div., U.S.
Steel Corp.

The Daily Pantagraph
Thomas A. Dean
DeForest's Training, Inc.
Deltox Rug Company
DeSoto Council, Knights
of Columbus
DeVry Corp.
Edison Dick
The Division Fund
Wm. Djidich
Dohl's Morton House,
Emil and Otis Dohl
J. L. Donoghue
R/Adm. John Downes,
USN (Ret.)
Wm. W. Downey
Thomas J. Downs
Alex Dreier
Brian J. Ducey
James W. Dunham
Theo. M. Dunlap
Dunn Coal Company

Edgewater Paint Co.
John Egan
George M. Eisenberg
Foundation
Electro-Motive Division,
General Motors Corp.
T. J. Ellerthorpe, YNC
USN

Enger Brothers
(R. M. & W.)
A. A. Englehardt
E. M. Erickson
Lee Ettelson
D. C. Everest
John W. Evers

Vincent M. Fagan
Fairchild Engine &
Airplane Corp.
The Falk Corporation
Harold S. Falk
John D. Farrington
Albert D. Farwell
Federal Die Casting Co.
Marshall Field, Jr.
William Finkel
The First National Bank,
Madison, Wis.
First Nat'l Bank of Chicago
Post No. 985, The
American Legion
First Wisconsin Nat'l Bank,
Milwaukee
Clarence P. Fisher
Fitz Simons & Connell
Dredge & Dock Co.
James Flett Organization,
Inc.
Flying Farmers of Prairie
Farmer Land
Robert M. Foley
Ford Motor Co.
James B. Forgan
Jack Foster
L. B. Foster Company
B. T. Franck
Rt. Rev. Msgr. Daniel J.
Frawley
Charles Y. Freeman

Fruit Belt Motor Service, Inc.
Fullerton Parkway Towers Bldg.
Philip Furlong

Arthur J. Gallager
Mrs. Daniel V. Gallery
Rev. John I. Gallery
A. F. Gallum & Sons Corporation
Garfieldian Publications
Geib, Inc.
General Coatings Corp.
General Dynamics Corp.
General Mills, Inc.
General Motors Corp.
General Outdoor Adv. Co.
General Steel Warehouse Co., Inc.
Gerzin's Georgian
G. H. Building Corp.
Giddings & Lewis Machine Tool Co.
Charles Gill
Gisholt Machine Company
Globe Corporation
Globe Steel Tubes Co.
Arthur Godfrey
Arthur Godfrey Foundation, Inc.
Joel Goldblatt
David N. Goldenson
Seth M. Gooder
W. A. Goodrich
Rt. Rev. Monsignor Wm. J. Gorman
Goshen Charitable Fund
Graham-Paige Corp.
Thomas A. Grant
Great Lakes Dredge & Dock Co.

Great Lakes Towing Co.
M. D. Greenspan
Wm. J. Griffin
John Griffiths & Son Construction Co.
Leonard H. Grosse
Grumman Aircraft Engineering Corp.

Cornelius J. Hagan
Ted Hagg
H. J. Hagge
George S. Halas
William J. Halligan
Hamilton Mfg. Co.
Paul Hammond
Jam Handy Organization
T. L. Hankins
Fred H. Hansen
Harnischfeger Corp.
David L. Harrington
Stanley G. Harris
Edward A. Hayes
Hazeltine Research, Inc.
Raymond J. Healy
Frank A. Hecht
F. T. Heffelfinger
The Heinn Company
Heled Charitable Foundation
Hevi Duty Electric Co.
Hilton Hotels Corp.
Edward Hines Lumber Co.
Orville Hodge
C. O. Hogland, Inc.
Paul V. Hogland
The Dave Hokin Foundation
Frances Hooper Advertising Agency
Albert L. Hopkins
Maurice L. Horner, Jr.

J. W. Hostrup
Huch Leather Company
Hudson-Sharp Machine Co.
Herbert K. Hulson
Hy-Alloy Steels Co.

Oscar Iber
O. Iber & Co.
Illinois State Council,
Knights of Columbus
Indian Trailer Corporation
Samuel Insull, Jr.
International Brotherhood
of Teamsters etc., Local
No. 731
International Harvester
Foundation
Irish Fellowship Club of
Chicago
H. R. Isham

V. V. Jacomini
James A. Jennings, Jr.
D. O. James Gear Mfg. Co.
James Manufacturing Co.
Jewel Tea Co.
Jewett & Sowers Oil Co.
The Johnson Foundation
Johnson & Higgins
Johnson Service Company
Joslyn Mfg. & Supply Co.
Fred A. Joyce & Son
Fred Joyce, Jr.

Wm. V. Kahler
Kanelos Bldg. Corp.
M. S. Kaplan Co.
Fred Katz
Kearney & Trecker Corp.
E. J. Keeley
J. H. Keeney & Co. Inc.
T. Lloyd Kelly

Kelso-Burnett Electric Co.
Hon. Martin H. Kennelly
L. B. Kidwell
Dan A. Kimball
Kimberley-Clark Corp.
Willard L. King
Harry G. Kipke
Milton Kirshbaum
E. W. Kneip, Inc.
Raymond J. Koch
Koehring Company
Kohler Co.
J. B. Kolko
Francis H. Kullman, Jr.

Lake Shore Engineering Co.
Lakeside Bridge & Steel Co.
Lake States Engineering
Corp.
William Landess
Lawrence Lapcinski
LaPlante-Adair Co.
M. E. Latimer
Lavelle Rubber Co.
Wm. A. Lee
Stephen F. Leo
Sylvia Letts and Marie
Stacel
Louis E. Leverone
N. W. Levin
Lewis Spring & Mfg. Co.
Lincoln Bag Company
Linehan, Inc.
Lind Plastic Products, Inc.
Lindberg Steel Treating Co.
Lion Manufacturing Corp.
Local 705, Chicago Truck
Drivers, Chauffeurs &
Helpers Union
Horace L. Lohnes
L. R. Lohr

George P. Madigan
Madison-Kipp Corp.
Magnavox Company
Wm. J. Maloney
B. N. Maltz
John J. Manley
Marathon Battery Co.
Marine Nat'l Exchange
  Bank, Milwaukee
Marquette Cement Mfg.
  Co.
Marsh Electric Co.
Marshall & Illsley Bank,
  Milwaukee
Material Service Corp.
Max A. R. Mathews & Co.
Harold Matson
Oscar Mayer Foundation,
  Inc.
Mrs. Marguerite Mayne
J. L. McCaffrey
McCarthy & Smith
F. B. McConnell
James G. McDonald
McGraw Foundation
John F. McGuire
Thomas P. McGuire
Donald R. McLennan, Jr.
Don McNeill
Merrill C. Meigs
Dr. L. Robert Mellin
Merkle-Korff Gear Co.
The Merrill, Lynch, Pierce,
  Fenner & Beane Char-
  itable Foundation, Inc.
Merritt-Chapman & Scott
  Corp.
Davis Merwin
Metropolitan Amusement
  Co.
Geo. J. Meyer Mfg. Co.
Gerhardt F. Meyne

The Miehle Foundation
Military Order of the World
  Wars, Chicago Chapter
Milled Screw Products Co.
Mills Industries, Inc.
Milwaukee Gas Light Co.
W. H. Miner, Inc.
Minneapolis-Honeywell
  Regulator Co.
Raymond T. Moloney
Larry Monahan
Edmond J. Moran
Edward M. Moran
John S. Morris
The Morton Fund
Sterling Morton
Motor Research Corp.
Murphy Lanier & Quinn

Naess & Murphy
National City Lines, Inc.
  Charitable Trust
Nationwide Food Serv., Inc.
Navy Club, Illinois
  Squadron
Akron Council, Navy
  League
Chicago Council, Navy
  League
Detroit Men's & Wowen's
  Navy League Councils
Kenosha Council, Navy
  League
Los Angeles Council,
  Navy League
Minneapolis Council,
  Navy League
Wisconsin Council,
  Navy League
Navy League of the United
  States
Nehring Electrical Works

Henry J. Neils
Nepco Foundation
August Neumann
Aksel Nielsen
Fleet Adm. & Mrs. C. W.
    Nimitz
Nordberg Mfg. Co.
George Norgan Inc.
Normennenes Singing
    Society
Norris Grain Co.
Northern Trust Co.
R. A. Northquist
Trygve Nostwick

James F. Oates, Jr.
Ohmite Mfg. Co.
V. Adm. F. P. Old, USN
    (Ret.)
Wrisley B. Oleson
LCDR E. W. Oliphant,
    USNR
Arthur T. Olsen
Rudolph F. Onsrud
John R. Orton
Albert E. Overton

Pabst Breweries Foundation
Paine, Webber, Jackson &
    Curtis
The Parker Pen Company
Lloyd C. Partridge
Christian P. Paschen
Frank Paschen
Charles A. Patrizzi
W. A. Patterson
B. R. and A. Paulsen
F. H. Peavey & Co.
Perfex Corporation
Harold E. Peterson
Pfister & Vogel Tanning Co.
Pickands Mather & Co.

John S. Pillsbury
John S. Pillsbury, Jr.
Pipe Line Service Corp.
The Pittsburgh Plate Glass
    Foundation
Platt, Inc.
Fred A. Poor
John A. Prosser

Quinn, Riordan, Jacobs &
    Barry

Ray-O-Vac Company
Ben Regan
Ray C. Reinhartsen
Janet Rex
Daniel F. Rice & Co.
A. J. Riffell & Co.
Rival Packing Co.
S. M. Roberts
Rodman & Linn
Lessing J. Rosenwald
    Working Fund
William Rosenwald Family
    Fund
R. Adm. Jas. M. Ross,
    USNR
Mr. and Mrs. Joseph F.
    Ross
Rotary Club of Chicago
Maurice L. Rothschild
Rubloff Investments, Inc.
Fred Rueping Foundation
H. L. Ruggles & Co.
Rust-Oleum Corporation
Willard M. Rutzen
Lawrence J. Ryan

Saint Ignatius High School,
    Class of 1918
Adm. H. B. Sallada, USN
    (Ret.)

Brig. Gen. E. H. Salzman, USMC (Ret.)
Peter Sampson
U. A. Sanabria
The Sanitary District of Chicago
Jos. Schlitz Brewing Co.
Philip B. Schnering
Rudolph A. Schoenecker
Schuster's
Gilbert H. Scribner
Sea Gulls Club of Naval Post
Searle Grain Co.
Sears Roebuck & Co.
Sheridan H. Serre
James G. Shakman
Shaw-Metz & Dolio
R. Adm. D. F. J. Shea, USN (Ret.)
Sheraton Hotel, Chicago Sheraton Corp.
J. P. Sieberling
Signal Delivery Service
Sigmund Silberman Foundation
Sincere & Co.
Small Motors, Inc.
A. O. Smith Corp.
Wendell E. Smith
Arnold Sobel
Speedway Wrecking Co.
John L. Spiczak
Spiral Step Tool Co.
Standard Oil Company
Steel Warehousing Corp.
Albert M. Stein
Stewart Warner Corp.
Russ Stewart
Carl Stockholm, Co-chairman

Stolper Steel Products Corp.
Doctors Strauss Foundation
Lewis Strauss
R. R. Street & Co., Inc.
Samuel Cardinal Stritch, Archbishop of Chicago
Arthur Sullivan
Patrick F. Sullivan
Sun Oil Co.
Sverdrup & Parcel, Inc.
Svithiod Singing Club
Swith & Co.

Teamsters' Joint Council No. 25
Thilmany Pulp & Paper Co.
Thomson & McKinnon
Frank Thornber
J. J. Tourek Mfg. Co.
Trackson Company
The Traffic Club of Chicago
Captain Earl Trosino, USNR
Calvin D. Trowbridge
Twain Manufacturing Co.
Twin Disc Clutch Co.

U & S Machined Products Co.
Union Refrigerator Transit Lines Div., GATC
United Aircraft Corp.
United Air Lines Foundation
United Mfg. Co.
United Specialties Co.
United States Motors Corp.
United States Steel Corp.
University of Chicago

Gordon H. Visneau
Anthony von Wening
Hamilson Vose, Jr.

C. R. Walgreen, Jr.
Walgreen Drug Stores
DeWitt Wallace
Wallace Furniture &
  Upholstery Shop
Basil L. Walters
Rawleigh Warner
Paul V. Warren
Warner M. Washburn
Waukesha Foundry Co.
Waukesha Motor Co.
Wausau Daily Record
  Herald
WBBM-TV
Paul Weir Co.
L. S. Wescoat
West Bend Aluminum Co.
William Whalen
John A. Wheeler
White Building &
  Maintenance Corp.

Roger Q. White
Thomas F. White
Lawrence H. Whiting
Willett Motor Coach Co.
Edward Foss Wilson
Wisconsin Electric Power
  Co.
Max A. Witz
H. M. Wolf
Wolfe Associates, Inc.,
  Columbus, Ohio
Frank Wood
The Aytchmonde Woodson
  Foundation
Worden-Allen Company
Herman Wouk
Philip K. Wrigley

Frank H. Yarnall
Summer B. Young

E. K. Zitzewitz
Frank Zotti

INTENTIONS FOR THE NIGHT SIGNAL, MAY 17

Incoming Dispatch—U.S.S. Guadalcanal   Information—172110Z

TOP SECRET

Course 180 Speed 14 Close Screen X Zigzag 10 at 0300 X We will be on hot trail tomorrow X Each escort draw up plans and organize a party to board capture and take sub in tow if opportunity arises.

PRECEDENCE   VISUAL

FM: CTG 22.3   TO: TG 22.3

LAST PAGE OF U-505 WAR DIARY—Page 60   LOG

Date and Time	Account of Position, Wind, Weather, Sea, Light, Visibility of the Atmosphere, Moonlight, etc.	Events
3/6/44	Northeast of Cape Verde Is.	
0800	DU 7539	
1200	DU 7536	Nautical miles carried
		over: 5922 1875
		2-3/6 14 34
		Total 5936 1909
1338	DU 7533	Surfaced.
	High cirrus screen.	Day's surface run for charging.
	Horizon clear.	
1540	DU 7285	Submerged.
1600	DU 7285	
2000	DU 7282	
2210	DU 7281	Surfaced.
2231		End of daylight.
2400	DU (sic)	
	N 2-3, sea 2, 1018 mb.	
	overcast, medium visibility	
4/6/44		
0213	DU 4796	Submerged.
0400	DU 4795	
0754		Beginning of daylight.
0800	DU 4792	
1200		Nautical miles carried
		over: 5936 1909
		3-4/6 78 24
		Total 6014 1933
1600	DU 4767	
2000	DU 4756	
2236		End of daylight.
2400	DU 4756	
	NE 3-4, sea 3, overcast.	
	Horizon misty, moderate	
	phosphorescence.	
5/6/44		

NOTE: The above is a translation of the actual War Diary of the U-505. Observe that although the sub was captured at noon the War Diary found on board runs to midnight and even records positions for 1600, 2000, and 2400. The explanation is that watches expected to be uneventful are sometimes written up in the log ahead of time during a long cruise. In this case the afternoon watch turned out to be a lot more eventful than they thought it would be.

THE BEST OF BESTSELLERS
FROM WARNER BOOKS

THE NEXT
by Bob Randall   (95-740, $2.75)

A growing boy! That's what Kate's ten-year-old nephew was. Yet during the weeks he was left in her care—while his mother recovered from a car accident—Charles was growing at an astonishing rate. Love can turn a boy into a man. But evil can do it faster.

THE FAN
by Bob Randall   (95-887, $2.75)

The Fan: warm and admiring, then arrogantly suggestive; then obscene, and finally, menacing. Plunging a dawdy Broadway actress into a shocking nightmare. "A real nail-biter . . . works to perfection as it builds to a surprising climax . . . the tension is killing."   —*Saturday Review*

FORT APACHE, THE BRONX
by Heywood Gould   (95-618, $2.75)

They were only rookies . . . two green cops blown away on the killer walkways of the Bronx. Now the Force is on the prowl under a tough new captain who is determined to shape up his last command for losers where life is mean, death is often murder, and the law of the jungle is the only law.

SEE THE KID RUN
by Bob Ottum   (91-123, $2.50)

A chilling race through the dark side of New York with a kid you'll never forget! Wanted: Elvis Presley Reynolds, aged 14½, who dreams of Mark Cross, Brooks Brothers and the Plaza—where one day soon he'll pass as "Somebody." He's an urban urchin with bottomless eyes and an incredible ambition to escape to the good life while there's still time.

THE TUESDAY BLADE
by Bob Ottum   (91-643, $2.50)

"We're looking for one guy carrying seven razors or seven guys carrying one razor each." That's how a cop summed up the case. But the killer they were tracking was just one girl—big, beautiful and armed with THE TUESDAY BLADE. "My current reading favorite . . . makes 'Death Wish' look like a kindergarten exercise."
                                        —Liz Smith, *New York News*

OUTSTANDING READING FROM WARNER BOOKS

THE EXECUTIONER'S SONG
by Norman Mailer   (80-558, $3.95)

The execution is what the public remembers: on January 17, 1977, a firing squad at Utah State Prison put an end to the life of convicted murderer Gary Gilmore. But by then the real story was over—the true tale of violence and fear, jealousy and loss, of a love that was defiant even in death. Winner of the Pulitzer Prize. "The big book no one but Mailer could have dared . . . an absolutely astonishing book."—Joan Didion, *New York Times Book Review.*

THE GLORY
by Ronald S. Joseph   (85-469, $2.75)

Meet the inheritors: Allis Cameron, great-granddaughter of the pioneers who carved a kingdom in southern Texas. Go with her to Hollywood where her beauty conquers the screen and captures the heart of her leading man. Cammie: Allis's daughter, who comes of age and finds herself torn between a ruthless politician and a radical young Mexican. They were the Cameron women, heirs to a Texas fortune, rich, defiant, ripe for love.

THE IMAGE
by Charlotte Paul   (95-145, $2.75)

The gift of sight came to Karen Thorndyke as the bequest of an unknown man. His camera, willed to the Eye Bank, enabled the beautiful young artist to see and paint again. But with that bit of transparent tissue came an insight into horror. With her new view of life came a vision of death.

CRY FOR THE DEMON
by Julia Grice   (95-497, $2.75)

Where the lava flows and sharks hunt, Ann Southold has found a retreat on the island of Maui. Here the painful memory of her husband dims, her guilts and fears are assuaged, and she meets a dark man who calls to her—a man who wants her more than any man has ever wanted her before. Out of the deep, a terror no woman can resist . . . CRY FOR THE DEMON.